*Warm, romantic,
ensual & charming...*

-blooded male, warm summer
ezes and a gorgeous setting:
cipe for an irresistible idyll...
ou could lose your heart!

n ITALIAN
UMMER

brand-new delicious romances
ader favourites Rebecca Winters,
ate Hewitt & Jackie Braun

An ITALIAN SUMMER

REBECCA WINTERS
KATE HEWITT
JACKIE BRAUN

*M&B™ and M&B™ with the Rose Device
are trademarks of the publisher.
Harlequin Mills & Boon Limited, Eton House,
18-24 Paradise Road, Richmond, Surrey TW9 1SR*

AN ITALIAN SUMMER
© Harlequin Enterprises II B.V./S.à.r.l. 2009

The Lucchesi Bride © Rebecca Winters 2009
Italian Boss, Housekeeper Mistress © Kate Hewitt 2009
A Venetian Affair © Jackie Braun Fridline 2008

ISBN: 978 0 263 87531 7

009-0709

*Harlequin Mills & Boon policy is to use papers that are
natural, renewable and recyclable products and made from
wood grown in sustainable forests. The logging and
manufacturing processes conform to the legal environmental
regulations of the country of origin.*

*Printed and bound in Spain
by Litografia Rosés S.A., Barcelona*

The Lucchesi Bride

REBECCA WINTERS

Rebecca Winters, whose family of four children has now swelled to include three beautiful grandchildren, lives in Salt Lake City, Utah, in the land of the Rocky Mountains. With canyons and high meadows full of wildflowers, she never runs out of places to explore. They, plus her favourite holiday spots in Europe, often end up as backgrounds for her novels because writing is her passion, along with her family and church.

Rebecca loves to hear from her readers. If you wish to e-mail her, please visit her website at: www.rebeccawinters-author.com

Don't miss Rebecca Winters' new book,
The Greek's Long-Lost Son, **coming
in October 2009 from
Mills & Boon® Romance.**

Dear Reader,

One of the great joys of writing is the fun of making up a story I haven't personally lived. For example, I was raised in a home with two loving parents who lived long, amazing lives. Recently I started thinking out of the box about my situation and started asking questions about what my life might have been like if I'd had two fathers for example? What if I loved them both? What then? Under what circumstances might that have occurred? With what results?

Ah – the results are terribly important and eventually lead the heroine to meet the hero. Both need each other desperately.

Before long I'd created a story called *The Lucchesi Bride*. This story gets even more exciting because Catherine must leave the stepfather she adores and travel to Naples to meet her birth father. This throws her into the entirely new world of Alessandro Lucchesi, whose unexpected entry into her life robs her of breath. Guess what? She never quite catches it again. Read my story and you'll find out why.

Enjoy!

Rebecca Winters

Dedicated to one of my dear sisters, a brilliant linguist, who attended the University of Perugia and travelled in Europe with me. She's my greatest fan and a lover of all things Italian, too. Remember the night I met your ship in Genoa? Will you ever forget dinner at our hotel with all those gorgeous Italian waiters who make every woman feel beautiful? The "*bellissima*"s were flying! This book is for you, Kathie!

CHAPTER ONE

"BRETT? Do you honestly think I should do it?"

Catherine's brother might be five years younger, but they always talked everything over.

"Let's put it this way. If I were in your shoes, I would have wanted to meet my birth father years ago. Now that you have the chance, I say go for it. Mom set something in motion for a reason. Dad's fine with it."

Catherine's hand tightened on her cellphone. She was horribly conflicted right now and really appreciated Brett's advice.

She knew her mom had gotten pregnant at nineteen, but since her mother had never told her any details about the man who'd impregnated her Catherine had left the subject alone. It had been after Catherine was born that Stan Dalton, a New Mexico rancher, had come along and married Catherine's mother. He'd always been Catherine's daddy and she adored him.

Naturally there had been moments growing up when she'd wondered about her birth father. There were some obvious differences between her and her family. The

Dalton men were blond with light blue eyes, built like tennis players. Catherine was a redhead, like her mom, with dark blue eyes, but her other traits and build belonged to the father she would never know.

None of it had truly mattered to her until her mother had contracted a severe lung infection six months ago and had been told it was terminal. The diagnosis had shattered the Daltons' world—they were going to lose wife and mother.

While Brett had taken spring semester off from the University of Albuquerque, Catherine had obtained a leave of absence from her job at the insurance company in town so both could be at home on the ranch to help their dad nurse their darling mother.

During those bedside discussions when Catherine and her mom had been alone, the truth had come pouring out about Catherine's birth father. Everything Catherine's mother had wanted to tell her beloved daughter but had held back because she had been afraid it would hurt Stan, who'd been so wonderful to Catherine.

Catherine had understood all of it—until her mom had dropped a bombshell just two days before she had died. Without anyone knowing about it, she'd already contacted Catherine's birth father, who was now a widower. They'd talked for quite a while, and now he wanted to meet the daughter he'd never known existed. There was more. After her mother died, Catherine could expect a call from him.

The call that had come a month later had changed her life, deepening Catherine's shock still further. For a stranger, her birth father had been surprisingly tender with her. Among other things, he had told her there was an airline ticket waiting for her.

"Since Elizabeth told me of your existence, I've longed to meet our little girl. If you could find it in your heart to visit me in Naples, it would make me happier than you will ever know."

The tone of his words, with its hint of melancholy, its sweetness, had wound its way into Catherine's troubled soul. Angry as she had been at her mother's death, and at her mother too, who'd done this to their family at the last minute, she had agreed to go. Her birth father had hoped it would be for a month, but Catherine couldn't think of leaving her dad that long, and she wasn't sure if her boss would give her that much time off. They had finally agreed on ten days.

"I agree Dad's been totally understanding, Brett, but then that's the way he is about everything."

"How come you're so hesitant?"

The tears dripped off her chin. At times her brother could be very intuitive. "I don't want to hurt Dad."

"This doesn't have anything to do with him."

"I know. That's what's so sad. All these years I've been his daughter. Now my birth father is suddenly in the picture. It's not fair to either of them."

Brett let out a low whistle. "I guess it all boils down to how much you'd like to meet the man who fathered you. If you want my opinion, I think Mom wanted you two to get to know each other for the most basic reason of all. He gave you life."

Catherine blinked at his insight. "Thank you, Brett. I needed to hear that. I'm going to leave tomorrow. Dad's driving me."

"Then I'll meet you guys at the airport. What time is your flight?"

"I have to be there at seven a.m."

"That's perfect. My first class isn't until nine."

"It'll be good to see you."

"You know what I think? This trip is going to be good for you. We'll probably never get over losing Mom, especially this soon, but you need to do this."

Her eyes filled again. "I think you're right, but what will Dad do while I'm gone?"

"He's a rock. I think he can handle your being away for ten days."

Of course he could handle it, but when Catherine saw his grief over losing their mom, it almost killed her to think about leaving him. "You're right." She sniffed. "I'll see you tomorrow. Love you."

"Love you too."

After they hung up, she flung herself across the bed and sobbed. She'd told her dad he didn't have to drive her, but he'd insisted. She thought of him watching her plane, knowing where it was headed. It wouldn't be easy for him.

"Sandro? Your secretary said you were busy, but I must talk to you now!"

Must? It looked like he would have to have a little chat with his secretary, who'd probably been told it was an emergency.

Gabriella Conti was not his girlfriend, let alone his fiancée. The fact that she thought she had the right to behave as if she was tried his patience. He could never be interested in her that way. The wife he'd lost in a freak accident while he'd been in college had left a hole no other woman could fill. If it hadn't been for their baby son, Benito, Sandro doubted he'd have made it through those first torturous years without her.

Since then there'd been women who'd provided temporary distraction, but he seriously doubted he would ever marry again. The thought of bringing a woman into the house who might not get along with Benito made him hesitant to take that step. Unfortunately Gabriella was determined to change his mind, and things were coming to a head.

Part of it probably had to do with the fact that she was the daughter of Mario Conti, a prominent Neopolitan widower who entertained on a regular basis and used Gabriella as his hostess. He and Sandro had done business together for a long time, and they had become good friends.

However, to Sandro's chagrin, Mario's daughter had started to insinuate herself into his life, always on the pretext of organizing for her father. Sandro had been trying to find a way to let her down gently without alienating her father who, unfortunately, had hinted that lucky would be the man who could claim Sandro for a son-in-law. Mario was a good man, one Sandro honestly liked and respected. That put the situation on a very slippery slope.

"I'm in the middle of an important conference, Gabriella. I'll have to call you back."

"This can't wait—Catherine Dalton is checked in at the Hotel Celestina. Papà told me to meet him there and he'd introduce us over drinks, but he's always late. That would mean I'd have to entertain her by myself. Since I've never met her, the thought is too daunting. When I told Papà he could have no comprehension of how I'm feeling right now, he suggested that I invite you to join us."

Sandro was certain that the idea had not come from Mario. He rubbed his eyes with the palm of his hand. Though irritated by the intrusion, he chalked up her peremptory demands to the fact that she was in shock. He had to concede that it wasn't every day you were told you had a twenty-six-year-old half-sister from America you hadn't known existed until recently.

In the time Sandro had known Gabriella it had always been clear she worshipped her *papà*. Her own mother had died some time ago, and Mario now had a serious girlfriend and was hoping to get married again. However, since Gabriella had learned he'd fathered a secret love-child with another woman before he'd married her mother, Sandro suspected Mario's halo had slipped a few centimeters.

For Mario to discover after all this time that he had another daughter living on the other side of the Atlantic must have come as a tremendous shock. No doubt both father and daughter needed some support.

Compassion for the situation, and Gabriella's fragile state of mind, tempered his response. He could at least be a friend and lend them his moral support. After checking his watch he said, "I'll meet you in the hotel foyer at five." That would give him time to wind up this meeting.

"Papà expects all of us to have dinner together."

"I'm afraid I can't."

"But—"

"I promised Benito," he interjected. "In truth it will be much better if the three of you spend time alone to get acquainted. Now, I have to go. *Ciao*, Gabriella." He hung up the phone before she could say anything else.

Since his son's school was out for the summer, Sandro had been spending as much time with him as possible. He needed to get closer to him. During the past school year Benito had become secretive and uncommunicative. It was something Sandro intended to get to the bottom of in a hurry.

Forty-five minutes later he asked for the limo to be brought around. While his driver maneuvered through the heavy traffic to the newest five-star hotel in Naples acquired by his company, he phoned his son.

Though he worked for Sandro in the warehouse, Benito still had a lot of time on his hands—particularly since his favorite older cousin Silvio had gone to South America on vacation. Sandro's two older brothers, Vito and Matteo, and their families would be gone for three weeks. When Silvio was around he was a good influence on Benito, who'd made some missteps this last year, causing Sandro a certain amount of grief.

Always in the back of his mind was the fact that the absence of a mother in the home since Benito's birth hadn't helped the situation. With the assistance of live-in housekeepers, Sandro had tried to make up for the loss, but he couldn't do it all. He thanked providence for his family and their support, but the fact remained that lately his son had a penchant for getting into trouble with the wrong crowd.

Vito had promised that when he got back he'd try to gain Benito's confidence and help straighten him out. Sandro was counting on it. In the meantime he'd decided to cut down his own workload in order to concentrate on his son.

He'd made a deal with him. If Benito put in six hours of work every day in the family's exporting department, with no skipping out on some excuse, they would do an activity together every evening and on the weekends. For the last three days everything had gone without incident, and Sandro and Benito had enjoyed boating together, both being accomplished sailors.

After telling him he'd be home by six-thirty at the latest, Sandro phoned their housekeeper, Angelina, and asked her to pack a hamper of food they could take out on the boat a little later. They chatted about a needed repair on the villa roof, where some tiles had come loose. He added that to his list of things to take care of tomorrow.

Before long he alighted from the limo. Asking his driver to wait, he strode through the glass doors to the opulent lobby in search of Gabriella. Once introductions were made, and she felt comfortable with her half-sister, he'd be able to make his apologies and leave.

His keen gaze took in the tourist activity while he

looked around for Mario and Gabriella. With her short, stylish black hair, plus her impeccable dress sense and slender, five-foot-nine figure, Gabriella was usually easy to spot. However, there didn't seem to be any sign of either of them.

Knowing her father wasn't a punctual man, Gabriella had probably determined to be late on purpose, or she'd already gone into the bar with her half-sister. Unfortunately Sandro had arrived ten minutes behind schedule himself, so, deciding it was probably the latter, he headed in that direction.

As he was passing a bank of phones, the sight of glorious red-gold hair flowing halfway down a curvaceous female body dressed in jeans and well-worn cowboy boots caused him to slow down—him and a dozen other men who didn't bother to hide their interest. She had "American" written all over her, but since there were hundreds of American female tourists in Naples at any given time it didn't mean this one was Signorina Dalton.

She appeared totally engrossed in her conversation, oblivious to the stares of male admiration coming her way. Finally forcing himself to continue his quest, Alessandro searched the bar area for Gabriella without success. Close to five-thirty now, there was still no evidence of her or Mario. It stretched the imagination, but maybe Gabriella had gone up to her half-sister's room for some reason.

Impatient to get home to Benito, he retraced his steps to the crowded foyer, unconsciously watching for the redhead while hoping he might see Mario. In the process of looking around, he almost bumped into the stunning young woman wearing the cowboy boots.

She flashed him an apologetic smile before hurriedly moving out of his way. As she did so their arms brushed, making him aware of the warm flesh beneath the navy silk blouse tucked inside the jeans hugging her alluring shape. Since she seemed to be waiting for someone, he acted on instinct and caught up to her.

"Signorina Dalton?"

Of medium height, she turned to look up at him, stirring the air with the subtle scent of flowers emanating from her. Her deep-set eyes framed by dark brows and long lashes reminiscent of Mario's matched the midnight-blue of her blouse. Except for those few traits, and her light olive skin, he saw little else of the Conti genes.

"Yes? Who are you?"

CHAPTER TWO

SANDRO found her accent as charming as the husky tone of her voice. Gabriella's was much higher pitched. The two half-sisters couldn't be more different.

Instead of answering her question, it dawned on him that he was making too many comparisons—like the fact that she was shorter in stature, like her father. Annoyed with himself for his preoccupation with her, he drew in a fortifying breath.

"My name is Alessandro Lucchesi, a longtime friend and business acquaintance of Mario Conti. I understand you're his daughter Catherine from New Mexico?" Mario had confided that information to him while they had been on the phone discussing contracts only recently.

"Yes," she said, sounding slightly nervous, if not breathless. "I've been waiting for him and Gabriella."

"So have I," he drawled. "Since it's evident something has arisen to make them late, shall we go to the bar for a drink? I'll inform the front desk so they'll know where to find us."

Her nod set some fetching red curls in motion. "That

would be very nice. Your English is amazing, by the way. Thank you for being so kind to me."

The sincerity of the woman wound its way to his insides. "It's my pleasure."

While she waited for him, he gave one of the desk clerks the information, then rejoined her. By tacit agreement they headed down the hall toward the bar.

Sandro quickly realized that he was the envy of every male they passed. If she was aware of their eyes riveted on her, he couldn't tell. Undoubtedly the imminent meeting with her new-found family was all her mind could process for the moment.

His thoughts flicked to Gabriella, who'd been her daddy's darling for the last twenty-four years. To suddenly have to share his love with a sibling, especially one who looked like Signorina Dalton, would take some getting used to. If Sandro was already adding up the differences between the two women, he could only imagine how difficult it would be for Gabriella.

The friendly hostess said hello and showed them to a table, and no sooner had they sat down than a waiter approached. His gaze lingered on the pretty woman, who asked for a cola.

"Coffee for me," Sandro said in clipped Italian, hoping the out-of-control employee got the message that there were other people waiting to be served besides the raving beauty who lit up the bar area like a torch. The waiter's cheeky smile vanished in an instant. Mario would certainly have his work cut out protecting this woman from unwanted advances.

Once the waiter had disappeared, she eyed Sandro curiously. "You must be a very good friend of Mario's to be willing to look after me, Mr. Lucchesi."

"He and I have worked on many important transactions in the past. Today we planned to finish up some final discussions on one while we were here." A little lie wouldn't go amiss in this instance. "He and Gabriella should be walking in any minute now."

She sat back, visibly attempting to gain a measure of calm, but it was clear she wouldn't achieve it until she'd met Gabriella.

"I met Mario alone in his office yesterday and everything went well," she confided. "However, I have to admit I'm apprehensive about meeting his daughter. How she must hate me—or at least hate the idea of me." The last was said in a trembling voice.

He stared at her through narrowed lids. "Hate is a strong word, *signorina*. I have no doubt she's simply as curious as you are."

"Curious is too kind a word," she fired back, causing her cheeks to flush. "I've tried to put myself in her place and know I would be so hurt for myself and Mario I wouldn't know how to handle it." Her eyes filled with pain. "After twenty-six years, my mother decided to break her silence about the name of my birth father and where he lived. All these years I've been content not to know anything." A tear escaped, forming a rivulet down her cheek. "No one asked for or wanted her deathbed repentance. I keep asking myself why she did it. My brother believes it was perfectly natural for her to want to unite us, but as far as I'm concerned I think it was a cruel thing to do to five innocent people."

"Five?" Sandro asked, while a rush of unexpected emotions swept through him. Sandro couldn't equate it with cruelty—not when he recalled the look of joy on Mario's face as he had told Sandro about Catherine.

"My stepfather and brother included." She buried her face in her hands. "He's the only dad I've ever known and I adore him. When Mom opened Pandora's box before taking her last breath, she wounded Dad in unimaginable ways."

Sandro had to agree the situation was much more complex than he'd realized. "Uniting a father and daughter ought to be a thrilling occasion."

"You'd think," came the mournful reply.

"I'm sorry you lost your mother. Was she ill?"

"She died of a rare lung disease. Before that she'd never had a really sick day in her life. We're all still in shock. Especially my dad."

So much grief. Mario hadn't confided those details to him. He had been too overcome with excitement that he had another daughter.

Sandro's gaze flicked to the waiter who'd brought them their order, this time without showing undue interest in Sandro's breathtaking companion.

Catherine quickly composed herself and drank from the glass. After draining half of it, she darted him a frank glance. "I'm sorry for falling apart like that. Please forgive me. I feel like a fool. Obviously the saying is true that it's easier to tell a stranger your problems. Knowing you're good friends with Mario didn't give me the right."

He sipped his coffee. "I'm glad you felt comfortable enough to confide in me."

"You're a good listener. I've been selfish, and I know next to nothing about you except that you're a businessman and obviously married." She eyed his wedding band. "Do you have a wallet full of pictures of your children? If so, I'd love to see them."

His lips twitched. "I have a seventeen-year-old son. Though there are several pictures in my office, I don't carry a picture of him. My wife was killed in an accident a few months after he was born."

"I'm so sorry," she whispered, before finishing her drink. "I don't know how you survived that kind of pain. My dad's devastated."

"He has you and your brother. Surely that's a comfort?"

"It is for us."

"How old is your brother?"

"Brett is twenty. He's away at college right now." Her eyes clouded over. "The thing is—my mother contacted Mario before she told my dad what she'd done. It hurt him so much—especially when he learned Mario had phoned me and insisted on paying for me to fly over so we could meet."

Sandro studied her for a long moment. "Are you sorry you came?"

Her wet gaze met his. "No. We spent several hours at his office talking. H-He's really wonderful," she stammered, "but it leaves me conflicted because—because—"

"You feel guilty for liking him?" He finished the sentence for her.

She nodded slowly. "Yes. I don't want my dad to think I've betrayed him by wanting to meet my birth father and spend some time with him."

The strongest urge to comfort her took hold of Sandro. "If he's been there for you all your life, then the love you two share can't be threatened and he'll be able to handle it. Give it time."

"That's what Brett said. You're a very wise man." She bit her lip. "I take it you're acquainted with my half-sister?"

He heard a question coming. "Yes." Sandro could be thankful he'd never once felt an urge to respond to Gabriella the way she'd wanted.

"Do you think she'll like me?"

No. There's nothing about you your half-sister will like. Not your looks, your sensitivity, your intelligence or your attractive personality.

However, Sandro's opinion wasn't for her ears. What he said was, "Why wouldn't she, once she gets past the initial shock of realizing Mario had feelings for another woman before he met her mother? A very beautiful woman, obviously. Was she a redhead too?"

"Yes." The slow smile that broke the corners of her pliant mouth stirred his senses. That hadn't happened for a long time. "Thank you."

"It's only the truth." He finished the last of his coffee.

"Sandro—"

Gabriella's cry reached his ears. She'd chosen the wrong moment to interrupt. He found himself wishing he had the whole evening to spend alone with Mario's other daughter. She was like a breath of fresh air.

Resenting Gabriella's intrusion for the second time in several hours, he got to his feet in time to see her glide through the bar toward them wearing a bright red dress. Sandro feared she'd chosen that particular outfit because her father would have told her Catherine had been born with flame-colored hair. The knowledge that the competition for favorite daughter was well under way disturbed him on several levels.

Without giving her half-sister a glance, Gabriella made straight for him, intent on staking a proprietary claim on something that wasn't hers. Gut instinct drove him to apply the only evasion tactic that would work. He moved behind Catherine's chair and helped her to her feet. Again he was assailed by the sweet fragrance emanating from her hair and skin.

Still using her as a shield, he said, "Signorina Dalton? May I introduce you to Signorina Gabriella Conti. Mario is a lucky man to have fathered two such lovely daughters. You must have many things to talk about in private. While you both get to know each other, I must excuse myself to go home. Benito's waiting for me, and I'm afraid patience isn't his strong suit."

He tossed some bills on the table. "It's been a pleasure meeting you, Signorina Dalton." Unable to help it, he shot her another glance before giving his attention to Gabriella. "When Mario arrives, tell him we'll talk business tomorrow. *A presto*."

Catherine watched in fascination as her half-sister unexpectedly ran after the tall, powerfully built Alessandro Lucchesi. The way she tried to detain him before he disappeared convinced her that Gabriella was in love with the sophisticated Italian widower, who had to be in his mid to late thirties. Ten years Gabriella's senior, anyway.

For the last thirty minutes he'd given Catherine his precious time, and had made her feel her troubles were more important than his own. What set him apart from other men was his unique ability to listen and empathize with a total stranger.

A close business friend of Mario's or not, he hadn't needed to put himself out for her the way he'd done. Such genuine kindness was a trait she couldn't help but admire.

There were other things about him that commanded her interest, of course, like eyes of jet so black they'd pierced while he'd studied her. The combination of rugged features and warm olive skin framed by vibrant black hair and brows made him more sensational than the legendary Adonis. Altogether the total man had no equal she could recall.

By alluding to her mother's looks he'd paid her a compliment she wouldn't forget. He too would be one of the haunting memories she took back to New Mexico in nine days' time. She didn't want to leave her dad alone any longer than that.

Stan Dalton had always said that when it came to

relatives, a good visit was a short one—and it was advice she intended to follow. Besides, being in a foreign country where she didn't know the language made her miss him horribly…except for those moments she'd spent talking with Alessandro.

What a fabulous name for a fabulous man, whose expensive-looking gray suit encased his hard-muscled body like an exquisite kid glove. During their conversation she'd found herself loving the way he spoke English with an Italian accent. He'd made every word sound exciting—provocative, even.

She enjoyed the way he unconsciously shrugged his elegant shoulders, the way he sat with his dark head slightly cocked as he took in everything she said. There was a certain male grace in the way he drank his coffee, in the way he did everything.

All these thoughts were running through her mind as Gabriella suddenly returned to the table. Except for her height, she resembled Mario, with her dark brown eyes and coloring. She was lovely.

"Hello, Gabriella."

"Hello."

She was so reserved. Catherine couldn't imagine breaking down that wall. "This is very awkward for both of us."

"Yes."

"Do you speak English?"

"Of course."

"I only meant— Well, it doesn't matter." Catherine spoke passable Spanish, but that wouldn't help her out right now. Sucking in her breath, she said, "Isn't Mario coming?"

"There was an emergency at his office. He will be here soon."

"Would you like to have a drink while we wait?"

Without a word she sat down opposite Catherine. "It looks like you've already had one with Sandro."

The mention of his name—his nickname—made the tension worse. She would have to proceed carefully. "He was kind enough to keep me company."

Once again the waiter approached with a broad smile. "Another cola, *signorina*? Or something stronger?"

"A cola will be fine, thank you." She didn't want another drink, but needed to do whatever she could to break the ice.

Gabriella rattled off something in Italian before he left them alone. She leveled unfriendly eyes on Catherine. "I asked him to come because I knew I would be late."

She was referring to Alessandro, of course. "I appreciated the company. Thank you." Gabriella had some kind of relationship with him apart from his business dealings with Mario, otherwise he wouldn't have done a favor of that nature for her. The knowledge disturbed something inside Catherine she couldn't readily identify.

In the interim she could hear Gabriella's mind working. She didn't know what her half-sister was going to ask next. Mario needed to arrive soon or Catherine wouldn't be able to deal with her.

"You are a cowboy?"

"Cowgirl," she corrected her, in case she really didn't know. "My family lives on a ranch."

"Papà said he met your mother when she came to Italy on a trip with her girlfriends?"

The mention of her mother drove another nail in deep. "Yes."

"You do realize he was not in love with her?"

Catherine's eyes closed tightly for a moment. According to her mom, Mario had begged her to stay in Italy, but his mother hadn't approved of her and had actually forbidden Mario from seeing her.

Mario had found a way around his mother to be with her, of course, but he hadn't been able to desert the family at a time when his father was ill. They had argued over an impossible situation. Catherine's mom had finally left Italy in tears and had never returned—but Gabriella didn't need to hear those salient details.

As long as her half-sister was being blunt, Catherine decided to oblige her and get this over with. "Mother explained it was an interlude, nothing more. That's why she never let Mario know she was having his baby. She didn't tell me or my father any details until just before she died."

Her dark head reared back. "Did she hate Papà so much for not loving her that she decided to try and ruin his life and mine with this news?"

CHAPTER THREE

GABRIELLA had asked a reasonable question, and one Catherine could understand. "No. I believe she didn't want to meet God knowing there were still secrets. In my opinion she should have kept them to herself. I don't blame you for hating her and me."

The waiter placed their drinks on the table and left. Gabriella stared at the cola. "You don't drink alcohol?"

"No. I don't care for it."

A smile that could be construed as smug lifted the corners of her mouth. "How fascinating."

"Many people don't drink."

"Since part of the Conti fortune comes from our vineyards in Taurasi, it is ironic that you don't." She lifted a glass of red wine to her lips. "This is our Lachryma Christi—but it would be wasted on you, is that not true?"

"You're probably right."

But her mother had loved it, and had blamed Lachryma Christi for aiding her pleasure the night Catherine had been conceived. That was another piece of information Gabriella didn't need to hear about either. Apparently

Mario had translated for her mom and informed her, "It means 'the tears of Christ.'" Their wine was famous all over the continent.

After returning to New Mexico, Catherine's mother had shed many tears upon discovering there'd been a consequence of that very romantic interlude at the base of Mount Vesuvius. The man she'd loved to distraction would never know he'd fathered a redheaded daughter.

Eyeing Catherine over the rim of her wine glass, Gabriella said, "You shouldn't have come here."

On the phone Mario had pleaded with Catherine to fly to Italy so they could really get acquainted. She'd felt Mario's emotion, and knew it hadn't been lip service talking, otherwise she would never have left home in order to satisfy that deep longing.

She cocked her head. "Is that how your father feels now that he's met me? It's all right, Gabriella. You can tell me the truth. I won't fall apart. Does he wish I were leaving tomorrow? I'll go if that's what he wants."

She seemed to pale. "No."

Under the circumstances, that kind of honesty was humbling. "Look—I'm not here to disrupt your life. My mother was the one who called your father, not the other way around. He in turn phoned me and asked me to come. I'm only going to be here through next weekend, then I'll be flying back to the ranch. My dad and my job are waiting for me."

At that revelation, Gabriella's rigid body seemed to relax. "You don't have a boyfriend?"

Catherine took a few swallows of her drink. "Not for

a while." She'd dated a lot in college, and after, but there'd been no affair of the heart. Brett accused her of being too picky, but she couldn't help it. Stan had been so wonderful to her mom, Catherine was unconsciously waiting for someone like him to come along.

"What about you, Gabriella? Is there someone special?" Though she knew the answer, she had to ask the expected questions.

"Yes. Sandro."

That was right. Alessandro Lucchesi. Catherine had already met the man who transcended her image of the ideal male. As she lifted her glass to drink the rest of her cola, she heard Gabriella's cellphone ring. The other woman answered and a rapid conversation in Italian ensued.

When she hung up she said, "Papà is out in front of the hotel with his girlfriend, Sofia. They have made dinner reservations for us at the Ristorante Umberto."

The name didn't mean anything to Catherine. "Do I need to be dressed up?"

"No."

She'd said no, but Catherine noticed her half-sister was beautifully turned out. Though she would like to run upstairs and change, she decided it would be wiser to go to dinner in what she was wearing.

The last thing she wanted to do was give the impression she was trying to upstage Gabriella. Not that she *could* do that. Tall and slender did wonders for the trendy red cocktail dress she'd worn to capture Alessandro's attention.

When he'd told her he couldn't stay because he'd made plans to be with his son, Catherine had seen Gabriella was severely disappointed. All that preparation to knock his eyes out the moment he saw her had backfired. Without turning around for a last look, he'd strode away on those long, powerful legs. Little did he know Gabriella wasn't the only one left behind who'd groaned in frustration over his abrupt departure.

If the truth be told, Catherine wished her time spent with Alessandro could have gone on, but it wasn't meant to be. Like ships passing in the night, she would never see him again—and had better get used to that unpalatable fact before she forgot why she'd flown to Italy in the first place.

Following Alessandro's earlier actions, she pulled out some euros and put them on the table. Again, she wanted to show Gabriella that she hadn't come to Naples to get something out of Mario like money. Catherine's father was a millionaire in his own right, although his money was tied up in the ranch property.

He certainly wasn't on a par with Mario or Alessandro, though. According to Mario, who'd been in negotiations with Alessandro before she'd arrived at the office, the well-known Lucchesi family had built up one of the foremost financial institutions in southern Italy. Alessandro, the youngest of three brothers and five cousins, was reputed to be *the* new driving force.

Now that she'd met the man, it didn't surprise Catherine. One thing she could say about Gabriella: her half-sister showed superb taste in her choice of future mate. But if he'd remained single for seventeen years, Catherine had a real presentiment he intended to stay that way. The line of women who hoped to become the next Mrs. Lucchesi had to stretch from one end of the Bay of Naples to the other.

Catherine was probably the only woman who wouldn't be joining that cast of a thousand rejectees he'd left in mourning. For one thing, Gabriella wouldn't stand for it.

A familiar rap sounded on the bedroom door of the villa. "*Buonanotte, Papà*. Thanks for tonight. I had fun sailing."

"I did too. But not so fast, *figlio mio*." Sandro had just come out of the shower. He wrapped a toweling robe around his body and told his black-haired boy to come all the way in.

"I'm kind of in a hurry," he said, standing in the aperture. Wearing the bottom half of his pajamas, the tall, lanky teen had the look of all the Lucchesi clan. He also had a hidden agenda.

"To do what?" Sandro inquired mildly. "It's only ten o'clock."

"Go to bed. I'm getting up early to swim with friends."

His son loved the water, but they'd been sailing every evening. Why the need to swim at dawn? "I'm afraid you'll have to give it a miss in the morning. I have plans for us."

By the frown on his expressive face, the news didn't sit well with Benito. "What plans? You said you had an important meeting tomorrow."

Sandro gave him a shrewd regard. "That's right, I did. But plans have a way of changing."

"What do you mean?"

"It's time you and I took a day off to have some fun."

Benito averted his dark brown eyes. "A whole *day* off?"

"Until your uncles get back, someone has to mind the company. Then we'll take a few weeks off."

He let out an unhappy sigh. "I'd rather do that another time, if you don't mind."

His son's attempt at politeness went a long way to make Sandro even more suspicious. Not that Benito wasn't a basically wonderful son, but the pull to be with the wrong kind of friends was compelling at his age. Before things went any further, Sandro intended to find out what was going on this summer.

"Actually, I *do* mind."

Benito blinked.

"Before I went in the shower I had a call from Mario. It seems Gabriella's grandmother in Rome has been taken to the hospital, very ill. He's flying there tonight with Gabriella. They don't know how long they'll have to be gone. In the meantime, Mario asked me if I would watch out for his other daughter, Catherine, who's here visiting."

Benito frowned. "I didn't know he had another daughter."

"It's complicated. I'll tell you about it later. The point is, he asked me to help her enjoy her time here until he and Gabriella get back. Mario wants her to fall in love with Italy so she'll end up spending her vacations with him—maybe even live here part of the year. One day he hopes she'll consider Naples her home too."

A scowl broke out on his face. "Why do *you* have to do it? When we go to his villa he's always got plenty of other friends around."

"Maybe it's because he knows I have a son who can help make it fun for her."

Sandro could tell Benito wasn't happy with the situation. "For how long will we have to show her around?"

"I guess for as long as Mario and Gabriella have to be gone. Probably a day or two. He tells me she's never been to Italy and doesn't speak the language. You can practice your English with her."

"Great." The sarcasm didn't show his son at his finest. "How old is she?"

"Twenty-six."

"Is she as uptight as Gabriella?"

No. "I only met her for a few minutes earlier today at the hotel. She's seems very nice. Maybe you can think of something we could do to entertain her that would make you happy too?"

"Tomorrow's the Moto GP in Mugello."

Sandro had had something closer to home in mind— like Naples. He eyed his teenaged son thoughtfully. Benito expected him to turn the idea down flat, but for once Sandro would surprise him.

"Why don't you suggest that to Signorina Dalton in the morning? If she's in agreement, we can fly there. Florence is nearby. We'll have dinner after the race and walk around so she gets a feeling for it."

His son flashed him a bewildered, half-impatient glance before his features closed up. "She won't want to go."

"You won't know unless you ask."

"She'll probably say yes to be polite."

"Then that's all right. She'll dislike something you want, and you'll dislike something she wants. Every tourist wants to see Florence. You'll both be winners."

Benito had nothing to say to that kind of logic.

Hoping to lighten his son's mood, he said, "Would you like to go out for *gelato*? I'll get dressed."

He looked shocked. "You mean now?"

The question was laughable, coming from his normally night owl son. "Why not?"

"No, thanks. I'm pretty tired after loading boxes today. I think I'll call it a night."

Sandro nodded. "In that case, set your alarm for six-thirty. We'll eat breakfast and take off by seven so we can get to the track on time."

Benito muttered something morosely vague before turning to leave. When he was almost out the door, Sandro called to him. "I promise that the person you were hoping to meet up with in the morning will be alive another day to involve you in whatever is going on you can't or won't divulge to me."

A guilty look crept over Benito's face, verifying Sandro's suspicions.

"The problem about being a Lucchesi is that if you're doing something immoral and/or illegal, word will leak out and it'll be all over the press before you can take another breath. You have to ask yourself if what you're doing is worth the price you'll ultimately have to pay. Think about it before it's too late. Sometimes the wrong choice changes the path destiny has in store for you. I know you don't remember your mother, but she would have wanted to see you rise to your full potential. When we found out you were on the way, we were both overjoyed. Remember that."

After a long period of quiet, Benito closed the door. As soon as he did, Sandro moved over to the bedside table to phone Mario's daughter. He needed to make arrangements with her before she was asleep.

"Hotel Celestina."

As he was connected to the front desk he said, "Signorina Catherine Dalton, *per favore*. I don't know her room number."

"Sì. Momento."

While Catherine was letting herself in her hotel room, she heard the phone ring. She thought that it was probably her dad calling from the ranch, and she dashed across the floor to answer it.

Although she'd promised to keep him informed, there wasn't a lot to tell him today, because she hadn't spent any alone time with Mario. In all fairness to him, it wasn't his fault. Throughout dinner Mario had been trying to placate three women at once—all of whom had wanted his attention.

While they'd been eating he'd received a phone call that had seemed to disturb him very much. He'd excused himself from the table and had been gone for quite a while, leaving it to Sofia, his girlfriend, to keep the conversation going between Catherine and Gabriella.

Then Mario had returned to the table and told them the bad news. He had to take Gabriella to Rome with him tonight. Her grandmother on Mario's side had been taken to the hospital with a heart attack and they had to leave immediately. He had asked Catherine to come along, but she had refused, knowing it would be difficult enough. He had sounded upset at leaving Catherine behind, but she had rushed to assure him that it was all right. She understood that he and Gabriella needed private time with their ill family member. Until they returned Catherine would get in some sightseeing on her own.

That was when he had told her not to worry about anything. He'd asked his good friend Sandro to see to her needs and stand in for him until he and Gabriella got back.

Catherine's breath had caught in reaction before she'd told him that wasn't necessary. Mario didn't need to give it another thought. She didn't require anyone else in order to enjoy being in Naples. Mr. Lucchesi was too important and busy a man to have to be concerned about her. The hotel Mario had booked her into was exclusive and offered every tour under the sun. She could have her own private tour guide if she wanted.

However, Mario hadn't been listening. He'd told her he'd already arranged everything with Sandro, and that she could expect him to call in the morning. Before she could say anything else he had left her in the lobby, with the promise that he'd call her from Rome and tell her when he'd be back home again.

With that conversation still on her mind, she picked up the receiver, anxious to tell her dad the latest development.

"Signorina Dalton?" sounded a deep Italian male voice she would never forget, no matter how many miles or years separated them.

"Hello, Mr. Lucchesi," she said a trifle breathlessly. "I just got back from dinner with Mario. We were talking about you."

"Good. Then you already know he's on his way to Rome with Gabriella. It grieves him that he has to leave like this, so he's asked me to do the honors and show you around until his return. Naturally you'll want to do some sightseeing while you're here, and explore the sights of Naples, but how would you like to see something further afield by helicopter first?"

Her stomach got butterflies just thinking about going anywhere with him. "That sounds exciting."

"Have you been in a helicopter before?"

"Yes, over the Grand Canyon."

"I've done that trip. There's no sight quite like it. However, I promise you'll love the sights here too. My son will be coming with us. I'm sure he'll enjoy your company. Since jet lag has probably caught up with you, I'll let you go and be by for you in the limo at seven. Meet us outside in front of the hotel. *Buonanotte*, Signorina Dalton."

She heard the click, but, like everything about their conversation, it seemed to have happened in a dream state, making her slow on the uptake. She'd come here to get acquainted with her birth father, yet tomorrow she'd be spending the day with his good friend instead.

If she'd turned him down, she had a feeling it would have offended him—and her father too. The best thing to do was go with him tomorrow, but that would be it. No matter how much longer Mario might have to be in Rome after that, she wouldn't presume another minute on Mr. Lucchesi's time.

CHAPTER FOUR

BEFORE his driver turned into the entry of the hotel, Sandro's attention was drawn to the redheaded woman in cowboy boots standing outside the doors. Today she was wearing a green ribbed top over tan pleated pants. With her glorious hair, he couldn't have looked anywhere else if he'd wanted to.

She walked right up to the limo and climbed in the back, opposite him and Benito. How nice to meet a woman who didn't keep them waiting. His son looked as dumbstruck as the waiter who'd served them in the bar last night.

"Benito? This is Signorina Catherine Dalton, who's flown here from the States." He spoke in English. "As I told you, she's Mario Conti's daughter."

A smile lit up her classic features. "Hi, Benito. So you're the famous son. Last evening your father cut short a meeting just so he could be with you. I'm living proof because I was there," she added impishly.

"*Buon giorno*, Signorina Dalton. It's very nice to meet you," Benito replied, but he spoke without a trace of a smile.

She in turn said, "Please call me Catherine."

Benito's eyes went back and forth between Catherine and his father. Sandro knew his son had been upset about having to come in the first place, and he seemed to like the situation even less now that Catherine had joined them. Normally he displayed good manners in front of a stranger.

"Catherine lives on a ranch in San Antonio, New Mexico."

"San Antonio...the Spurs?" he blurted.

She flicked Sandro an amused smile before giving Benito her full attention. "No, they're in Texas. My San Antonio is out in the middle of New Mexico, kind of near some other little towns you've never heard of."

Sandro chuckled, before translating some of the nuances of her explanation. Benito's English was coming along. When he went to the university in England next year, it would improve in quantum leaps.

His son's gaze traveled to her boots. "You are a cowboy?"

"Not really, but my brother Brett is. He rides in the rodeo. I only wear these boots because there's so much dust around at home, and they're more comfortable than regular shoes."

Again Sandro helped his son understand.

"You have a horse?"

She nodded, causing her hair to shimmer. Sandro could almost hear it rustle.

"What is its name?"

"Tootsie." As she obliged him, her mouth curved

provocatively. Again Sandro's senses were affected. He wished he hadn't noticed.

"How long are you in Napoli?"

"She isn't sure," Sandro inserted smoothly.

"According to my ticket, nine more days," she corrected him. "I came to get acquainted with my father and see a little of Naples."

"Do you like sport bikes?"

"My brother does. He's got an old Yamaha he rides around on at the ranch with a couple of his buddies."

Sandro tried not to smile, because he could tell the news had surprised his son.

"Do you have one too?" she asked.

"Yes."

"I bet it's a Ducati. My brother says the Italian make is the best, but he couldn't afford it."

When his son wasn't forthcoming fast enough, Sandro said, "Benito's asking because there's a Moto GP race in Mugello today."

"You're kidding?" she cried. "Where is Mugello?"

"Near Florence."

Her eyes met Sandro's. "Could we go? Brett would die to see one. I'll take pictures. He'll be so jealous."

Well, well. "It could be arranged—don't you think?" he prodded his son.

Benito nodded, but grew silent after that. Before long they arrived at the Lucchesi headquarters. The helicopter on top of the complex was standing by. They rode to the roof, where Sandro nodded to his pilot before helping Catherine inside. Benito sat next to her, while

Sandro took the co-pilot's seat. Everyone buckled up before the blades started rotating.

Catherine let out a hushed cry as the helicopter flew them over the city and headed north, leaving Vesuvius behind. The pictures in the geography books of her childhood could never do justice to the surreal landscape spread beneath them. It was an awesome sight.

She hadn't expected to do any real sightseeing on this first trip. Time constraints wouldn't allow it. Her only thought had been focused on meeting Mario before she had to turn around and go back home. Whatever he'd planned for her would be fine. Hopefully the grandmother's heart attack had been a mild one and they'd be back soon.

Right now Catherine would concentrate on her surroundings. The day would be over soon enough. She had the distinct feeling Benito wasn't happy about this trip. In fact with her trying to fall in with his wishes he seemed to be even more upset.

Like Gabriella, Benito made her feel like she was intruding on his life. But neither of them had to worry. Tomorrow she would insist on being on her own, no matter how long Mario had to stay away. Alessandro was being wonderful to her, but she didn't expect him to drop everything because of her—not even for his good friend.

If Mario had to be away too long, she'd fly back to the States and come another time. Maybe it would be better that way? In time Gabriella would get used to the fact that her father had another daughter. On the next visit it was possible she'd be more friendly to Catherine. If not that, at least more accepting of the reality of the situation.

Just watching Benito's reaction, she saw that he wanted his father's whole attention. Without a wife and mother, the two had to have been so close all these years, and it gave her insight into Gabriella's reaction to her. If Catherine suddenly had to share her dad's love with a sibling she hadn't known about it would be hard for her too. She could understand Gabriella's jealousy. She really could.

After flying on jets, and standing in line for hours to collect luggage and dealing with the crowds, she decided getting around Italy in a helicopter was the only way to travel. They swooped down from one venue to another.

First they watched the exciting sports bike Grand Prix. She filmed parts of it with her video camera. For a little while Benito became so engrossed watching his favorite cyclist he was more pleasant to be around. They ate lunch after the race, then flew to Florence and landed on the roof of the Lucchesi Palace Hotel, overlooking the pristine Piazza D'Azeglio.

Alessandro installed them in the penthouse with adjoining suites. Once they'd freshened up, they left the hotel on foot and headed directly for the Accademia Gallery that housed the real David of Michelangelo. They had to walk fast to see it before the place closed for the evening.

"In my opinion, this is the most important piece of art in Florence," Alessandro said in his deep voice as the two of them walked around the tall statue. Benito had stopped to look at another piece of art. For the moment she was alone with her host. "The architecture of the city itself is an art treasure, but this statue is the representation of man, God's greatest creation."

Even before he'd spoken, she'd been moved to tears looking at it. Alessandro enhanced the experience with the reverence in his tone. Though she'd seen pictures of David all her life, it was bigger than she'd realized and absolutely breathtaking. Between the beauty of the stone and the beauty of the face and body Michelangelo had created, Catherine was awestruck.

She heard one of the tourists standing nearby comment that it was anatomically perfect. In Catherine's mind, so was Alessandro. Throughout the day she'd watched him at moments when he didn't know she was looking. She couldn't help thinking what a masterpiece Michelangelo might have created if Benito's father had been his inspiration. But, as she was finding out, he had other qualities beyond merely the physical. The way he handled his son while going out of his way to add to the pleasure of her trip when he didn't have to was truly exceptional.

"What are you thinking?" he asked in a quiet tone.

Praying her face didn't look as hot as it felt, she said, "That this is one of the most memorable days of my life."

"I've enjoyed it too—more than you know. It's been years since I brought Benito to see this the first time. I think he was seven. This time I can tell he's definitely growing up. The *Ratto delle Sabine* statue has grabbed his attention."

Catherine knew what piece of sculpture he was referring to. They'd passed the Rape of the Sabine before coming into this room. It would fascinate anyone. When her eyes lifted to Alessandro's, his were studying her face with an intensity that sent a jolt through her body like a current of electricity.

"The museum's closing. Let's go." Benito had found them, breaking her trance. He sounded bored and wanted to leave.

Alessandro's lips twitched. "I think someone's hungry. There's a place near the Giotto Tower that serves the best steak *carpaccio* in the city. It's Austrian-run and they make a Sacher dessert to die for. But if you'd prefer an all-Tuscan meal, just say the word."

She smiled. "I wouldn't dream of depriving you of something you've been craving."

His expression sobered. "I don't have that many cravings, but the ones I do have are fairly strong."

Catherine averted her eyes, sensing he'd meant something else—but maybe he was just teasing her and it was foolishness on her part to imagine it could have been interpreted differently. That was the way this day had been. Out of this world because of him… She didn't want it to end.

Anxious to appease Benito, she moved ahead of them to reach the entrance. Within ten minutes they'd reached the restaurant, and after a fabulous meal they walked by the Arno river and crossed the medieval Ponte Vecchio bridge.

Despite her protests, Alessandro bought her a pair of

earrings from one of the little jewelry shops. He made the purchase so fast she didn't see what they looked like until they'd arrived back at the penthouse.

While Benito disappeared into the bedroom to watch the sports news on TV, Alessandro handed her the little box before she went to her room. "Go ahead and open it."

With trembling fingers she lifted the lid. Inside were two tiny gold replicas of David, spinning inside a delicate outer gold sphere the size of a dime. She knew they were expensive, but it was the significance more than the price that sent a spurt of warmth through her body.

"There's a lot of gold in your red hair."

Her head flew back as she looked up at him. "I've never been given a lovelier gift." Her voice trembled. "I'll always treasure them. But when Mario asked you to show me around, I'm sure he didn't mean you had to buy me gifts."

In the silence that followed she felt his mood change. "Today's trip was something he would have done for you under normal circumstances. The earrings are something *I* wanted to do."

She swallowed hard. "Thank you very much."

"You're welcome."

The gleam of satisfaction coming from his dark eyes confused her. She moved to the door that separated their suites, then turned to him. "Goodnight, Alessandro. Please thank Benito again for explaining the finer points of the race to me."

"Thank *you* for helping me deal with a crosspatch."

Catherine chuckled. "It's his age." Plus the fact that

he wanted his father to himself. "My brother went through a similar stage, but he's come out of it."

"That helps to know. We'll see you in the morning. Plan to come to our room at eight, and we'll set up an itinerary for the day over breakfast."

"Maybe Mario will be back tomorrow?"

"Possibly."

"I don't want to be an imposition, Alessandro."

"You're not. In fact you're doing me a favor. Keeping Benito away from Naples right now is the best thing that could happen. I'll tell you about it tomorrow, when he's not in earshot. Sleep well."

After she got ready for bed, she phoned her dad to tell him about her amazing day. That led to an explanation about Gabriella's grandmother and Mario's request that his friend Alessandro take her sightseeing until he returned. All the while they spoke, she fingered the earrings Alessandro had bought her.

Once they'd hung up, she fell asleep, exhausted. The next morning she found them by her pillow. She quickly showered and washed her hair. Then she undid her studs and put the earrings on, remembering what he'd said about the gold in her hair while she blow-dried it.

She decided to wear pants again, yellow ones, with a yellow-and-white-striped top. Pants were much safer when you had to climb in and out of a helicopter. More often than not she felt Alessandro's gaze on her, making her all too aware of his masculine presence. After slipping on the new bone-colored leather sandals she'd bought her first day in Naples, she felt ready to join the others next door.

The truth was, she couldn't wait to see Alessandro. He'd been the last person on her mind last night before she had fallen asleep, and when she'd awakened this morning her thoughts had been filled with him again. To her dismay, she didn't remember Mario until she was packing her things.

Guilt pricked her to realize how far her thoughts had wandered from her only reason for being in Italy. She needed to go back to Naples before she enjoyed being with Alessandro too much. He could become an addiction if she weren't careful. How disastrous would that be?

There were so many reasons this was wrong. She was crazy to keep this up. Benito couldn't wait to see the end of her! And Gabriella would have a fit to find out just how much time Catherine had spent with Alessandro already. As for him, he was doing this favor for Mario, and no other reason. Then there was her dad, who missed her horribly. So did her brother. They were a family, who needed each other to get through this period without her mom.

When she eventually knocked on the door to announce she was coming in, she'd made up her mind to go back to Naples after they'd eaten. Alessandro had made a comment about keeping Benito away from there for a reason, but he could still do that. It was just that *she* couldn't afford to spend any more time with him.

"Buon giorno," Alessandro greeted her the second she stepped over the threshold into the sitting room. He

stood there with his legs slightly apart, dressed in jeans and a silky-looking cream-colored shirt open at the neck while he drank his coffee. Their gazes fused, sending her pulse soaring. "Coffee or juice?"

"Juice, please." She moved closer to the coffee table spread with a variety of rolls and fruit.

As he handed her the glass, his eyes lighted on her earrings. "They suit you." His deep voice sounded like velvet brushing gravel.

"Thank you." She took a steadying breath. Everything he wore suited him. "Where's Benito?"

"In the shower. He'll be out in a minute."

"Alessandro—"

"Obviously you have something important on your mind. But before you say anything I'd like to talk to you about my son before he joins us."

"Of course. What is it?" She sipped the juice, thankful for something to do with her hands.

"He's had some problems this year, being with the wrong friends. When Mario asked me to show you around, he unknowingly provided me with an excuse to get Benito away from their influence. Until we hear from Mario, would you be willing to work with me to help my son?"

Her brows formed a gentle frown. "What do you want me to do?"

"Be willing to do some of the activities he enjoys— like we did yesterday. My son's fragile right now. He has secrets. If I can spend enough time with him, I'm hoping he'll break down and confide in me."

She both saw and felt his concern. After being with

Benito and witnessing his moody behavior, Catherine had to concede Sandro's worries were legitimate.

"Papà?" He unexpectedly wandered in to the sitting room, pulling on a T-shirt. When he saw Catherine he halted.

"Good morning, Benito."

"Hi," he said, without enthusiasm.

Alessandro glanced at his son. "Now that we're all together, where shall we go today?"

"If you're planning to tour the Uffizi Gallery, I'll stay here."

"That destination didn't come up," his father stated. Catherine had to give him marks for not letting his son rile him. "This is as much a vacation for us as for Catherine. Any suggestions?"

Benito glanced at her out of the corner of his eye. "Ever heard of the Count of Monte Cristo?"

"I must have read the book a dozen times."

He didn't look particularly pleased with her answer. "Want to see the island of Monte Cristo?"

"I'd love it!"

CHAPTER FIVE

SANDRO told the pilot to set them down at Cala Maestra, the only part of the island where they could land.

"*This* tiny little island is Monte Cristo?" Catherine almost squeaked after they jumped down from the helicopter. "It's full of rocks and nothing else!"

Benito tossed one in the water. His back was turned toward Catherine. In the next breath Catherine broke down in rich, feminine laughter. Her incredible blue eyes swerved from his son to Sandro.

"Thanks for suggesting we come, Benito. The joke's on me. Obviously Hollywood decided not to film it here. There's no place to hide the treasure."

Sandro had let his son have his fun. No woman of his acquaintance would have been happy about being brought to this desolate hump of earth in the middle of the Mediterranean, but Catherine appeared to genuinely enjoy it. She was a rare person not to take herself seriously. Benito looked over his shoulder.

She grinned at him. "What's our next stop? Elba? I studied a map of Italy before I left New Mexico. Do I dare get out of the helicopter, in case you banish me like the government did poor Napoleon?"

It was Sandro's turn to laugh out loud, but his son didn't join in. Before it subsided, his cellphone rang. He pulled it from his pocket and walked a little distance away so neither of them could hear the conversation.

"Mario?"

"I'm glad you answered so I didn't have to leave a message. Gabriella's grandmother died a little while ago."

"I'm very sorry to hear that."

"Don't be. Her suffering is over, but there's a problem."

"I understand. Your family needs you to help plan the funeral."

"Exactly. It may be three or four days before we can get back to Naples."

The news shouldn't have elated Sandro—not when his son was more than ready to drop Catherine off at the Celestina and be done with the whole business.

"Don't worry about Catherine. The three of us are enjoying ourselves, and will continue to do so until your return."

"I knew I could count on you. When she hears, she'll probably say she should fly back to the States."

Sandro could guarantee it. In little ways she'd been pulling away from him all day. "It's not going to happen," he vowed. The thought of her leaving was worse than imagining the day without the sun. In just a short time she'd added something to his life that would rob him if she left.

"*Grazie.* I owe you, Alessandro."

"That's what friends are for. Concentrate on Gabriella."

He cleared his throat. "Is Catherine there?"

"Yes."

"Let me talk to her."

Sandro turned around and walked toward her. "It's Mario." Ignoring the question in her eyes, he handed her the phone and moved toward Benito, who'd started throwing rocks again.

He put his arm around his shoulders. "Gabriella's grandmother died, so we'll be spending a few more days with Catherine. As soon as she's off the phone we'll fly to Capri. I'm depending on you to show her around the Blue Grotto. We'll stay there tonight. Starting tomorrow, we'll give her the definitive tour of Naples. Keep in mind that if Mario had married her mother, Naples would be Catherine's home. Try to think about that while you're being intentionally rude to our guest."

Over the next three days Catherine felt she'd seen and learned so much about the city she could be a tour guide. They did everything, from visiting museums and churches to exploring the network of caves beneath the city. Every night she went to bed exhausted.

Mario had virtually begged her not to leave Italy. In the end she hadn't wanted to. But in the dark hours of the night in her hotel room she had to admit Mario wasn't the only person who kept her here.

She'd spent the better part of a week with Alessandro, eating, laughing, walking, communicating eighteen hours a day. But there'd been a downside, because the more she craved being with him, the more Benito retreated into his shell. For his sake, and her own self-preservation, she didn't dare leave herself open on the chance she found herself alone with Alessandro again.

Today, at the National Archaeological Museum while they'd been looking at the frescoes from Pompeii, Catherine had turned to make a comment to him but he hadn't even heard her. Instead his eyes had been concentrated on her mouth.

If Benito hadn't been with them, and there hadn't been any tourists in the room, she knew he would have kissed her. There'd been too many signs over the last few days that he was barely holding back. The chemistry had been there from the moment he'd introduced himself to her in the hotel lobby.

But they hadn't crossed that line yet, and she was determined they wouldn't. Thankfully Mario had phoned a little while ago. He and Gabriella were returning tomorrow, and Mario planned to come for her around noon. As far as Catherine was concerned Alessandro's obligation to her father was now over. With only a few days left before she went home, she intended to spend all of it with Mario.

Too restless for bed yet, Sandro walked out on to the balcony off his bedroom. For once he didn't see the view that drew tourists from around the globe to capture it on film. To his chagrin, images of Catherine filled his mind to the exclusion of everything else.

He couldn't lie to himself any longer. It didn't matter that Mario was coming home tomorrow. Sandro *wanted* to see her again. In fact she was all he'd been able to think about since dropping her off at the hotel.

From the beginning, his desire to be with her had been too intense to ignore. But Benito thought Mario's return signaled the end of their time with Catherine, and couldn't be happier this day had come. Sandro groaned, because he knew his son would become more difficult if he did decide to pursue her.

No woman had ever come between father and son before. If she were the right woman, it shouldn't have to be that way. With time and patience surely it could work?

How many times had both Vito and Matteo told Sandro he needed to risk loving again, otherwise life had no meaning? That was easy for them to say. They hadn't lost their spouses. No one could know the pain he had suffered except someone who'd been through it also.

He rubbed his neck absently. In order to get on a more intimate footing with Catherine he would of necessity hurt Gabriella's pride and cause Mario unnecessary concern when he already had enough on his plate. The whole business went against Sandro's natural code of ethics.

Like Benito, who was struggling to make the right choices in life, Sandro found he too had a choice to make. The high road or the low. Which one would it be?

A caustic laugh escaped his throat. How ironic that he'd been lecturing his son all week about straightening out his life when Sandro himself was on the verge of doing something that could be construed as dishonorable in certain people's eyes.

One wrong move could injure Benito, not to mention the added possibility of opening himself up to the kind of pain he'd been careful to avoid since his wife's death. Something serious had to be wrong with him to even consider seeking Catherine out. A week with her should have been enough.

Yet even while he reasoned this way, and gave himself mental lashings for his weakness, no argument could deter him from going back into the room and reaching for the phone to call her hotel room. If she didn't pick up, then maybe he would have dodged a bullet, as the Americans put it so well. But if she answered, then *she* would be the one forced to make the next choice. Though he might be damned for what he was doing, he couldn't summon a conscience over it. He was too far gone for that.

While Catherine was putting on a fresh nightgown after her shower, she heard the hotel phone ring. It was probably Mario, who had told her that he'd phone again tonight to finalize their plans for tomorrow.

His intention was to pick her up by twelve-thirty at the latest. This time it would be just the two of them. She hoped nothing had come up to change their plans. They were going to take a drive into the country, and Mario wanted to show her where he'd been born and had grown up. Where he'd met her mother. He'd promised they would talk.

She'd told him that was what she wanted. It was

really the only reason she'd come to Naples. There would be no more time spent with Alessandro. Everything had become way too complicated.

By the time she picked up the receiver, she was feeling incredibly emotional. "Hello?" She almost said Mario's name.

"Catherine?"

Alessandro—

She sank down on the side of the queen-size bed to gather her wits. After he and Benito had dropped her off earlier, she hadn't thought to talk to him again tonight. At this point she felt as if she were doing something forbidden—yet he was the one who'd called.

Her pulse sped up. "Yes?" she finally answered, when she could catch her breath. He would always have that effect on her.

"I can tell there's something wrong. Don't try to deny it."

His instincts were uncanny.

She swallowed with difficulty. "Are you a psychic, as well as the dynamic power who moves mountains at Lucchesi?"

"Neither one," his voice rasped. He was not fooled by her attempt to inject some levity into the conversation. "I'm aware the situation between us is explosive for a number of reasons."

All week Catherine had been making a list of them. Neither she nor Alessandro needed to have things spelled out to understand. This ability to eavesdrop on each other's minds without words really shook her.

"The fact is, Mario's a fine man—as you're coming to find out. Someone you'd be happy to claim as your father. But you're afraid to open up because you know how hard this is on Gabriella."

It was getting even harder on Catherine. During their delicious seafood dinner with her father last week, Gabriella had confided to all of them that she and Sandro were getting closer, and that it was only a matter of time before they began to date exclusively. Catherine knew for a fact it wasn't true, but as long as Gabriella believed it nothing else mattered—because she'd made her claim on Alessandro.

Catherine's hand tightened on the receiver. "With that kind of insight, Mr. Lucchesi, you're positively frightening. Poor Mario is trying so hard to keep Gabriella and Sofia happy, without me adding more problems to the mix."

"That's why I'm calling—to take you out of that mix for a while longer. I'm coming for you early in the morning."

The announcement she shouldn't have been waiting for filled her with alternating waves of joy and fear, making it almost impossible to articulate an answer.

"I—I can't," she faltered. "Mario's picking me up at noon. It'll take me that long to get ready. He wants to show me his world."

Silence followed her response, and then she could hear him saying as clearly as anything, "*Naturalmente.* He's your *papà.* He wants to make up for all the years you've lost. You're blood of his blood, heart of his heart.

You represent that period of his life when he knew what it was like to be in love for the first time. But I want to show you my world," he said in a husky tone.

When Alessandro spoke, she was so deep in thought she didn't know if she was reading his mind or if he'd said the words aloud.

"Catherine?"

He was prodding her. Just hearing the way her name sounded on the tip of his Italian tongue released a fresh spurt of adrenalin. She felt like jumping out of her skin.

"I heard you tell Benito you had work in the morning."

She heard his sharp intake of breath come through the line. "I have to fly to Sardinia in the morning on business," he continued in a low tone, knowing she was at war with her conscience. "Benito's coming with us. You'll enjoy the island. At this time of year it's a flower garden."

Her mouth went dry. She rocked in place. "I'm sure it's beautiful." So beautiful she was afraid that if she went it would be the kind of mistake you couldn't undo.

Aside from all the reasons she shouldn't be with him again, she had no business getting to know a man who could have nothing to do with her life when she returned home to her dad in America in a few days. She had a life in New Mexico that had nothing to do with the Lucchesi family here. Alessandro had responsibilities, friendships, relationships. There'd be a ripple effect on everything and everyone. Gabriella. Benito and Mario. The risk would be too costly.

"Think about my invitation. I'll come by the hotel in the limo tomorrow morning at seven. If you're not out in front, then I'll know you needed your sleep. *Buonanotte*, Catherine."

She heard the click, but like everything about their conversation it seemed to happen in a dream state, making her slow on the uptake. Nothing had been decided. To spend any more time with Alessandro would guarantee she'd go home with thoughts of him she couldn't do anything about.

If she slept in tomorrow then it could all remain a dream. No harm done to anyone or herself.

Catherine let out an agonized cry. What a lie *that* was! There was harm done by virtue of her very desire to do something wrong—even if she didn't follow through. Alessandro had set the idea afloat in her mind. Now she would burn with it like a fever for the rest of the night. What a fool she was even to consider it.

Once she'd prepared for bed and slid beneath the covers, she decided to let her natural body rhythm make the decision. If she slept in until eleven, so be it. If she was pacing the floor at six, then she'd think long and hard about the consequences of giving in to something she wanted more than she could have imagined.

CHAPTER SIX

"I THOUGHT we were going to work."

Sandro glanced at his unhappy son, who was sitting opposite him in the back of the limo. "I asked the driver to make a short detour first."

Benito's eyes narrowed. "Is *she* coming with us *again*?"

"Maybe. Maybe not."

He made a noise before throwing his head back. "Is that why you're so uptight this morning?"

Sandro supposed he was. "If you want to know the truth, I'm struggling with something that could get me into trouble. Would that bother you?"

His son's face screwed up. "What kind?"

"An ugly kind," he muttered. It had already impacted Benito.

"You mean like embezzlement or something?"

Sandro's jaw hardened. "Worse."

"Worse than going to prison?"

"There are different kinds of prisons."

"You're starting to scare me, Papà."

"Then maybe you understand how I feel."

Benito's brows furrowed. "Do you want to talk about it?"

Sandro couldn't remember the last time his son had thought out of his own sphere long enough to worry about his father. This had to be a first.

He was tempted to tell him, because it was the perfect lead-in for the conversation they needed to have, but the timing was all wrong. The limo had already entered the drive leading to the front entrance of the hotel. There were a few people coming in and out, but his gut twisted when he realized Catherine wasn't anywhere around.

That was good, he decided, letting out his breath. She'd chosen. Yet the second the limo came to a full stop he opened the door and leaped out. "I'll be right back."

Sandro had promised himself that if he didn't see her standing there he'd tell the driver to head for the office. So much for promises.

In a few swift strides he entered the lobby. A grimace stole over his features because she wasn't there either. He knew which room she was in, but he preferred not to draw the staff's attention by going there.

Feeling out of control at this point, he moved over to the elevators. His watch said five after seven. In case she was on her way down, he'd give her another minute before he walked away for good. It would be better this way. Better for Benito. Better for everyone. Don't let anything get past the point of no return, then there'd be no pain. After losing Andrea he'd had enough hurt to last a lifetime.

The lights above the elevator doors indicated movement. Traffic had started to pick up, but it was clear she wasn't coming. Two minutes went by before he wheeled around, his face set, and started for the entrance.

A few feet from the glass doors leading out to the curb, he felt a soft tap on his arm from behind.

"Alessandro?"

His heart did a double clutch. Only one woman could own that slightly husky voice. Sandro had to tamp down his elation before he turned to her. "*Buon giorno*, Catherine."

Her eyes clung to his for a brief moment. "Good morning."

He could swear she'd been running, and that thought pleased him even more. Her breathing had grown shallow, drawing his attention to the Levi's and turquoise top she was wearing. The cowboy boots were back.

The attraction between them was palpably real—otherwise she wouldn't have willingly passed the danger point that said "Proceed from here at your own peril."

"Have you eaten?"

"I called Room Service for juice and a roll."

That meant she hadn't been able to sleep either. His instincts hadn't let him down. But she'd fought a hard battle, before showing up late enough to give him a heart attack.

"We'll eat a more substantial meal when we arrive in Sassari. Shall we go?" He cupped her elbow—any excuse to touch her. Together they walked outside to the limo. The occasional brush of her leg against his shot fire through him.

In order to cool off, he helped her into the limo next to Benito, then sat down opposite them.

Their eyes met again. This time he saw worry lurking in those dark blue depths. She raised questions for which he didn't have answers yet. All he knew was that, despite the problems a relationship with her would create, he felt young again.

After he'd buried his wife, he'd assumed you only got one chance in life for that kind of happiness. All these years he'd been coasting along in a drab existence, falling deeper into an apathetic groove. Then out of nowhere he had caught sight of the exquisite woman who now sat across from him.

So help him, whatever obstacles she threw in their way—and she would; already he could sense her retreating behind her fears—he intended to explore what might happen between them.

He had half a mind to send Benito home and simply whisk her away. But in this mood he might never bring her back, and could add kidnapping to his growing list of worries.

When they reached his office, he helped her out of the limo. "One more elevator ride. Are you ready?" He'd put his hand behind her waist. Her quivering response was all the answer he needed.

This time when the helicopter took off the pilot flew them over Pompeii and Mount Vesuvius, where Catherine was given a close look at the river of lava. Mario's vineyards lay somewhere down there at the foot.

She'd come to meet Mario. It had never occurred to her that her whole world would turn inside out the instant a tall, dark, brooding stranger stopped her in the hotel lobby and asked if she was Signorina Dalton. From that moment on a force had been unleashed that had rearranged the molecular structure making up her physical existence. From here on out she would mark time in terms of B.A. and A.A. Before Alessandro and After Alessandro.

In B.A. time she'd enjoyed her life, her family, her friends, her job. Except for her mother's death and the revelation about her birth father, nothing monumental had disturbed the tenor of her life.

In A.A. time she didn't know herself any more. None of the old rules applied. This was new, uncharted territory, consisting of one man unlike any other. Judging by Mario's praise of him, the youngest and brightest Lucchesi brother who'd invaded her universe appeared to draw women and men alike.

Gabriella was in love with him. His pilot revered him. Mario thought the world of him, and Benito clearly adored him—despite his apparent uninterest. All this Catherine had absorbed in just a week's time.

If there was such a thing as casting a spell, he'd done it with the mere flash of his eyes and a toss of his head. This morning she'd awakened at five, with the knowledge that if she couldn't be with him she didn't want to be anywhere else, with anyone else. The realization was terrifying enough without the awful guilt of knowing Gabriella had fallen under his spell first.

She wasn't just any woman. She was Catherine's half-sister! Mario was hoping the day would come when Alessandro took a romantic interest in Gabriella. He'd whispered as much to Catherine at dinner that night.

Yet here she was, accompanying Alessandro Lucchesi on a business trip in his private helicopter at seven in the morning, and no one else knew about it—except Benito, of course.

While she was deep in torturous thought, she heard Alessandro's vibrant voice through the microphone. He sat in the co-pilot's seat with his headgear on, bigger than life. She and Benito were in back.

"We're approaching Sassari, Catherine. It sprang up in the Middle Ages. Later we'll go exploring. Right now the pilot is flying us over the oak cork forest before we set down. I'm thinking of purchasing more for the company."

"Tell me about it," she called out, needing something to distract her from staring at him.

"With cork harvested from these trees, one division of our company makes several products which we export—including corks for wine. You'll be interested to know Mario started buying them from us several years ago. It's an arrangement that has benefited all concerned."

Until the mention of Mario, Catherine had wanted to know everything about Alessandro and his work. Now her stomach clenched. Someone who worked here was bound to find out she'd come with Alessandro, and the news would leak back to Mario and Gabriella.

It was one thing to sightsee, but another to be here—

of all places. Even if she weren't introduced to anyone, her red hair and cowboy boots would be a topic of conversation that might reach Mario's ears. What possible excuse could either of them offer him or Gabriella if that happened?

Sardinia was like one fantastic flower garden—an Eden. To have flown here with Alessandro represented the thrill of a lifetime. But they would have to establish some ground rules or she wouldn't step outside.

The pilot circled the treetops to give her a close-up view, then he set them down in a clearing near a cluster of outbuildings and cars. Once the blades stopped rotating, Alessandro took off his gear and turned to her. He looked incredible in cargo pants and a cream shirt open at the neck, where she could see a dusting of black hair.

"You think I don't know what's going through your mind? But you can stop worrying," he said in a low voice. "I'm taking Benito inside to meet with the manager. This is a trial run for him, to see how he handles things. In a few minutes I'll return. We'll take a company car and find us a place to eat along the coast. Then we'll come back for him."

Relief made her body go limp.

"See you later, Benito."

He eyed her speculatively. She couldn't imagine him ever liking her. *"Ciao, signorina."*

Alessandro darted her a private glance. His penetrating black eyes set her heart tripping. "I won't be long."

Hurry, she wanted to cry out.

"I will," he murmured, once again reading her mind before he left to catch up with his son.

Catherine sat there, stunned by what had just occurred. The feeling of oneness between them wasn't a fluke. It was so strong they might have been bound in another life.

While the pilot talked to someone on his cellphone, she rested her head against the seat. Soon she was going to be alone with Alessandro. The anticipation made it impossible to quell the frantic beating of her heart. This was insanity. She absolutely *had* to get her emotions under control before he came back for her.

CHAPTER SEVEN

TEN minutes later Sandro concluded his business with the manager, then took Benito aside. "You're about to watch the stripping process. It's fascinating."

"But not as fascinating as watching Catherine Dalton?" he came back unexpectedly. "What is she to you, Papà?"

Benito's blunt question had been expected, but he was surprised about one thing. His son sounded as grown-up and serious as one of Sandro's brothers. He felt the impact of his question like he'd slugged him in the mid-section. "She is Mario's daughter."

"So is Gabriella. But you've never taken *her* anywhere with us—let alone to work."

His eyes narrowed on Benito, he said, "Suppose you tell me what's on your mind?"

Benito acted a trifle uncertain. "You're angry with me, huh?" Just then he looked like he had when he was a little boy, knowing he'd done something wrong.

A frown marred Sandro's features. "For your behavior, yes. For your question, no."

After a slight hesitation, "Do you still miss my mother?"

With that question, Sandro had just been given the answer he'd suspected. He expelled the breath he'd been holding. "Your mother was my life."

Benito released a huge pent-up breath.

"But I won't lie to you, Benito. Catherine has become important to me."

Benito scuffed his toe against the wood floor in reaction. Then he flicked his gaze to the manager. "I've got to go."

Alessandro checked his watch. "I'll be back for you at ten-fifteen."

His son eyed him as if he didn't believe him. Sandro gave him a pat on the shoulder and watched him disappear before he went outside. At least it was out in the open with Benito now. While his son pondered the ramifications, Sandro had been given two hours of freedom that he was sure were going to change his life.

He got in the car he'd arranged for and drove around to the helicopter—where he discovered Catherine asleep, proof of her restless night. Though he might be in a sleep-deprived state himself, he'd never felt more alive than at this moment. Her hair was splayed over the headrest in enticing disarray, and he was tempted to muss it further and watch it flicker like live flame.

"Catherine?" he called to her. She stirred. He said her name again. It brought her awake. Her lids fluttered open.

Those cobalt eyes ignited, sending a rush of adrenaline through his being. They roved over him as if she needed to make certain he was really there. During that unguarded moment he heard her cry his name on a distinct note of longing. His pulse pounded at the temples.

"We can go now." He couldn't get her alone fast enough.

Catherine quickly exited the helicopter and climbed into the front passenger seat of the car. She smelled like the wild flowers growing in clusters everywhere. The need to touch her had become paramount to his existence.

He started the car and drove on a winding road beneath the trees. When they were out of sight and secluded, he pulled to the side and cut the motor. In a blind move he turned to undo her seat belt, catching her by surprise.

"What are you doing?"

"What do you think, *bellissima*? A whole week without being able to really touch you? Come to me, Catherine," he cried in an aching voice, and reached for her.

"I'm afraid," she cried.

"But not of me—otherwise you wouldn't have come." Filled with primitive need, Sandro gathered her compulsively against him. Her warm, sweet breath mingled with his before he covered her trembling mouth with his own. The feminine mold of her body sent desire arcing through him.

"Open your mouth to me, *squisita*. Don't hold back." His lips roved her satin cheeks and throat. "I couldn't bear it."

Her body gave a final shudder of surrender, allowing him access until they were tasting each other's mouths with a hunger that refused to be appeased. The rush of euphoria assailing him was too indescribable to put into words. For the next little while he settled down to a sensual feasting that took him to a sphere beyond his comprehension.

How had he lived this long without her?

The sun rose higher in the sky, but he was no longer cognizant of anything but this feeling of ecstasy. She gave kiss for life-giving kiss, until he'd memorized every centimeter of her enchanting features. He cupped her face, lifting it so she was forced to look at him.

"You're the most heavenly sight these eyes have ever beheld. Do you have any idea what you've done to me?" His voice throbbed. He twisted the red-gold curls around his fingers. "I want to eat you alive."

She moaned. Through swollen lips she murmured, "I thought that was what I was doing to you." Her avid mouth found his once more. It was like a hot desert wind, fanning the fire building inside him. "I could no more deny you than I could deny breath, and that's the truth of it," she admitted against his neck.

The rapture she brought him went beyond words. He never wanted her mouth to stop doing those marvelous things to his. He never wanted to let her out of his arms.

"I didn't know I could feel like this," she cried, raining kisses along his jaw. "If this is how my mother felt when she met Mario on vacation, then I understand a lot of things I didn't before."

He pressed his face in her hair. "Mario said your mother was the great love of his life," Sandro related.

"He was devastated that he couldn't go after her, but his whole family depended on him."

Alessandro was so enthralled with Catherine it took him a while before he realized his cellphone was ringing. The intrusion angered him. He didn't want anything to mar their pleasure in each other. Whoever was calling could wait. The knowledge that he had to fly her back to Naples by noon was tearing him apart. If it had been anyone but her father she was meeting…

A few minutes later she murmured dazedly against his lips, "That's the third time your phone has rung. It might be important. Maybe it's Benito?"

Why would his son be calling when he knew they'd be back for him? He drew another deep kiss from her mouth, wanting to forget everything, but she slowly managed to ease out of his grasp. Smoothing back the strands of crimson hair he'd been playing with she said, "What time is it?"

Rebelling against this injustice, he had no choice but to check his watch. "Twenty after ten." *Diavolo!* It couldn't be.

His phone rang again. She sat up straighter. "I can't believe we've been here all this time!"

He lifted his hand to trace the luscious curvature of the lips that had been giving him heart failure. "Forgive me for not taking you to breakfast, but I quite forgot we were in this world."

"So did I," she admitted quietly. Her honesty was one of the things he loved most about this incredible woman. "I—I don't know what came over me."

"Do you really need an answer to that?"

She looked away from him. "No."

Already he'd discovered that Catherine had a shy, and also a passionate side to her nature. Both were beguiling. In time he intended to learn all the wonderful parts that formed her unforgettable make-up.

"Now that we've been forced to catch our breath for the moment, would you have preferred we played tourist this morning?" Sandro liked all his Ts crossed.

She caught his hand between both of hers, pressing her lips to the top of it. "You know better than to ask." Her voice sounded unsteady. "You've bewitched me."

Unable to resist her, he leaned across the seat and wrapped his arms around her neck. "Let's agree we've done that to each other," he whispered against her ear, biting her lobe gently. "The strength associated with Samson's long black hair has nothing on *your* fiery mane. It ensnared me before you even knew I existed."

"*When* did you see me?" She drew back so she could look at him.

"You were having a conversation with someone on the phone in the lobby. Every male's eyes were glued to the breathtaking *testarossa* outfitted in cowboy boots."

"*Testarossa?*"

"Redhead. I took one look and was stopped dead in my tracks."

A soft blush entered her cheeks. "I'd promised to phone my dad."

The phone rang again. At this point he knew exactly

who it was. No one else had the sheer nerve to pester him to this degree.

"Please get it." Catherine was starting to panic.

He pulled the cellphone from his pocket. Verifying the identity of the caller, he turned off the ringer.

She made a sound of frustration. "Why did you do that?"

"Because I'm otherwise occupied."

She eyed him with more than a twinge of fear in her eyes. "It's Gabriella, isn't it? She hasn't been able to find you and has probably discovered I'm not at the hotel."

Resigned that Catherine wasn't going to let this go, he said, "Let's listen to her message, shall we? I'll translate." He turned on the mini-speaker and pressed the button.

"Sandro? Why haven't you answered? I've been calling everywhere for you. Papà has a party planned at the villa tonight at eight. He asked me to make sure you would be there. Since he has to spend time with Catherine this afternoon, before she leaves for the States, he's afraid you won't get the message in time. Come early, and we'll have a drink together before everyone else arrives. You hurt my feelings last week when you didn't stay at the hotel, but I forgive you because I know you have to be with Benito. Bring him with you. He can swim in the pool with the others. *Ciao, caro.*"

Catherine turned away from him. "We have to go, Alessandro. I wouldn't like to keep Mario waiting when he's planned his day to be with me."

No. She couldn't do that. His hand caught the curls

cascading against the back of her neck and brought them to his lips. "I'll let you go on one condition."

She quivered. "There can't be any."

"It's me you're talking to." His voice grated. "Surely by now you recognize a fire's been lit? After Mario takes you home from the party tonight I'll come for you. We have to talk."

She shook her head. "I can't believe I've done the very thing that happens to thousands of women who fly off to Europe on vacation and meet some gorgeous Frenchman or Italian and have a fling. It's humiliating to discover I've fallen into the same trap as my mother. We're much more alike than I thought—but it's not going to have the same ending for me."

"I can guarantee that," Sandro interjected savagely.

She bit her lip. "I refuse to let this go any further."

"For your information, we haven't even gotten started yet." His comment briefly silenced her. "What has gone on between us has no resemblance to the typical phenomenon you're referring to. Let me make it clear that if all I wanted was a one-night stand with you, as you Americans call it, I would wait until you left Italy and follow you until I tracked you down. We would have a night's pleasure and that would be the end of it. But that isn't what either of us wants or has in mind, and that's why we have to talk. Otherwise we'll inadvertently hurt Mario. He's the one person who needs to hear the truth from us before the inevitable gossip reaches his ears. I want to honor him by asking his permission to pursue his daughter Catherine."

"No—" she cried. "Promise me you won't say anything to him yet. What will he think? How will he explain to Gabriella without it damaging her? She's known you for a long time and is hoping for an intimate relationship. I realize you don't have those feelings for her, but that's not the point. Already Benito feels threatened, and I wouldn't want to hurt him for the world. Don't you see how impossible this situation is?"

"All I know is that you and I feel something that goes deeper than our skin. If we don't explore it, we'll be setting ourselves up for a kind of misery I have no intention of tolerating. We passed the point of no return when you met me in the lobby this morning. You couldn't stay away from me any more than I could you. That's not going to change. Our desire for each other is only going to grow. You're too intelligent a woman to pretend otherwise."

He started the car. Once he'd turned them around he said, "Should you have any idea of keeping me locked out of your hotel room tonight, let me disabuse you. Lucchesi owns the chain of hotels that recently acquired the Celestina."

She tossed her head back. "Alessandro— Please listen to me—" Her cry sounded anguished.

His jaw hardened. "Expect me after the party tonight. We'll decide when and how to approach Mario."

The rest became a blur as they picked up Benito and headed back to Naples. During the flight, Alessandro's deep voice drifted to the rear of the helicopter as he chatted in Italian with his son. While they discussed business, it gave Catherine a chance to try to recover from those hours of being in his arms. A wave of physical pleasure swept through her with such force, she couldn't think.

"Signorina Dalton?" Benito's voice broke her concentration. She jerked her head toward him. He gestured for her to gaze out the window. "This is the best view of the volcano."

Even if he didn't like her, Alessandro's son was trying very hard to be accommodating—no doubt because his father expected his cooperation.

She did his bidding. Sure enough, Naples was in the foreground—with Vesuvius looming quite ominously in the background. From this approach she could see the famous bay photographed by millions. Everything shimmered. She smiled at him.

He pointed further in the distance. "Sorrento!"

"It's magnificent—like viewing it through diamond dust."

"That's typical for this time of year," Alessandro explained. Though he sat in front, he was aware of everything that went on. "The water vapor in the air produces that light haze. Diamond dust is the perfect description."

As Alessandro translated for his son, the pilot made a beeline for the Lucchesi office complex in the distance. Time and civilization had encroached on their incredible morning together. Now it was over. Combined with the sudden drop in the helicopter's altitude, she felt like she'd been flung into a void where it would be impossible to get her bearings again.

The three of them alighted and took the elevator to the main floor. A limo stood parked out in front. Catherine purposely walked on Benito's other side toward it, in order to avoid brushing against Alessandro by accident. However, when he helped her in the back his hand slid from her shoulder to her hip in one sinuous glide.

Maybe it was accidental? She didn't know anything any more, and almost collapsed from the sensation. His son could be forgiven if he thought she sounded incoherent when she said goodbye to him.

"Benito and I will see you tonight," Alessandro reminded her in his deep, compelling voice. The teen stared at his father with a puzzled expression. "That's right," he continued in English. "We've been invited to a party for Catherine at Mario Conti's villa."

Catherine could see he was surprised, but she had something else on her mind and needed Alessandro's attention. "What if Mario is already at the hotel? If he sees me in your limo—"

"He won't." His features had hardened, as if he didn't like being reminded. "I'll tell the driver to drop you off at the corner of the *piazza*. When Mario sees you walking, you'll be able to tell him in all honesty that you were sight-seeing and the scenery was…out of this world."

He trailed a finger down her hot cheek before closing the door. She felt its imprint on her skin all the way to the spot where the driver deposited her, near the hotel.

After thanking him, she got out and started across the busy intersection. Almost at the hotel entrance, she saw a familiar male figure dressed in light blue pants and a white sport shirt come out the doors. She waved to him. Mario returned her wave and started walking across the *piazza* toward her, faster and faster. They reached for each other in a spontaneous hug.

Not more than an hour ago she and Alessandro had been devouring each other in the car. The man Mario would love to see be a part of Gabriella's life. It was the bitter mixed with the sweet and Catherine could hardly bear it.

For a person of forty-seven years, Mario was still a fit, striking man, with dark brown hair and eyes. At twenty-one he would have broken many hearts. According to Alessandro, her mother had broken Mario's. It killed Catherine to think her mom had lived all these years not knowing what she'd meant to him.

Catherine didn't even want to think what it might have been like if they'd been a family because it hurt too much. Images of her grieving dad back home on the ranch kept flashing through her mind. His heart was breaking too.

The situation was so sad she wanted to cry, but she couldn't. Today she had to put on a happy face for this man she knew instinctively would have been a wonderful father to her, but who had been denied all knowledge.

"If you are ready, we will go," he said in heavily accented Italian. "There is much I want to show you, and so little time."

He was right about the time. The delightful afternoon spent touring his vineyards while they talked passed in a flash. These were her roots—something she could hardly take in during one outing. They talked about her mother, and the illness that had claimed her life. Yet there were still so many things to discuss. Before she knew it the time was gone and he had to return her to the hotel. Neither of them wanted it to be over.

"I will wait in the *piazza* for you while you change. Then we will go to my home. My friends will find you as enchanting as I do, *figlia mia*."

His daughter…

When she felt his arms go around her, it felt right—natural. Though she hadn't talked about it with her mom, growing up she'd wondered secretly at times what her birth father was like. In the act of dying her mom had finally made it possible for Catherine to get to know him.

The hours spent with him this afternoon had managed to take her anger against her mother away. This was a gift from beyond the grave she was only starting to comprehend and be grateful for.

One more hug and she rushed up to her room to shower and get ready for the evening. After only a day of being together, she felt the bond that connected them. So many physical traits and small mannerisms revealed they were truly father and daughter.

Now, when she looked in the mirror to do her make-up, she saw him in the way their eyebrows grew, their similar widow's peaks. As she zipped into a black crêpe dress, and slipped on her black high heels, she thought about their discussions. They felt the same way concerning many issues. He had told her how he had met her mother and they had both laughed and wept. The only subjects they had stayed away from had been Gabriella and Stan—the two people they loved and wanted to spare any additional hurt.

As she started to leave the room, the phone rang. It was eleven a.m. in New Mexico. She supposed it could be her dad calling, but so far he'd let her set the pace for their talks. Maybe it was Mario, just checking to know how much longer she would be, but by the hammering of her heart she had a feeling it was Alessandro. A thrill of alarm traveled through her body.

She stared at the phone in a quandary. Alessandro functioned according to his own dictates. She could try to outguess his intentions, but she wouldn't succeed. With a mixture of trepidation and a deep yearning, she started to pick up the receiver—then dropped it like a hot coal and flew out the door. She'd told him it was over. It *had* to be.

CHAPTER EIGHT

FIFTEEN minutes later Catherine entered her father's three-story villa in the northern part of the city. Italian pop music was playing in the background, and a noisy group of twenty or so beautifully dressed people Mario's age and younger wandered about the rooms with a drink in hand. Alessandro wasn't among them, which filled her with a mixture of relief and misery.

Everyone, including Mario's girlfriend, crowded around them while he introduced Catherine. Their interest made her feel as if she were a celebrity. They had a good laugh when they learned the vintner's daughter didn't drink any alcohol!

Her mother had told her Neopolitans had a reputation for hearty, even boisterous behavior. Every gathering meant lots of delicious food and the enjoyment of life. This was a part of Catherine's heritage. Already she was drawn to the warmth of Mario's friends who, like him, embraced living with more enthusiasm than the average person.

"I don't see Gabriella," murmured Mario. "She's

probably out on the terrace. Come with me and we'll find her."

Though the ceilings were tall and corniced, dating the villa to a hundred years at least, the rooms had been decorated with comfortable contemporary furnishings. They walked through a dining room, where the table was laden with marvelous-looking Italian food. At the end of it the French doors opened wide onto a veranda, with steps that ran the length of the house.

She followed him to the long, oval-shaped pool below, where a dozen or so people were treading water while they chatted—Gabriella among them.

"Excuse me for a minute while I talk to her."

"Of course," she said, glad to stay in the background for a minute. While she stood there, her attention was drawn to two strong male swimmers who were racing each other to the end of the pool with tremendous speed.

Alessandro heaved his magnificent body out of the water with athletic grace. As he slicked his hair back, his glittering black gaze suddenly met hers. She felt the impact, and for a moment it robbed her of breath.

Embarrassed to be caught staring at the amazing sight, she tore her eyes from his to concentrate on Benito, who came in a close second. He leaped to the edge of the tiled pool, but the moment he saw her his smile faded.

Full of remorse because she'd gone with them this morning, she turned away to go back inside—but Alessandro didn't let her get far. Within seconds he'd caught up to her.

While he reached for a towel to dry off, his eyes

swept over her, turning her legs to jelly. "How was the rest of your day?"

"I wish I could thank my mother for giving me the gift of my father."

His expression softened. "Mario must be overjoyed."

She nodded, and would have said more, but her father was urging her to join him. Only at that moment did it hit her that she truly thought of him as her father now. "I'll be right there!"

Alessandro tossed the towel over one broad shoulder. "I too would like to thank your mother. The gift she gave you thrust you into my life. I haven't been the same since, and I can relate to your father, who looks and sounds happy in a brand-new way. You have that effect on people."

"But not on Benito or Gabriella," she said in a haunted whisper, before backing away from him. "I—I have to go." People were looking in their direction. Gabriella was staring daggers at her.

His features took on a chiseled cast. "I'll let Mario take you away from me for now." The implicit warning that this wasn't over chased her all the way to the other end of the patio.

Twice throughout the rest of the evening Catherine saw her half-sister talking to Alessandro, who circulated with Benito, but neither man came wtihin range of Catherine. At one point they left the villa.

Possibly because Gabriella didn't feel threatened, she opted to drive Catherine to the hotel with Mario after their guests left. Catherine climbed in the back seat, prepared to do anything to keep the peace. *En route*,

Gabriella acted friendlier than usual and that seemed to please Mario. When he pulled up the drive in front of the hotel, he turned to look over his shoulder at her.

"I'll come by for you at nine. We'll need all day to do a thorough visit of Pompeii."

"I can't wait! Thank you for today. I won't forget it for as long as I live."

"Neither will I, *piccina*. I still can't believe I have two *piccinas*." Mario beamed at her and Gabriella.

When she slid out of the back seat, to her surprise Gabriella joined her. "I'm going to walk Catherine to her room, Papà." In the moonlight she looked stunning, in a silver lamé designer dress with spaghetti straps. Catherine wished they would grow to be friends.

"Don't be too long. It's late, and we have a big day tomorrow."

She didn't know if he'd cautioned Gabriella because he was exhausted and needed to get to bed, or if he was concerned over leaving his two daughters alone—both of them still virtual strangers. Catherine had a feeling it was the latter. He wasn't fooled and neither was Catherine. Gabriella had an agenda.

When they reached her room and Catherine opened the door, Gabriella said, "Can I come in? I want to ask you something."

"Of course. Please."

She moved inside. Catherine shut the door while Gabriella looked around. There wasn't anything to see—Catherine traveled light.

"Do you want to sit down?"

"No. I want to ask you a few questions. We got in from Rome a little earlier than expected. I came by to see if you wanted to go sightseeing, but you didn't answer your door."

Uh-oh. "I'm sorry. I wish I'd known you were here. It's so exciting to be in Italy I left early to walk around."

Gabriella studied her intently. "Tell me what you said to Sandro about me."

No one could get to the point faster than Gabriella. "We didn't talk about you. He and Benito have been my tour guides."

"I'm referring to that first day, when you had drinks with him in the bar. I know you discussed me with him."

Catherine frowned. "He said only that he came at your invitation and would wait with me until you arrived before joining Benito. Since Mario had told him the situation, he mostly listened while I explained how terrible I thought it was that my mother had hurt so many people—including you." Everything she'd just told her was the truth.

"Sandro was different after I joined you."

Gabriella looked so vulnerable it twisted something inside Catherine. But she couldn't help her or everything would escalate out of control. In a minute her half-sister was going to ask another searching question. Catherine had to head her off before that happened.

"I don't know about you, Gabriella, but I think it's been a long day and it's late. I still have to call my dad. He expects me to phone him now that the party is over. Do you mind?"

She eyed her speculatively for a moment. "No."

"Then I'll see you and Mario in the morning." Catherine walked her to the door. She was already feeling panicky. She'd told Alessandro she couldn't see him again, but she knew he had other ideas.

After Gabriella left, Catherine fell limp against the closed door. Though she was hurting for her half-sister, and exhausted from lack of sleep, her senses were on full alert. When the phone rang, she jumped. Fortifying herself with a deep breath, she moved over to the bedside table to answer it.

"Hello?'

"At last," he muttered. "I'm outside in the limo, waiting for you."

"I-I'm not coming, Alessandro." Her voice trembled. "You know why. Benito isn't ready for this kind of change yet. He is too young. He needs the same *papà* who has been raising him all these years. And I have a grieving father who has lost his wife and is afraid he might be losing me too. Tomorrow I'll be spending another day with Mario, who's trying to help Gabriella feel secure while at the same time welcoming me.

"Even if you do own this hotel, and could walk into my room at any minute, I know you won't because you're an honorable man. This has to be goodbye. Th-Thank you for everything." Her voice shook. "I'll never forget you, or our time together," she said before hanging up the phone.

Those words stopped Alessandro cold. He clicked off.

Benito stared at him in the semi-darkness. "Isn't she going to come?"

Wouldn't his son give anything for this to be the end of it? "No. We won't be seeing each other again."

Catherine was being strong for both of them—and maybe she was right. Benito wasn't ready. Alessandro heaved a sigh before signaling his driver to take them back to the villa.

"Why not?"

"There are too many complications," Sandro ground out.

A long silence ensued before Benito said, "She doesn't like me, does she?"

Benito, Benito…

Sandro sat forward. "Wrong, *figlio mio*. In fact she told me I've done a wonderful job raising you." He raked a hand through his hair in frustration. "Let's just say she doesn't want to interfere in our lives."

Benito stared out the window. "She's so different from Gabriella. I can't believe they're related."

"That makes two of us."

"I guess I can see why you like her. She's better-looking than any woman you've ever been with—except maybe my mother."

"There's more to a woman than looks, Benito."

"I know."

"None of that matters now. She'll be going back to the States in a few days. Her mother passed away recently and her dad needs her there."

"What does that have to do with her not wanting to be with you?"

"For one thing, she's afraid a relationship between us will hurt Mario."

"I don't get it. Oh—wait a minute. She knows Gabriella has a thing for you?"

Since when did his son get so smart? "Under the circumstances, Catherine has decided to leave well enough alone."

"But she likes you?"

He lowered his head. "Even if two people like each other, the conditions have to be right for something to happen."

"Like they were for you and my mother?"

"Exactly."

Eventually the limo pulled up to the front of the villa. They both got out and went in the house.

"Want to watch some soccer with me, Papà? I recorded the game."

Now that Catherine was history, Benito's moodiness was gone. This might be a good time for that talk with his son about the friends who'd been getting him in trouble.

"There's nothing I'd like better. I'll grab the drinks." It would have to be soda for both of them.

CHAPTER NINE

"From 200 B.C. the Romans ruled Pompeii, until that fateful day in 79 B.C. when Vesuvius unleashed its fury on twenty thousand inhabitants," said the tour director in English. "However, this tragic event that ended their lives—the ash that buried their town and mummified it—captured a moment in time. Under the ash everything remained the same as it was. Artwork was preserved, buildings…clues. These clues give us little glimpses into the past."

Throughout the exceptionally hot day Catherine spent with Mario and Sofia, those words and images had never left her mind. When they dropped her back at the hotel at seven that evening, she showered and ate a meal in her room while she phoned her dad and told him all about her trip.

Gabriella had chosen to stay away until tomorrow. Catherine knew it bothered Mario, but he hadn't let it ruin the wonder of their day trip together. Sofia's friendliness made up for a lot. And tomorrow they would all go out on his yacht, for Catherine's last day in Italy.

As for Alessandro, she tried hard not to think about him. But of course that was futile. She threw herself across the bed. He hadn't tried to get hold of her since their phone conversation last night. There was no light on her phone indicating a message was waiting. Part of her wished he'd missed her so much he'd show up at her hotel room door this instant. But he'd obviously thought everything over and decided the end didn't justify the means. It would destroy everyone they knew. Catherine could return to New Mexico with the knowledge that she'd hurt no one.

Except her own tortured psyche, that would never know the great joy of being with him again. The ache in her heart had become physical. Every beat actually hurt.

While she was in this state, the phone rang. She rolled over and grabbed for it, in case he'd broken down and called her after all.

"Hello?" she inquired shakily.

"Signorina Dalton?"

She blinked and sat up. "Benito?"

"*Sì.* Papà's sick."

Catherine jumped to her feet in alarm. "Did you send for the doctor?"

"He said he didn't need a doctor, but I think he does."

"Is your father asking for me?"

"No, but I think he will listen to you. I am outside the hotel. Please come. *Ciao.*" He rang off, making it impossible for her to ask any more questions.

It sounded like Alessandro needed help. She dressed in tan pants and a light blue knit top before grabbing her purse. With a feeling of *déjà vu*, she found herself rushing down to the foyer. The fear that something might be seriously wrong with him had her flying out the doors to the drive, where she saw Benito waiting at the side of the limo with the door open.

She ran up to him, out of breath. "How did he get hurt?"

"On his sailboat."

"Were you with him?"

Benito nodded, before helping her inside and shutting the door. The limo driver didn't waste any time driving through the city. Before long they veered off the coast highway to a private road that led to a villa overlooking the water.

She could see a pier in the distance, and several boats. To her surprise the driver pulled up in front of the house itself. She'd thought they were going to his boat. Maybe Benito had helped his father inside the villa first?

He helped her out of the car. "Follow me."

Another time she would have loved to explore the three-story house that was very much like Mario's, inside and out. They both lived in the same district of Naples. But at the moment her only concern was for Alessandro.

Benito led her down a hallway off the foyer to a set of paneled double doors. He pointed. "In there."

With her heart in her throat, Catherine carefully opened one and walked inside what turned out to be a man's elegant den, with plush décor and a wall of books. A small brass lamp gave out enough light for her to distinguish Alessandro, seated at his desk.

The lower half of his jaw had a five o'clock shadow and his hair looked like he'd been running his hands through it. In a maroon crew neck and white shorts, he certainly could have just come in from sailing, but he appeared to be recovered enough to work. Her gaze fell on the bottle of Scotch and a glass next to the computer.

"Alessandro?" she whispered.

He spun around so fast she jumped. "Catherine—" Now that he was facing her, she thought he looked pale. "What are you doing here?"

She swallowed hard. "Benito phoned me at the hotel. He told me you were sick and said I should come. He brought the limo for me."

His powerful body sprang from the leather chair. He looked incredulous. "My son told you I was *ill*?"

"Yes. He said something about the boat, and I thought you must have been injured. When I asked if you'd seen a doctor, he said no, but that he thought you'd listen to me."

He moved closer to her. "We've been out sailing all day and came in a little while ago. I was just answering my brother's email." She heard him inhale abruptly. "Do you know what this means?" His voice sounded husky.

"Yes. That he worries about you."

"He knows I've been going out of my mind since you told me goodbye. If he could get you here, then there would be no need for a doctor. You realize from him doing all this on his own he doesn't exactly dislike you?"

She couldn't believe Benito had tricked her.

"The real miracle is you came."

"How could I not when I visualized you bleeding or—or worse?"

"I'm anything but." Without conscious thought he picked her up like he was about to carry his bride over the threshold and crushed her against him. "I wanted to do this when I got out of the pool last night, *bellissima*."

She buried her face against his chest. Her shy side charmed him. "Where are you taking me?"

"Down to my sailboat."

"I don't think that's a good idea."

"It's the only idea that makes sense for us."

"Alessandro—"

A few minutes later he'd stepped inside the boat and carried her down to a dimly lit bedroom. "Don't be afraid. I'm not about to ravish you without your permission, but I wanted us to be alone in a safe place. I'm too well known at the hotel, and I'd prefer not to set the staff gossiping by sneaking you into my bedroom tonight. It's your reputation I'm worried about. Not mine. You're Mario's daughter, and that makes you a target."

"I do understand that." The words came out muffled.

"If Benito hadn't taken things into his own hands I would have come for you myself later tonight, regardless of who would have seen me enter your hotel room. I've been *living* to get you alone," he whispered into her hair.

"Even if we both have, you know it's wrong." Her voice shook. "Gabriella came up to my room last night to talk. She thought I said something to you in the bar that turned you off her. I denied it, of course. How could I have told her that you and I decided to give in to our primitive wants and fly to Sardinia for a morning's interlude?"

"It was much more than that," he thundered. "But to get back to Gabriella—today I told her no when she asked me to join your family outing tomorrow. She's spoiled, and doesn't like to be turned down. Naturally she would say anything to you rather than face the truth that I'm not interested in her and never could be. It's her immaturity talking. She'll outgrow it one day."

Catherine's body was trembling. She burrowed deeper into him. "That doesn't help the situation now."

He sat down on the side of the bed with her. Unable to help himself, he lowered his head to kiss the side of her neck. Her little moans of pleasure drove him to find her luscious mouth. After a slight hesitation she slid her arms around his neck, to bring them closer. Suddenly they were kissing each other once more.

Exultant, he fell back and pulled her on top of him. He needed to feel *all* of her. Cupping her gorgeous face in his hands, he cried, "I want you with a terrible hunger, Catherine."

"I want you too. So much it frightens me." She pressed a passionate kiss to his mouth, holding nothing back. When he finally allowed her to breathe again she said, "I can only imagine how your wife must have felt."

Sandro blinked.

"At the same time Mario told me he never forgot my mother, he also confided that your wife was the great love of *your* life."

It took a minute before the thrust of her words sank

in. When they did, a frown marred his features. This conversation had taken a strange turn. He rolled her onto her back so he could look deep into her eyes.

"What are you getting at?" Her trembling lower lip was a temptation he kissed quiet.

"Seventeen years without remarrying is a testament to the ties that still bind you." Her eyes misted over. "Was she your first love?"

He smoothed the hair off her forehead. "Yes—but what does that have to do with *us*?"

"You can only have one of those," she whispered sadly. "She got your youth and your passion. Your dreams. The dreams of Alessandro Lucchesi must have really been something."

He ran his hands up her arms to her shoulders. His gaze probed hers intently. "Where has all this come from?"

She shook her head. "I don't honestly know. I'm an emotional wreck right now. You don't meet a person one day and fall into his arms the next."

"We did."

She groaned. "I can't believe I'm the same woman who left San Antonio."

"You're not. Nor am I the same frustrated man who agreed to run by the hotel and support Gabriella out of respect for Mario. You and I met. The attraction was a cataclysmic event for both of us. We're living proof of the fallout. Tell me, if you can, who made up the rule that says such a thing is impossible?" he demanded.

"You know what I meant."

"It's obvious you can't answer that question." Her

lack of response prompted him to ask another question. "Was your parents' marriage shaky?"

Pain filled her eyes. "Why do you ask that?"

Sandro cocked his head. "Because something's not right. Why do I get the feeling you're projecting your dad's feelings rather than your own? Putting two and two together: your mother had another man's baby; if she didn't make Stan feel secure, he might have considered himself second-best. That insecurity could have rubbed off on you from the beginning—thus the reason you're so anxious to protect him and yourself from further hurt."

She averted her eyes. "Is that what I'm doing?"

"Until the outing with your father yesterday, you gave me the impression you were angry with your mother. It would explain why you're apprehensive about *our* relationship."

He felt her try to pull away from him, but he refused to let her go.

"We might be physically attracted, Alessandro, but we don't have a real relationship." Her voice faltered. "We can't!"

His hands tightened on the warmth of her upper arms below the short sleeves of her top. "So you've decided to cut me off? Do you think repeating the same kind of sin your mother committed by leaving Mario will serve as some sort of recompense to Stan? You *do* realize you can't fill a husband's needs for him?"

She turned her head away. "I wasn't aware I was trying to do that."

"Then maybe you want to punish me before I hurt you the way Mario hurt your mother? Is that what this is all about?"

"Don't be absurd. I don't want to hurt you."

"Not consciously, perhaps," he conceded.

"Not unconsciously either!"

"Nevertheless, you seem to have drawn a parallel between us. Be careful, Catherine. I'm not Mario. I'm not in the situation he was in when he met your mother. You're not your mother."

She made a sound of exasperation. "All I'm saying is that our situation is going to hurt other people."

"It will be simplified once your father realizes how it is with us."

"Dad would never understand."

"What? That you have met someone who altered your whole life within seconds of meeting him? I would imagine that's all it took your father to decide he wanted your mother."

"Probably—but right now he's in mourning, and he can't deal with any shocks. Surely you of all people can understand that, since you never remarried after losing your wife? I think Mario's in shock too."

"Mario's a strong, stable man, and he has Sofia. We'll face him together and explain what has happened. His experience with your mother will lend him automatic understanding."

"You've forgotten Gabriella—"

"Hush." He silenced her with his mouth. "She's resilient. One day, when she's all grown up, she'll fall in love and it will be the right match. After you get back from your outing tomorrow we'll talk everything over and make plans. I'll send the limo for you."

She moaned. "Is it still out there?"

"No. If you really want to leave I'll drive you back in my car. It's parked at the villa. All you have to do is say the word."

Except for a heavy sigh of defeat, silence followed his offer.

He buried his face in her hair. "That's what I thought. Right now I need to hold you all night. That's part of getting to know each other better. Surely it isn't too much to ask?"

"I don't know," she cried softly.

"I do. What you need is a good night's sleep with me. Tomorrow you'll need your strength to snorkel off the island of Ischia."

"I've heard of it. Don't scuba divers hunt there for old Roman galleons?"

"All the time. My brothers and I did our share. Those waters have been my backyard since I was born."

"I can't relate. My family lives on a dry, landlocked plateau, where the sight of any water—even a tiny stream—is like stumbling on pure gold. No diamond dust, just…dust."

Sandro chuckled. "I want to hear it all." He got up to turn off the light and put a quilt over them. Then he stretched out and drew her into his arms. "But first I want to finish the kiss we started in the den."

No matter how many arguments she'd raised to

prevent them from being together, the instant he searched for her mouth she was ready for him—as if her life depended on it.

CHAPTER TEN

CATHERINE lay on the lounger, soaking up the late-afternoon sun. In the distance was Ischia—or the Emerald Isle, as Mario had referred to it. She could hear him and Gabriella swimming on the starboard side of his small yacht. A little while ago Sofia had gone below to take a shower. For the moment Catherine was alone. She enjoyed the gentle rocking motion that lulled her in and out of a light sleep.

Last night she and Alessandro had clung to each other, kissing and talking until oblivion claimed them. His control was nothing short of miraculous—but he'd promised she'd be safe with him, and so far he had always kept his promises.

He'd said everything would look clearer to her in the morning, and those had been prophetic words. Upon their awakening at seven, he'd fixed her a fabulous breakfast in the galley before his limo had arrived to take her back to the hotel. When he'd fed her slices of a juicy peach for dessert, kissing her after every swallow until she drowned in rapture, she'd realized she was in love.

Before she'd left New Mexico she hadn't known what that emotion felt like. Then she'd come to Naples. Alessandro had lit Catherine's world in unimagined ways, but one fact remained. He'd already been married and he didn't need a new wife. Once Catherine left Italy he'd meet other women who would provide diversion and his life would go on.

As for Catherine—when she got back to the ranch she would take better care of her dad and find herself a more fulfilling job. Alessandro Lucchesi would remain a cherished memory. He was her first love and she didn't want another. He'd been married to his first love and had lost her in death. A seventeen-year track record of going it alone made it clear he would continue on the same path.

He had Benito. They belonged to a big family, with nephews and nieces who loved them both. Alessandro's success as a mega-entrepreneur and pillar of the Neopolitan financial world occupied the greater part of his life. It was enough for him.

"Catherine? Are you awake?"

She opened her eyes to discover Sofia had pulled up another lounger. Catherine liked the attractive, soft-spoken blond woman so much. She clearly made Mario happy.

"I was never asleep." Alessandro's touch still radiated through her body. A constant fire burned deep beneath the surface of her skin.

"I have a confession. When Mario told me about your mother calling to tell him he had a daughter, I'm afraid I felt like Gabriella and was prepared to dislike you. But the opposite has happened. You're a lot like him. Kind. He loves you."

Her words moved Catherine to tears. "Thank you for saying that. I love him too. For your information, he feels exactly the same way about *you.*"

"We want to get married—but as you've probably noticed Gabriella isn't helping. In fact she's very discontented right now. Her hope that Sandro would be interested in her has not materialized. I could have told her he never saw her in that light, but I didn't dare."

Her assessment of Gabriella was exactly right. She was spoiled, and young for her years. Mario had a hard time saying no to her. For once Catherine could be objective about her half-sister.

She sat up. "Listen, Sofia—Mario and my mom didn't get married, but you don't know the real reason why. It was because *his mother* didn't like my mom."

"What?"

"It's true. Mario needed my mother to be strong, but she was too timid and unsure of herself to deal with his mother."

"Your mother told you that?"

"Yes. Don't be like my mom, Sofia. Marry Mario right away. Do it because it's right for both of you. Then the two of you can deal with Gabriella on an equal footing. If you let her win, then it will be twice that Mario has missed out on what he really wants."

Sofia put a hand on her arm. "I love you very much, Catherine. You are amazing, and incredibly wise."

"No. It's just that I've had a lot to deal with since my

mother made her deathbed confession. Certain things have opened my eyes." And a certain someone.

The feelings Catherine had for Alessandro had forced her to see things as they really were and act on them. She felt much better having made the decision to go home to America tonight. She'd booked a night flight before Mario had picked her up. He had no idea the suitcase she'd brought on board held everything. When they left the port, she would ask him to drop her off at the airport instead of the hotel.

He would want to know why, of course. She'd tell him a good visit was a short one—especially now he had his wedding to plan. Maybe that would light a fire under him.

She'd already checked out of the hotel. When she didn't answer her phone or the door, Alessandro would eventually realize she'd gone. However, by that time she planned to be in San Antonio—a world light years away from the Lucchesi empire.

He might want her to stay. She represented a change from the women he associated with. But before long it would grow old. No woman could hold him indefinitely.

"You're getting a little sunburned," Sofia warned her.

"I feel sticky too. I think I'll go down and take a shower." She'd wash off the sunscreen and shampoo her hair. By the time her dad and Gabriella came back on board she'd be dressed and ready to go. "See you in a little while."

"Catherine—I'm thankful you came. You've given me courage."

"Good." Now all Catherine had to do was summon enough of it to carry through with her own plan.

Benito brought the sailboat alongside the pier without bumping into it. Sandro clapped his hands.

"*Grazie*, Papà."

As his son leaped onto the dock to tie the ropes, Sandro's cellphone rang. At a glance he saw it was the Hotel Celestina calling.

The manager had orders to phone him when Catherine returned from her outing, but it was too early in the day for them to be back...unless they'd decided not to go to Ischia. That set off an alarm bell in his head. He answered the call.

"Signor Lucchesi here."

"I am so sorry, *signore*, but it seems Signorina Dalton paid her bill and checked out this morning, before you phoned me."

This morning. Sandro shot to his feet.

"I've had everyone at the front desk watching for her. Then just now someone from Housekeeping mentioned that she'd checked out around nine."

"Thank you for letting me know."

Sandro's lips formed a white line of anger. He clicked off before letting go with a curse.

"What's wrong, Papà?"

He turned to Benito. "Catherine checked out of the hotel this morning."

"You think she already went back to the States?"

"I'm not sure." Maybe Mario had decided they would

stay out on the yacht overnight and he'd drive her to the airport tomorrow morning. But Sandro didn't think so.

"Do you want to go to Ischia?"

Sandro nodded. "Let me grab my wallet and keys and we'll take the powerboat." Thanks to Gabriella, he knew exactly where to find them.

Within a few minutes they undid the ropes of the other boat and got in. Sandro started the motor and took them out of the cove at wakeless speed before he gunned the motor. They ripped through the water.

"Whoa, Papà—" Benito hurried to sit down before he fell. "You've got it so bad for her you'd better marry her."

Sandro jerked his head around. "You wouldn't mind?"

"No. You should have seen the look on her face when she thought something bad had happened to you."

"Yeah?" Sandro grinned.

"Yeah. She really loves you."

Full of emotion, he reached out to muss Benito's hair. "I really love *you*."

Now the trick was to catch up to Catherine. He could read her mind. She planned to disappear on him before everything exploded—but she'd made a tactical error. At this point he would do what he should have done at Mario's villa the other night. The gloves were off.

Within the hour Catherine was dressed in a pair of jeans and a white blouson-styled shirt with short sleeves. Being on the ocean, her hair would stay damp for a while, even with the aid of her blow-dryer.

Sofia had been right. They'd all picked up a lot of sun. Heat poured off her arms and face. Catherine needed no blusher—just lipstick. When she was ready, she slipped on sandals and left the cabin to join her father on deck.

To her surprise she discovered two tall male figures near the bow with him and Sofia. At first she thought they must be members of the crew, who wore white casual pants and T-shirts. Her father, looking tanned and relaxed, was dressed the same. He waved when he saw her.

"Look who has joined us, *piccina*!"

When she glimpsed Alessandro's distinctive profile she got a suffocating feeling in her chest. Where had he and Benito come from? Her heart started to run away with her. How could she disappear on him *now*? Catherine should never have underestimated him for a second.

She looked around quickly. There was no sign of Gabriella. She must have gone below to her cabin to shower. As Catherine closed the distance separating them, she felt Alessandro's dark, penetrating gaze. It assessed her from her toes to the crown of her head, missing nothing in between. The intimacy of his slow perusal turned her cheeks to flame.

"You're a vision," her father murmured, before slipping an arm around her waist.

"I quite concur, Mario." Alessandro's eyes didn't leave her face.

"*Ciao*, Benito. *Come va?*" She had to say something to break the tension Alessandro created by simply occupying her space.

"*Ciao*, Catherine." He lifted his index finger. "Very good." He grinned at her, no doubt amused she was using the few Italian words Mario had taught her.

Her father chuckled. "This number one daughter of mine is a quick learner."

Alessandro flashed her a white smile. He had to be the most gorgeous man on the continent. "She takes after you, Mario. That must be the reason I like her so much, I'd like your permission to go on seeing her."

The world suddenly reeled. Catherine sagged against her father, unable to credit what she'd just heard.

After a slight pause, Mario spoke again. "What do you mean 'go on'?" Naturally Mario needed clarification. The blood pounded in Catherine's ears. She averted her eyes, furious with Alessandro, yet helpless to stop what he'd unleashed. Any hope she'd nursed to avoid this situation evaporated in the sea air.

"When I met Catherine in the lobby of the hotel last week there was instant chemistry between us. In fact the day you came back from Rome I went to the hotel early and convinced her to fly to Sardinia with me and Benito on business. I thought she'd enjoy seeing the fruit of a Conti-Lucchesi merger."

The hand around her back slipped away. Mario turned so he could look into her eyes. Incredibly, he broke into a smile. "So the whole time I was telling you about the process of wine-making you already knew all about my corks?"

"Well, not all," she confessed.

Sofia's laugh made everything seem more normal.

Catherine came close to fainting with relief. If the glint in her father's brown eyes was anything to go by, he wasn't upset. On the contrary—she had a feeling that on some level the news pleased him.

One glance at Alessandro's smile of satisfaction let her know there was more to come. Catherine felt sorry for his business adversaries who had to go up against him. They could never win. She folded her arms in an effort to brace herself for the rest. He was unstoppable now.

"Last night after she came back from Pompeii I pursued your daughter further. But she wasn't happy about it because she came here to be with *you*. The last thing she wants to do is hurt you. I could tell you Benito and I were just out here enjoying a boat ride and happened to see your yacht, but that wouldn't be the truth. Earlier today the manager of the Celestina phoned to let me know Catherine had checked out."

Catherine's quiet gasp coincided with that revelation. It prompted Mario to flick her a searching glance.

"In my fear that she had decided to fly back to the States tonight in order to avoid me, I opted for a pre-emptive intervention to see if we can't come up with a solution that will satisfy everyone."

Mario looked amused. "I'd expect nothing less from you. Go on."

She felt the full heat of Alessandro's gaze as it rested on her. "As Catherine is coming to find out, I'm a very possessive man about something I want. If she's willing, and doesn't have to get back to her job right away, I'd like her to be my guest at the villa for a while. Benito's English ought to have improved some-what by then."

"*Papà*—"

Everyone laughed at Benito's outburst before Alessandro said, "Catherine and I need time to get to know each other—but we want to fit it in around your schedule, Mario. That way you can spend as many hours as you want with both your daughters."

Mario eyed Alessandro with a half-smile. "As usual, you have a way of sewing up a deal that is advantageous to both parties. I guess the only thing remaining is to find out what Catherine wants." His curious glance darted to her. "Naturally I don't want you to go home yet. In a perfect world you would live here forever." The loving tone in his voice said everything. "It's up to you, *piccina*."

Catherine weaved in place. Feelings of euphoria and turmoil made her lightheaded because of the impact this would have on Gabriella. "I'm not sure I can stay. It depends on several things." Her dad for one. "But I do know I don't want to leave you yet," she con-fessed to Mario.

"Nor Sandro, it seems." He patted her arm.

"Then it's settled," Alessandro announced, capturing her gaze. The way he was looking at her, he might as well have been kissing her. Her insides were melting.

"What's settled?"

Gabriella had come on deck, looking terrific in tan shorts and an orange top. Fear sent adrenalin gushing through Catherine's nervous system.

Mario moved toward Gabriella and put an arm

around her shoulders. "Catherine is going to be a guest at Sandro's villa for a while. I'm told Benito could benefit from some English lessons. It looks like both our families will be enjoying more vacation time together. Just what the doctor ordered."

He looked over his shoulder. "Come on, Sofia—Benito. The steward has set up our dinner on the other end of the deck. I don't know about anyone else, but I'm starving." He winked at Catherine before ushering both women away from her and Alessandro. Benito took up the rear.

A shudder passed through Catherine's body. No matter how masterfully her father had handled the tension-filled moment, Gabriella's shock and hurt had to be enormous.

A strong hand slid to her neck beneath her hair. Alessandro massaged the skin gently. "This was the only way to handle the situation," he whispered. "Your father gets it. He's remembering the first moment he met your mother. Once you feel that chemistry, no power on earth can make it go away."

She lowered her head. "That may be true, but I don't want to flaunt it in front of Gabriella. If I'd hoped that she and I could be loving sisters one day, this has probably put that miracle off until the next life."

His fingers inched their way into her hair, sending little trickles of delight through her body. "You don't give her enough credit. She's not the fragile flower you imagine. I'm much more concerned about *you*. Your father needs to know what's going on. While I join the others, you're welcome to use my cellphone."

He pulled it from the pocket of the pants he wore and put it in her hand. "When you're ready to call him, I'll be happy to get on the phone and reassure him of my intentions. I realize you're a twenty-six-year-old woman who doesn't require anyone's help or permission about anything. This would be for me." His voice trailed. "I'd like to let him know what a remarkable daughter he has."

Catherine didn't have to think about it before she handed the phone back to him. "Thank you, but I'll make my call tonight—when I'm alone."

"Alone with *me*, you mean," he asserted, in that deep, velvety voice.

Still refusing to look at him, she said, "Nothing's firm yet, Alessandro. Right now my father has planned a lovely dinner. He's already received one shock this evening. We need to join him and help pick up the pieces if we can."

"I'm ready when you are."

"Please don't sit by me."

"Do we have a choice if your father has arranged it otherwise?"

I don't know. I don't know anything.

He moved his hand to her shoulder and squeezed it before letting her go. "Don't worry. I'll work out something with Benito. His English may need help, but he has proved to be very bright and he may already have thought of a plan."

Obeying a force he had no power against whenever he got near her, he kissed the corner of her mouth. "Forgive me. I had to do that first. Shall we go?"

CHAPTER ELEVEN

Sure enough, as the two of them walked to the other end of the yacht where their meal was being served *al fresco*, Alessandro saw that his son had saved a place at the large round table between him and Sofia. Smart boy.

Benito saw them approaching. "Catherine? Come. You can teach me the names of these foods in English."

"I'd love to."

Alessandro felt the rigidity leave her beautiful body as she practically ran to the chair he held out. Mario sat on Sofia's other side. That placed Alessandro next to Gabriella.

"*Buonasera*, Gabriella. I haven't seen that top before. The orange color is very becoming on you."

"*Grazie*," she muttered, through gritted teeth.

He helped himself to the *brusceta* and dipped it in olive oil. The others had started on their cannelloni. Through veiled lashes he watched Catherine enchant his son.

"Why didn't you tell us at the party you'd taken Catherine to Sardinia with you?" Gabriella said it loud enough that everyone at the table picked up on her question.

"I didn't think it was information the guests needed to hear—do you?"

"I'm not a guest."

She had no intention of letting this go. "That's true, but I hadn't spoken to your father yet."

"Since you'd already slept with her, it hardly mattered, did it?"

"Gabriella Conti!" Mario said in a stern voice. "You'll apologize to Catherine and Sandro immediately."

Her jaw set, she jumped to her feet. "Why? You slept with Catherine's mother before she'd been in town twenty-four hours and my grandmother knew it. So why the outrage?" She threw down her napkin and disappeared below.

"Let her go," Sofia pleaded with Mario, who'd started to get to his feet. "She's hurting right now, but she'll get over it."

Sandro took one look at Catherine's crumpled expression and got up from the table to reach her. He put his hands on her trembling shoulders, wanting to comfort her.

"Sofia's right, Mario. All that emotion was bound to come out sooner or later. It's part of growing up, no matter how painful. No one blames her."

Sofia squeezed Mario's hand. "Sandro did the right thing to get it out in the open before Gabriella felt truly betrayed."

Catherine shook her head. "That girl is heartbroken. I shouldn't have come."

"Don't ever say that!" Mario's voice shook. "Don't ever think it! You're my daughter as surely as she is. What I want to know is, when did her grandmother talk to her about Elizabeth? Gabriella has been given a distorted version of the truth."

Sandro saw a look pass between Catherine and Sofia before the other woman said, "I know something about that."

While Mario stared at her in bewilderment, Sandro said, "Under the circumstances I'm going to take Catherine and Benito back to the villa with me now."

"Until I've talked with Gabriella, that might be for the best."

"Feel free to come by at any time—day or night."

Mario nodded. "I'll phone you later, *piccina*."

"All right."

"I'll get your suitcase," Sofia offered. She looked at Catherine. "Is everything packed?"

"Yes."

"I'll be right back."

"Oh, Papà—" Catherine threw herself into Mario's arms and sobbed. Sandro's throat swelled with emotion. "I'm so sorry."

"I'm not. When your mother called me and told me about you I rejoiced. Nothing could have kept me from you once I knew. We'll find a way to deal with all this."

She wiped her eyes. "We will. You're so wonderful! That's why this is so hard on Gabriella. She worshipped you first."

It was Mario's turn to weep. Sandro looked at Benito,

whose eyes were suspiciously bright. He hoped his son realized how important it was to tell the truth up-front. Sandro was still waiting for Benito to confess what he'd been up to this last year.

While his son went ahead with her suitcase and started the engine, Sandro helped Catherine down the ladder into the powerboat. He put a life jacket on her. "I'm going to take care of you now."

Catherine lifted wounded eyes to his. "No, Alessandro. I have to go home tonight. Seeing Gabriella so upset makes me realize I've been too focused on things here and I've neglected my dad. When I came to Italy I only expected to *meet* Mario. I didn't know I would develop such strong feelings for him. Then I met you—everything has changed—" Her voice shook. "It's—it's almost like I've forgotten my own family. Gabriella's pain has reminded me I can't do this to my dad. When I look at her and Mario all I see is suffering. Dad's suffering too. He's been there for me my whole life, and now he's alone. I have to be there for him! That's where my life is—where it has to be. This has all happened way too fast. You have to understand."

"I do," he murmured. "The time spent with you has changed my life drastically too. It did happen fast, but let's give it another few days at least—for us to think things over and work something out, Catherine."

She shook her head. "I can't. Don't ask me."

"Not even for *us*?" He was ready to explode with pain.

"Considering how much my dad is hurting, my wants and needs can't be compared. He loves me even though

I'm not his birth daughter. And I love him and owe him everything."

"Do you have any conception of *my* wants and needs?"

She couldn't look at him right then, because she was too swamped by guilt and pain.

They made the rest of the trip back to Naples in silence. He stood a few feet away with his arms folded, his legs slightly apart. With his black hair slightly mussed he cut a dashing figure, but his mood had darkened, giving him a more forbidding countenance. The sight of his masculine features standing out in stark relief sent a little chill down her spine. She'd hurt him too.

"I'm sorry, Alessandro—" she cried.

A cruel smile broke out on his sensual male mouth. "So am I. We're almost to the dock. Give me a moment to send for the limo, and then you can be gone whenever it suits you." With lightning speed he pulled out his cellphone and made the call.

His swift capitulation surprised her. "Thank you for not fighting me on this."

"Figurati, signorina." His hands made the gesture her father always made, that meant "no problem." "A businessman with a modicum of experience senses when something is fatally flawed, and he knows when to back out before there's too great a price to pay."

Fatally flawed?

The bitterness in his tone left her reeling. "Alessandro—"

"Fly back to your arid world. I give you my word I won't come after you." His voice sounded cavernous. "Believe me, you're safer from me now than before we met."

His narrowed black eyes no longer blazed with desire for her. Instead they flicked to the limo that had just arrived at the end of the pier.

"Help at last." His mockery stung her to the quick. He reached for her suitcase.

Catherine had never seen this cold, dark side of him before. It was like a force field she couldn't penetrate. She didn't know him like this. It left her scrambling to get out of the boat before he could help her.

Steady footsteps sounded behind her as she hurried toward the limo. The driver greeted her and opened the door. After she climbed in, Alessandro put her suitcase on the seat opposite hers. Before he backed away he shot her a withering glance that left her desolate.

"Have a good life, Signorina Dalton. *Arrivederci*."

When he'd shut the door, the driver headed for the main road. As images of the rapture they'd shared flashed through her mind, Catherine felt like a drowning victim, going down for the third time.

Sandro entered the kitchen. His son was on the phone— no doubt with his friend Faustino—but when he saw him he quickly hung up.

"Where's Catherine?"

He inhaled sharply. "She's gone."

"What do you mean?"

"I mean she's no longer in my life."

He laughed. "Come on."

Wild with pain—desolate—he opened the fridge and pulled out a beer.

"Can I have one too?"

"No." Sandro drank half the bottle without taking a breath.

"Do you want to talk about it?"

"No, but I'd like to know how much trouble *you're* in, and why." After draining the rest of it he turned to Benito. "How about you come clean with me?"

His son squinted at him. "If you'll tell me what happened between you and Catherine first."

Maybe he was making headway with Benito? He cocked his head. "Nothing happened. *That's* what happened. She wanted to go home and that's what she's done." After a pause, "We won't be seeing each other again."

"You mean you're not going after her?"

Sandro braced his body against the counter. "Now, why would I do that?"

"Maybe so I won't have to live around a bear with a sore head!"

That brought Sandro up short. "I'm sorry, son. I didn't mean to be sarcastic."

"Hey—it's okay. Uncle Vito has been afraid you'd never fall in love again. Looks like he was wrong. You and Catherine were sickeningly happy in Sardinia."

He shut his eyes tightly. "We were—for a little while."

"I don't get it." By now Benito was standing in front of him. "Doesn't she want to marry you?"

That brought his eyes open again. "I didn't ask her."

"Why not?"

"It won't work."

"But you've always told me that a Lucchesi strikes on his first instinct and works out the details later."

Sandro's mouth twisted in self-mockery. "I did say that. But then I met Catherine. Too many demons are haunting her. Her attachment to her dad in America is too strong. She feels guilty about our relationship. So guilty it has prevented her from letting me in. I can't fight that."

"That doesn't sound like you, Papà."

He eyed his son lovingly. "Your difficult behavior this last year doesn't sound like *you* either. Why not let me listen to your problems now? It will help me get my mind off mine."

"Promise you won't erupt if I tell you?"

"I swear."

Benito paced the floor for a minute, then stopped. His head came up. "You know that diver who was caught stealing shipwreck artefacts off the coast of Turkey last year?"

It had been in all the papers. Good grief. *"Sì?"*

"Well, I guess he paid the fines, and now he's doing it again off the coast of Ischia. Faustino met him out boating in the fall, and he has been helping him for a percentage of the salvage they bring up."

One plus one made… "You've been helping too, I presume?"

"Not all the time."

"Have they found anything?"

"A lot of stuff—but I don't know how much it's worth."

"Have you been paid?"

"Any time now. He has to sell it to private collectors, and says it could be until the end of the summer before he sees the money."

"That's the best news I've heard all day. You do know the laws are changing? The penalties for destroying our underwater heritage could land you in prison."

"Yeah, I know. I've been getting nervous about that. But Faustino just laughs it off."

"If he isn't careful he'll be laughing behind bars. First thing tomorrow morning we're going to sit down with my attorney and talk about how to get you out of this mess before the police catch up to you."

Benito suddenly gave him a bear hug. "Thanks, Papà." The relief in his voice revealed that his son had been carrying around his guilt for a long time. He and Catherine had a lot in common.

Sandro squeezed his shoulder. "I owe you, after the way you've been helping me out."

"I'm sorry about Catherine. She'll miss you like crazy after she gets home."

Missing him like crazy didn't compete on the same level as a needy, bereaved father who'd just lost his wife and tugged on his daughter's emotional heartstrings without conscious thought. Stan Dalton had twenty-six years on Sandro. There was no contest.

"I've got an idea, Benito. After we've been to see my attorney, let's take a trip."

"Are you serious?"

"Completely. I need to get out of here. Anywhere you want to go except the States. We won't come back until the family does."

"Whoa."

CHAPTER TWELVE

THE second Catherine saw her father standing by his car outside of the airport terminal in Albuquerque, she practically threw herself into his arms. "Oh, Dad—if you hadn't been here I don't know what I would have done."

"You're a sight for sore eyes." He rocked her for a long time. "It's good to have you back, honey. Come on. We'll talk on the way to the ranch."

"Where's Brett?"

"He'll drive out later tonight."

As she was fastening her seat belt, he studied her features. "On the phone you told me that getting to know your birth father was a wonderful experience, but you don't look in the least happy."

The tears gushed. "I am—about him. I'd like to be a part of his life as much as it's possible."

"Good. I was hoping you'd say that. Your mother loved him enough once to have his baby. She wanted him to know the truth. He didn't have to call you. That tells me he's an honorable man."

"He is," she said. "But everything else is a disaster."

"*What* everything else?"

How to say it? "I met someone."

"You mean Alessandro."

"Yes," she said quietly.

"Go on."

"Oh, there's no point in talking about him. It was impossible to begin with, and Gabriella's in love with him, and he's got a son who's his life, and—and—"

"You're in love with him?"

Catherine buried her face in her hands and sobbed.

"Well, well, well. I was beginning to wonder if it would ever happen. Much as I love you, honey, I haven't relished the thought of having an old maid daughter on my hands forever."

She gasped. "Dad—"

He chuckled. "Okay, so what's wrong? Doesn't he love you? Is that what this is all about?"

"He's never said the words."

"Well, he must have done something to get you into this state."

"He-he asked me to stay at his villa for a while—but I couldn't!"

"Why not?"

"Because I wanted to get home to *you*."

After a long silence, "More than you wanted to be with him?"

"Yes— No— I don't know—" she cried.

"Catherine Dalton. Did he ask you to marry him?"

She wiped her eyes. "No."

"I see. So you think he just wanted an affair."

"He's been single since his wife died. That was seventeen years ago. I don't think he wants a wife."

"But you didn't stay long enough to find out what he wants? Too bad he thinks I'm the one to blame."

Catherine stared at her dad. "Blame?"

"That's right. You've got this notion in your head that I can't get along without you, when nothing could be further from the truth."

That was the last response she'd expected to hear. "Dad? Haven't you listened to anything I've said?"

"Yes. You've just told me you said goodbye to an exciting man, by all accounts. Evidently he's a man Mario would like for a son-in-law, but you have this misguided idea that I need you here and won't understand your decision. You don't give me much credit, Catherine."

She cringed. "What are you saying?"

"I adopted you because I *wanted* to, honey. I loved your mom even knowing she'd been in love with someone else first. It happens. I want you to have a life of your own and live it to the fullest. If I've seemed burdened down with grief, it's because I feel so bad that you've missed out on all these years getting to know your birth father."

Her heart leaped. "I didn't realize that."

"Obviously not. Something tells me Alessandro believes you're too tied to me to let go. If that's the case, it's no wonder he didn't prevent you from leaving."

Catherine was incredulous. "You think *that's* the reason?"

"I don't care how good a friend he is to Mario. No man as successful as he is would continue to squire you around all week with his son in tow if his deepest emotions weren't involved. Think about that while we drive back to the ranch."

It was all she *could* think about. As soon as they arrived, she ran into her room to phone Mario at his office. She was desperate to hear how things were going with Gabriella. And of course it was important he learned that she'd flown home instead of staying at Alessandro's villa.

His secretary put her on hold. She had to wait five minutes before he came on the line.

"Piccina—" She smiled through the tears. "I've been waiting for your call. I phoned Sandro's villa a little while ago. The housekeeper informed me there was no house guest and that Sandro and Benito have left for Australia on vacation."

Australia?

"That came as a shock, I can tell you."

To Catherine too. With that astounding piece of information, her soaring spirits had just plummeted to a new, all-time low. "I couldn't stay with Alessandro, Papà. Don't ask me all the reasons." There'd been too many.

"Only one is important. When you have figured it out, let me know."

After the illuminating conversation with her dad, she'd already done that. All that was left was to talk to Alessandro again. It might not change anything, but if her dad was right…

"In the meantime, Sofia and I have been talking. We're getting married in a quiet ceremony at the winery three weeks from tomorrow. Just a few friends. You met them at the party."

"That's fantastic!" Her mind was racing ahead with an idea.

"I'm glad you approve. I'd like both of my daughters there, but if neither of you comes because you can't bring yourselves to do it, for your own private reasons, I'll understand."

Sofia had gotten to him. She bit her lip. "Will you be inviting Alessandro?"

"Yes. He's been a good friend. Under the circumstances, however, it's possible he might not attend either. The next time you come to Naples—whenever that is— you will stay with your *papà* at the villa. It is your home. Understand?"

Her eyes filmed over. "Yes."

"I love you."

"I love you too. I'll talk to you very soon."

"Ciao, piccina."

"Signor Lucchesi? Your next appointment is here."

He scowled. "I'm through for today, to attend a wedding in the country later on. It appears you've made a mistake on the calendar."

"No mistake. This was a write-in at the last moment."

"I don't take write-ins." His secretary knew that. "I'm in a hurry."

He had to go home and change out of his lightweight

shirt into a summer suit—a painful task after his run-in with a creature from the reef. Even with his wetsuit on, it had penetrated. The wound had affected his left shoulder and was still sore. It surprised him. He'd thought it would be cleared up by now.

"This one insists."

"I assume it is Signor Conti's daughter?"

"Yes."

Sandro bristled. *Gabriella.* He hadn't seen or heard from her since that disastrous dinner on board the yacht three weeks ago. What a loving daughter she was, not to be at the winery supporting her *papà*!

Knowing she'd come to his office escalated his irritability—which, as Benito had commented just last night, when he'd mentioned Catherine's name by accident, was off the charts.

"Stall her until I've gone down to the garage." He pushed himself away from the desk and started for his private elevator. As the door was about to close he saw a woman with a mane of flowing red-gold hair enter his office on high heels. His heart knocked against his ribs before his view was cut off.

Frantic, he tried to get the door to reopen. But it was too late. Letting out a curse, he pressed the stop button, halting his descent mid-floor two stories down. If she left before he made it back to his office…

Finally he was ascending. Soon the door opened. He rushed into the room. "Catherine?"

"I'm right here."

Sandro wheeled around and came face to face with

her. A tight band constricted his lungs. She wore a filmy pansy-blue dress that hinted at the beautiful mold of the feminine body beneath. He couldn't do anything but feast his gaze on her.

A pulse beat a tattoo at his temple. "Why didn't you tell my secretary who you were?"

Dark blue eyes studied him anxiously. "After the way we parted at the dock, I didn't know what kind of a reception I would receive."

"You're the one who left," he accused. "I never expected to see you again."

He watched her swallow. "In the state I was in, I wasn't sure I'd be back."

"So it took Mario's wedding to get you to Italy again?"

"Yes."

His hands formed fists. "The ceremony isn't taking place in my office. Why in the hell did you come *here*?"

"Because Papà told me he'd invited you. I hoped we could go together—that is if you weren't planning to attend with someone else?"

"Who might that be?" he demanded with bitter sarcasm.

Her softly rounded chin lifted a trifle. "I have no idea. I just didn't want you to think that I would assume anything where you're concerned—or…or presume on our former relationship."

"What relationship? According to you, we didn't have one."

"I said a lot of things that seemed to make sense at the time."

"But now they don't?"

"Alessandro—"

"I'm surprised you could leave your father again," he threw out. The reality of her being in the same room within touching distance of him had him tied in knots.

"He wanted me to come." Her voice trailed, because her eyes were watching him attentively. "What's wrong with your shoulder? You keep rubbing it."

"Nothing you need to be concerned about."

She moved closer. "Every time you touch it you wince."

"It'll pass."

"You didn't have a wound the night of Mario's party. I know because I saw you get out of the pool. Are you ill? You *are* pale. Did something happen to you in Australia?"

Mario had kept her well informed. "Benito and I were doing some diving and—"

"And you had a brush with a stingray or a jellyfish?" she cried in alarm.

"No. A bristle worm. I had to have a couple of spines removed with forceps."

"Please may I see?"

"Here?"

"Yes. Right now."

"It hurts to take off my shirt. Since I have to change before going to the wedding, I only want to do it once."

"If the pain is that bad, then I insist we drop by the nearest hospital and have it looked at, in case you've developed more infection. You'll need to get going on an antibiotic before we leave for the wedding."

"I've just finished a series."

"Then you need more." She put a cool palm to his forehead. "You're warm, Alessandro. I can tell you're running a temperature. That settles it. We're leaving now."

She hurried into the elevator ahead of him and waited. He followed more slowly, studying her gorgeous face whose expression bordered on fear—for *him*. No one had worried about his well-being to this extent in years.

Within ten minutes Alessandro's driver had deposited them at St. Joseph's Hospital. The doctor in the ER examined his wound right away. Catherine insisted on being in the cubicle with him. Sure enough, it was infected. There were a few red streaks around the puncture wounds.

"It is good you came in. These kinds of wounds can get nasty if left untreated. We will put you on a new regimen of drugs and a heavier painkiller until it clears up. Go by the pharmacy on your way out to get these prescriptions filled."

They left the ER and went around the corner for the pills. "Could we have some water, please? Signor Lucchesi needs to take his medicine immediately," Catherine asked.

The mention of Alessandro's name sent the pharmacist running to be of help. Catherine breathed more easily once he'd swallowed the pills. She put the bottles in her purse and held on to his good arm as they left the hospital. The drive to his villa didn't take too long. The driver helped her get Alessandro into the foyer.

"Let's go straight to your bedroom. I'll help you off

with that shirt, and then I want you to lie down for a little while before we leave for the wedding. We still have four hours until the ceremony, so you can rest for three and then we'll take the helicopter."

"I had no idea you were so bossy," he murmured, but once they entered his bedroom he turned out to be very obedient.

"Here. Let me." She undid the buttons on his shirt, then eased the sleeves off his shoulders as carefully as possible and put it on a nearby chair. "Come on. You're going to bed." She walked over to the king-size bed and threw back the covers.

As he lay down and stretched out, all splendid six-feet-three of him on his back, she heard him sigh with relief. He'd been holding himself tense because of the pain, the poor darling. She took off his shoes, so he wouldn't have to lean over and strain himself.

"I'll keep your medicine in my purse until we come back tonight. Your next pill is due at the time of the ceremony, so you'll take it just before we go inside. Now, what else can I do for you?"

He reached out with his good arm to grasp her hand. The fiery black eyes sweeping over her held a devilish gleam. "I need a nurse to rub the skin around the wound. It's itching like mad."

She gave it a squeeze. "Turn on your right side. I'll get behind you so I can go to work."

A small smile lifted the corner of his mouth, tempting her to kiss him senseless. But first things first. Easing her hand out of his grasp, she hurried around the other side of the bed and slid across. After adapting her body to his, like two spoons, she raised herself on her right elbow and began gently touching the skin of his left arm and shoulder.

Sounds of pleasure came from deep in his throat. "That feels like heaven. Don't ever stop."

"I don't intend to. If it soothes you, that's all that matters. Did Benito get hurt too?"

"No. He came home without a scratch."

"What about his problems? Did he ever confess?"

"Yes. He and his friend have been helping a diver bring up treasure from shipwrecks illegally. Fortunately my attorney got him to turn state's evidence against the man, who has since been arrested. Benito and Faustino have to do public service for a year, to atone for their part of the crime. Luckily no money had changed hands yet, so they didn't have a fine to pay as well."

"Do you think he's learned his lesson?"

"I do. As he told me, lying is more terrible than facing the truth. He saw how complicated things grew with *our* situation. It made him think. I believe my son has made it through the worst of his teens."

Alessandro's speech had slowed down. The painkiller was starting to work. His body had gone limp. He needed sleep. She would be his alarm clock.

"Did I ever tell you every son needs a father like you?"

"Every father…needs a…wife like you."

Her heart turned over and over.

Alessandro—

CHAPTER THIRTEEN

"ALESSANDRO?"

He heard a familiar voice calling to him from a long way off.

"Catherine?"

"Yes, darling."

She'd just called him darling. She wouldn't have done that if the worst of her demons were still pulling her apart. His emotional state had just gone from darkest agony to joy beyond bearing.

"You need to wake up."

"I'm awake." His eyes were still closed. The drug had been powerful. "You called me darling."

"Did I?" she teased quietly. Now she was standing next to the bed in front of him. He could smell her fragrance.

"You know you did, and you can't take it back."

"What if I told you I don't want to?"

"Come closer and tell me again."

"Later. Right now I have to help you get ready for the wedding. We need to leave the villa within a half-hour to make it on time."

He opened his eyes. "*Now*, Catherine."

"Well—" Her slow white smile enraptured him. "I'd say that rest did you a lot of good."

"Please, *amorata*. I'm begging you."

She put her hands on her hips. "Did I hear the great Alessandro Lucchesi begging a mortal woman?"

"For the love of heaven, Catherine. You know what I need."

"If I didn't need the same thing I wouldn't be here." He felt the mattress give as she sank down on the side of the bed. Putting her hands on either side of his head, she lowered her mouth until it hovered above his. Her hair made a glowing red curtain around them.

"To make sure you understand, I want you to know that I love you. I'm desperately in love with you, Alessandro. Ask me again, and I'll tell you I want to stay with you in this villa for as long as you'll have me."

He brushed his lips against hers. "Even when I'm old and gray?"

"That'll be the best part. It will mean we've had a lifetime of loving together. Children. Grandchildren. Dad can't wait to be a grandpa. He can't wait to meet *you*. I'm afraid you and I will be making lots of trips to the ranch."

"Benito can't wait for you and Brett to teach him how to ride."

"I love you."

Their mouths merged in a deep kiss that resonated to the very core of his soul. When she finally lifted her head, he asked the question. "Till the end of time?"

"Yes," she whispered feverishly, kissing every part of his face and mouth.

"Catherine—"

She put a finger on his lips. "I know. There's nothing I want more than to lie down with you and forget the world. But our time is coming later. First we need to go to a wedding. Think how it will make my *papà* feel when he sees his firstborn daughter and his very good friend walk in with their arms around each other to help celebrate this important occasion. He deserves to have joy on his wedding day. Our presence will go a long way to make it happen—even if Gabriella can't bring herself to be there."

"I'm hoping she'll show up," Sandro murmured.

"So am I. He adores her."

He pressed another kiss to her lips. "Your coming to me today is a miracle. Maybe the gods will be kind and grant us one more."

She nodded. "Are you ready to try getting up?"

"I think I'm capable now."

He'd been quite capable since she'd told him she was in love with him. With her help, he rolled on his side and sat up so his legs touched the floor. Needing to feel all of her, he pulled her down on his lap with his good arm.

"One more for the road, *bellissima*."

She hid her face in his neck. "We can't. One more won't be enough for either of us."

"I swear I'll stop in time. Look. No hands."

The curve of her compelling lips intensified. "You don't need hands. Your mouth can do it all."

"Is that so?" He smiled back. "Our wedding night's coming up soon. By then I'll have the full use of my left arm, which ought to improve things considerably. Right now I'll settle for being in a semi-handicapped condition—as long as you're the one seeing to my exacting needs."

"Then let me do all the work this once." She wound her arms carefully around his neck and gave him a kiss unlike any other. The promise of a wife who would love him and stand by him forever was implicit in its urgency, filling all the aching, lonely spots inside his being.

Within the hour, the helicopter had landed in Taurasi. A car was waiting to drive them to the winery, several miles away. Three weeks before, Catherine had been to the wonderful old ochre-colored farmhouse, sitting in the middle of a vineyard. It had a large covered patio where the guests had already assembled on chairs in front of festively decorated tables. The abundance of flowers filled the air with the unmistakable fragrance of a wedding about to take place.

A five-piece orchestra was playing music in the background. Four chairs sat conspicuously empty in front of an arbor draped with garlands.

"We didn't get here any too soon," Alessandro whispered, grazing her cheek with his lips. "You shouldn't be so enticing."

"I was going to tell you the same thing," she said in a trembling voice. His touch was like a heat ray that melted her on the spot. She looked around. "Do you see Gabriella?"

"No."

They made their way to the front, smiling at everyone before they took their places. The second Catherine sat on his good side, Alessandro put his arm around her and pulled her close against him.

"Don't worry about her now, *amorata*. Let's concentrate on Mario and Sofia."

"You're right. This is *their* day."

The music stopped as the priest came out of the house and walked toward the arbor. Mario and Sofia followed. She looked lovely, in a creamy two-piece suit with lace, but Catherine's eyes fastened on her father, looking striking in a dark blue formal suit and tie. She'd expected to see the look of an eager bridegroom. Instead she saw a sad, solemn expression that seemed completely out of character for him.

Her heart twisted—because she knew the reason for it.

Then they turned to face their guests. The second Mario saw her and Alessandro seated there, holding on to each other, the sad expression turned into a smile that slowly radiated through his body.

Just before the priest took his place in front of them, Catherine heard footsteps. Both she and Alessandro turned their heads at the same time. In came Gabriella, looking beautiful in a flowing soft rose dress. She'd come with an attractive guy close to her own age, and they quickly took their places.

Catherine saw the loving glance that passed between

Mario and his second-born. He was so happy his eyes filled with tears. Catherine clutched Alessandro's arm. "It's going to be all right, darling," she whispered, with tears in her voice.

"It certainly is. We have our second miracle."

Alessandro twined his fingers with hers, in affirmation of the life they had waiting for them. Catherine lowered her head, her heart full of joy at too many blessings to enumerate—the greatest one being the man holding on to her.

Her first love. Her greatest love.

Italian Boss, Housekeeper Mistress

KATE HEWITT

Kate Hewitt discovered her first Mills & Boon®
romance on a trip to England when she was
thirteen, and she's continued to read them ever
since.

She wrote her first story at the age of five, simply
because her older brother had written one and
she thought she could do it too. That story was
one sentence long – fortunately, they've become a
bit more detailed as she's grown older.

She has written plays, short stories, and magazine
serials for many years, but writing romance
remains her first love. Besides writing, she enjoys
reading, travelling, and learning to knit.

After marrying the man of her dreams – her older
brother's childhood friend – she lived in England
for six years and now resides in Connecticut with
her husband, her three young children, and the
possibility of one day getting a dog.

Kate loves to hear from readers – you can contact
her through her website, www.kate-hewitt.com.

Don't miss Kate Hewitt's new book,
Royal Love-Child, Forbidden Marriage,
coming in November 2009 from Modern™.

Dear Reader,

Italy in summer…can you think of anything better? Sun-drenched afternoons idling in a boat on the lake, pavement cafés enjoying tiny cups of espresso and baskets of pastries, street markets with barrels of mozzarella and ropes of garlic – writing this story was a feast of the senses.

My hero, Leandro, is a man who's sworn off such earthly pleasures, and all because of a scandal in his past. It takes his feisty American housekeeper Zoe to reawaken his need and desire for not just pleasure, but love.

I was so thrilled to be able to be part of this anthology, and I hope you enjoy these wonderful stories of men and women discovering both passion and love during one memorable summer in Italy…

Kate

CHAPTER ONE

ZOE CLARK slipped the sunglasses off her nose to survey the discreet grey limousine idling at the kerb.

'Nice,' she murmured as the uniformed driver opened the door with a flourish. He'd already taken her one beaten up suitcase and stowed it in the boot.

Now she slipped into the cool leather interior of the luxury car and leaned her head back against the plush seat.

This was going to be a *fantastic* summer.

A smile bloomed and grew across her face as she leaned forward and flipped open the mini-fridge.

'Is this complimentary?' she called to the driver.

He stiffened before answering in heavily accented English, 'Of course.'

Zoe grinned and plucked a bottle of orange juice from the fridge. She'd rather have had the little bottle of cognac, but she didn't think it would be prudent to meet her future employer with brandy on her breath.

She took a swig of juice as the limousine pulled away from Milan's Malpensa Airport and into the teeming traffic.

The sky was cloudless and blue, the sun glinting brightly off the cars that zipped and zoomed their way across half a dozen motorway lanes.

Zoe sipped her drink, feeling the first familiar wave of fatigue crash over her. She hadn't slept much on the plane, and now a bit grimly she wondered if her employer would expect her to start work that morning.

For a moment she imagined him greeting her at the door of his villa, a feather duster and frilly apron in hand. What exactly did the temporary housekeeper of an Italian villa in the lakes do?

The job description had been surprisingly pithy—a scant two lines of tiny print in the back of the *New York Times*. Blink and you'd miss it. But Zoe had had a lifetime's experience of looking at such ads, circling them in red ink—usually with a pen that was sputtering or leaking or had lost its life altogether—before handing them hopefully to her mother.

What about this one?

There was always something better, something great right around the corner. There had to be.

The driver turned off the motorway, leaving behind the rolling hills of Lombardy as well as the endless traffic of the capital's outskirts for a smaller road lined with plane trees. Zoe glanced at the small road sign that read 'Como: 25 kilometres' before leaning her head once more against the soft leather seat and closing her eyes.

She must have dozed—she could sleep anywhere, except perhaps on planes—for when she woke the car was climbing higher into the hills, the dark green, densely forested peaks of the mountains providing a stunning backdrop.

She rapped on the dividing window, and with a long-suffering air the driver pressed a button so the glass slid smoothly away.

'Are we almost there?'

'Sì, signorina.'

Zoe sat back, taking in the ancient winding road, and the wrought-iron gates that presented themselves at intervals, guarding the wealthy residents within, whose villas could barely be glimpsed through the heavy foliage of rhododendrons and bougainvillea. As the car continued up the twisting road the lake shimmered enticingly at each bend, before disappearing again, and Zoe found herself turning around to look at it, to find its brilliant blue promise winking at her from between the trees.

'This is beautiful,' she said to the driver, before realising belatedly that he'd already pressed a button to return the dividing glass to its original place.

Then the car was turning smoothly into a narrow lane, and the driver spoke into an intercom affixed to an ancient crumbling wall. Zoe couldn't hear what was spoken, but after a moment the iron gates swung inwards, and the car proceeded up the lane.

Foliage crowded the car densely on both sides of the drive, so that when it finally fell away to reveal the villa Zoe let her breath out in a sharp, impressed exhalation.

Wow.

A sweep of jewel-green lawn led up to a villa that

seemed more like a palace—a *palazzo*—than the villa Zoe had been imagining.

This place was a *castle*.

And she was supposed to clean it all?

She counted twenty-two multi-paned windows glinting in the sunlight before she stopped.

The car pulled round the circular drive to the front of the villa. A pair of solid oak doors, looking as if they'd survived the Dark Ages, remained ominously shut.

Zoe climbed out of the car before the driver could come round, earning his continued disapproval. He took her suitcase from the boot and deposited it on the crumbling portico.

'Here you are, *signorina*.'

It took Zoe a moment to realise he was leaving.

'Wait—you're going?' she demanded, hearing an annoying edge of panic creep into her voice. 'Don't you work here?'

'I am hired only,' the driver replied, his voice stiff with disdain, before he slammed the door and drove away.

As the sound of his motor faded into the distance, Zoe was conscious of how surprisingly silent it was. A bird twittered nearby, and the breeze, cool and fresh from the lake, rustled the leaves of the palm trees that fringed the great lawn.

The owner of the villa—her employer, Leandro Filametti—obviously knew she was here. Someone had answered the intercom and opened the gates. So why the silent treatment now?

Squaring her shoulders, Zoe marched up to the front door, lifted the heavy brass knocker and let it drop. A deep, melancholy boom reverberated through her bones—and hopefully through the house—and then there was silence.

Zoe waited. The bird twittered again, fretfully this time, its tranquillity disturbed. Zoe raised her hand to the knocker once more, her fingers curling around the sun-warmed metal, but before she could drop it to sound the boom again the door opened, pulling her with it.

'Argh!' With a surprised yelp she tried to disentangle her fingers from the knocker, and in the process nearly fell headlong into the man who had opened the door.

Firm hands curled around her shoulders and righted her once more. Zoe was conscious of a sudden sense of strength and power, although she couldn't really see the man in front of her. Once she was steady, she looked up, and found her breath coming out in a rush once more.

The man was beautiful. Zoe didn't know if he was her employer or a gardener, but she certainly liked looking at him. His hair was light brown and a bit ragged, touching the back of his collar. Eyes the same colour as the lake—a deep blue-green—were narrowed against the sunlight, or perhaps in disapproval. He didn't look very friendly.

Zoe straightened, unable to keep her gaze from wandering down the length of him. He was tall, a few inches over six feet, dressed in a faded grey tee shirt and worn jeans that hugged his long powerful legs. His feet were tanned and bare.

Zoe swallowed. 'Hello…um… *Ciao. Il mi…*' Her few words of Italian, snatched on the plane from a battered phrasebook, seemed to have leaked out of her brain. She smiled with bright determination. 'I'm Zoe Clark.'

'The housekeeper.' He spoke with little accent, his voice cutting and precise. He stepped back, opening the door wider, yet somehow the gesture still seemed unfriendly. 'Come in.'

Zoe stepped into a foyer, the black and white marble cool even through her flip-flops. The light was dim, and as her eyes adjusted she saw a sweeping spiral staircase in front of her, ornate and yet also clearly in disrepair. Her glance took in sheet-shrouded tables, and a bronze statue of a cupid that looked in need of some serious polish.

The man cleared his throat and her gaze snapped back to him. 'Are you Leandro Filametti?'

'Yes.'

The one word was spoken with a brusque flatness that made Zoe want to recoil. Instead, she jutted her chin and thrust out her hand. 'Nice to meet you.'

Leandro Filametti regarded her hand silently for a moment before he shook it. His touch was light, yet firm, and all too brief. He dropped her hand without ceremony and turned to walk out of the foyer, clearly expecting Zoe to follow—which, with some resentment, she did.

Leandro led her down a narrow passageway to the back of the *palazzo*. From the peeling paint and chipped woodwork, Zoe could tell the palace needed a good deal of TLC. More, she suspected, than her limited capabilities allowed.

Leandro stopped on the threshold of an enormous

ancient kitchen. Zoe regarded the huge blackened range and the scarred oak table with both awe and dismay. A single plate and glass, she noticed, had been washed and placed on the drainer by the sink. In the huge space, clearly meant for cooking meals for twenty or more, they looked incongruous and lonely.

'You can start here,' Leandro informed her.

'Start…?' Zoe stared around. She couldn't even see so much as a broom—and, frankly, she wouldn't know where to begin. How did you scrub away years of grime and dust? Did you start with the cobwebs or the mouse nests?

'Yes,' Leandro replied, his tone sharp with impatience. 'You do know what housekeeping entails, don't you?'

'I do,' Zoe replied, her tone matching his. 'But I also know that my suitcase is still on your front steps, I've been travelling all night and I haven't even washed my face or had a drink of water.' Juice, perhaps, but not water.

Leandro did not even look abashed. 'If you'd like a few moments to freshen up, by all means take them,' he said, with just a trace of sarcasm.

'Could you show me my room?'

'Top floor. Take any room you like,' he replied. 'And you can get acquainted with the house as well as with your responsibilities.'

With that he turned on his heel and disappeared down another passageway, leaving Zoe open-mouthed and fuming.

* * *

She wasn't what he'd expected. Back in the sanctuary of his private study, Leandro ran his hands through his hair before dropping them with ill-concealed impatience. In truth, he hadn't known *what* to expect; he hadn't thought to expect anything at all. He hadn't considered the housekeeper he'd hired beyond her ignorance of Italian society and, most importantly, the Filametti family. He wanted someone anonymous; someone to whom *he* could be anonymous.

Yet when he'd surveyed Zoe Clark on his front steps, anonymous had not been the first word that came to mind. She was, in fact, all too familiar—all too similar to the women of his past. His father's past.

Fast and flighty. Cheap and easy. Unprincipled.

Even now his mind conjured the image of her standing there, dressed in a skinny-strapped top and shorts that showed far too great an expanse of smooth, tanned leg. Her hair, silky and dark, framed her face in choppy waves, and her eyes were a warm honeyed brown, almond-shaped and luxuriously fringed. Everything about her, Leandro thought, reeked of sensuality—a confident sexuality that he recognised, remembered. How he loathed that knowing feline smile, the glint in the eyes of a woman so arrogantly confident of her own paltry charms. And yet his father had fallen prey to those charms time and time again.

He would not be the same.

Yet even as that resolution fired his soul, another part of his body already recognised there was something about Zoe Clark that he both resented and wanted. She was sexy, and he was man enough to respond to it. That didn't mean he would act upon it. Ever. The world—*his* world—was waiting for him to make the same mistake his father had. To fall. To humiliate himself, his family, the ancient Filametti name. He knew it, had always known it, and even in the lonely solitude of the villa he recognised the dangers within himself.

He didn't need the complication of a sexy house-keeper; he didn't want it.

Except even as his fingers had wrapped around hers for that brief, tantalising moment, he had.

Leandro muttered an oath under his breath and sat down at the huge mahogany desk that had once belonged to his father. He hated that desk, its connotations and memories, yet some perverse part of his psyche insisted on using it. Redeeming it—or perhaps avenging it was the better term. He gazed sightlessly at the pages in front of him, with their endless equations, numbers and squiggles that represented a lifetime of research and achievement, and yet right now they signified nothing. He swore again.

The less he saw of Zoe Clark, the better, he decided. She could sweep and mop and dust and stay completely out of his way.

He didn't need distractions—and ill-timed, inappropriate desire was just one of many he'd have to push resolutely away.

Zoe found the servants' staircase—a steep, narrow, dismal set of steps—and cautiously made her way up. The gloom was intensified by a gossamer net of cobwebs suspended from the ceiling, and the only sound besides her own breathing was the resentful squeak of the steps as she made her way upwards.

She passed a dark, silent floor of closed doors and more shrouded furniture and then went up to the top floor, gazing in dismay at the four rooms available there. Each one was small and depressing, containing only a chest of drawers and a narrow bed whose mattress was questionable in both comfort and hygiene.

It was also stiflingly hot.

'At least the view is good,' she muttered, as she forced open a pair of peeling shutters and gazed out at the terraced gardens that ran down directly to the lake. The gardens were in as much disrepair as the villa, but they showed it less. Bougainvillea run rampant, Zoe decided, was pretty. Dust run rampant was not.

With a sigh she turned back to survey the room. Sweat trickled down her back and between her breasts, and with sudden clarity and determination Zoe decided she was not going to suffer up here while a dozen bedrooms below went unused.

Leandro Filametti be damned. She deserved a little comfort if he expected her to tackle this lot.

Twenty minutes later Zoe had settled on one of the more modest bedrooms on the second floor. Painted in a faded lemony yellow, it was a smaller room, whose shuttered windows afforded a stunning view of Lake Como. After locating a dented bucket and an old mop in one of the kitchen's many cupboards, Zoe spent most of the afternoon cleaning her own bedroom, airing the mattress and scrubbing and dusting what looked like a dozen years' worth of dust and dirt.

Why was this villa such a mess? she wondered more than once. It was a prime piece of property, yet it looked as if it had been empty for years.

She felt as dirty as the room had been by the time she'd finished cleaning, and she seriously doubted the villa was equipped with a decent shower.

The sun was starting its descent towards the lake, but the air was still sultry and warm. With a defiant shrug Zoe decided she'd make use of the natural resources on hand, and after slipping on a bikini she made her way downstairs.

All was silent, and Leandro was nowhere to be seen. Just as well, Zoe decided grimly. If she saw him, she might give him a piece of her mind—and that could get her fired.

She picked her way through the overgrown gardens to a set of stone steps that led directly to an old jetty. The water shimmered with late-afternoon sunlight and after a second's hesitation Zoe dived in, gasping as the shock of surprisingly cold water hit her near-naked body. She swam underwater for a few lengths, before surfacing and flipping onto her back, her eyes closed.

She floated pleasantly in an almost half-doze before she became conscious of another presence. She didn't know what alerted her, but something prickled along her skin entirely separate from the cool water. She lifted her head, treading water, as her eyes scanned the shoreline and came in direct contact with Leandro Filametti.

His expression was neutral, his eyes narrowed

against the sun, his hands fisted on his hips. Even so, Zoe's heart slammed in her chest and she found herself strangely conscious of everything: her own rather bare body, the coolness of the water, the brilliance of the sun. And the cold, hard look she could now see in Leandro's eyes—could feel emanating from him just as if she were standing in front of a freezer.

He didn't speak, and Zoe forced a breezy laugh as she raised an arm in greeting. 'Come on in. The water's lovely.'

Wrong thing to say, she decided, as Leandro's neutral expression darkened into a scowl.

'I see you are availing yourself of the comforts of my home,' he said after a moment, and before she could stop herself Zoe gave a little laugh of disbelief.

'Comforts? I'm afraid, Signor Filametti, that your home affords very *few* comforts.'

In answer he arched one eyebrow, coldly sceptical. Zoe was getting tired of treading water, so she swam to the side of the jetty and hauled herself up. Sitting on the sun-warmed stone, dripping wet, she felt Leandro's gaze rove over her, and was conscious yet again of the skimpiness of her bikini. She was also aware that she didn't have a towel.

'What have you been doing this afternoon?' Leandro asked, his tone one that suggested Zoe had been lolling by the lakeside for hours, eating bonbons and reading novels.

'Making a bedroom habitable,' she replied sharply. 'When an ad says "room and board provided" it usually means just that. But none of the bedrooms in your villa were fit for human habitation, Signor Filametti, so I spent the afternoon making sure I had a place to sleep tonight.'

Leandro was silent for a long moment, and when Zoe glanced at him she saw his expression was as dark and foreboding as ever.

'I'm sorry,' he said finally, surprising her. 'I didn't think... I am involved in important research at the moment, and such considerations escaped my notice.'

Zoe jerked her head in a nod of acceptance. 'I couldn't find any sheets,' she added, a bit petulantly.

Leandro's mouth quirked upwards in an unexpected glimmering of a smile. 'Or towels, I suspect. Those I have, I brought with me. Although if I recall the beds on the top floor are single—'

'That shouldn't be a problem,' Zoe replied, 'because I chose a bedroom on the second floor.' She glared at him, ready for a battle, but after a tiny pause he just shrugged.

'As you wish. When you come up to the house I'll provide you with some sheets...' His disapproving glance took in her wet length once more before he added, 'And a towel.'

He shouldn't have gone down to the lake, Leandro knew. He was angry with himself that he had. He hadn't made the decision until he'd heard the sound of splashing and realised Zoe Clark must be down there. Swimming. In a swimming costume.

This realisation had presented his tired mind with far too many intriguing images that he'd pushed resolutely away. He'd been without a woman for too long—

without companionship of any kind for too long. Normally a woman like Zoe Clark would disgust him. Bold, obvious, inappropriate, cheap. All the qualities he despised in a woman.

The few women he'd taken to his bed had been sophisticated, classy and most importantly discreet. They'd understood the nature of short-term, expedient affairs and they'd wanted the same thing. Pleasure. Satisfaction. And a painless goodbye.

Not, he thought grimly, money. Or, worse, love.

He didn't know what Zoe wanted, but he knew what women like her were capable of. And even if they weren't, he knew what the tabloids were capable of. He'd seen firsthand how whispers could destroy a person. Already he imagined the headlines if someone got hold of his situation: *Like father, like son. Leandro Filametti in a flagrant affair with his housekeeper.*

He pushed the thought—and the temptation—away.

Upstairs in the villa Leandro dug through the supplies he'd brought to the villa from his flat in Milan and found a set of clean sheets and a couple of towels. He should have considered the whole matter of her bedroom, but he hadn't wanted to consider her at all. Thinking about a housekeeper meant thinking about the villa, and even though he'd spent every day of the last month within its walls he didn't want to think about it.

He didn't want to remember.

As he headed downstairs his stomach gave a growl, reminding him that it was nearing suppertime and the only thing in the fridge was half a portion of pasta, left over from the restaurant where he'd eaten last night. He'd brought it home for lunch and forgotten about it completely. Somehow he didn't think Zoe Clark would consider it suitable fare—and she would be quick to point out that room and board meant feeding her too. He knew her type; she would insist on her rights.

The only option was to take her out to a restaurant. Of course there was always the danger of being recognised, but Lornetto was small enough and its few residents were close-mouthed and loyal. Annoyed, Leandro realised he was almost looking forward to the prospect of the evening ahead. He was being so weak…as his father had been weak. Grimacing, he headed for the kitchen.

He found Zoe dripping and shivering by the range, her arms wrapped around her sides. She dropped them as soon as she saw him.

'This kitchen is huge,' she remarked. 'I'm not sure where to begin.'

Leandro shrugged. 'You just need to clean it.' He thrust the sheets and towels into her arms. He couldn't keep himself from noticing the lithe perfection of her body, tanned and taut and so very bare. She wasn't curvaceous, but she had enough of a rounded shape to please a man and make his mid-section tighten uncomfortably. 'Once you're dressed, we'll go out to eat. Perhaps tomorrow you can go to the shops for food and whatever else you'll need. Do you cook?'

Zoe raised an eyebrow. 'That wasn't in the job description, but I can rustle up a few meals, if that's what you're asking. Is it just the two of us here?'

Although the question was basic, it seemed to reverberate through the air, conjuring up an uncomfortable intimacy, and Leandro instinctively sharpened his tone. 'Yes. I'll see you in a few minutes.' He turned on his heel, striding quickly out of the room before Zoe had a chance to say another word.

CHAPTER TWO

SHE shouldn't be looking forward to sharing a meal with as ornery a creature as Leandro Filametti, yet Zoe was honest enough to acknowledge that she was. She gazed briefly at her reflection in the tarnished mirror in her bedroom, happy enough with her appearance. No need to impress her employer, she decided, knowing that any attempt to do so would most likely achieve the opposite effect. She'd settled on a pair of jeans and a yellow silky top with skinny straps. She left her hair loose and damp, and eschewed any make-up. Leandro was waiting, probably counting the minutes or seconds to determine how tardy she was. He seemed the type.

Humming under her breath, Zoe headed downstairs. Just as she'd expected, Leandro was waiting in the foyer, and Zoe saw immediately that he'd changed. He wore a cream-coloured button-down shirt and tan trousers—a boring outfit if there ever was one. And yet on him it looked far too appealing. The sleeves were rolled up to expose strong, tanned forearms—how did someone closeted all day doing research get tanned?—and the trousers emphasised a trim waist and long, well-muscled legs.

Zoe tore her gaze away; there was no point ogling her employer. She didn't want to get involved with someone like Leandro Filametti, who could only see her as the hired help—a drudge to be treated with disdain or at best grudging respect. She knew how *that* scenario played out. But he was nice to look at.

'There is a restaurant in Lornetto, the nearby village,' Leandro told her. 'We can walk, if you like.'

'Sounds great,' Zoe replied breezily, causing a brief frown to pass over Leandro's face like a shadow. What a stickler, she thought, with a little burst of annoyed amusement. She wondered what kind of research he was doing. He was probably an accountant, or something equally dull.

Yet there was nothing dull about the flash of aware-ness that tingled up her arm when he took her elbow and guided her down the crumbling steps of the portico. He dropped it as soon as they'd navigated the wrecked stone, but Zoe was still conscious of a strange, shivery warmth where he'd touched her.

She shrugged the feeling away, determined not to be distracted. She hadn't come to Italy for a relationship; she'd come to get away from one, and she'd do well to remember that.

The sun set as they walked down the lane, leaving vivid violet streaks across the sky, and although the air was still warm and scented with lavender there was a hint of coolness too, as the evening breeze rolled in from the mountains.

They walked in companionable enough silence for a few moments along the lake road—La Ancina Strada, from Roman times, according to the guidebook Zoe had leafed through—until a village—no more than a huddle of stone buildings along a narrow cobblestoned street—came into view.

There was certainly something charming about the scattering of tables under a faded striped awning, Zoe reflected as Leandro guided her to an outdoor café along an even narrower side street. Dusk had fallen, and the night cloaked them in cool softness as he pulled out her chair. There was, she thought with an uneasy sort of pleasure, something almost romantic about the situation.

That notion was quickly dispelled as Leandro took a seat across from her, folded his hands in businesslike fashion and launched into an extensive list of her duties.

'I'm selling the villa,' he stated bluntly, 'as soon as it's in decent condition. You are required to keep it as neat and clean as possible. I understand the difficulty, since so much of it is in disrepair, but there will be workmen coming in to deal with much of the damage, and as their work continues so yours should become easier.'

Zoe nodded, although she hardly thought navigating workmen, falling plaster and all manner of unknown hazards would make her job easier.

A waiter came, and without a glance at her Leandro ordered for both of them. Annoyance prickled along her spine at this presumption—although she recognised fairly that she knew an appallingly little amount of Italian.

'What did you order?' she asked after the waiter had left. 'Just out of curiosity.'

'A local pasta dish,' Leandro replied with a shrug. 'Made with tomatoes and basil—simple enough.'

Zoe nodded. She wasn't about to kick up a fuss over something so small, yet it still irritated her that Leandro had ordered for her without even asking. It spoke volumes about how he viewed his station in life...and hers.

And yet, she asked herself, determined to be honest, why should she care? She'd had years of experience in menial work; her impressive listing of chambermaid and waitressing jobs was undoubtedly what had secured her this position in the first place. Yet for some reason, in the enforced intimacy of their situation, it rankled.

'May I have a drink?' she asked a little pettishly, and Leandro's eyes narrowed, his lips thinning in obvious disapproval.

'The waiter will bring water—were you thinking of something else?'

Zoe almost said she'd like a glass of wine after the day she'd had, but she decided she'd pressed enough. She shrugged her acceptance instead and switched subjects. 'Why are you selling the villa? Is it a business investment?'

Leandro's expression hardened briefly and he shrugged in reply. 'Something like that.'

Zoe took a thoughtful sip from the water glass the waiter had placed on the table. 'Why is it in such a state?'

'Isn't it obvious? No one has lived in it for years.'

'Yes, but...' Zoe set down her glass. 'Why not? It's beautiful, and it's the type of property that would go in a heartbeat—or so I would have thought.'

'You know very much about real estate in the region?' Leandro asked with an arched eyebrow.

Zoe shrugged. 'I read gossip magazines. Celebrities are always buying up places like this for millions.'

'This villa hasn't been for sale.'

There was an ominously final note in Leandro's voice that made Zoe wonder what he wasn't saying. Still, she decided to drop the subject.

'You mentioned getting supplies in—would I find them here?'

'Probably not. Lornetto is no more than a fishing village. There is a market town across the lake—you can take the boat.'

'The boat?' The idea of jetting across the lake on her own gave Zoe an unspeakable thrill.

Leandro must have sensed it, for he narrowed his eyes. 'Have you ever driven a powerboat?' he asked. 'It is a small one, but still...'

Zoe opened her eyes wide. 'I'm sure I can manage.'

A reluctant smile quirked the corner of his mouth before disappearing completely, replaced by the more familiar disapproval. 'It is not so simple. I'll drive you tomorrow. After that...' He shrugged. 'We'll see.'

The waiter came to the table bearing two steaming

bowls of pasta, fragrant with fresh basil and oregano. Zoe's mouth watered. She hadn't eaten anything all day, and she was starving.

Neither of them spoke as they dug into the pasta, and after a few moments Zoe became aware that Leandro was watching her with a mixture of amusement and disapproval.

'Do you always attack your meals with so much gusto?'

'When I haven't had anything to eat all day,' she replied, swallowing a mouthful of pasta, 'yes.'

Leandro did not look remotely abashed. Zoe wondered what kind of women he was used to. No doubt stick-thin models from Milan, who toyed with a lettuce leaf and called it a meal. Her mouth twisted in cynicism. He was wealthy, good-looking, powerful. Men like that liked ornaments on their arm, nothing more. Ornaments they quickly discarded...or shattered.

Pushing those memories away, Zoe smiled brightly at Leandro as their pasta bowls were cleared. 'What kind of research do you do?'

'You wouldn't understand it,' Leandro replied, and her interest—and annoyance—were piqued.

'Try me.'

He shrugged. 'Risk analysis. I'm an actuary—I work in financial forecasting. Cashflow studies, you'd call it.' At Zoe's blank look he continued, amusement lurking in his eyes, 'Statistical modelling, stochastic stimulations, pricing role?'

Zoe shook her head. 'Nope, nope and nope.'

The amusement in his eyes made its way to his

mouth, and Zoe's heart rate jumped and then kicked up a notch at the sight of his full-fledged grin. Did he know of its dazzling effect? she wondered, feeling almost dizzy. Was he aware of how it lightened his features, brightened his eyes, and made him all too approachable?

'I told you you wouldn't understand it,' he said with a shrug, and at this dismissal Zoe's heart rate settled right down again.

'Well, it's obviously made you rich,' she said bluntly.

Leandro's mouth tightened, his eyes flashing with something close to anger. 'Yes, it has. Although it is of no concern to you. I started my own company, and it has done well.'

Clearly he'd had enough of the subject—and of her—for he rose from the table, signalling for the bill with one autocratically raised hand. Zoe rose as well, and in a matter of seconds Leandro had dealt with the bill and was striding out of the restaurant, clearly expecting her to follow. He didn't look back, and with a little stirring of resentment, she made her way down the dusky street to join him, matching his brisk pace.

By the time they'd left the lights of Lornetto behind, the road was dark and filled with shadows. There were no street lights or passing cars, only the silvery glint of moonlight on the lake. Zoe stumbled on the uneven pavement and Leandro reached out to steady her, grabbing her elbow in a firm grip before she righted herself again.

'And you didn't even have a glass of wine,' he said, his voice a murmur in the dark. 'Although I think you wanted one.'

There went her heart rate again—skittering all over the place, stupid thing. Zoe could see his eyes and teeth gleaming in the darkness, but nothing more. 'How did you know?' she asked, a bit unevenly.

Leandro dropped his hand from her elbow, his face partially averted. When he spoke, his voice was coolly dismissive. 'A girl like you…what else would I expect?'

It took Zoe a moment to process his implication. She came to a stop in the middle of the road. 'What do you mean, a girl like me?' she asked, feeling a sudden icy pooling in her stomach. It was so close to what Steve had said, what he had *thought*.

Leandro turned around, exasperated. 'What do you think I mean?'

It was clearly a rhetorical question; there was no doubt, Zoe thought bitterly, in either of their minds what he meant. Resentment bubbled within her.

'The implication is hardly complimentary,' she said, her voice sharp.

Leandro just shrugged. 'It is what it is. Now, I don't fancy standing in the middle of the road in the dark. Let's go.' Without waiting for a response, he turned and started back down the shadowy road.

Fuming, Zoe followed.

A girl like her. If she felt like being charitable— or *he* did—she might think that simply meant some- one who was fun, friendly, full of life. A few months ago she would have made that assumption—before she'd realised exactly what kind of assumptions men like Steve and apparently Leandro were making about her. *A girl like you.* Loose, easy, cheap. Basically, a slut.

Her mouth thinned and her eyes narrowed as she followed Leandro up the villa's private lane. The *palazzo* was no more than a huge shadow in the darkness.

She shouldn't be offended by Leandro's words, Zoe told herself. She shouldn't care what *a man like him* thought. She understood that going from place to place, job to job, made men think she was as loose as her lifestyle. And projecting a certain image—fun-loving, free—kept her safe. Protected her heart. She revelled in her reputation, in her freedom.

She could pick up or drop down at a moment, discarding homes and relationships with insouciant ease. That was who she was. That was who she *had* to be, to protect herself from getting hurt.

So why, for a moment, did she not like a man like Leandro assuming it?

A man like Leandro... What did that mean? She didn't know him at all, Zoe realised. He was rich, he was well connected, he was a buttoned-up accountant. No, an actuary. Whatever that was. But beyond the basics she had no idea what kind of man he was.

'The kind of man who thinks he knows all about a girl like me,' she muttered, and Leandro, now at the front door, turned round.

'Did you say something?'

'No.' Her voice came out in a petulant retort, but Leandro merely arched an eyebrow.

Zoe jabbed him in the chest with one forefinger; even

with just the tip of her finger she could feel the hard definition of sculpted muscle underneath his shirt. 'You don't know me, *signor*. So don't go telling me what kind of girl I am.' She sounded ridiculous, Zoe realised distantly. She also realised her finger was still jabbed in his chest. And yet she didn't move it. If she wasn't so tired, if her brain didn't feel so fuzzy and light and disconnected, she wouldn't have mentioned anything. She certainly wouldn't have touched him.

Instead, her brain registered in that same disconnected way that he'd wrapped his own hand—warm, strong, dry—around her finger and raised it to his lips. His eyes were dark, and Zoe detected a spark of anger in their depths. She wondered who he was angry with. Himself or her.

She watched, fascinated, as her finger barely brushed the softness of his parted mouth. His eyes darkened even more, to almost black, and his mouth thinned into a contemptuous, knowing smile as he dropped her hand and it fell limply to her side.

'I wouldn't presume to tell you anything,' Leandro replied curtly. 'I don't need to. You say it plainly enough.'

With that he turned and disappeared into the darkness of the house, and Zoe realised it was the third time that day he'd walked away and left her standing alone.

He was playing with fire. Touching her. Needing to touch her. And enjoying it.

Leandro flung himself into his desk chair and closed his eyes, but he couldn't banish the image of Zoe Clark at dinner, wearing that silky top, her hair dark and soft around her face. He pictured the way her eyes had danced with amusement, the way those silly little straps had slipped off her tanned shoulders. The way he'd wanted to push them off.

And she would have let him.

He could still feel the barest brush of her finger against his lips—what had he been thinking, teasing her like that? Teasing himself?

He certainly wasn't going to act upon the latent desire that hummed inside him—between them. If he were a different man he might have. He might have said to hell with good intentions and higher principles, and taken what was so blatantly on offer. He'd enjoy it, for a time, and then he'd walk away—tabloids, colleagues, family be damned... All for the sake of desire.

But he wasn't a different man.

He wasn't his father, and he wouldn't cheapen and enslave himself to desire. Not for a woman like Zoe Clark—a woman like all the others who took and took and didn't care who she stepped on to get what she wanted.

Who she hurt.

It's obviously made you rich.

His mouth thinned in distaste at the memory of her words. Another woman on the prowl. Well, she wouldn't get anything from *him*. He wouldn't give her the chance.

Stifling a curse, he pulled his papers towards him, one hand fumbling for the spectacles he'd discarded on his desk. He switched on the desk lamp, and with a grim, determined focus bent his head to his work.

CHAPTER THREE

ZOE awoke to bright lemony sunshine pouring through the windows, a fresh breeze from the mountains ruffling the rather tattered curtains.

She lay still for a moment, enjoying the feel of the sun and the breeze, before memories of last night filtered through her consciousness and started to spoil her mood.

A girl like you.

You say it plainly enough.

Leandro Filametti had made it clear how little he thought of her. She shouldn't be surprised, Zoe knew. She'd faced far worse in her years as a chambermaid or short-order cook, in the endless parade of dead-end jobs she'd determinedly revelled in. Zoe Clark—the girl without a plan.

Tomorrow will take care of itself, sweetie. Hasn't it always?

And with the dead-end jobs had come the leering looks, the men who assumed *a girl like her* was always on offer.

And when she'd finally chosen to be involved with someone, to give her body and yet keep her heart safe, she'd still had her ego stamped on. She pictured Steve's sneering face before resolutely pushing the image away.

She wouldn't let Steve hurt her any more—she'd let him hurt her enough already—and she wouldn't let Leandro hurt her either.

Except last night Leandro's carelessly delivered condemnation *had* hurt. It had pierced her armour of indifference, and she didn't even understand why.

Why was Leandro Filametti different? Why did he make her feel different?

'He doesn't,' Zoe said aloud, her voice sounding strange, echoing in the empty room. She shrugged off her covers and jumped out of bed, determined to enjoy the beautiful day, so fresh and bright, and not to think about Leandro.

Not to care.

She was good at that; she always had been. And now would be no different.

The villa was silent as Zoe made her way downstairs, stepping through pools of sunshine. She skidded to a halt when she saw Leandro sitting at the huge kitchen table, drinking a cup of coffee.

'Sleeping Beauty finally awakes,' he said, his voice a mixture of amusement and acerbity.

'What—?' Zoe glanced inadvertently at the clock, and gasped when she saw what time it was. 'Eleven a.m.!'

'It must be the jet lag,' Leandro said laconically. 'In future I hope you intend to have a little *less* beauty sleep.' He rose from the table, taking his mug to the sink.

'If you're dressed, we might as well head to town. I can't spend all day fetching and carrying, and it's already near lunchtime.'

'Fine.' Zoe pushed her hair away from her face, and her stomach rumbled audibly.

A smile flickered across Leandro's features, then disappeared. 'And we'll get some breakfast as well.'

Zoe followed Leandro outside, through the gardens and down to the jetty, to where a weathered speedboat was moored. It was a small craft, clearly meant for functional use, yet despite its age Zoe could tell it was well made and expensive.

Like Leandro, she thought with a trace of humour. Nothing showy or ostentatious, nothing obvious, yet he still emanated the sort of arrogant assurance that could only come from a lifetime of money and power.

She repeated that mantra to herself as she climbed into the boat, sinking into one of the comfortable leather seats as Leandro slid into the driver's seat and the boat thrummed to life.

Zoe knew she should stay angry with Leandro, remind herself of all the assumptions he'd made, but with the sun sparkling on the water as if the lake were strewn with diamonds, and the day stretched out in front of them filled with enticing possibility and adventure, she found her indignation trickling away…at least for the moment. She slipped on her sunglasses as they pulled away from the jetty. The breeze was fresh, and just a little bit sharp.

'This is fabulous!' she shouted to Leandro over the

sound of the motor. He glanced across at her, a smile lurking in his eyes, and suddenly Zoe wanted to see it on his mouth, see his face transformed, alive. 'Can you go any faster?'

For a moment his mouth tightened, as if he disapproved of the question, its implications and innuendoes. Then with a shrug he pushed the throttle forward and the speedboat jumped ahead, singing through the sea. A gurgle of laughter escaped from Zoe's throat, and she turned to see Leandro grin.

His teeth flashed white in his tanned face, his eyes, the same colour of the lake, sparkling with humour, and Zoe felt herself react, her heart skipping a beat, her insides tightening.

This was dangerous, she acknowledged, even as she grinned back. She knew what getting involved with a man like Leandro meant. What it felt like. Yet for that moment, recklessly, she *wanted* to be just a little bit dangerous. She'd keep her wayward heart under lock and key.

She held his gaze, silently challenging him, her grin changing into a seductive smile. He looked away first, his smile disappearing, and Zoe felt a flicker of disappointment. She sat back, enjoying the simple beauty of the alpine forests that stretched straight to the shore, dotted with the terracotta tile and crumbled stone of the region's many hamlets and villages.

After a quarter of an hour Leandro steered the boat towards the shoreline of one of the lake's larger towns. A promenade fronted the water, lined with villas, shops and street cafés. Leandro moored the boat at the public dock, and leaped gracefully out of the boat before extending a hand to Zoe.

She took it, not wanting to make a fool of herself by scrambling inelegantly out of the speedboat. And, she admitted silently, she liked the feel of his hand encasing hers—although he dropped it almost immediately.

'You should be able to get what you need in the shops here in Menaggio,' Leandro said as they walked towards the centre of town. 'Did you bring a list?'

She hadn't even thought of a list, but Zoe smiled brightly. 'Of course.'

Leandro's lips twitched even as his eyes narrowed. 'Why do I have trouble believing that?'

Zoe met his gaze directly. She was good at brazening it out; she'd had loads of practice evading landlords, bosses, men with groping hands and leering looks. Widen the eyes, smile confidently, keep the voice firm. It was easy. Too easy. 'I don't know. Why?'

Leandro shook his head. 'Because you don't seem like the kind of girl who even thinks about lists.'

Another judgement. 'You seem to have fitted me neatly into a box,' Zoe said, her voice a little shorter than she'd intended. 'And it's *woman*, please. Not girl. I'm twenty-eight.'

'Are you?' Leandro murmured, his tone and smile both sardonic. 'And don't you think you fit into that box?'

Zoe glanced at him sharply. 'No one belongs in a box. Not willingly, anyway.'

'Perhaps not,' Leandro agreed in a drawl. 'But even so the box can still fit.'

Zoe bristled, but Leandro ignored her, gesturing to a row of small quaint shops lining one of the town's squares.

'Perhaps we should have a coffee first, and you can actually *make* that list?'

'All right,' Zoe agreed, her voice still stiff. Hunger won over pride. 'I am starving.'

Leandro led her to a small street café, its tables shaded by brightly coloured umbrellas and situated perfectly to watch the lively bustle of the square.

Zoe's eyebrows rose when the owner of the café came out, speaking in rapid Italian, fawning over Leandro as if he were some kind of celebrity. Zoe saw a few other patrons glance their way, heard the speculative murmur of hushed whispers and wondered just what was going on.

Just who Leandro was.

Leandro answered the owner tersely before leading Zoe to a table at the back. He ordered two espressos and a basket of pastries, affecting an air of unconcern even though Zoe was conscious of a few more open stares and another round of whispers.

'You're famous,' she stated baldly, and Leandro shrugged, his mouth tightening.

'My family is from this region, that is all.'

At least that was all he was going to say, Zoe realised, although she imagined there was quite a bit more to the story. Shrugging, she started to write her list on the back of a napkin.

After a moment Leandro peered over at her writing. '"Cleaning supplies",' he read, his voice dry with amusement. 'That's a bit general, don't you think?'

'In *general*, I need everything,' Zoe replied. 'I looked around yesterday and couldn't find so much as a sponge.'

'Fair enough.' Leandro shrugged. 'The villa's been vacant for years, so I'm not surprised.'

'You mentioned it hasn't been for sale,' Zoe said. She'd added *'food'* to the list. That was pretty general, too. All she'd seen in the kitchen was a plastic takeaway container and a packet of coffee.

'Yes, I did.' Leandro's tone was guarded.

'Who owned it? And why did they sell now?'

The waiter came with the coffee and rolls, and Zoe took one from the basket, biting into it with relish. Leandro watched her, sipping his own coffee.

'They didn't sell,' he said at last, and then forestalled any of the questions which had clamoured to Zoe's tongue by raising one hand. 'Eat up,' he told her brusquely, dispelling any notion of friendliness. 'We have a lot to do, and I want to get back to the villa. You should, too. I'd like to see you earn your keep.'

The shops lining the square were small, yet surprisingly well stocked. Within an hour Zoe had found nearly all the cleaning supplies she needed, as well as the basic food provisions she wanted to make some simple meals. Leandro arranged for it all to be delivered to the boat, and they were heading back to the dock when Zoe saw a small outdoor market set up in another smaller, leafy square.

She skidded to a halt, strangely mesmerised. 'Oh, let's stop!' The stalls, with their barrels of spices and baskets of fresh fruit and vegetables, beckoned enticingly, unexpectedly. Kerchief-clad housewives haggled over bins of lettuce and joints of beef, their hard bargains tempered by shouts of laughter.

With a sigh and a little shrug, Leandro gave his acceptance, and soon Zoe was lost amid the stalls, touching fabrics, chatting in her broken, nearly useless Italian, happier than she'd been in a while.

When she'd said she could make meals, she'd meant it; but she'd envisaged plates of pasta with tinned sauce—staples from her nomadic existence. Yet now the ropes of garlic, the bunches of fresh basil, the huge rounds of mozzarella floating murkily in brine, made her want to be unaccountably domestic, providing real meals—meals for a home, a family.

Ridiculous.

She'd never had a family or a home—didn't even *want* one—and Leandro Filametti's decrepit villa hardly counted as one anyway. Still, she couldn't keep herself from loading up a wicker basket with plump red tomatoes and mozzarella wrapped in wax paper, a kilo of ripe peaches and the freshest asparagus she'd ever seen.

'I hope you're planning on actually cooking with this,' Leandro muttered, taking the basket from her.

Zoe gave him a quick grin. 'Absolutely.'

Half an hour later he finally pulled her away and they headed back to the boat. It was well after lunchtime, and Zoe had a brief spasm of guilt for having taken so long.

'I'll make you a really nice lunch,' she promised as they got in the boat.

'Never mind about that,' Leandro replied tartly. 'I'll

settle for dinner. You can spend the afternoon doing what you're paid for.'

As soon as they returned to the villa, the bags and boxes were loaded into the kitchen, then Leandro disappeared into his study. Zoe felt momentarily bereft without him; she'd enjoyed their outing more than she wanted to admit even to herself.

With a pragmatic shrug, she began to put all their purchases away. She'd start on the kitchen first, she decided. It needed a good scrub, and she didn't relish the idea of cooking in a such a dirty space. She wrapped a kerchief around her head, got out the new mop and sponge and set to work.

Three hours later the kitchen was as clean as it would get without a complete overhaul, and Zoe was filthy. She considered another dip in the lake, but decided to opt for a shower instead. She didn't want Leandro thinking she was slacking off the job… Except, Zoe asked herself in exasperation, why did she care what he thought?

Why did she care at all?

She never had before.

Even as she'd scrubbed and mopped he'd intruded on her thoughts. Questions, images, memories. Why had he bought this villa? Why had the people in the café recognised him and whispered about him? What was his life normally like? Did he have a girlfriend? A wife? A family?

Stupid questions, she told herself as she stripped off and stepped into the shower. Ones with answers she shouldn't care about, shouldn't even consider. She twisted the taps on and let the water stream hotly over her. Many of the villa's bathrooms looked as if their plumbing was at least fifty years old, but she'd found a renovated one on the upstairs hallway, and she revelled in the strong stinging spray.

Until the door opened.

To her credit, Zoe didn't even yelp. The shower door was fogged completely, so she could barely see Leandro...although she could make out that he was only in a towel, his chest bare and bronzed. She resisted the urge to wipe away the steam so she could see a little more.

And she wondered how much he could see.

Enough, she determined. For he froze in the doorway, and Zoe saw his eyes sweep her hidden length, felt tension and awareness stretch tautly between them, before, with a muttered apology—or was it an oath?— he slammed out of the bathroom.

Zoe leaned her forehead against the wet glass, her heart pounding, her head swimming. Even her knees felt weak.

Desire. Molten, liquid, hot. It coursed through her, stronger than she'd expected or even wanted. It made her wonder what Leandro was thinking. Feeling. And what might possibly happen between them.

Stop. Her mind screeched such musings to a halt. She didn't want to get involved with a man like Leandro. Hadn't she learned that lesson already? For a moment— a second—she pictured Steve's sneering face.

A girl like you... What did you expect?

A girl like you. The same words Leandro had used. The same condemnation. The judgement had hurt then, and she wasn't about to let herself feel that again. She refused to be used by a man who had too much power and wealth for anyone's good.

Even if he looked amazing in just a towel.

Still a little shaky, Zoe turned off the taps and stepped out of the shower, wrapping a thick towel around her, and another to cover her hair. Safely swaddled, she stepped out of the bathroom, glancing instinctively for Leandro, but he was gone.

And she felt disappointed.

Leandro raked his hands through his hair, his heart beating fast and erratically. He felt every latent instinct tightening into need at just seeing the vague outline of Zoe's delectable body.

From outside his bedroom he heard the bathroom door open and close, and cursed himself for hiding in here—away from her, away from temptation.

For he *was* so unbearably tempted. In that brief moment of seeing her fogged shape behind the shower glass he'd wanted her. He'd wanted to slide the door open and step under the spray, pulling Zoe's wet naked length against his, feeling her—feeling the smoothness of her skin against his palms, the sweetness of her lips against his. He'd wanted that touch, both the thrill and the comfort of a body close—joined—with his.

It would be so easy. The desire was there between them, stretching, simmering. Why not take advantage of it? Why not enjoy it and let Zoe enjoy it? He could be discreet; perhaps so could she?

Why not?

Such enticing, enchanting little whispers, stroking his conscience to sleep. He didn't use women. He didn't discard them as his father had, time and time again. He didn't let them enslave him, wrapping him around their little fingers, cheapening himself, his name, his family.

He wouldn't be that man.

It's not the same… You're in control. No one would know. There could be no scandal, no shame. Just mutual pleasure… Surely you can see that?

Leandro cursed aloud. Had his father had such thoughts? Been led astray by such damning whispers?

You've been without a woman for so long…what are you trying to prove?

Nothing. Everything.

Resolutely Leandro turned away from the door, away from the image of Zoe imprinted on his brain—away from the desire coursing through his body, convincing his mind just how easy—and wonderful—it could be.

Downstairs in the kitchen, Zoe pushed the memory of Leandro's intrusion into the bathroom firmly from her thoughts. It wasn't as easy as she would have liked.

She found herself becoming cross, banging pots and cupboard doors as she assembled the ingredients for a simple pasta dish.

She should just get Leandro Filametti out of her mind, she told herself. Maybe giving in to temptation would do the trick… For a moment she imagined it.

What would Leandro be like as a lover? How would he kiss? Would his lips be soft? She remembered the brief touch of them against her fingers and knew they would be. Soft lips for a hard man.

She exhaled loudly, forcing the treacherous images away. She wanted to be sensible. She was *going* to be sensible. She'd learned her lesson with Steve. She shook her head in self-disgust. At least she'd *thought* she'd learned her lesson. Steve had been the first man she'd let close, and look what had happened. She might not have loved him—she wasn't *that* stupid—but she'd let herself care.

And she'd learned her lesson. Don't care. Not about anyone. Certainly not about a man like Leandro, who treated *girls like her* with careless contempt.

She turned her attention to the meal, determined to enjoy the simple pleasure of slicing ripe red tomatoes, the fragrant aroma of basil wafting through the kitchen. The sounds and scents of a home. While the sauce was simmering she went out to the garden and picked a bunch of soft pink oleanders, holding them to her nose to inhale their sweet fragrance.

She was overwhelmed for a moment by the simple pleasures of food and flowers. The large, dank space of the kitchen was somehow transformed by the bubbling pots on the stove, by the sense of space being used and enjoyed.

She was being silly, she knew, silly and romantic. But she couldn't help it. Somehow this decrepit old villa was growing on her, winding its way around her heart.

She didn't even notice Leandro come into the kitchen, and when he spoke from the doorway she gave a little jump, nearly dropping the flowers.

'That smells good.'

'Thank you.' Zoe busied herself with putting the flowers in an old glass jar.

'It looks much better in here too,' Leandro added.

Zoe dug a pair of ancient black scissors out of a drawer and snipped the ends off the flowers.

'That's my job.' She glanced at Leandro, her heart giving a now-customary lurch, and saw his hair was damp, brushed away from his forehead, curling along the nape of his neck. He was dressed simply in a white tee shirt and faded jeans that hugged his long muscular legs. Zoe swallowed and looked away. 'I thought we could eat on the terrace,' she said, turning to needlessly stir the sauce bubbling on the range top. 'It's so hot in here.'

'Fine.' Leandro was silent for a long moment, and Zoe kept her focus on the pans bubbling away on the stove. 'I'm sorry about earlier,' he finally said. 'I'll install a lock on the door.'

'Or just listen for the sound of running water?' Zoe returned, her voice somewhere between a scold and a joke.

Leandro was silent again, and Zoe almost looked around. Almost.

'I did,' he finally said, and she whirled around in surprise. He was gone.

By the time the meal was ready, the sun had set and the first stars were twinkling on the horizon. Zoe had laid the small wrought-iron table outside for two, conscious of the intimacy of the gesture. The soft night air swirled around her. The lights from a few boats glittered on the smooth surface of the lake, competing with the stars above.

Zoe gazed at the table and wondered if Leandro even expected her to join him. Perhaps he wanted to eat alone? In other circumstances she would never have presumed to share a meal with her employer. Unless he asked.

Why don't you join me? Steve again, reminding her of how pointless and pathetic getting involved with her employer was—how false this situation really was.

'Ready?' His voice, like a low hum, seemed to creep right into her bones and swirl around her soul. Zoe turned with a bright, fixed smile.

'Yes, I'll just bring it out.'

A few minutes later she came out onto the terrace with a large steaming bowl of pasta, returning to add salad, bread and a jug of water.

Leandro surveyed the spread with the barest flicker of a smile. 'I haven't eaten this well in weeks.'

'Takeaways and coffee aren't exactly a healthy diet,' Zoe agreed, and he glanced at her as she sat down.

'I imagine you survive on the same,' he said. 'Or similar. Am I right?'

Discomfited, she shrugged. It was no more than the truth, but she didn't want to be reminded of it now. 'I like cooking when I get the chance.'

'And when is that?' He'd placed a napkin on his lap and now began to serve them both pasta.

'When there's more than just me, I suppose.'

Leandro glanced up at her, his eyes heavy-lidded

and sensuously speculative. 'And is there often more than just you?'

'You'd probably assume there was,' Zoe replied, a bit crossly. 'But, no, actually, there isn't.' She didn't let anyone get close enough. Or else she wasn't given the chance.

Leandro's smile widened briefly before he took a bite of pasta. 'This is delicious. Is it from a recipe?'

'I just made it up,' Zoe admitted, absurdly pleased by his casual compliment. 'I put in all the things I liked.'

'Why am I not surprised?'

She should be annoyed by his assumptions, Zoe supposed, but somehow she couldn't be. Not when the night air was as soft as silk, and the stars glittered like tiny diamonds strewn on a velvet cloth above them. Not when Leandro looked at her with that lazy sensuality that made her toes curl and her heart hammer and her mind go wonderfully blank.

And he was attracted to her, too. She could feel it— sense it the way you sensed a storm coming, when the atmosphere grew heavy and an energy snapped and buzzed through the air. She became achingly aware of everything: the cool heaviness of her fork—sterling silver, undoubtedly—the cool water sliding down her throat, the distant lap of the lake against the jetty.

Did Leandro feel it too? Was he wondering, as she was, what might happen after dinner? What *would*?

For suddenly there seemed a wonderful and frightening inevitability to their coming together. All her sensible self-warnings melted into nothing as the delicious tension stretched agonisingly, achingly between them.

They hardly spoke for the rest of the meal. Yet even so, as Zoe cleared the plates, she almost expected Leandro to come up behind her and wrap his arms around her waist. She was waiting for his touch, needing it, caution thrown to the winds, senses scattered.

But that didn't happen. He helped her carry the plates and bowls back into the kitchen, and then set about brewing coffee while she washed up. It was a strangely domestic and intimate scene, like that of a husband and wife. Or perhaps lovers. Zoe's whole body seemed to tingle with awareness and expectation as she waited for—what?

What did she want Leandro to do? What did she want to happen? Zoe pushed those questions out of her mind; now wasn't the time for thinking, it was for feeling. For waiting and wanting.

Yet as soon as the coffee was brewed Leandro took his mug and retreated to his study. Disappointment swamped her as he left, and the sudden heavy expectancy was dispelled, the storm clouds of desire blown clean away.

It was better this way, she told herself, struggling to be pragmatic. Better and safer.

It was late by the time Zoe finished with the dishes, and she prowled restlessly through the darkened rooms of the villa, taking in the swathed furniture, the paintings covered with sheets. The villa was completely furnished, she realised. Whoever had once lived here had left it suddenly, sorrowfully. Or was she letting her imagination run away with her?

Why had it been left to decay and rot? She felt like a magician, being asked to transform the empty rooms into something liveable and clean. A fairy godmother, longing to make the decrepit villa a happy place—a home.

Yet how on earth could she accomplish such a task? She, who had never known a home? Zoe gazed at the tattered drapes at the windows, suddenly remembering her childish effort at making curtains from a cut-up dress that had no longer fitted her. They'd been ridiculous raggedy things, the hems stapled because she'd never learned to sew. Yet Zoe had been so proud of them; they'd lent something warm and alive to the sterile hotel room with its plastic shades and stained bedspread. Her mother, however, hadn't even noticed.

Zoe sighed, the memory depressing her. Why was she thinking of such things now? Was it simply because she'd never cleaned a house—a home—before? She'd kept to hotels and restaurants, impersonal places, jobs and people you could walk away from.

And you'll walk away from this one…in three months.

The thought only made her sad.

She let her finger trace a line through the thick dust on a windowsill and realised again that she wanted to bring this villa back to life—which was stupid, since Leandro would just be selling it on anyway. And yet for the summer it could be more than just a property.

She stood by the window and watched the moonlight shimmer on the lake, imagined the people who had once lived here. Had they loved this home? Had they laughed and danced and loved in these rooms?

She wanted to believe they had. It was important to her, and she didn't even know why.

Isn't it obvious? a sly little voice mocked silently. *This is everything you never had.*

And never would. Leandro's voice echoed through her mind. *Girls like her* didn't have homes like this. Didn't want them or need them. She should never forget that.

A rustling from the drawing room's chimney startled her, and she jumped back. A trapped bird? Or a rat? Suppressing a shudder, Zoe backed out of the room, wanting to escape the alarming noise—as well as her own thoughts.

She decided to go for another swim.

Leandro was still locked in his study as Zoe came down in her swimming costume, a towel over her shoulders. She picked her way through the darkened garden, the scent of roses heavy on the sultry night air.

The stone of the jetty was cool under her bare feet and she surveyed the water gleaming blackly with only a tiny bit of apprehension before she dropped her towel and dived cleanly in.

She surfaced, the cold water a pleasant shock to her senses, and swam a few lengths before turning back. She was barely aware of a shadow on the jetty before someone else dived in, and a moment later Leandro surfaced a few feet away from her, his teeth gleaming in the darkness, his hair slicked back from his face.

'I thought I'd join you.'

Zoe's heart rate accelerated even as she tossed her head, pushing her hair back with her hands. 'How refreshing.'

'I thought so.'

The expectancy was back, Zoe thought hazily. The storm was coming. In a desperate effort to clear her head, she ducked underwater and swam away from Leandro.

What was she thinking? Doing? She knew what he wanted from her, what she wanted, and yet...

She wasn't ready to get involved again. To give her body again. She knew how little he expected from *a girl like her*. Was she willing to accept it? Was it enough?

Her lungs near to bursting, she swam to the surface— only to have Leandro grab her shoulder. She gasped aloud, and he turned her around in the water to face him.

'I thought you'd drowned!'

'I'm a good swimmer.' His hand didn't leave her shoulder, and a desperate, aching weakness flooded through her, making it hard even to tread water. 'I'm ready to get out,' she said, a bit stiffly.

Shrugging off his hand, she swam to the ladder by the side of the jetty. She felt Leandro's eyes on her as she climbed up, grabbing her towel and wrapping it securely around her. Desire and fear warred within her, and she didn't know which would win. Which she wanted to win.

Leandro hauled himself up, dripping wet and utterly magnificent. Zoe couldn't keep her gaze from roving over the taut muscles of his body gleaming in the moonlight. Her breath caught in her throat and her mind turned blank as sensation—the expectation of sensation—took over once more.

Leandro looked down and held her gaze, his eyes

dark and compelling. Zoe forced herself to breathe. In. Out. And again. Despite her best intentions, her breath came out in a shudder, and Leandro lifted his hand.

Zoe stilled, tensed, waiting for his fingers to tangle in her damp hair and draw her inexorably closer. She wouldn't resist. Yet he didn't move his hand, and the moment stretched between them, suspended and endless.

Her head fell back, her lips parted. Her throat was open and vulnerable to his caress. Slowly Leandro let his fingers trail down her cheek, along her jaw, her throat working as he dropped his hand lower, to touch the vee between her breasts.

It was such a small, simple touch, and yet it left fire in its wake. Fire and yearning. Zoe swayed, and reached out a hand to steady herself. Her palm encountered the slick, taut muscle of Leandro's chest and she felt him jerk in response. She reached up with her other hand and laid it flat against him. They remained that way for a moment, suspended on the threshold, and then suddenly Leandro stepped away.

Zoe's hands dropped, her arms falling limply to her sides, and her eyes flew open. She saw Leandro's mouth harden into a thin line and distaste flickered in his eyes. Disappointment—and something deeper—swamped her.

'It's late,' he said brusquely. 'Goodnight.' And without another word or look, he turned and disappeared into the darkness.

CHAPTER FOUR

THE next morning Leandro was already enclosed in his study when Zoe awoke at the much more reasonable hour of seven o'clock. She dressed in her oldest clothes—a faded tee shirt and cut-off shorts—and after a cup of strong coffee in the kitchen determined to begin tackling the drawing room.

Faded yellow curtains covered every window, and when Zoe pushed them aside a cloud of musty dust rose in the still air. She coughed, wincing, and then moved to the next window.

Last night had been a wake-up call of sorts. Seeing the distaste in Leandro's eyes—perhaps it had even been disgust—had acted like a bucket of ice water, drenching her senses and her desire. For a moment or two she'd been wrapped up in the seductive promise of pleasure given and received. Shared. Of seeing her own desire reflected in his eyes, of feeling wanted. And perhaps she'd even deceived herself that it meant something more.

Well, it didn't. The look in his eyes had confirmed

that. Yes, Leandro Filametti might *want* her, but that was all. And when the wanting was over he'd discard her, dump her like a bucket of dirty water, disgusting and forgotten. Like Steve had.

Zoe stilled, remembering the similar look of disgust in Steve's eyes. His snide rejection had stung her pride more than her heart, because she hadn't let her heart get involved—even when she'd finally given a man her body, she'd refused him her heart. Her love. Not that he'd wanted either.

Zoe's mouth twisted cynically as she plunged her mop into a bucket of soapy water. She'd avoided love and commitment for so long she barely remembered what that craving felt like. That deep, endless well of need. And she didn't want to feel it again—the hope, the disappointment, the unfulfilled longing that swamped the senses and the heart.

Yet she didn't want a fling either. Her one attempt at a fling had left her more hurt and embittered than she ever wanted to be again. So what was left?

A sigh escaped her, a heavy sound. Nothing was left, and the thought was unbearably depressing.

She forced her mind away from such ruminations as she tackled the drawing room, mopping the old parquet floors with a determined ferociousness. She'd emptied the bucket of dirty water half a dozen times, and each time she'd hauled it to the kitchen she had found herself looking around for Leandro. She hadn't seen him at all.

Later in the morning a crew of workmen arrived to start on the roof, and Zoe glimpsed Leandro talking to them on the front driveway. He disappeared back into his study without so much as a word or glance in her direction.

At noon she ate some leftover pasta alone in the kitchen, half wondering if she should knock on Leandro's study door and offer him some. She decided against it, for her own sake.

After she'd eaten she offered coffee and some *biscotti* she'd bought at the market to the roofers. The three men threw up their hands and exclaimed over her kindness and beauty, with shouts of *'Magnifico!'* and *'Bella!'* as Zoe handed around mugs. She laughed, feeling cheered by their easy friendliness. *This* was the Italy she'd expected—not Leandro's taciturn disapproval.

'What were you doing?' He stood in the foyer, hands on trim hips, as she returned with empty mugs and a plate scattered with crumbs.

'Feeding the work crew,' she replied a bit tartly, even as her heart started skittering once again. 'It's hot out there.'

Leandro grunted his assent and Zoe dared to ask, 'Would *you* like a coffee? Biscotti?'

Leandro gazed at her for a long moment, his expression foreboding and yet also fathomless. What had she done to earn such disapproval? Zoe wondered. Gone for a swim? Acted a little light-heartedly? What made him—men like him, men like Steve—judge her so quickly and harshly?

Or was she judging herself?

'No,' he said at last, and Zoe almost thought she heard a thread of regret in his voice. 'No, thank you.'

He hesitated, and for a moment Zoe thought he might say something. Then he turned to go back to his study, and she went back to work.

By late afternoon the drawing room was resplendent in all its faded glory, the now clean floor and walls somehow emphasising the threadbare condition and peeling gilt of the antique sofas and chairs.

Zoe perched on the edge of a chair and surveyed the room with a strange aching pride. Afternoon sunshine streamed through the wide, now sparkling windows, pooling in golden puddles on the floor.

She'd pulled away the dust sheets from the furniture and paintings, intending to wash them—although she realised the villa might not even possess a washing machine. Yet even so she could imagine the curtains and sofas restored, the room blazingly beautiful once more.

With a little sigh she rose from the spindly chair and walked over to one of the paintings, an ancient-looking oil portrait of a rather austere man in nineteenth-century dress. Had he lived here? she wondered. He looked halfway to a scowl—so close to the way Leandro looked at her.

Then her gaze rested on the tarnished placard at the bottom of the picture, and her heart skipped a surprised beat.

Alfredo Filametti, 1817-1888. Her breath caught in her throat before she expelled it in a slow hiss. Glancing quickly up at the figure depicted in the painting, she realised there actually *was* a passing resemblance to

Leandro—in the set of the mouth, the deep aquamarine of the eyes. Alfredo Filametti was Leandro's ancestor. The villa had to be his family home.

Her mind was still spinning with this new information as she showered, and then repaired to the kitchen to make dinner. She grilled some chicken breasts with lemon and basil in the huge oven, and tossed a quick salad. She set the meal on the terrace, looking forward to Leandro's company more than she knew she should.

At a little after seven, the meal she'd made steaming and fragrant, the table decorated with wild orchids from the garden, Zoe knocked on Leandro's study door—and was answered with an indistinct noise halfway between a snarl and a hello.

'Dinner's ready,' she called, and inwardly winced at how wifely she sounded.

'Leave a plate by the door,' Leandro barked back, and Zoe stiffened.

She shouldn't be hurt or disappointed, she reminded herself fiercely. Had she actually *expected* Leandro to eat with her every night? They might share a simmering attraction, but he was clearly showing her what kind of relationship he intended them to have now. And that was probably for the best.

She forced the feelings back, and even managed a shrug. 'Fine.' She took a plate from the terrace, unable to keep from noticing how romantic the table looked, with its flowers and fripperies. Unable to keep from feeling like a fool.

Resolutely she made him up a plate and brought it to the study, leaving it outside his door with a perfunctory knock. There was no response.

She ate alone in the kitchen, and afterwards took her cup of coffee out to the terrace, sipping it with a rather disconsolate air as she watched the sailing boats and pleasure yachts bob lazily along the lake.

Suddenly the summer stretched in front of her, endless and lonely. What was she supposed to do with herself all alone? she wondered. She could hardly expect Leandro to entertain her, yet she chafed at the idea of night after night spent alone, empty and aching with a need she could barely name... A need she'd always refused to acknowledge, or even feel...

She watched as a couple came out onto the prow of a yacht. Even squinting, Zoe could barely make out their forms, although she suspected they were tall and slim and elegant. Rich. People like Leandro. Accustomed to wealth and power and luxury. People who looked down on skivvies like her.

She watched as the couple embraced, the woman's slim brown arms twining around the man's neck with sinuous ease.

They looked so happy, so in love. Zoe could almost hear the low murmur of their voices, the rumble of the man's laughter. They had everything, she thought with a sudden, surprising bitterness. Not just wealth and power, but happiness too. Love.

A pang of sorrowful longing pierced her, making her hurt in a way she'd kept herself from hurting for so long. Deep inside, in the empty well of her soul that insisted human beings were made for love, for togetherness and belonging, for a *home*.

She didn't want to feel this way. She'd come to Italy for an escape, not for a revelation about her life and its shortcomings. She *liked* her life; she always had. It suited her fine and it would continue to do so.

She'd never allowed herself another choice.

Zoe set her chin, forcing the sorrow and the emptiness—the longing—back deep inside, where it could stay good and buried. There was no reason why she couldn't enjoy herself this summer. Why she couldn't have fun. Lornetto might not be much of a hot spot, but there were surely other villages nearby, with bars, clubs—places she could go and meet people like herself. Girls like her, men like her, people who wanted to laugh and dance and have a good time. If you had a good enough time you forgot about the loneliness and the need. You filled up the emptiness…if only for a moment.

A little voice whispered inside her that she didn't want any of that right now—maybe not ever again—but Zoe pushed it away. She'd told herself she was going to have a fantastic summer, and she *was*.

'Where are you going?'

Zoe turned, her hand still on the handle of the front door. 'Out,' she said sweetly. 'It's nine o'clock at night. I assume my duties are over for the day?'

'Yes…' Leandro admitted reluctantly. 'But where do you think you're going dressed like that?'

Zoe glanced down at the strappy jewel-green sundress. It was on the skimpy side, but she hardly thought it deserved Leandro's look of contempt. 'Out,' she repeated, and added a smile that was only a little bit brittle with determination.

Leandro scowled. She hadn't even seen him in four days, and now he looked like a surly bear woken suddenly from his hibernation. He had several days' stubble on his jaw, and his hair was tousled, sticking up in a dozen different directions. He wore an old tee shirt and jeans, but the casual clothes just emphasised his lithe and yet powerful frame.

'Out where?' he demanded.

Zoe reined in her temper. She couldn't decide if Leandro had been avoiding her or was utterly indifferent to her presence in the villa, but after four days of non-stop cleaning and silent, solitary evenings, she was ready for a change.

'To Menaggio,' she said. She'd discovered a bus timetable in a drawer in the kitchen, and had realised she could get there on her own. 'Tomorrow's Sunday—my day off,' she reminded him. 'So don't worry if I'm back late.'

'What will you be doing in Menaggio at this hour?' Leandro asked, but the condemnation in his voice provided the answer.

'Having fun,' Zoe tossed back defiantly, and with a waggle of her fingers she flounced out of the villa, refusing to look back.

He had no right to interrogate her like that, she fumed as she strode down the villa's drive. No rights in her life at all. And she wouldn't think of him once this evening—she'd find a club in Menaggio, meet people, dance and chat, and have fun for as long as she liked. She *would*.

And she would like it.

Leandro stared unseeingly at the front door of the villa, the sound of its slamming echoing remorselessly through his mind. Zoe Clark had every right to do as she pleased in the evening, he knew. There was no absolutely no reason why she shouldn't go out and enjoy the region's attractions. Yet the thought of her in some seedy bar in Menaggio, dancing and drinking and flirting, made Leandro's gut tighten and his mouth pull into a grimace.

Of course he should have expected no less. If *he* wasn't going to provide her amusement, she'd damn well find it somewhere else. He should be amazed that it had taken her so long. He knew what she was like—what women such as her were like.

Yet at that moment he wasn't thinking of his father's women; he was thinking only of Zoe.

He'd *liked* knowing she was in the villa—listening to her move about, sometimes humming or whistling under her breath. He'd caught glimpses of her wringing out a mop in the sink or washing windows, her hair caught up in a ponytail, and he'd felt that tug of desire.

He'd always retreated before she saw him, knowing he couldn't get any nearer. She was dangerous. *He* was.

He'd been avoiding her for days—ever since he'd come so close to pulling her into his arms after their evening swim. She'd been irresistible then, dripping wet, her skin almost silver in the moonlight. She'd wanted him, wouldn't have resisted, and that had made it all the harder to step away.

Even now he wondered why he had.

Why not take what was on offer? Why not enjoy it?

He could make his expectations clear; perhaps she wanted the same thing? A quick, easy affair. No strings, no promises.

He'd had such arrangements before—he was a man, after all—but they'd been with women of his own world, his own class, women he could trust.

Could he trust Zoe? He didn't know—and, worse, he didn't know if he could trust himself. Already he sensed in himself a deeper need for Zoe than he'd had for other women, and that was dangerous.

Suddenly he could hear his father's desperate, wheedling voice.

It never meant anything, Leandro... I couldn't help it... I was lonely... A man has needs...

And what of his family's needs? His family left bankrupt and shamed by his father's illicit lifestyle? What about his mother, left not just heartbroken but utterly destroyed by his father's faithlessness?

And was he, Leandro, going to act in the same manner? Chasing after whatever bit of skirt caught his fancy? Weren't the tabloids waiting for him to do so?

He wouldn't give them the pleasure. He wouldn't give *himself* the pleasure of sampling a woman like Zoe either. He knew what she was like—what women like her were capable of: selling their stories, blackmailing his family, holding out for more and more and more. Always more. Until there had been *nothing* left.

For a mere second he wondered if he was judging Zoe Clark too harshly. Yes, she was fun and easy, even loose— but a blackmailer? A thief? Utterly unscrupulous?

Leandro shrugged. Perhaps he was too harsh, but he refused to change his opinion. It was his safety net. The only thing that kept him from taking Zoe into his arms and making her his…to his shame.

He let out a growl of frustration and turned away from the door, heading outside to the terrace. The air was fragrant and cool, the evening light bathing the lake in shimmering golds and reds.

There were too many memories here, Leandro knew. They were haunting him, mocking him. Tormenting him. Making him feel—when he'd spent the last two decades refusing to feel, to care, letting his obsession be work, success. Wealth. Then there was no time to think—to remember all he'd loved and lost.

He didn't have to stay, he told himself. He could return to Milan, hire someone to oversee the workmen, the repairs. Zoe.

It would be running away.

He'd hidden from the past, from memories, for too long already. He knew this instinctively—had known when the villa had come into his possession that he needed to face its ghosts. And so he would.

He would face the ghosts of his past, of his family. His father. Exorcise and exonerate them. And then he would move on.

Yet meanwhile the days passed with painful slowness. He couldn't concentrate on his research—important research, that would bring him new clients, more money, even celebrity status in his profession.

What are you trying to prove?

He had so much to prove, to account for, that he ached with it. Burned with it. With the ferocious desire to atone for the past, to absolve his father's sins and his family's shame.

Having a fling with Zoe Clark would not help his cause at all. It would accomplish the opposite—taking him further from his goal, making him more like his father than he ever wanted to be. Yet, even so, he couldn't keep this other burning from consuming him, images and imaginings of Zoe leaping through his fevered brain.

It would be so easy...too easy. And too dangerous.

It was several hours past midnight when Zoe pushed open the front door to the villa with a cautious creak. Her feet ached both from dancing and walking; she'd missed the last bus from Menaggio and, after hitching a ride halfway, had been forced to walk alone in the darkness along the old rutted road.

It had not been a happy time.

To be truthful, the entire evening had been borderline wretched, a fact that annoyed her. She'd gone out in search of a good time, she'd been determined to have one, and she hadn't.

She'd moped instead.

Oh, she'd danced, chatted, flirted—done everything she could think of to ensure a successful evening. But inside she'd moped. Wanted to be back in the villa. Wondered what Leandro was doing.

Stupid Leandro, who probably hadn't thought of her at all. Why should he? She was just the slutty housekeeper.

'You're back.'

In the process of taking off her heels, Zoe froze, one hand still wrapped around her ankle. Slowly she straightened. In the gloom of the hallway she could barely make out Leandro's form, although his eyes blazed through the darkness.

'Yes,' she said inanely, and he grunted.

'I wondered if you'd be back this evening at all.'

Zoe stiffened at the implication. After a second's hesitation she threw back her head, smiling in the darkness. 'I didn't have *that* good a time.'

'No?' Leandro stepped closer, and with a lurch of something between alarm and attraction Zoe realised his chest was bare. He wore only a pair of loose drawstring pyjama bottoms. She could feel the heat radiating from him coiling inside her too. 'How good a time *did* you have, Zoe?'

She lifted her chin. 'Why do you care?'

Leandro was silent for a moment. Zoe could see the beat of his heart, the pulse in his throat, and felt her own jerk and leap in answer. 'I don't know,' he said finally. 'God knows, I shouldn't. Shouldn't even…'

His voice thickened, almost slurring, and Zoe held her breath as his hand reached out and brushed a strand of hair away from her face, his fingertips trailing her cheek.

'Want...'

Want. That was what was between them. Heavy and pulsing, a magnetic tidal force she had no strength or desire to avoid. She wanted it—wanted to be pulled under, to lose herself in the moment and the man... Even if that was all it was. A moment.

'Why shouldn't you?' Zoe whispered, afraid to break the moment for either Leandro or herself. Afraid to stop it, yet also afraid to begin.

'I don't know,' Leandro confessed raggedly, and then his hand stole around to the back of her head and he drew her unresistingly to him.

The first touch of his lips against her was sweet, tentative, tender as they tested and tasted one another. Yet even as that sweetness unfurled and bloomed within her it was already changing, deepening and darkening into something primal and ferocious and hard.

It took another split second to adjust, and then she felt the answering need blaze within her. She returned the kiss's ferocity, her hands coming around his bare shoulders, digging into skin, their bodies pressed against one another now, pressed and pushing, proving something.

Was she exorcising the memory of Steve and the shame he'd made her feel? Proving to herself that she could handle one more no-strings affair? Showing Leandro just what kind of girl she was?

But I'm not that kind of girl, and I don't think I ever really was.

Zoe pushed the questions and doubts away. She wouldn't—couldn't—think. Couldn't imagine what a man like Leandro had to prove—why he shouldn't *want*…want her.

For right now there was a great deal of wanting going on.

He pushed the straps of her dress off her shoulders, his lips hot and seeking on the sensitive skin of her nape. They both stumbled back and Leandro landed hard on the stairs—cold, slick marble against bare skin. Uncomfortable, difficult, and yet somehow it didn't matter, somehow it was still urgent and desperate and *angry*.

Why were they both so angry?

For that was the emotion pulsing to life between them, Zoe realised hazily as they exchanged kiss for kiss, brand for brand. It wasn't what she wanted, and from some inner reserve of strength she pulled away from Leandro, her bare back biting into the staircase's wrought-iron railing, and gasped, *'No.'*

Leandro was breathing hard, his face flushed, his eyes blazing blue fire. He dropped his head back, raking a hand through his hair.

'Cold feet?' he asked sardonically, yet Zoe heard the bite of another, darker emotion underneath his cynicism, and he didn't look at her.

'Something like that,' she admitted shakily. She pulled up the straps of her dress, covering herself. 'I don't want it to be like *that*,' she said quietly, after a tense silence when the only sound had been their ragged breathing as they recovered from the shock of experiencing something that Zoe didn't think either of them had expected. Or wanted. 'We're attracted to one another, obviously,' she continued, trying to regulate her breathing, her heart rate, her heart itself, 'but…not like that.'

Leandro half rolled away, his face and body averted from her, one arm thrown over his eyes. 'No,' he agreed in a low voice. 'Not like that.'

Zoe stared at him, at his dejected, defensive pose, heard the ache of self-loathing in his voice and wondered just what had happened…and why. She curled her fingers around the cold iron banister and hauled herself up.

'Well, then.' She'd meant to sound light, but there was a telltale wobble in her voice that made her wince.

Leandro didn't answer. Still sprawled on the stairs, his face averted, his head bowed, he simply waved one hand—whether in dismissal or entreaty, Zoe didn't know, but one thing was clear. He wanted her to go. So she did.

He *was* that man. Leandro listened to Zoe's heels click up the stairs and the distant slamming of her door before he let out a long, shaky breath. And then a curse.

What had he been thinking? Doing? Risking everything he'd worked for in a moment of lust?

He knew what he'd been *feeling*: desire, desperate and angry. More than he ever had before. He didn't *want* to want Zoe Clark. He didn't want the complications or reminders, the fears and suspicions confirmed. He didn't want to be pulled under by desire, to lose himself to lust when he never had before, when he'd always—*always*—been in control. A moment ago he hadn't been. A moment ago he'd wanted to lose control, to lose *himself*.

He wanted her too much, more than any other woman, and that was the problem. The danger. *He* was.

Leandro let out a shuddering breath. He didn't want to be proved wrong. Or right. He didn't know which it was, but one thing was glaringly, terribly obvious from this evening's encounter: he was his father's son.

Zoe walked to her room on shaky legs and aching feet. A slice of moonlight bisected the room, and in its silver wash she peeled off her dress, shrugged out of her underwear and fell onto the bed. She shouldn't feel this way, she told herself. She shouldn't feel so...*lacerated*. Her soul, her mind, her heart in tatters.

Steve had never hurt her this much, and the realisation that she'd allowed it only added to her pain. *Why* had she let Leandro affect her? When had she become so vulnerable?

She closed her eyes, longing for the oblivion of sleep. She certainly felt exhausted, yet sleep eluded her. Memories did not.

Leandro, his eyes darkening with desire, his fingers caressing her cheek, his voice confessing raggedly, '*I shouldn't want...*'

Why shouldn't he? Zoe wondered now, as she tracked the moon's voyage across the sky and waited helplessly for dawn. In her experience men like Leandro Filametti—rich, powerful, arrogant men, men like

Steve—took what they wanted when they wanted, and damn the consequences.

Wasn't that what Steve had done with her? She still remembered the scalding sting of shame as he'd tossed a few crumpled twenties across the unmade bed. *For services rendered.* She'd thought they had a relationship; he'd seen her as no more than a prostitute—just another chambermaid in his daddy's hotel who gave a little extra on the side.

Zoe closed her eyes again, wishing she could block out that moment as easily as the moonlight. At least her heart hadn't been broken, because she hadn't given her heart to anybody. That had been her one saving grace.

Yet her pride, her self-esteem, her very *self* had been damaged in that moment. For Steve's careless actions had shone a glaring light on her life and its choices. Was this the kind of woman she wanted to be mistaken for? The kind of carefree, careless life she wanted to lead?

The life her mother had led?

She might have been far more inexperienced and innocent than men like Steve—or Leandro—assumed, but the fact that they even assumed at all hurt. She knew what image she projected, and she was beginning to understand its cost. It had kept her safe—yet had it really? Why was she now feeling so hurt?

She was on the brink of making the same mistake with Leandro Filametti that she'd made with Steve Rinault. And the frightening thing was this hurt *more*.

Except Leandro was no Steve. The thought made Zoe's eyes fly open, and she stared blankly at the moon once more. What was Leandro hiding? Why was he selling his family's villa? And why had there been so much anguish in his voice, his body, as he lay on the stairs and waved her away, a man broken by desire?

The questions swirled in Zoe's mind without answers, and as the first grey fingers of dawn edged the lake she finally fell into a restless, dreamless sleep.

She awoke to sun streaming through the window, filling the room with the heat of late morning. Guiltily Zoe threw off the covers and hurried to dress. She didn't need to be derelict in her duties on top of everything else.

Several workmen were hammering away on the roof as she came downstairs, making her wonder how she'd managed to sleep through the noise.

The rest of the house was silent and still, however, and a peek at Leandro's door showed it ominously closed. Forcing herself to shrug—not to care—Zoe got to work. Mop and pail, broom and dustpan.

She'd managed to clean most of the downstairs reception rooms, with their panelled walls and shrouded paintings—a few sneaking glances under dustsheets revealed more of Leandro's ancestors—and then she decided to head upstairs and tackle the bedrooms.

Cleaning was a mindless activity, and that, Zoe knew, was what she needed. Scrub and sweep and don't think. Don't remember the aching humiliation of Steve's dismissal, the fresher hurt of Leandro's anger. Or, even more painful, the endless well of loss and need of her unhappy childhood.

Can we stay here? Please, just this once? I like it here, Mum. I don't want to go…

Don't think.

Yet her thoughts kept intruding even as she washed windows and swept floors, feeling like a modern-day Cinderella without her prince. Memories, questions. Desires. Regrets.

It's better this way, sweetie. The next place will be better, I promise. Don't you want an adventure?

And of course she'd always blinked back the tears and smiled. *Yes, of course I do.* Because that was the kind of girl she was—the kind of girl she'd made herself be.

Yet somehow, for some reason, being in this villa, being with Leandro, made her question everything she'd ever forced herself to believe.

Don't *think*.

'What are you doing?'

Zoe whirled around, a dirty dustsheet crumpled in one hand. Leandro stood in the doorway, dressed in faded jeans and a mint-green shirt open at the throat, looking fresh and cool. In contrast she was hot and sweaty, dirty and dishevelled, and at a distinct disadvantage.

'Doing my job,' she replied, a bit tartly. Already the sight of him was causing memories to stir within her; she couldn't quite take her gaze from the hollow of his throat where last night she'd put her lips and tasted the salt of his skin. And then asked him to stop.

'Yes, I realise that,' Leandro replied dryly. He wasn't smiling, but neither did he look as ferociously moody as he normally was. 'However, as you reminded me yesterday, today is your day off. Sunday.'

'Oh.' A blush swept over Zoe's face and she dropped the dustsheet. When had she *ever* forgotten her day off? 'I must have…' Her throat was dry from the dust of the room. 'The workmen,' she justified lamely. 'They made me think… Why are they working on a Sunday?'

'I'm paying them extra to get the job done,' Leandro replied, a brusque note entering his voice. 'I need to get this villa on the market in the next few months. I hope they didn't disturb your beauty sleep?'

'No…' Zoe trailed off, wondering why she couldn't grin challengingly at Leandro and snap back a witty retort—something about how she didn't need any beauty sleep to begin with. That was what she would have normally done. Yet all her witty retorts and snappy rejoinders had trickled from her mind—and, even worse, from her heart. She didn't feel capable of making one, or even *wanting* to make one.

Instead questions clamoured in her throat, desperate for answers. Why are you selling this villa? Why were you so angry last night? What is haunting you?

Who are you?

And who am I, wanting things I never did before?

'So.' Leandro cleared his throat, absently swiping at a few strands of cobwebs from the gilt doorframe. 'Do you have exciting plans for your day off?'

'No, I don't have any plans,' Zoe admitted. 'I suppose I could go for a swim…' Only that conjured up memories of her last swim with Leandro, the water beading on his moonlit skin, the kiss they'd almost shared, and she blushed again. What was *wrong* with her?

'In that case,' Leandro said, clearing his throat again, 'would you like to see some of the sights of the region?'

'With you?' Zoe blurted, the surprise in her voice cringingly blatant to both of them.

Leandro's mouth tightened, and his eyes shadowed before he managed a tiny smile. 'Yes, that was the idea.'

Zoe bent to retrieve the dustsheet, smoothing it out before folding it in an effort to hide her confusion. Why was Leandro asking her out? If that was indeed what he was doing? Was this a peace offering? Or an offer of something more?

What did he want? What did *she* want?

'All right.' She looked up, smiling, although Leandro's expression was carefully neutral. 'That would be nice.'

Nice. Such an innocent, innocuous word. Would this outing be the same? She didn't know, wouldn't think. She'd just enjoy, or at least try to. It was something— better than a day spent moping alone.

'Good.' He nodded briskly. 'I'll meet you downstairs in half an hour.'

'All right,' Zoe repeated, and then he was gone.

CHAPTER FIVE

ZOE showered and dressed quickly, choosing a demure pink tee shirt and khaki shorts, her hair swept up in a ponytail. It was armour, of a kind—a way to keep Leandro at a distance. She wasn't sure who needed the protection, him or herself. She refused to consider the issue too closely.

Leandro was waiting by the front door as she came down the stairs. He smiled briefly when he saw her, the cool smile of a friendly employer, nothing more, and Zoe knew they'd both put the boundaries in place, both donned the armour of an impersonal employer-employee relationship.

It was better this way, she told herself. Safer. So there was absolutely no reason to feel disappointed.

'I thought we'd take the boat,' Leandro said, and led her through the kitchen and the gardens to the shore.

A few minutes later they were seated on the speed-boat, jetting smoothly through the lake's tranquil waters, the sun high and bright above.

'What are you going to show me?' Zoe called over

the sound of the motor, and Leandro slotted her a quick, knowing smile.

'Everything.'

Zoe sat back and tried to ignore the tingle of anticipation—awareness—at his words. Had he meant to sound so provocative? Already the boundaries were slipping, changing. Weakening. And so was she. Because she didn't even mind.

She pushed her sunglasses down, determined to simply enjoy the day and not second-guess everything Leandro Filametti said. Not to wonder or want. It would, she knew, be a difficult task.

Leandro glanced across at Zoe, reclining in the seat across from him, her long, tanned legs stretched out in front of her. She looked carelessly relaxed, yet he didn't think he'd been imagining the guarded look in her eyes when he'd invited her out for the day.

And why had he done that, precisely? He'd had no intention of even seeing her today, having closeted himself in his study before she'd woken. Yet he'd spent the morning gazing sightlessly at figures, listening for the sound of her steps on the stairs, the slam of the front door as she went out in pursuit of a day's pleasure.

By eleven o'clock he'd had enough, and had gone in search of her. He'd looked on the jetty, in the gardens, expecting her to be swimming or sunbathing or just lolling around. The last place he'd expected her to be was upstairs, cleaning as if the devil was driving her.

And his invitation had surprised him as much as it

had her. He couldn't fathom why he'd made it; he'd determined to ignore her completely after last night. To forget her.

Yet he couldn't. And even now Leandro knew he was deceiving himself, thinking he could take his house-keeper to see the sights as some sort of friendly gesture, something almost paternal and innocent.

It was anything but.

He'd invited her out today because he wanted— needed—to see her, to be with her, and the realisation ignited both his fury and despair. Why must he be so weak when it came to this woman? A woman who was totally unsuitable, ridiculously inappropriate. A woman who reminded him of every showy, lipsticked tart his father had picked up and paraded, to his family's shame.

And Leandro was just the same—taking her out, showing her off… Didn't he realise how dangerous this was? How dangerous *he* was? At least when it came to Zoe.

They rode in silence for half an hour, before Leandro slowed and they approached a crumbling jetty sur-rounded by dense forest that led directly to the shore.

'An island,' Zoe said in surprise. A tiny island right in the middle of the lake, which looked practically deserted.

'Isola Comacina,' Leandro confirmed. 'Lake Como's only island. It doesn't have much on it any more, but it has a colourful history.' He tied up the boat, exchanging greetings with a wrinkled, round-cheeked man who sat in a rickety wooden chair on the jetty, presumably to welcome visitors to this undisturbed oasis. Zoe scrambled out of the boat, avoiding the impulse to take Leandro's extended hand, and he dropped it without a word.

'The island has been somewhat of a haven over the years,' Leandro told her as they followed a path from the shore to the island's heart.

The air smelled sweet and dry, and the forest cleared to reveal a meadow of long grass and a few twisted plane trees.

'Oh?' Zoe picked her way across the tufted mounds of grass, half wishing Leandro would offer his hand again. The chunky-heeled sandals she'd chosen to wear were far from practical, yet she was honest enough to admit she wanted to hold his hand for another reason. She wanted to feel its cool, dry strength, his fingers wrapping possessively—promisingly—around hers.

She wanted his touch.

'How is it a haven?' she asked, swallowing as she looked away from the sight of his arm swinging loosely at his side, his fingers within reach.

'The inhabitants of Lake Como—the wealthiest ones anyway—took refuge here when the barbarians swept in over a thousand years ago. The island looked a little different then—covered with houses and churches.' Leandro pointed downwards, and Zoe saw a foundation of ancient crumbled stone. 'Not much left now.'

'No,' she agreed. It was hard to imagine this lonely, deserted landscape busy and bustling with life. The only sound now was the rustle of grass as they walked through the meadow, and the distant cawing of a gull.

'What happened then?' she asked, and Leandro shrugged, his hands in his pockets.

'They had several hundred years of prosperity when they formed an alliance with Milan. Then Como and Milan declared war on each other, and soldiers came here and burned everything. A decree was made that nothing could be built on the island—no houses, churches or fortresses. That was over eight hundred years ago, and no one has really lived here since then.'

'I guess they took that decree kind of seriously?'

Leandro smiled faintly. 'I suppose. A curse was put on the island, actually, by Bishop Vidulf: "No longer shall bells ring, no stone shall be put on stone, nobody shall be host, under pain of unnatural death."'

'And that frightened people off good and proper?' Zoe returned, but a shadow had passed over Leandro's face, and there was a haunted, almost hunted look in his eyes.

'Yes… It must be terrible to live under a curse.' His words fell into the stillness, rippling and disturbing the tranquillity, and somehow Zoe felt he was speaking from experience.

'Well, here's one building that's still standing!' she said cheerfully, for they'd come upon a little church, with a high bell tower looking out over the little island.

'Yes, a few buildings remain. Fifty years ago this was a retreat for artists. Their cottages are on the other side, along with a hideously over-priced restaurant that caters to tourists.'

'Shall we eat there?' Zoe asked innocently, and couldn't help but smile at Leandro's firm shake of his head.

'Indeed not. There are far better places to eat.'

They didn't speak much as they wandered around the rest of the island, gazing at the ruins, with the lake sparkling like a jewel in the distance.

There was something lonely and sad about Isola Comacina, Zoe thought, although perhaps she was only being fanciful, thinking of the bishop's curse. Yet she wasn't being fanciful in noticing that a pall had come over Leandro's mood. He seemed guarded and distant, his mind on other matters, other memories.

What are they? Zoe wanted to ask, wanted to know. Yet she knew she had no right to such information. Still, she wondered what ghosts haunted Leandro, what had made him kiss her last night with such angry desperation before turning away in self-disgust.

They took the boat over to Bellagio, an ancient village with steep cobblestoned alleyways lined with flowerpots and sidewalk cafés.

Leandro led her to a café tucked away on a tiny alley. They were the only patrons, and the hostess, a smiling woman with greying, flyaway hair barely kept by a headscarf, fussed over them, bringing menus and bread and a plate of olives swimming in herbs and oil.

'*Signor Filametti, è stato così lungo,*' she exclaimed, and Zoe looked up with a jolt of surprise. She didn't understand the Italian, but she recognised Leandro's name. He was known here. He was known—just as he was in Menaggio.

He *was* famous.

And why shouldn't he be? Zoe reminded herself as

she spread her napkin across her lap. If the villa belonged to Leandro's family—had done so for centuries—then of course he would be known in the region. Fussed over as a man of consequence, wealth, power.

Except he didn't wear his family's history and power like a mantle, with a sense of entitlement as Steve had. Leandro wore it like a yoke. A burden.

The realisation surprised Zoe, even though it was so glaringly obvious. After a few rather tersely exchanged words, Leandro opened his menu, effectively dismissing the friendly hostess, who promptly scurried to the back of the restaurant. Yet Zoe had the feeling that he acted more out of self-preservation than anything else.

'She knew you,' she commented, scanning the lines of incomprehensible Italian on her menu.

Leandro hesitated for half a second, his eyes on his own menu. 'Yes,' he replied flatly, and Zoe decided not to pursue that line of conversation.

'What do you recommend?' she asked instead. 'I can't understand a word.'

Leandro looked up, smiling faintly. 'I thought on your CV it said you knew Italian?'

Did it? Zoe bit her lip. 'I do—a bit,' she said. '*Sì, ciao, grazie…*'

Leandro's smile deepened. 'You're practically fluent.'

'I bought a book,' Zoe replied, her smile matching Leandro's. 'And I even looked at it once or twice.'

He shook his head, but Zoe could tell for once he was not annoyed. 'You're hopeless.'

'Why did you hire me, then?'

He glanced up, his expression sharpening. 'Because you suited my needs.'

'Which are?' She held her breath, waiting, wondering what he would say. Admit.

'Someone who doesn't know me or my family,' Leandro said flatly. 'A perfect stranger.'

His expression had darkened as he spoke, and when he turned back to his menu it felt like a dismissal. A rejection.

Yes, Zoe agreed silently, she was that indeed. A stranger. But why had Leandro wanted a stranger as an employee? It was an odd requirement, and one that made Zoe wonder yet again about his past. His secrets.

The mood remained sombre over lunch—huge plates of pasta and a shared salad that should have created a cosy, intimate mood, yet missed by a mile.

Leandro had retreated back into himself, and with a prickle of hurt annoyance Zoe realised she felt like an irritation to him now—as if she'd insisted on coming along rather than come by his own unexpected invitation.

'Where to now?' she asked as she followed Leandro out of the restaurant.

'Back to the boat, I should think.' Leandro scanned the sky. It was already well into the afternoon, and a few gauzy pink clouds streamed like ribbons across the horizon. 'I'll show you a tour of the lake's most spectacular sights from the boat, and then we should head back to the villa. I need to accomplish something today.'

'Important research?' Zoe surmised, falling into step beside him.

'Yes, actually. I have a client in Zurich, and my numbers analysis could affect the outcome of his bid by several million euros.'

'Wow.'

'Indeed.'

Back in the boat, Leandro perched at the helm, speeding them through the water with a distant, distracted air. Zoe gazed out at the gentle swells the boat created, trying to ignore the vague, yet growing sense of disappointment that gnawed at her insides and ate at her hopes.

What had she expected from today? From Leandro? Surely no more than what he was giving her—a friendly, if impersonal tour of Lake Como. Yet last night and all of its implications remained between them, unspoken, stretching the silence as taut as a wire. For a moment Zoe relived the touch of Leandro's lips on hers, his hands on her body, skin against skin.

Had it really been no more than a mistake? An aberration? It seemed that was how Leandro was going to view it. And there had been something *wrong* about it—something angry. Yet even that realisation could not keep her from remembering the sweetness of his touch, and Zoe sighed, restless, unsatisfied, not knowing what she wanted or how she could even begin to get it. If Leandro could even provide it… For surely she wanted more than he was willing to give?

Leandro cut the motor, and they were both plunged into a tranquil silence that somehow made Zoe feel more tense than ever. He pointed at the near shore.

'Villa Carlotta.'

Zoe glanced at the villa whose impressive façade was reflected in the still water. The densely forested mountain towered behind, the tops of the trees reaching for a few wispy clouds. The terraced gardens, surrounded by hedges, led right down to the water. It was like looking at a postcard—something too fabulous to be real.

'It's amazing,' she said, and Leandro nodded.

'One of the more spectacular villas on the lake.'

'Yours is pretty spectacular,' Zoe ventured, trying for a light tone. Leandro just shrugged. 'It *is* yours, isn't it?' she pressed. She didn't look at him, but leaned over the side of the boat to trail her fingers through the smooth silky water.

'Of course it is,' Leandro replied.

'I mean it belongs to your family.' Her words seemed to fall into the silence, rippling and disturbing the stillness just as her fingers were. 'I saw some paintings as I was cleaning. Portraits of your ancestors. Filamettis.'

'Ah.' Leandro's fingers clenched around the steering wheel, his knuckles whitening, although his tone was deceptively light. *Still*, Zoe wasn't fooled. 'Well, yes, as a matter of fact. It has been in the Filametti family for generations. But it now belongs to me.' There was implacable resolution, a hardness to his tone, and he turned his head away from her, squinting into the sunlight.

'But why are you selling it?' Zoe blurted. 'It's your family's. It must have such a history, a *legacy*—'

'That it does.' Leandro shrugged one shoulder, his muscles rippling under his shirt. 'But it's not one I admire or care for, so it hardly matters.'

That, Zoe thought, was not true. Oh, she believed the first part, but not the second. Every line of Leandro's powerful body was taut with tension, with suppressed anger. Whatever his family's legacy was, it mattered very much indeed.

'Did you ever live there before?' she asked, and Leandro was silent for so long Zoe didn't think he was going to answer.

'Yes,' he finally said tightly.

'For how long?'

'Thirteen years, as you're so curious. I grew up there.'

Zoe shook her head slowly. She thought of the rooms full of antiques, portraits and keepsakes of a family that stretched on for generations. She remembered her fanciful imaginings of the people who'd lived and loved there. Leandro had, his ancestors had, for hundreds of years.

It was a dizzying thought for someone like her— someone who had no family or home, who knew no one but the mother who refused to answer questions, who preferred to pretend they'd both somehow sprung fully formed upon this earth, like Venus from the waves.

So much history, so much heritage, so many people and memories. And Leandro was giving it all away as if it was worth nothing. 'I can't believe you're selling it,' she said, her voice somewhere between a sigh and a scold, and Leandro turned to look at her sharply.

'Why shouldn't I? I can hardly live there now.'

'Why not? Or at least when you marry, start a family—' She swallowed, her mind suddenly filled with images of Leandro playing happy families—a child on his shoulder, an elegant, *appropriate* wife by his side.

'I'm not going to marry or start a family,' Leandro stated flatly.

Zoe raised her eyebrows. 'Ever?'

'Ever,' he confirmed with a cold smile. 'I shouldn't think that would surprise *you*,' he continued. 'You don't seem the marrying kind either.'

'Don't I?' Zoe kept her voice light, but she bent her head, letting her hair fall forward as she trailed her fingers through the cool water again. She didn't want Leandro to see how much those words stung. Hurt.

'No, you don't,' he told her, his voice blunt and hard.

Zoe stiffened and looked up, and saw him gazing at her with a critical shrewdness that she didn't like. At all.

'You seem like the kind of girl who takes what she can get when she can get it. Who enjoys the ride and damns the consequences. Who doesn't care…about anything.'

His voice was cutting, brutal, and Zoe blinked under the verbal onslaught. She was too shocked to feel anything at first, but as Leandro flicked the motor back on the feelings came. Hurt and humiliation, causing her cheeks to flush and her eyes to sting, making her remember the money Steve had thrown across the bed as he'd sneeringly told her he'd had enough.

Yet this wasn't about Steve. It was about Leandro— the man sitting across from her, his body taut with tension and memory, his words an accusation and a judgement.

Anger fired through her, fuelling her. She reached out and grabbed Leandro's arm, forcing him to slow the boat. He turned his head, his eyes flashing, his mouth no more than a thin, hard line.

'You don't know anything about me,' Zoe said, her voice clear and hard.

Leandro's lips thinned into a cold smile. 'I've seen and experienced enough.'

'Oh?' She raised one eyebrow, still high on outrage. 'You want to make assumptions, Leandro? Then I'll go ahead and make a few of my own. You're a man who is completely blinded by his past. I don't know what your family did or didn't do that's made you so disgusted, so angry, but I do know that if I had a house like that—a *history* like that—I wouldn't go throwing it away. I wouldn't spit on it the way you are.'

'You don't know—'

'No, I don't. And you don't know me either. You have no idea who I am or where I come from, what I've lived or seen or felt. *You don't know.*' Her voice shook, and she felt tears at the corners of her eyes. She drew a shaky breath and forced herself to continue. 'So why don't you just keep your lousy assumptions to yourself and take me home? Or should I just say back to the villa, since it obviously was never a home to you?'

Leandro stared at her for a long moment, his face expressionless, ominously blank. Then with a jerky nod he pushed hard on the throttle, sending them skimming across the water in angry silence.

They didn't speak as Leandro tied the boat up to the dock, and Zoe scrambled onto the jetty without his help. Once inside the villa he disappeared into his study, and Zoe made her way upstairs to the sanctuary of her bedroom.

Except no respite was to be found there. She lay on the bed and watched the sun sink towards the horizon, her mind numb, her heart empty. Leandro's words hammered relentlessly through her mind, her heart.

You seem like the kind of girl who takes what she can get when she can get it. Who enjoys the ride and damns the consequences. Who doesn't care...about anything.

He'd summed her up so pithily, condemned her so readily—and in many ways he was right. That *was* who she'd been, who she'd had to be—at least on the outside. Act as if you don't care—or, better yet, *really* don't care. Then you won't be hurt when it's time to move on, when Sheila decides she's had enough.

Don't cry, Zoe. The next place will be better...

And the next, and the next, and the next. There was always something better somewhere else. That had been her mother's maxim, and Zoe had taken it as her own. She'd never known another way to live, and it was a *safe* way to live—you kept your heart guarded and had no home or family, nothing to care about.

Except somehow now she did. She hadn't come to Italy to care. She'd come to escape, to forget Steve. And yet as she lay on her bed she realised Steve hardly mattered any more; he was no more than a smokescreen for the true feelings she had—feelings which scared her.

She cared.

She cared about Leandro, about the villa, about the charade of domesticity she'd been acting out in the last few days. For the first time in her life her home was more than a bedsit or a grotty hostel. Her life was more than a meaningless job.

How pathetic to think she'd found something here. Hadn't Leandro made it clear what he thought of her?

Yet it both saddened and angered her to think that he had all this—all that she'd never had—and he was throwing it away.

Zoe brushed at the tears she hadn't realised were falling, silently streaking down her face. Now, as dusk began to blanket the lake, causing long shadows to melt into each other, she fell into an uneasy doze.

When she awoke, disorientated and still drowsy, night had fallen, and the room was illuminated only by a sliver of moonlight. A shutter creaked and then banged shut in a gust of evening air—a haunting, lonely sound that propelled Zoe from her bedroom in search of some comfort, if not company.

She made her way downstairs, picking her way carefully through the dark, and found some more leftover pasta in the kitchen, eating it cold while standing by the sink.

She felt bruised all over—lonely and heartsore and just plain sad. Gazing out at the unending darkness—even the lake was empty of boats and their comforting lights due to the wind—she decided to retreat back to her bedroom. Then, on the bottom stair, she heard a noise from the drawing room.

She hesitated, her hand curling around the cold iron railing as she listened. It had been two sounds, she realised: the clink of crystal and the more human sound of a sigh.

Still she didn't move, weighing her options. Leandro had to be in there, alone. Did she want to see him? Talk to him?

Even as these thoughts and their implications flitted through her brain, she was already turning, drawn towards Leandro with the irresistible force of a magnet. With need. She hesitated for no more than half a second on the threshold—surely no good could come of this?—before pushing the door further open with her fingertips.

'Well, hello.'

Zoe stiffened at Leandro's unaccustomed drawl. The room was shrouded in darkness save for a single lamp in the corner, next to the chair he was sprawled in. His hair was rumpled, the top two buttons of his half-tucked shirt undone, and he held a tumbler of whisky in his hand.

Zoe hesitated, not sure how to handle Leandro like this. There was something sad, and even vulnerable about him, yet she refused to let her sympathy overcome her sense. His harsh words from this afternoon still reverberated in her mind, stung her soul, and even in the dim room she could see a dangerous glint in his eye.

'Hello,' she said a bit stiffly. 'What are you doing?'

Leandro cocked an eyebrow, and Zoe flushed. It was a stupid question. 'Isn't it obvious?' he said, lifting his glass. 'I'm drinking.'

'Drunk?' Zoe interjected, and Leandro laughed, a sound without humour.

'Not quite. Not yet.' He gestured to the half-empty bottle on the sideboard. 'Care to join me?'

'No, thank you.' Zoe knew she sounded prissy, but

she didn't care. She didn't like Leandro in this mood—didn't know what he might say. What could happen.

'I thought you'd be good for at least one drink.'

'You thought a lot of things about me,' Zoe returned sharply.

'So I did.' Leandro turned his glass around in his hands, the lamplight making the whisky glint amber and gold. 'Are you trying to say they're not true?'

'Considering you summed me up as a mercenary trollop, then, yes, that *is* what I'm trying to say.' Zoe clenched her fists, her nails biting into her palms.

'Maybe I was too harsh,' Leandro replied musingly. 'But then so were you.'

'About what?'

He was silent, still rotating his glass between his palms, and after a moment Zoe wondered if he'd even heard the question. Then he looked up, and her breath came out in a soft rush at the sorrow in his eyes.

'You told me I was completely blinded by my past. That I'm spitting on my history, my family.'

He lapsed into silence again, his expression distant, and Zoe waited, caught between impatience and interest. And hope, strangely.

'I don't know why that disturbs me,' he finally said. He looked up at her again. '*You* disturb me.'

'I don't mean to.'

'Don't you? You're just like them, you know. At least I thought you were. Like all the others.'

He shook his head, and Zoe frowned. 'What do you mean, all the others?'

He brushed her question aside, setting his glass down on the table with a clatter before sweeping his arm to take in the shabby faded room, the whole villa. 'This villa was beautiful in its day. Do you know how long it's been in the Filametti family? Five hundred years. It was given to my ancestor by Ludovico Sforza, for his help in the wars against Venice and Florence. And my family held on to it through Spanish and Austrian domination, the Napoleonic wars, the devastation of the Fascist party. Through all of it we survived.'

He shook his head—whether in disbelief or something darker, Zoe couldn't tell.

'So, if your family managed to survive all that, why are you selling it now?' It was the obvious question, yet she still felt intrusive—insensitive—for asking it.

Leandro turned to look at her, and for a moment his eyes burned blue fire, pure rage. Then that brief light was extinguished, and he slumped back in his seat once more. 'I'm proud of my heritage,' he said. 'Despite what you think. That is why I'm so ashamed of what has happened.'

Zoe took a step into the room, and then another. 'What *has* happened?'

'The Filametti family was ruined,' Leandro replied simply, his voice more matter-of-fact than bleak. 'Completely ruined.'

CHAPTER SIX

THE statement seemed to have brought a new lucidity to Leandro, for he rose from the chair in one brisk yet fluid movement, and drained his glass before putting away the bottle of whisky.

Zoe watched him, unspeaking, not knowing what to say. There was a brittleness, she saw, to his movements; his face was averted from her. When he'd finished his tidying tasks he moved to the window, his back to her, his hands shoved deep into his pockets, and gazed out into the night.

'I used to play football out on the front lawn,' he said after a moment. 'My father loved the game. We played together.' He spoke in the same flat voice he'd been using all along, yet Zoe thought she heard a thread of wistfulness underneath, a ghost of memory.

She moved a bit closer to him, still wary and uncertain, treading dangerous, uncertain ground. 'And then?'

Lost in his own memories, Leandro didn't seem to hear her. Or perhaps he chose not to hear. He simply continued talking. 'We had parties in the summer, on the terrace. My sister and I used to hide under the tables and listen to the adults talking. They never said anything remotely interesting, though. There was always delicious food…*panettone, pastiocciotti*. We'd steal some when no one was looking.' He shook his head, and as Zoe drew closer to him she saw the glimmer of a smile on his face, although his eyes were hard. Unforgiving.

'And then?' she asked again, for she knew instinctively that this was the beginning of the story, not the end.

'Natale—Christmas—here was magical,' he continued, as if trying to explain something to her. Prove something, even. 'Candles in every window, a Yule log burning here in this room, and we'd walk to Midnight Mass in Lornetto. Once, even, there was snow. I tried to make a snowball, but it was no more than a dusting and it fell apart in my hands. My father laughed, and told me he would give me a snowball for Christmas. And he did. I don't know how he managed it—he must have sent someone to the mountains to collect snow. He hid it in the freezer and made a treasure hunt for me to find it.'

Leandro lapsed into silence and Zoe stood next to him, her heart aching. These were the kinds of memories she had always dreamed of, longed for, and from the taut set of Leandro's jaw she knew they were precious to him too. Precious and yet desecrated somehow—by what? What had happened to him? To his family?

She couldn't bring herself to ask, *And then?*

'It's those memories that I can't bear to lose. They matter more than all my so-called heritage.' He half turned to her, the faint smile now full-fledged, hard and cynical. 'Pathetic, really.'

'I don't think so,' Zoe said quietly. 'I'd love to have memories like that.'

'Would you? Even if what happened afterwards ruined everything—coloured it so it all seemed absurd and false?'

Zoe blinked at the ragged harshness in his voice. 'At least you *have* memories.'

'What are you saying?' Leandro demanded. 'You must have had parents—a family of some kind?'

'I had—have—a mother.' Zoe cut him off, her words flat.

Leandro stared at her for a moment before repeating her own question. 'And then?'

'I don't know who my father is,' Zoe told him. She felt heat rush up into her face and tried to control it. 'I don't think my mother does either.' She'd never told anyone this—never exposed the shaming paucity of her childhood. 'We didn't have a home—not a villa like this, not a house or apartment, not anything.'

Leandro frowned. 'What do you mean?'

Now Zoe found herself smiling just as cynically as he had. 'It's hard for you to imagine, isn't it, Leandro? You don't even realise the luxury you had growing up. I'm not even talking about wealth or prestige. I mean a family. Two parents, a sister—more for all I know.' She shook her head. 'Something normal.'

'It was far from normal,' Leandro cut in harshly.

'It sounds pretty wonderful to me,' Zoe challenged.

'Christmas, parties, football. It sounds like an American television show—happy families, Italian-style.'

'Well, as I soon found out, it wasn't.'

'No? What happened?' Zoe felt a flaring of anger, and it surprised her. Why did she care what had happened to Leandro's family? What he'd felt or done about it? Why did it matter to *her*?

Yet it did; she couldn't bear to see him throw it all away, no matter how bitter he was. He'd had something, something wonderful and he didn't even realise it, wouldn't acknowledge it.

'What happened,' Leandro said, his voice as sharp as broken glass, 'is my father gambled everything away. Lost it all—squandered it, even.'

'Like you're doing.'

The silence following her pronouncement was both chilling and profound. Leandro's eyes darkened, the skin around his mouth whitening with rage. 'Are you comparing me to my father?' he asked in a quiet, lethal voice, and Zoe knew that was the worst thing she could have done.

Still, her anger—as unreasonable as it might have been—fuelled her. 'There seem to be some similarities.'

Leandro's hand slashed through the air. 'I am nothing—*nothing* like my father!' His voice came out in a cry of desperation, a plea for mercy. 'Nothing like him,' he repeated in a savage whisper. His features twisted with regret, memory, fear.

'What did he do that was so terrible?' Zoe whispered.

Leandro was silent for so long, his face averted from her once more, that she wondered if he would ever answer. The room was dark save the one small circle of light from the delicate table lamp.

'Do you know why I hired you?' Leandro asked finally. His back was still to her, his voice was flat and unemotional, yet Zoe sensed the deep current of anger and disappointment underneath.

'You told me earlier today it was because I didn't know you,' she replied evenly. 'A perfect stranger, you said.'

'Yes. Exactly. I wanted someone who had never heard the name Filametti. Who hadn't seen my father and his trollops splashed across the tabloids. Who didn't see my family as either a tragedy or a laughing stock.'

'Well, you succeeded there,' Zoe replied, struggling to maintain a calm tone. Leandro's words were branding her brain: tragedy, *trollop*. 'I'd never heard of you.'

'Nearly everyone in Italy has,' Leandro replied diffidently. 'Georgio Filametti—my father—made sure of it. Oh, he was famous enough to begin with—although I don't think I realised it as a child. How could I? As a child you simply accept the way things are as the only way they can be. You don't know any different…or any better.'

'I suppose that in your case that was true,' Zoe replied, thinking it had certainly not been *her* situation. Even from a very young age she had been aware there was something unusual and even unnatural about her upbringing—her mother's frantic flitting from anonymous city to anonymous city, her confused and unhappy daughter in tow.

'He had everything going for him,' Leandro said, and now there was disgust in his voice. 'Related to royalty, Italy's golden child, adored and intelligent too. He could have accepted everything as his due, given to him on a golden plate, but he worked hard. He was in finance, banking, and he made his own money.'

'He sounds like a good man,' Zoe said after a moment, when Leandro lapsed into silence once more.

'I thought he was,' Leandro agreed, his voice caught between bitterness and grief. 'I *thought* he was. But he proved me—us—the whole of Italy wrong.'

Zoe kept silent. She could not imagine what Leandro's father had done that was so unbearably unforgivable. Then Leandro dragged in a breath and told her, each word spat out like a loathsome, poisonous confession.

'He lost it all,' he said. 'Gave it away. And for what? A few nights' sordid pleasure.' He glared at her in accusation, and Zoe recoiled. She didn't understand, but somehow this felt personal—as if Leandro were accusing *her*.

'What do you mean?' she asked, struggling to raise her voice above an uncertain whisper.

'My father was an addict of sorts,' Leandro explained coolly. 'Addicted to women—cheap women, mercenary women, glossy, but from the gutter all the same.'

'He had affairs?' Zoe clarified, and Leandro smiled mirthlessly.

'Oh, he didn't just have affairs. He had torrid, sordid, *pathetic* encounters. *He* was pathetic... Those women took him for everything he had. And I don't just mean his money. I mean his dignity, his self-respect. His business began to fail, he started embezzling, and then one of his paramours began blackmailing him. Eventually it all came crashing down—a grand exposé in the papers, grainy photos of everything.' Leandro's mouth twisted. 'And my father couldn't face it. So he ran away. Disappeared to Monaco with what was left of his money, and left my mother to face it all.'

'And you?' Zoe surmised softly. 'How old were you when this happened?'

Leandro looked surprised by the question. 'Thirteen,' he said shortly.

Thirteen. Zoe's heart ached. Almost a man, and yet such a child. 'And then?' she asked quietly.

Leandro shrugged. 'I haven't seen him since. My mother died two years ago, and she never saw him again either. He'd left her shamed, a virtual pauper, smeared and ridiculed in every newspaper, and yet she still couldn't hate him.'

Because you hated him enough already, Zoe finished silently. She shook her head. It was a sad story—a tragedy, just as Leandro had said—and yet it seemed to her all the more tragic that he was selling this villa, throwing away the few good memories he had.

'If your father lost everything, what happened to this villa?'

'It couldn't be lost,' Leandro replied. 'It was never his to begin with. It was my grandfather's, and when he died last year it passed to me. Of course no one had the funds to restore it—my grandfather had spent all his money paying my father's debts. He managed to hold on to the villa only barely.'

'So the villa's ownership skipped over your father?'

Leandro smiled grimly. 'My grandfather made that provision in his will after my father showed his true colours. Chasing after every tart who took what she could get.'

Zoe nodded, digesting this even as another echo began its insistent, remorseless beating in her brain. *You seem like the kind of girl who takes what she can get when she can get it. Who enjoys the ride and damns the consequences. Who doesn't care...about anything.* Shock rippled icily through her, pooled like cold acid in her stomach. She was beginning to understand why this felt so personal.

'And you think I'm just like them?' she whispered, cruel comprehension making her feel sick, ashamed, though she knew she had nothing to be ashamed of. 'Your father's women—those heartless, blackmailing scum! You think I'm just like them. That's why...'

Dizzily she stepped back from him, reaching for a chair to steady her, her fingers curling slickly around the burnished wood. She didn't know why the realisation should hurt so much, should make her feel as if her heart was breaking. Her heart wasn't even involved. It *couldn't* be. Yet at that moment she felt as if someone had reached right down inside and wrenched it apart. She felt torn up inside, shattered into pieces...

It all made a kind of sickening sense now—why Leandro resisted his attraction to her, why he judged her so harshly.

I shouldn't...want...

He was afraid of becoming like his father, of *being* his father—risking and ruining everything for *a girl like her*. A tart, a trollop, a cold-hearted, *blackmailing*—

Bile rose in her throat and she choked it down, willing herself not to cry, not to care.

Wasn't that how she'd kept herself safe all these years? First as a child, losing best friends and favoured 'uncles' when her mother had decided it was time to move on, and then later, as an adult, when she'd followed in her mother's footsteps, quite literally, never staying long enough to know or be known, because she was afraid to try any other way. Afraid to be hurt.

Yet now she *was* hurt. Now she hurt all over.

Leandro turned slowly to look at her. There was a new, naked desolation in his face, a bleakness in his eyes that somehow seemed strangely vulnerable. 'No, Zoe,' he said quietly. 'I don't think that. You're not like them at all.'

Tears, treacherous tears, gathered at the corners of her eyes and she dashed at them angrily. 'But you said—'

'I think I was trying to prove to myself that you were. And you must admit you *do* project a certain image.' Leandro's sudden wry smile took the sting out of his words.

'Image...' Zoe repeated numbly. It was all about image. Who she pretended to be because it was safer. It wasn't who she really was—who she'd *ever* been.

'Is it just an image?' Leandro asked softly. 'Who are you really, Zoe Clark? Why did you come to Italy? What are you running away from? Because I am beginning to think you have secrets—perhaps as many as I do.'

Yes, she did. And the fact that he'd guessed made Zoe ache. She almost *wanted* him to know, to tell him all of it, to finally be known. Understood. Accepted.

Loved.

His hand reached out slowly, hypnotically, to brush a strand of hair away from her cheek. 'And,' he added, his voice lowered to a rasp, 'why can't I get you out of my mind?'

'I can't get you out of mine either,' Zoe admitted shakily.

They stared at each other, silent, still, and Zoe knew it was a moment for making decisions. For turning away if they could. And surely that was the safer, saner course of action? She already knew she was in way too deep—cared far too much. Yet she couldn't—didn't even want to. Under Leandro's penetrating stare she felt vulnerable, emotionally bare, and even though it terrified her it was something she wanted. Craved. To know and be known. *Finally.*

She didn't know who moved first, who gave in before the other. It didn't matter. One moment they were simply staring at one another, and the next they were a tangle of arms, of legs and lips and skin, seeking and finding again and again, like deep-water divers desperate for air.

She stumbled backwards, tripping on the frayed fringe of the carpet, and Leandro's arms came around her, steadying her. Holding her. She never wanted him to let her go.

She could feel him pressed against her, felt the hard length of his thigh, the chiselled muscles of his chest. Felt his lips on her skin, touching her bare shoulder, the nape of her neck, her jawbone. She shuddered under his caress, wanting more. Needing more.

There was nothing desperate or angry here; there was, instead, something precious. Something beautiful. Or so Zoe wanted to believe.

Her fingers threaded through Leandro's hair, drawing him closer. He kissed her again, deeply, drinking her in, and Zoe let him—let herself open to his touch in a way she never had before.

Leandro drew back, tilted her chin so she was forced to meet her gaze, and somehow it felt even more intimate than a kiss.

'Zoe…are you sure?'

Her heart thudding in her ears, desire coursing wildly through her veins, her senses alert and her thoughts blurred, there was nothing Zoe wanted more than to give a simple yes.

Yet as Leandro's gaze burned into hers she found that single word so difficult to say.

Yes. What was she agreeing to? A single night of pleasure? A one-night stand with her employer, who would walk away from her in the morning?

She was worth more than that. She *wanted* more than that.

'Zoe?' Leandro said softly, his fingers caressing her cheek. Such a light, simple touch, and yet it reached deep inside her—made her ache from its tenderness.

'Yes,' she whispered, praying she wouldn't regret her decision, knowing that when Leandro looked at her like that she was powerless to say anything else. To walk away, to stay safe. 'Yes, I'm sure.'

He led her by the hand, silent and accepting, through the shadowy, moonlit corridors of the villa. Everything was hushed, as if even the house around them sensed the expectancy of the moment.

In his bedroom he stopped before the wide double bed with its navy sheets and turned slowly to her.

'Let me look at you.'

Zoe fidgeted under his sweeping gaze, the airy confidence she'd cloaked herself with falling away. Had anyone really looked at her before? Had anyone seen who she truly was? Had *she*?

Steve had, she supposed. He'd seen her naked. Yet this felt like so much more than a physical baring. She felt as if her senses, her soul, her whole self were being bared. Exposed. And the strange thing was that she didn't mind. She *wanted* it.

Slowly Leandro reached out and pushed the straps of her top off her shoulders. With the barest shrug the garment slithered off her, leaving her nearly naked save a skimpy pair of pyjama shorts. Zoe felt goosebumps rise on her arms even though she wasn't cold. Leandro was still looking at her, and she fought not to cover herself, to stand there proud and bold, willing to be vulnerable.

He reached out to stay the arm she hadn't realised was already moving closer, protectively, towards her body.

'Don't. You're beautiful.'

'So are you,' she admitted with a little smile, and then reached out to lift his tee shirt over his head and shoulders. He shrugged it away completely and she let her hands drift down his bare chest. His muscles flexed under her touch.

'What you do to me,' he murmured. 'I've been helpless to resist you since I first saw you on my doorstep.'

'And that infuriated you?' Zoe whispered, her hands resting on his belt buckle.

Leandro helped her to unclasp it. Such a simple task. Yet she felt as shy and uncertain as the virgin she almost was—for even though she'd had a physical relationship she'd never felt like this.

'Yes,' he replied. 'I didn't want to want you. But I did. God knows, I did.'

'And now?' She shouldn't ask the question, shouldn't be so desperate for its answer.

'I *do*.' He pulled her towards him, her breasts colliding against his chest, and murmured against her hair, 'Can't you tell?'

Yes, she could. But she wondered at the war that had raged within Leandro. Would he hate her in the morning? Hate himself? Could she stand it?

His hands stroked her body, reached up to cup her breasts with sleek yet gentle movements that still managed to stir her up inside, and it was all too easy to push away that scared little voice and give herself up to feeling. Feeling wanted, desired. Treasured, even.

She wouldn't think about the morning.

* * *

Yet morning came, as Zoe had known it would. She lay in Leandro's arms as dawn crept along the horizon, sent its pale pink fingers streaking along the floor. A gentle breeze rustled the curtains. She'd been awake most of the night, caught between regret and wonder. It was an uncomfortable place.

Her body still tingled and ached from their lovemaking; Leandro had touched and caressed her with an intimacy that even now astounded her. He'd touched her everywhere, fingers and lips seeking, exploring, yet it hadn't simply been about the physical pleasure, amazing and intense as that had been. It had been something more, something deeper, and she'd seen it reflected in Leandro's eyes. This wasn't the one-night stand they'd both silently agreed on.

She'd seen it in Leandro's eyes when she'd touched him, felt it when he'd shuddered and almost—*almost*—tried to resist her caress. As if he'd been afraid it was too much. Too intense, too wonderful.

They were both afraid, Zoe had realised with a thrill of understanding as she'd traded caress for caress with Leandro. They were both protecting themselves, trying not to care, and yet now it was all stripped away.

When he'd finally entered her it had felt like the purest form of communication.

Yet now, as sunlight slanted across the floor and Leandro slept next to her, the doubts crept in. Last night she'd never felt so physically vulnerable, so emotionally exposed. Or was she just feeling that way now? Lying in his arms, waiting for him to wake up, having no idea what the expression on his face would be?

Disgust? Desire? Indifference? Irritation? The range of possibilities was frightening. Zoe had never felt so hesitant, so uncertain, and she knew why. She wasn't in control. She hadn't played it safe.

She'd let herself care.

CHAPTER SEVEN

LEANDRO lay on his side and watched Zoe sleep. It was an hour or so past dawn and she looked exhausted. Her lashes fanned on her cheeks, shadows showed under her eyes, yet she was still so beautiful.

His gut tightened—and so did something a little higher, a little more vital and frightening. His heart.

How had he come to care for this woman?

He meant what he'd said last night; he knew she wasn't like the women his father had chased after. Those women had been grasping, shallow, obvious. Zoe might only be after a good time, but Leandro knew she was far from the greedy blackmailer he'd been determined to see her as. He thought of her taking such simple pleasure in buying peaches, serving *biscotti*. She was a woman who in her unguarded moments looked thoughtful and even sad, and he knew she'd never been the schemer he'd wanted to believe her to be.

Gently he brushed a tendril of hair away from her forehead and she sighed softly in her sleep. Leandro smiled at the sound. What was she hiding? he wondered.

He thought of her guarded references to an unhappy past—a lack of home and family—and wondered just what had made Zoe Clark determined to treat the world with such insouciant indifference.

Determined not to care, as he was determined not to care.

His gut clenched again, and so did his heart. It was a warning, a reminder that Leandro could not afford to ignore. He couldn't afford to get involved.

He knew what happened when you did. He knew how much it hurt.

Determinedly he pushed away the wave of desire—and, more fearfully, something deeper—and rolled away from Zoe, vainly searching once more for sleep.

Zoe realised she must have finally fallen into a doze, for when she awoke the sun was high in the sky and Leandro was still sleeping—although now his back was to her. Even in the ignorance of sleep it felt like a rejection, and Zoe tried to prepare herself for the dreaded morning-after conversation. Confrontation, more like.

As if Leandro had sensed her thoughts, he stirred and slowly rolled over, blinking sleep out of his eyes only for a second before he was instantly alert.

'Good morning.'

His tone was expressionless, impossible to discern, and it gave Zoe no clue as to how she should behave. She gave a little smile that could mean anything—or nothing—and tossed her hair out of her eyes, drawing the sheet protectively over her in a casual gesture that Leandro still noticed.

'Good morning.'

They stared at each other, silent and unblinking, for a long moment, before Leandro smiled lazily and said, 'How about some breakfast?'

So there was to be no conversation. No confrontation. At least not yet. Zoe didn't know whether to feel disappointed or relieved. She stretched sleepily to mask her confusion, buy herself time. She didn't know how to act—couldn't afford to be honest. Didn't even know what honesty would look like, sound like. Her feelings for Leandro were so new, raw and untested. She was afraid to try them out and see if they were real.

'All right,' she said after a moment, and slipped quickly from the bed, throwing on her discarded clothes with her back to Leandro. Still she felt him watching, and a rosy blush spread over her whole body.

When she turned around again, Leandro had pulled on his pyjama bottoms. His chest was still magnificently bare. Zoe averted her gaze, feeling awkward and gauche.

'I'll let you off the hook this morning,' he said. 'I'll cook breakfast.'

He was as good as his word, and as Zoe sat at the kitchen table, sipping coffee, Leandro cracked half a dozen eggs into a bowl and began to briskly whisk them.

'I can't make much,' he told her, 'but I can do a decent omelette.'

'Sounds good,' Zoe replied lightly.

And it smelled good too, when, a few minutes later, Leandro placed an omelette in front of her, steaming and fragrant with basil and tomato.

He sat across from her and handed her a fork. 'Dig in.'

They ate silently for a few moments, the sun streaming through the wide windows, glinting off the lake. It should have been a pleasant, comfortable, even happy moment, yet Zoe could only feel the tension uncoiling in her belly, wrapping around her heart.

What is this? she wanted to ask. *What are we?* A one-night stand? A summer fling?

Was she actually thinking it might be more?

She choked on a bite of omelette and reached desperately for her half-drunk mug of coffee. Leandro watched her in concern. When she'd recovered herself, she found she had a bit courage as well, and she set her mug down with careful determination.

'So...'

Leandro sat back in his chair, his arms folded, as if he'd expected this. 'So?'

His expression was guarded, yet not unfriendly. Neutral, Zoe decided, which could mean—or could hide—anything.

She licked her lips, her mouth and throat suddenly dry, the words she'd intended to speak evaporating into thin air. 'What do you want, Leandro?' she finally asked. 'From me?' And then she held her breath and waited. Worse—hoped.

For what?

Leandro was silent for a long moment. He raked a hand through his hair, let out a long sigh. Not good signs. 'We had a good time last night, Zoe.'

Something in Zoe wilted. Withered. *A good time.* That

was all she was good for, the kind of girl she still was. To him, at least. Inside she didn't feel like that at all.

'Yes,' she agreed, and reached for her mug once more, desperate to disguise the disappointment she felt rolling through her in consuming waves. Surely Leandro would be able to see it in her eyes, her face? 'Yes, we did,' she repeated, her voice stronger now. She was able to meet his gaze directly.

'So?' Leandro shrugged, smiling a bit. 'You're here for…what…? Another two months?'

'So we can have two months of good times,' Zoe filled in for him, feeling sick.

Leandro frowned, and Zoe saw something crystallise and harden in his eyes. 'Is that not what *you* want? You seem like you'd…' He trailed off, shrugging, and Zoe forced herself to smile.

'I know what I seem like.'

'I'm not judging you,' Leandro told her quickly. 'You know that?'

Zoe nodded slowly. 'Yes.' And he wasn't—not really. She was judging herself. She rose from the table, clearing the plates—mindless tasks, because she couldn't think, didn't *want* to think, about how she was feeling. How much she hurt.

'Zoe…' Leandro rose as well. 'I feel as if I've said something to offend you.'

'Offend me? No, of course not.' She leaned against the sink, a damp dish towel in one hand. 'Like you said, we had a good time last night, Leandro. There's no reason for it to stop, is there?' She swallowed, forced herself to continue. 'As long as we know what to expect, no one gets hurt—right?'

'Right,' Leandro agreed slowly. He didn't move, and Zoe turned determinedly back to the dishes. When he spoke again his voice was low and final. 'If you were expecting…more, I'm afraid I don't have it to give, Zoe.'

'Why should I expect more?' she asked, her back to him. She heard the brittleness in her voice, felt it inside.

'It's not about who *you* are,' Leandro said. He crossed the room in a few long steps and reached out to stay her arm, his fingers curling around her wrist, burning her bare skin. 'It's who *I* am.'

Zoe's fingers clenched around the dish towel. She looked down, blinked hard. 'I see.'

'Do you? Do you remember when I said I didn't plan to marry or have children? Any of that?'

Blink again. Quickly. 'Yes.'

'I meant that. I'm not—' He shrugged, releasing her arm. 'After everything, I'm not capable of that. And I didn't think you wanted it either.'

He had said as much. Not her. Yet she wasn't about to point that out now. 'No, not really,' she said instead. She pushed her hair back from her face and found a smile. 'We've had a good time, Leandro, like you said. And there's no reason why it can't continue.' Except for the fact that her heart was splintering apart at every damning word he said.

'All right, then.' Leandro smiled, and then drew her into his arms.

Zoe went, unresisting, recognising her own shaming

powerlessness. He kissed her once, deeply and sweetly, and her splintered heart seemed to squeeze together again, still hoping—

Then he released her.

'I'll see you later, then. I need to do some work.'

Mutely Zoe nodded and watched him leave, thinking sadly that he was always the first to go.

Too distracted and weary to start on her own work, she took a second mug of coffee out onto the terrace and sat curled in a chair, gazing blindly at the lake now full of sailboats and pleasure yachts. Above her there was the steady clatter and hammer of the roofers, working hard to make sure Leandro could sell his villa.

His home.

Except he refused to think of it as a home—didn't *want* a home. And with a growing sense of desolation Zoe realised what that meant for her.

She wanted a home. She wanted a family. Children, love, laughter, safety, warmth. She wanted it all, and she wanted it with Leandro.

Her mouth twisted cynically. How could she fall in love so quickly, so hopelessly? How could she want something so impossible—as impossible as the neat little houses with their window boxes and lace curtains that she'd seen from the window of a bus, *en route* to another town, another adventure. She'd drawn them secretly on scraps of paper and crumpled them up before her mother saw, knowing she would pour scorn on those dreams.

She should crumple up these new dreams too—hide them away before Leandro could guess her true feelings.

He'd be horrified, she knew, to realise just how much she wanted from him. Even if he no longer thought of her as an unscrupulous tart, he probably still considered her to be the kind of girl who enjoyed whatever came her way for a time, and then moved on.

And that was the kind of girl she was—whether she liked it or not. The kind of girl she would have to be.

Zoe took a sip of coffee; it had grown cold. She knew she would accept Leandro's offer, take what she could get even though she wanted so much more. It would simply have to be enough.

Leandro stared at the letter on his desk, the crabbed writing, barely legible, and felt a wave of disgust roll over him, tinted—*tainted*—by the faintest trace of pity.

Too little, too late. He wasn't remotely ready to forgive. He never would be.

He pushed the letter aside, raking a hand through his hair before dropping it to his side. It wasn't just the letter that was making him feel restless; it was Zoe.

Their conversation this morning, meant to put everything on a neat, clear footing, had left him instead with a deepening sense of unease and dissatisfaction.

It wasn't enough.

It would have to be.

Last night, he acknowledged with the flicker of a smile, had been wonderful. Wonderful was too simplistic a word; it had been...transcendent. His smile deepened cynically; he was sounding like some lovesick poet.

Yet he couldn't deny that last night had changed him,

touched him in a way he'd never expected. There had been an openness, an honesty to their lovemaking he'd never experienced with another woman. As if they had not just been baring their bodies, but their souls. And joining them as one.

Leandro let out a sigh of sardonic disgust. Really, he was sounding positively fanciful. The truth was, he hadn't been with a woman in a long time, and the enforced intimacy of the villa had created a false sense of—what?

Connection? Closeness? *Love?*

Leandro snorted again and pushed away from his desk. He couldn't work, but neither did he want to think about Zoe. She occupied too much of his mind already.

He'd enjoy their liaison for a few months more, and then he'd leave. So would she. Easier for everyone. Easier and safer. The best thing, really, and Leandro almost—almost—believed it.

Zoe didn't see Leandro for the rest of the day, which passed with a sorrowful, aching slowness. She was eager to see him again, yet she also dreaded it.

Wasn't this what she'd always tried to avoid? This hopeless disappointment? People left. Either they did or you did. No one stayed for long.

Still, Zoe told herself with brisk determination, she had over two months. Leandro had offered her that much, and she would take it and enjoy it.

It was dusk when he found her, attempting to grill two chicken breasts. She peered into the massive oven, which was ominously dark and cool.

'Something's gone wrong, I think,' she said, as Leandro came up behind her. She felt a little frisson of surprise as his arms slipped around her waist and he kissed her neck, sending even more frissons rippling up and down her spine.

'Has the oven finally given up the ghost? It is old— at least thirty years. Our cook, Maria, used to complain of it. She had a love-hate relationship with that thing.'

'I can understand why.' For a brief moment Zoe let herself lean back against the hard plane of Leandro's chest, allowed herself the luxury of relaxing into his arms, of feeling safe and loved.

'Never mind about the oven,' Leandro murmured against her hair. 'Let me take you out to a proper restaurant. Somewhere in Como, maybe.'

His arms tightened around her, his hands sliding along her ribcage. Zoe felt a trembling thrill of desire at the easy caress. 'Are you sure you don't want to stay here?'

'Well, now that you mention it…' His voice rumbled with suppressed laughter. 'Still, there is time. Let me take you out, Zoe.'

And it was so wonderfully, pitifully easy to say yes.

She slipped on a sundress in a pale, shimmering lavender, added a spangled shawl and strappy sandals and she was ready.

Leandro had changed into a suit of dark blue Italian silk, and he looked devastating. Zoe could hardly believe he was hers.

For just over two months. She must never forget that. Even if now it felt like for ever. She took his hand and he led her through the darkened gardens to the boat. They sped through the darkness, arriving at Como's dock in less than half an hour.

Leandro moored the boat and then helped her up. His fingers remained twined with hers all the way to the restaurant.

It was a small, intimate, expensive place—the kind of restaurant that only had half a dozen items on the menu, but all were sinfully delicious. They shared *tiramisu* for dessert, Leandro's eyes dark and heavy-lidded in the candlelight, and then he led her back to the boat.

It was magical being on the lake at night, with the smooth surface of the water reflecting the stars above. Leandro cut the motor so they drifted in the middle of the lake, the only sound the lap of the water against the sides of the boat. Zoe stood up, her hands curling around the railing. A slight breeze rippled her hair, and she pulled her shawl around her shoulders.

'I love it here,' she said quietly. 'A night like this…I never want it to end.'

Behind her Leandro stiffened slightly, and too late Zoe realised what she had said—how it had sounded. She opened her mouth to take back the words, then closed it again. Let Leandro make of it what he would.

His hands came up to her shoulders, slipping under her gauzy wrap to warm her skin. 'A night like this need never end,' he said softly, and kissed the nape of her neck. Zoe shivered. 'Zoe…'

He pressed against her, her name a supplication and a thanksgiving. Zoe leaned back, her arms reaching up to twine around his neck, and for a split second she remembered the couple she'd watched with such bitter envy on the boat.

Now she was like them, happy and loved. For a time.

Banishing the thought, she turned so she could embrace Leandro fully, her lips seeking his, her body needing the caress, the release, yet her heart still wanting so much more.

The days slid by all too quickly; July melted into August. Zoe tried not to count, not to think of it. She refused to register the passing of the weeks, or the fact that the roofers were nearly done. She simply wanted to enjoy, to revel in Leandro's attention, in the nights in his bed, the days in his company.

They'd fallen into a routine of sorts, both working most of the morning before coming to the kitchen to share a coffee. Zoe was surprised at how easy it was to talk with him, to laugh and chat and speak of simple things, with the sunlight slanting through the wide, high windows.

They'd mostly return to work after lunch—although almost as often they'd find themselves upstairs, in bed, whiling away the lazy summer afternoons, loving each other.

In the evenings they often stayed in; Zoe would cook a meal they'd enjoy on the terrace, and then they'd curl up on one of the sofas in the drawing room and read or chat or even play chess. Leandro, laughing, had taught her, and was amazed at how quickly she'd picked up the game.

It felt, Zoe thought, as if they were reclaiming the

villa. The past. Filling the rooms with laughter again, with love. For she loved Leandro—loved him with a completeness that cast out fear and left only a strong, happy certainty. She even let herself hope—believe— that he felt it too.

How could he lie with her in his arms night after night and not feel it? How could he swim and laugh and dance with her and not be in love?

She even let herself daydream—something she was usually wary of. She pictured the rooms of the villa restored and decorated again, filled with family. Their children, even.

Dangerous, Zoe knew, to want this much. To hope this much. Yet she couldn't help it. She was happy, and happiness did that to you. It made you believe.

For a little while, anyway.

The day the roofers finished up and left was cold and grey and drizzly. Zoe plied them with cups of coffee and freshly made *biscotti*, not wanting them to go. Not wanting to admit that it was all inexorably coming to an end.

Eventually they left, and she stood on the portico— a mason had repaired the crumbling step—and watched their van disappear down the drive, past the new red and white sign stuck to the iron gate.

A chill that was far colder than the needling drizzle swept through Zoe. The sign read *'Per La Vendita'*. For sale.

Zoe gazed at it for a moment, unblinking, as the coldness penetrated her bones, her heart, made her shiver deep inside. Of course she'd always known

Leandro planned to sell the villa. She'd expected it, and yet…she hadn't. Somehow she'd managed to convince herself it wasn't really going to happen.

The drizzle strengthened to a downpour, and Zoe realised she was getting soaked. She turned back inside.

A glance at the calendar by the kitchen telephone told her it was the end of August. She could hardly believe it; they'd been lovers since the beginning of the summer. Her plane ticket was booked for next week.

Zoe sank into a kitchen chair and dropped her head into her hands, her mind buzzing. One week. Seven days. That was all she had left.

It's not enough. Her mind screamed it, her heart begged for more. And sitting there, alone in the kitchen, as the rain streamed down the windowpanes and turned the lake to no more than a dank grey mist, she realised she was going to get it. More. At least she was going to ask.

She'd even hope for an answer. The right answer. The belief that Leandro loved her even if he didn't want to admit it to himself. Even if it didn't feel safe.

She rose from the table, her mind still buzzing, a strange new courage fizzing through her. That courage took her all the way to Leandro's study door, and after a second's hesitation she knocked. There was no answer. Another second and she turned the knob, opening the door with careful slowness.

The room was empty.

She'd only been in Leandro's study a handful of times; he told her he'd clean it himself, as he didn't want his papers disturbed. Looking at the messy scattering of papers across the desk's burnished mahogany top, Zoe wondered how they could be *more* disturbed.

She walked slowly around the room, taking in the masculine leather chairs, the bookshelves lined with dusty, musty tomes. This must have been his father's study, she realised, and wondered why Leandro had chosen it for himself. Punishment or retribution?

There were so many papers on the desk, some even scattered on the floor, that she didn't know why one small crumpled ball on top of the wastebasket intrigued her. She couldn't explain why she reached down to take it, laid it on the desk to smooth out the wrinkles. Perhaps because it had been more crumpled than the rest— savagely twisted into the tiniest ball possible. She remembered doing that with her own childish drawings. This was something no one must see, yet she couldn't bear to destroy it completely. Silently she scanned the single sheet; it was a letter, written in Italian. She could only understand a few phrases. They were enough.

Il più caro Leandro… Sono così spiacente… Lascilo vederlo… Il vostro padre votato…

Dearest Leandro… I'm so sorry… Let me see you… Your devoted father.

Leandro's father. He'd written him, after all these years, and Leandro had clearly thrown the letter away. Zoe stared at the words, trying to make more sense of it. The picture Leandro had painted of his father had been of an entirely unscrupulous man, corrupted by lust and driven by desperation. A man who had abandoned his family without a single backward glance, never to see them again.

Yet this letter showed a man who longed for forgiveness, for healing. Leandro, it seemed, was determined not to give it.

'What are you doing?'

Zoe looked up, tensing at Leandro's harsh voice—a voice he hadn't used with her for weeks. Months. It was, she knew, the voice of a judgemental stranger.

She also knew how it looked. She'd been snooping in Leandro's study, going through his rubbish and reading his personal letters. A blush rose from her throat to stain her cheeks. She pushed the letter away, as if to distance herself from it.

'I'm sorry.'

Leandro cocked one eyebrow, his mouth curling into an unpleasantly cynical smile. 'Are you? What for, Zoe?' He moved closer, with soft, lethal grace, and Zoe had to keep herself from taking a defensive step backwards.

'I—I was looking for you,' she said, stumbling over the simple explanation. 'I thought you'd be in here…'

'But I wasn't,' Leandro finished softly. 'So you decided to snoop around.'

He was so close to her now, his eyes bright with an anger Zoe didn't even understand. 'I'm sorry,' she said again. 'I didn't mean to snoop. I don't even know why I read that letter…'

'What?' His eyebrows rose in disbelief. 'You didn't read them all?'

'No!' Zoe shook her head, her hair brushing against her face. 'Leandro, why are you being so…so…?' She stopped, not wanting to finish the question. So cold. So hateful. So unforgiving.

'Why were you snooping, Zoe?' Leandro asked, in a voice no less hard for its softness. 'What were you looking for? My chequebook? My bank balance? A few bits and baubles?'

'What?' It took a full thirty seconds for comprehension to trickle coldly through her, while Leandro watched with scornful assurance. 'You think I was…? You still think I'm like one of your father's bimbos?'

Leandro cursed and turned away. 'No…of course not… I don't know what to think!'

The last came out in a cry of anguish, and Zoe grabbed the letter and shoved it towards him. He caught it reflexively against his chest, glancing down at the lines of scrawled writing, his brow furrowed.

'I was reading *this*,' she said heavily. 'A letter from your father. I can't understand all the Italian, but I know enough to realise he's sorry and he wants to see you.'

Leandro's fingers tightened around the wrinkled paper before, with deliberate, supreme indifference, he crumpled the letter once more and tossed it back in the bin. 'So?'

'So?' Zoe shook her head. 'Leandro, this is your *father*—your family.' She glanced at the crumpled ball of paper and felt all her hopes blow away like insubstantial dust. It had been such a deliberate dismissal of his father, his family, *everything*. Everything she'd begun to believe. 'You're never going to change, are you?'

'Change?' Leandro's voice sharpened, his eyes narrowing. 'Why should I change?'

'I thought…' Tears welled at the corners of her eyes, and only with effort could she blink them back. She felt disappointment and something deeper pouring through her, scalding her. She'd been so utterly foolish. 'I thought you'd change,' she finally said, and heard the ache of longing in her own voice. 'I thought you were changing—that what we had together…' She shook her head, not wanting to articulate just how deluded she had been. 'But I realise now I was wrong.'

'Yes, you were.' Leandro's voice was cold. 'I told you how much I had to give, Zoe. I never deceived you. I thought you were like—'

'Like you. Yes, I know.' She gave a tired imitation of a laugh and felt the tears sting her eyes again. 'But you see, I've come to realise this summer that I'm not really like that. I'm not sure I ever was. I know how I acted, how I wanted to be seen, but inside…' She shrugged. 'I want what I never had growing up. My mother was just like me. More, even. We travelled from place to place and we never stayed long—a few months at most—before she'd get itchy feet and have to pack up and leave. Always a new adventure, new school, new friends. Except they never really were friends—we never had time. I suppose I grew used to it, and I convinced myself that was how I wanted to live *my* life. Safer, really. You never get hurt, because no one ever gets close enough.'

A muscle ticked in Leandro's jaw, and for a moment he looked as if he might speak. But the silence just stretched on, endless, agonising. Zoe forced herself to continue.

'But now I know what I want, Leandro, and it's not just a good time. I don't even think I've ever *had* a good time—you were only my second lover, you know. I'm not the girl you thought I was. I'm not the girl *I* thought I was.'

'Zoe—'

Leandro broke off, and Zoe knew whatever he wanted to say he couldn't. He was right; he didn't have any more to give. He couldn't give her what she wanted—which was everything.

'I don't want a good time, Leandro. I want a home, a family. Love.' Her smile curled the corners of her mouth. 'I want it all, Leandro. And I thought maybe you did too…with me. I thought that even if you felt you didn't have enough to give you'd still want more. But you don't.'

Leandro was staring at her, his face horribly expressionless, making Zoe feel even more vulnerable. She'd exposed more to this man than anyone else, and he didn't even want it. *Her.*

'It's funny,' she finally said, breaking the taut, uncomfortable silence. 'It took a letter from your father to make me wake up from the dream I was living in. Because this was all a dream, wasn't it? Living here together like it's a home…our home…' Her voice cracked and she swallowed down the howl of sorrow that threatened to erupt out of her. 'If my father ever wrote to me like that I wouldn't throw away the letter. I'd keep it, and I'd see him. Because no matter what he did, Leandro, he's sorry now, and he loves you—'

'You can tell all that from a few badly translated lines of Italian?' Leandro's voice rang with contempt. 'You have no idea, Zoe.'

Zoe gazed at him, at his powerful frame and blazing eyes radiating scorn and rage, and she shook her head. 'Nor do you. Consider this my notice.'

Ducking her head so he couldn't see the tears that had begun to slip silently down her cheeks, she hurried out of the room.

Leandro watched her go, his chest aching as if he'd run a marathon, as if his heart were breaking.

But of course it wasn't. He didn't love Zoe Clark; he didn't love anybody. He'd made sure of that.

He cursed under his breath, wishing he'd never hired her, never met her, never loved her—

No. He did *not* love her. They'd been having a perfectly fine time, a *good* time, and she'd ruined it with silly schoolgirl dreams he'd thought her too savvy to possess.

I want it all. A home, family, love.

Didn't she realise those were all illusions? They didn't last, even if they were real in the first place. His had been torn apart by his father's lust and deceit, and she expected him to *forgive*?

Leandro cursed again. He would *never* forgive his father—no matter how many letters he wrote. He'd never allow him back in his life, his heart—

Or anyone?

The little voice that whispered inside him wasn't sly, only sad.

Leandro slumped in the chair behind his father's desk. A sudden memory pierced him with its sweetness: climbing on his father's lap while golden sunlight streamed through the window, playing with his pens and papers. His father had only chuckled, never minded, never swatted at his hands or told him to leave.

Not as he'd told Zoe to leave.

His father had always had time for him, always listened and loved him, and when he'd walked away that was what had hurt most of all.

Was he going to do the same? Prove once and for all he was just like his father—at least in that?

As the grey day turned to darkness, Leandro felt a fresh sorrow wash over him and he closed his eyes in regret.

In the end it was all too easy to creep out of the villa with her one beat-up bag. She left a note on the kitchen counter, asking for her last pay cheque to be sent to a postal box she kept in New York. Leandro's study door was firmly shut, and Zoe decided against knocking. There was nothing more to say; it had all, sadly, been said.

She walked down the driveway in a twilit drizzle, hitched her way to Menaggio, and then caught a bus to Milan. A few hours of waiting for a standby flight, and less than twenty-four hours after her confrontation with Leandro she was home.

Home. Home was hardly the word for the hostel she'd found in New York City's Meatpacking distract.

It was a grotty room with a single bed, a battered bureau and a cracked sink. After the warmth and beauty of the villa, crumbling as it had been, it seemed all the more appalling—yet it was within Zoe's budget.

The next morning she took a newspaper and a red pen to a local diner, and over coffee and scrambled eggs began circling ads. Chambermaids, temp work, anonymous dead-end jobs. Her usual.

Yet after a few minutes she set the pen and newspaper aside and took a sip of her cooling coffee. She didn't want to do this any more.

Yet she didn't know what else to do; how did you begin finding a life for yourself? She'd taken a chance once and it hadn't paid off. Tears leaked out of the corners of her eyes and she blew on her coffee, trying to distract herself. She didn't want to burst into tears in the middle of a grimy diner.

'You're the devil to find.'

Zoe stilled, tensed, unable to believe the voice she was hearing. Then she looked up slowly and blinked. Twice. Leandro didn't disappear.

He was dressed in jeans and a shirt, sporting a full two days' growth of beard. He looked wonderful. He couldn't be real.

Yet he was.

'What are you doing here?' Zoe asked when she'd finally found her voice. Her heart was beginning to thump with loud, painful hope.

'Looking for you. I had no idea you'd run out on me so quickly.'

'You made it clear that you didn't want what I wanted,' Zoe said quietly. She felt the tears again, and one trickled shamefully down her cheek.

'I did, didn't I?' Leandro agreed. He gestured to the vinyl seat across from Zoe. 'May I?' he asked, and when she nodded, slid into the booth.

Leandro was silent for a long moment, and a waitress sauntered over to take his order with a loud crack of her gum.

'I'll have what she's having,' Leandro said, and when the woman had left them alone he confessed in a voice so low Zoe could barely hear it, 'Zoe, I was afraid.'

'Afraid?' she whispered.

'You were right. It is safer to keep your distance. To never let anyone in. That's how I've been living my life since my father left, but somehow someone got in anyway. And I didn't realise how close until she was gone.'

'*How* close?' Zoe asked in a whisper, and Leandro smiled.

'Close enough to make me realise how many mistakes I was making, letting bitterness and fear guide me instead of love.'

Love. One simple, wonderful word. Zoe's heart ached. 'Love?' she repeated, and heard the longing in her voice.

'I love you, Zoe.' Leandro's voice was steady and strong. 'You've shown me so much…given me so much…and I almost threw it all away.' He reached across the table and brushed another tear from her cheek. 'I don't mean to make you cry.'

'I don't want to cry,' Zoe admitted with a choked laugh, two more tears streaking down her cheeks. 'I want to believe…'

'Believe me. I spent a great deal of time thinking yesterday, while I thought you were still in the villa. If I'd known how quickly you were going to leave—' Leandro shrugged ruefully. 'But, no. I needed that time. I suppose I'm a slow learner.'

'And what have you learned?'

'To forgive. To let go. To love.' Leandro's smile was endearingly crooked. 'I wrote to my father. I took down the "For Sale" sign. And I came to find you.'

Zoe's heart felt as if it was being squeezed even as it expanded with hope and joy. 'I can't believe you found me.'

'It took a lot of money,' Leandro told her wryly. 'I greased quite a few palms, trying to find what flight you'd taken, and then what address you'd given the cabbie. But in the end…I'm here.'

Zoe swallowed. 'Yes, you are.'

'And, frankly, I'd rather be somewhere else.' Her eyes widened and Leandro smiled. 'I'd rather be home,' he said softly. 'With you. Will you come home with me, Zoe? As my wife?'

Home. Wife. Words she'd never thought to hear, to hope for. Zoe could barely see Leandro through the shimmery haze of tears, yet she knew that the hardness was gone from his eyes, the bitterness and anger had melted away. There was only love shining there, perfect and true.

Home.

She reached across the table to twine her fingers with his. 'Yes,' she whispered, and knew there was no other place she'd rather be.

A Venetian Affair

JACKIE BRAUN

Jackie Braun is a three-time RITA® finalist, three-time National Readers' Choice Award finalist and past winner of the Rising Star Award. She worked as a copy-editor and editorial writer for a daily newspaper before quitting her day job in 2004 to write fiction full time. She lives in Michigan with her family. She loves to hear from readers and can be reached through her website at www.jackiebraun.com

Don't miss Jackie Braun's new book, *Boardroom Baby Surprise*, **coming in August 2009 from Mills & Boon® Romance.**

Dear Reader,

We've all met men who are shameless flirts. Maxwell Kinnick is just such a man. Or is he? As my heroine soon discovers, much more is percolating beneath his charming exterior. In fact, you could say Max uses flirting as a defence mechanism, especially when it comes to his lovely business partner, Dayle Alexander.

But real relationships take total honesty, something that neither Max nor Dayle is quite ready to offer…until fate forces their hand.

I hope you enjoy what happens when Max and Dayle find themselves alone in lovely Venice planning Dayle's wedding to another man — and both secretly wondering if maybe a different groom should be saying "I do."

Best wishes,

Jackie Braun

For Mark. I'd marry you all over again.

CHAPTER ONE

DAYLE ALEXANDER leaned against the doorjamb to Maxwell Kinnick's office and watched him fuss with his tie. He was standing in profile to her, using his reflection in the glass of a display case to rework the Windsor knot. He had a meeting with a client in half an hour. Dayle's bet was that the client was female.

"New tie?" she inquired.

He glanced over and grinned, not embarrassed in the least to be caught preening. They had known one another a dozen years and had been business partners for eight. If Dayle knew one thing about the man, it was that he took great care with his appearance and appreciated fine things. The silk tie and tailored suit he wore were proof of that.

"I picked it up in Milan last week." His smile turned wicked. "Same place I bought those red panties for you. Have you worn them yet?"

The man was a shameless flirt. Benign but shameless. And this was an old game.

"Maybe," she offered.

"I'll take that as a yes." He turned his head slightly and regarded her out of one eye. "So, how do they look on?"

"You'll have to ask Ryan," she replied, referring to her longtime boyfriend.

Max placed a hand over his heart, his expression shifting from wily to wounded. "You're killing me, Dayle. You know that, right? Absolutely killing me."

Unfazed by his dramatic proclamation, she nodded. "It's all part of my evil plot to take over the business."

Together they owned Globetrotter Sales, an import-export company that Max had started from nothing more than a dozen years earlier. The company had been in its infancy when Dayle had hired in as his assistant. The pay had been so-so, the hours horrendous, especially since she'd been trying to squeeze in business classes at New York University at the time. But she'd been glad for the job and eager to be totally self-sufficient after a particularly nasty divorce. Before that, she had been a coddled and overprotected only child.

Four years after hiring in, their business relationship had changed. Dayle had a good eye for investments, one reason she had amassed a tidy sum in her stock portfolio. While she didn't believe in taking big risks, she did believe in exploring opportunities. She'd seen expanding Globetrotter's as one such opportunity. Initially Max had specialized in high-end imports. Dayle had written up a business proposal suggesting that he consider more midrange options and add exports. She'd included an analysis of expenditures and then she had boldly suggested they use her nest egg to fund the expansion.

Max had taken an agonizingly long time to study the

proposal. Afterward, he'd said, "That would make you my partner."

"Exactly." She'd held her breath.

"I've never had a partner before."

His reply hadn't been quite yes. Even so, Dayle had stretched out her hand. "Well, now you do. Deal?"

Even after all these years she could clearly recall the slow smile that had spread over Max's face and the heat that, for some reason, had suffused her own. He hadn't taken her hand to shake it. Instead he'd used it to pull her forward, into his arms. Then he'd kissed her full on the mouth.

"Deal," he'd murmured afterward.

At the time, she'd been shocked—not just by the intimate nature of the kiss, but by the high-voltage current of desire that had zipped through her body during it. After her disastrous, four-year marriage the last thing Dayle had wanted was to become involved with a man, but she had been—and she remained—especially determined to steer clear of handsome charmers like Max. He was too smooth, too ready with a compliment. And his effect on her pulse— even before that kiss—had been a little too reminiscent of the effect her good-looking, good-for-nothing ex had had.

Still, she hadn't backed down about becoming Max's partner, even if she had made it clear that business was the only thing she had in mind. They'd worked side by side, putting in many long days and weekends to expand Globetrotter's. Afterward, they'd moved their headquarters to its current trendy location in a revitalized Lower Manhattan neighborhood.

Dayle saw to the details and kept an eye on the fine print, searching out goods and products to be shipped abroad or brought into the United States. Max continued to work the sales end. The man was a natural at cutting deals and getting people to sign on the dotted line, and he loved to travel, spending more time outside of New York than he did in it. Their partnership was perfect in many ways, and though the man still flirted outrageously with her, even bringing back red silk unmentionables whenever he went on trips abroad, he'd never kissed Dayle on the mouth again.

Max buttoned his coat now and faced her. "How do I look?"

Drop-dead gorgeous was the phrase that came to mind, but as Dayle levered away from the jamb, she merely shrugged. "How do you always look?"

"Come on, sweetheart," he coaxed, his voice turning low and liquid. "Just this once, say it."

He looked like something out of an old Hollywood movie. The jacket fit his broad shoulders perfectly. She'd never met a man who wore clothes half as well, and that included her boyfriend. Whether dressed down in jeans or decked out in designer suits, Max always looked sophisticated, elegant and decidedly debonair. Old Hollywood, she thought again, but she shook her head.

"You'll get no compliments from me, Kinnick. I don't believe in feeding your already enormous ego."

"You know what they say. Big ego…"

She felt her lips twitch, but forced her expression to

remain stern. "You're lucky we're partners or this conversation would constitute sexual harassment."

"Only if the advances were unwanted and the work environment was deemed hostile." He took a step toward her. "Nothing hostile here."

"Move any closer and that could change."

Max merely laughed. "When are you going to dump Ryan and admit that you're madly in love with me?"

"Oh, about the same time you decide you can commit to one woman and one woman only." Dayle did smile now. "In other words, it's not going to happen."

"Variety is the spice of life. You should try it."

"You should try monogamy."

"I am monogamous. I don't believe in cheating." This he said emphatically.

Dayle might have wondered about that, but he'd moved closer, bringing the seductive scent of his cologne with him. It curled around her like a lover's embrace. She exhaled sharply.

"You don't have to cheat, Max. Your relationships have the shelf-life of a carton of milk." She crossed her arms over her chest. "It's called commitment phobia."

Her pronouncement didn't bother him in the least. He tapped the tip of her nose with his index finger, and then ran his knuckles lightly over the curve of her cheek. It took all of her willpower not to tremble.

"You know, a woman who's been dating a man for years and has neither moved in with him nor set a wedding date really shouldn't lecture someone else on commitment."

She cleared her throat, reminded of the reason she'd stepped into his office. "Funny you should mention that."

For just a moment, she swore Max's easy smile faltered. But then his lips curved, his dark eyes lighting. "Don't tell me you're finally going to put that poor bastard out of his misery and cuff him with the old ball and chain?"

"I've accepted his proposal of marriage, yes."

"You say tomato…" He shrugged. "Congratulations, sweetheart. So, may I kiss the bride?" He didn't wait for an answer. He leaned forward and bussed her cheek.

"Thank you."

"So, when did this come about?" he asked.

"Over the weekend."

He studied her, eyes narrowing just a little. "It's Thursday and you're just now getting around to telling me? Worried that you might change your mind? Or worried that I might *help* you change it?"

She didn't like his conclusions, especially since the former held a nugget of truth. Dayle wanted to be over the moon with excitement about her decision. Instead she felt…what was the emotion? Not resignation. No, certainly not that. Realistic? Marrying Ryan made sense, especially now. She supposed that was to be expected since their relationship was based more on pragmatism than passion.

"I'm not going to change my mind." She said it resolutely, for her own benefit as well as for Max's, before turning to leave. He fell into step beside her.

"Well, don't keep me in suspense. When is the big

day?" He draped an arm around her shoulders as they walked to her office, which was right next to his.

"The last Saturday in June." She casually removed his arm and scooted around to the opposite side of her desk, putting five feet of solid oak between them.

"This June?" He pursed his lips in dismay. "That gives you less than six months to make plans."

Dayle laughed. "You sound like my mother." And, oh, was Lorna McAvoy displeased with the situation, even though she was ecstatic that after years of fence-sitting Dayle had finally begun to make plans for a wedding. "When I told her, she pitched a fit. She's determined that I should have a big, splashy affair since I eloped when I married Craig."

That had been back when Dayle was young and stupid. She'd been eighteen and so blind, trusting her husband completely when just months into their marriage he had begun to work late. Then weekend meetings started taking him out of town, but she still hadn't caught on. It was only after she came across a credit card statement that she realized he'd not only been cheating on her but charging everything from hotel rooms and fancy dinners to expensive jewelry to their jointly held card. By the time their marriage was legally dissolved she'd been brokenhearted and broke, wounded but far wiser. She wouldn't make the mistake of marrying a flirt a second time. Ryan—solid, stable and dependable—was anything but a ladies' man.

"You're her only daughter. That's all but a sin."

Dayle fought the urge to roll her eyes. Her mother

had adored Max from the moment they'd met and no wonder given the way he catered to Lorna's strongly stated opinions.

"I'm thirty-six years old and I've been to the altar once."

"Even if the bride won't be blushing, she deserves a day filled with style and romance."

Dayle liked the idea of both, but said, "I think those can be managed on a smaller scale than what my mother has in mind."

She picked up the jade-handled letter opener he'd brought her from Taipei and began opening the day's mail.

"Lorna only wants the best for you."

"Don't take her side, Max, or, swear to God, I'll have to hurt you." She pointed the opener's sharp end in his direction.

"Promises, promises."

His gaze turned sensual and the smile he offered would have done Lucifer proud. As it was, it sent the familiar burn of sparks shooting up Dayle's spine. She'd never managed to become completely immune to such sparks, but she wasn't about to let them determine her future, let alone sabotage it a second time.

Max started for the door. "Off to my meeting. It's likely to run late." Dark brows bobbed meaningfully. "I won't be seeing you again until tomorrow morning…or perhaps the afternoon."

She set the letter opener aside. "Actually, Max, I was wondering if you would have dinner with me this evening."

He stopped, clearly surprised by the invitation. They

didn't socialize outside of work, even though they sometimes attended events thrown by clients or other
business-related functions. Ryan always escorted Dayle.
She no longer tried to remember the names of the
women who accompanied Max.

"You're asking me out? Feeling caged already, hmm?"

"This is serious. I need to talk to you about something
important. It's about us and the future," she blurted.

The easy smile slipped. For a moment, something
enigmatic took its place. "Does that mean Ryan won't
be accompanying you?"

"No. This is between you and me."

"How can I resist when you put it like that? Do you
have a place in mind?" he asked.

"I was just thinking of something casual so I won't
feel out of place in my work clothes." She smoothed
down the front of the navy blazer she wore over a silk
blouse and wool trousers.

She should have known Max would object. "Go
home and change into something eye-catching. I'll pick
you up at your apartment and we'll dine at Daniel."

She whistled through her teeth and for good reason.
A meal at the premiere French restaurant was going to
set him back a few hundred dollars at least. Too intrigued by the possibility to dismiss it out of hand, she
asked, "Do you think you can get reservations on such
short notice? I've heard you should make them at least
a month in advance."

"I know someone who knows someone." He
shrugged. "What do you say? We can toast your

nuptials, maybe check out the private dining room as a possible wedding location."

She should decline and suggest another, less pricy restaurant. She opted for a compromise. "We'll go dutch and I'll meet you there. Is seven okay?"

He rubbed his chin thoughtfully. "I think I can wrap things up with Janiece by then."

"Janiece?"

"The glass artist in SoHo who stopped by the office last week. Tall and blond with a very firm...handshake."

She found it impossible not to chuckle. "God, you're incorrigible, Max. Truly incorrigible."

"That's only because I try." He winked and was gone.

CHAPTER TWO

MAX jingled the change in his front trouser pocket as he walked through the doors at Daniel. Nervous, that's how he felt and had for the better part of the afternoon.

Ever since talking to Dayle.

Max wasn't the nervous sort, which made his present state all the more perplexing. He preferred knowing what was coming and usually he did, but he couldn't see around this particular corner. He blamed Dayle for that. Despite her utter predictability, she was the only woman who'd ever managed to confound him—and on a regular basis no less.

Glancing at his watch, he realized it was five minutes past the time they had agreed upon. Punctuality had never been his strong suit, especially outside of work. What surprised him, though, was when the maître d' told him that Dayle hadn't arrived yet. Promptness was the woman's middle name. Where was she?

He ordered a cocktail and sipped it as he waited at their table, hoping the vodka martini would sand down the roughest edges of his apprehension. What did she want to talk about? She'd nearly KO'd him with the announcement of her engagement earlier in the day. He hadn't seen that particular punch coming, even if she had been dating Ryan for years. Max had just managed to find his footing again when she'd suggested that they meet for dinner so that they could discuss the future.

It was never a good thing when a woman said she wanted to chat and then used the F-word. He gave his cocktail a stir.

Max had made it a hard and fast rule not to discuss anything past the next twenty-four hours with females. If they seemed bent on going beyond that, he derailed the conversation with sex. A good, drawn-out, make-'em-weep orgasm was all but guaranteed to numb the mind and force a woman to forget all about such trivialities as where a relationship was heading.

But seduction wouldn't work this time. This was Dayle. She wasn't a woman to be wooed, won and then gently dispatched before too much entanglement ensued. She was his partner, his friend, his better half…in business.

He spied her then, winding her way through the white linen-topped tables. Business was forgotten. She'd taken his suggestion and had changed her clothes. And, oh, what a change.

Dayle rarely wore skirts to the office—a pity in Max's mind since she had a first-class pair of legs. Her legs, among other things, made an appearance tonight thanks to a clingy black slip of a dress that showcased her every curve. As a connoisseur of the female anatomy, Max liked what he saw. Indeed, he liked it a little too much if the uncomfortable fit of his jockey shorts at the moment was any indication. He reached for his martini and reminded himself that not only was she his business partner, but she was now engaged to be married. He'd meant it when he said he didn't cheat. Nor did he believe in getting involved with those who did.

When she reached the table, Max stood and offered a smile that was just this side of leering because he knew that was what she expected. With a dismissive nod to the mâitre d', he took both of Dayle's hands in his. Holding her an arm's length away, he murmured, "Well, look at you."

Barefoot, Dayle stood nearly five-ten, so in her three-inch-high, pencil-thin heels they were the same height. Some men might be intimidated by that. He'd always found it a turn-on.

"Hello, Max."

"Hello. Are you sure you want to marry Ryan?" he asked.

She blinked. "Wh-why do you ask?"

He let his gaze meander downward. "Because that little black dress you're wearing is telling me otherwise."

"You're hearing things again," she replied on a laugh, turning her head and leaning in for his kiss.

Max's lips brushed her cheek and he forced himself to back away when he felt tempted to move a little lower and to the left. He'd kissed her on the mouth only once, and years ago now, but he knew better than to do it again, even in this crowded, upscale restaurant where things couldn't progress to anything that could remotely be deemed sensual.

"You do look lovely." He pulled out her chair and, when she was seated, dropped a kiss on her nape, which her upswept hair had left exposed. She turned, eyes the color of amethysts opening wide. "Couldn't resist. You have a very nibble-worthy neck," he said with an apologetic shrug before coming around to take his place.

"Sorry I'm late."

"Don't be. You made quite an entrance." And he meant it. Heads had turned; heads belonging to men. Max had felt both smug and proprietary when she'd come to him.

"That wasn't my intention," she said, looking dismayed.

Of course it wasn't. Dayle wasn't the kind of woman who resorted to pretense. It was one of her qualities that Max admired. One of the many.

"It's not like you to be late. I was worried." He didn't realize how true the words were until they were out. Sitting there alone, waiting, he had been concerned and not just about the future she'd said she wanted to discuss.

"Really?" In the soft light of the dining room her fair, flawless skin glowed. Most of the women he knew were tanned, whether from idle time spent in the sun somewhere or at a salon. Not Dayle. She was decidedly pale. And perfect.

As his fingers tightened on the stem of his martini glass he vowed with intentional overstatement, "Practically beside myself. I was ready to call out the National Guard."

"Well, thank God you showed some restraint. The

truth is I couldn't decide what to wear. I even made Beth come over to help me." She touched the side of her head. "She did my hair."

"Your friend is a true talent." He lifted his glass in salute.

"I'll tell her you said so. I wanted to look my best." Just when he began to feel flattered that maybe meeting him for dinner had something to do with her uncharacteristic fussing, in an awed whisper she added, "This place is so amazing."

Max swore he heard his ego deflate. "Isn't it, though?"

She was glancing around. "I didn't want to feel underdressed."

One side of his mouth rose. "And so you wore that itty-bitty number?"

Her gaze snapped back to his. "It's not too…you know."

"Oh, no. Not nearly, especially for my taste. You always look classy," he assured her. And he meant it.

A waiter stopped for her drink order then and she glanced over at Max's half-empty glass. "What is that you're having?"

"A vodka martini." On a wink, he added, "Dirty."

She frowned.

"It's made with olive juice," he clarified.

"I'll have the same," she told the waiter.

Once they were alone, he asked, "Feeling adventurous tonight?" He'd never known Dayle to sip anything other than a crisp white wine.

"I guess I feel the need for a little kick of courage."

"You won't find that in a glass," Max told her.

"No, but then I won't care, will I?"

Nerves tingled again, causing his right foot to tap under the table. "Why don't you tell me what you wanted to talk about? My curiosity, among other things, is begging to be satisfied."

The suggestive comment earned no reprimand. Instead she asked, "Are you sure you don't want to wait until after we've had dinner?"

"That unappetizing?" He plucked up the small wooden skewer from his glass and ate one of the olives.

"Of course not." But Dayle's nervous laughter offered little reassurance.

"Come on. I'm all ears."

Max ate the remaining olive as he watched her moisten her lips. She'd painted them red tonight. Red, the color of passion. And the color that accompanied warnings of danger.

"Well, as you know, Ryan and I will be getting married this summer," she began.

A sharp pain lanced Max's breastbone. He'd felt its twin earlier that day, back at the office upon first hearing the news. This time he chalked it up to the vodka. He really shouldn't drink on an empty stomach, a couple of olives notwithstanding. Yet he raised his glass and sipped again after saying, "Unless I can persuade you otherwise."

"Right." Her gaze flicked toward the ceiling. "Well, one of the reasons we decided against a lengthy engagement is that he's accepted a new position. It's an excellent opportunity for advancement in his field."

Ryan was an engineer of some sort. "Good for him."

"Yes." She moistened those red lips again. *Danger! Danger!* his brain screamed as she added, "But it involves a move."

Both of Max's feet were tapping now. He thought he could hear the muffled thuds of his wingtips as they slapped the carpet. Or was that his heart? "Here in the city?" he managed in a casual tone.

"No." Dayle plucked at the linen tablecloth, her own nerves showing. "Actually in California."

The thuds had definitely come from his heart and it was now in Max's throat. He sought to dislodge it with a discreet gulp of his martini. "That's the other side of the country."

"Gee, Max, your grasp of geography is impressive."

Where he usually enjoyed her barbed comebacks, just now he was feeling too dazed for such repartee. "Are you moving, too?"

"Yes."

He stated the obvious. "To California."

No razzing this time. She nodded. "San Francisco."

"Am I really losing you, Dayle?"

Her brow furrowed. "Losing me?"

He took another liberal sip of his cocktail, giving him time to resurrect his easygoing façade. "You know, as a business partner. Are you asking me to buy you out?"

That was his major concern, Max told himself. He didn't need her. The company did.

"Of course not. We're partners, Max. I'm in for the long haul. It's just that I can do my job from anywhere thanks to technology and the Internet. Half the time you and I are on opposites of the globe."

It was true, but no matter where he went, he always felt connected to her, anchored in a way that he didn't care to analyze, especially now.

"Besides," she was saying, "we've talked about expanding again. This is the ideal time, not to mention that California is the ideal location. I can head up a West Coast office."

Dayle's proposal made perfect sense, he thought, while he listened to her expand on it for the next several minutes, during which time her drink arrived and he finished his. As always, she'd done her homework. She'd come armed with facts, statistics, ideas and her customary enthusiasm.

As a businessman Max knew she was right. Yet as his feet tapped faster under the table, the only thing that registered was that the one person he'd considered a permanent fixture in his life soon wouldn't be there to greet him when his wandering feet grew weary and brought him home.

CHAPTER THREE

OVER the next couple of months, while Max concentrated on Globetrotter's expansion, Dayle concentrated on her wedding plans. That proved the more trying of the two endeavors, but only because her mother insisted on calling three times a day to find out what she'd come up with and then making contradicting suggestions.

Dayle wasn't exactly ecstatic to be relocating to San Francisco, her expanded duties at Globetrotter's aside. She was a born and bred New Yorker, and her friends and family were here. Which brought her to the city by the bay's key selling point: it was three time zones and a long flight from Lorna.

"I'm going to be in Italy in April," Max announced one morning in mid-March. He stood framed in Dayle's doorway like a piece of pricy artwork in his crisp white shirt and cashmere jacket. "I've got a meeting in Milan about Bruno's new fall line and I'm going to Venice to meet with a couple of potential clients, including a sculptor I met on the previous trip."

"Is this trip business or pleasure?" she asked, arching one eyebrow in speculation.

"Business." But then his tone turned sly. "And it's entirely my pleasure."

Dayle sighed. "How long will you be gone?"

"Missing me already?"

"Always," she replied, but without inflection.

In truth, though, she did miss Max when he was away. She enjoyed his company, the give-and-take of their banter. She even enjoyed his clever double entendres and endless flirting. His friendship was another of the reasons that the thought of moving to San Francisco was proving so difficult.

He entered her office as she called up the master calendar they kept on the computer. Instead of taking a seat in one of the chairs, he hiked up a pant leg and settled his hip on the edge of her desk, as was his habit. Pointing to the calendar, he said, "I'm thinking of leaving on that Monday, staying in Rome a couple days, and then heading to Venice. I should be back by the end of the week."

Dayle typed in the dates and ignored the way his cologne tangled up her hormones. God, the stuff was potent. Sex in a bottle. "Has Cara made your travel arrangements yet?" she asked, referring to the secretary they shared.

"Yes. I'll be at the Gabriella in Rome and staying at the same place I did last time while in Venice."

"The Marquis? Again?" That surprised her. Usually Max liked to mix things up. "Any special…reason?" It was code for woman and he knew it.

"Not how you mean. The rooms were first-rate and the service was excellent, especially with so much going on."

"A wedding, right?" Dayle said, trying to recall the old conversation.

They always went over everything when he came back from a trip. Sometimes, he even called her at home, regardless of the hour, just to tell her that he'd returned and to recap the high points. Not everything they discussed had to do with business. He told her about the sights, the sounds, the interesting people he'd met and the new foods he'd tried. She enjoyed his travelogues almost as much as he enjoyed telling them.

"A wedding? Oh, no." Deep laughter rumbled. "This was Bridezilla, a philandering groom and thirty-two temperamental guests, according to the concierge." He winked then, before adding, "We played cards one evening."

"Let me guess. Strip poker?"

"Please. The concierge was a man. Now, had I managed to talk a couple of the very lovely clerks from the front desk into joining us…" He let his words trail off on a wolfish smile.

"You work too hard, Max," she drawled. The leather of her chair groaned softly as she leaned back, subtly putting more distance between them. Even so, the scent of his cologne followed her and seemed to beckon.

"I do work hard, every bit as hard as you do. The only difference between us, Dayle, is that I play hard, too."

He had her there, so she picked up a fountain pen, a gift he'd brought her from London, and said nothing.

Max went on. "You needn't stay chained to your desk, you know. I've told you often enough that you're welcome to travel. In fact, as head of our new West

Coast office, some buying trips might be inevitable, at least at first. I still haven't found a competent counterpart for me."

"That's because you're one of a kind."

A grin creased the hollows of his cheeks. "I'm glad you finally realize that, sweetheart."

Her telephone rang. Before she could reach for it, Max had snatched up the receiver. "Globetrotter's. We bring the world's goods to you and your goods to the world."

Dayle rolled her eyes. He seemed to come up with a new business slogan every week.

"Ah, Lorna. I was just telling your daughter how sorry I was that I wasn't here yesterday when you stopped in."

Dayle rolled her eyes again, but didn't reach for the telephone. She was hardly eager to talk to her mother for what would be the second time that day. And it wasn't even noon.

"Dayle?" Max was saying. "Actually she's right here. Yes. I'm in her office, trying to persuade her to dump that bum she's engaged to and run off with me." He chuckled softly at something Lorna said, before adding, "We'd give you beautiful grandbabies."

He stroked the side of Dayle's face as he said it and she shivered. His eyebrows rose fractionally. She glanced away, busying herself with paperwork.

"So, what's new with the wedding plans?" he asked, eliciting a groan from Dayle. "Really? No, your daughter didn't mention that. Three hundred guests." He whistled between his teeth. She issued an oath and felt the headache she'd chased away with three aspirin a couple of hours earlier throb back to life. "Well, I'll let you speak to Dayle. Yes. Nice talking to you, too."

Before handing her the telephone, he said softly, "Deep breath and then exhale, sweetheart. And remember, the woman gave you life."

Hand cupped over the receiver, Dayle muttered, "Yes, and for that reason she feels she's entitled to run it."

"In and out, in and out," Max said, motioning with both of his hands as he stood.

Dayle sent him a black look and brought the telephone to her ear. "Mom, hi." She managed this in a cheerful voice that had Max nodding in approval before he slipped out of her office. Once he was out of earshot, Dayle snarled, "Three hundred guests! Mother, I thought we agreed to no more than half that."

"We can't exclude my cousin Arlene's family." Lorna's tone was reproachful. "They were so good to me after your father died."

"Yes, but I wasn't aware Arlene had so many children."

"Don't be ridiculous, Dayle. If we include Arlene, then you know we must include her neighbors, the Thompsons. They've invited us to all of their children's weddings. And then, of course, there are the Bakers. They're such nice people."

Dayle tuned out at that point. Now she remembered exactly why she'd opted to elope the first time around. Her wedding to Ryan was turning into a three-ring circus rather than the intimate and romantic affair she'd imagined.

After talking to her mother, she called Ryan with a summary of the conversation, eager for an ally.

"So she wants to invite people you haven't seen in a decade. Is that really so bad?" he asked.

His response wasn't what she'd hoped to hear.

"I want something small and tasteful. You, me, a couple of attendants, our folks and a smattering of close friends. I told her that. I've told her that repeatedly. Now I have three hundred people coming to watch me prance down the aisle."

"You don't need to prance," Ryan said on a chuckle.

Dayle ignored his attempt at humor. "She doesn't like the dress I picked out or the cake's design. She wants a band rather than the nice string quartet I interviewed. With three hundred people, we're going to need to find a bigger reception hall." She tapped the tip of her pen against the deck blotter in irritation. "I don't even know that I can get the deposit back at this point."

"Don't worry about the money," he soothed.

"It's not the money. It's…her. She's taking over just like she tries to take over everything in my life."

"She's just excited, Dayle. For that matter, so is my mother. From what I understand, they've had their heads together," he said.

She groaned and was half hoping he would take her seriously when she asked, "Can't we just elope?"

"No. Now that I've finally convinced you to be my wife, I want a proper wedding. Something we both will remember well into our golden years."

"This is promising to be memorable for all the wrong reasons."

Ryan sounded slightly impatient when he replied, "It's just one day, Dayle."

After she hung up, she wilted back in her seat on a sigh. "It's just one day. But it's supposed to be *my* day."

When she glanced up, Max was standing in the doorway. "Want to talk about it?" he asked.

She straightened. "How long have you been there?"

"Long enough."

"Were you eavesdropping?"

"Shamelessly," he agreed on an affable grin. "I came by to see if you wanted to go to lunch with me and heard you talking. Unfortunately I could only hear your side of the conversation. You can fill me in on the parts I missed over a glass of wine," he invited.

"I have a bottle of water in the fridge."

"I'll throw in a Cobb salad," he replied, upping the ante.

He had her attention, but she held firm. "I brought tuna made with light mayo on marbled rye."

He wrinkled his nose. "Save it for tomorrow or, better yet, take it home and feed it to your cat."

"I don't have a cat."

"Give it to a stray, then. I know this cozy little bistro that makes the best soups—the perfect accompaniment to that salad I mentioned."

Dayle gave in as her stomach growled. "Why not?"

The cozy bistro turned out to be a gourmet restaurant in the theater district where the waitstaff knew Max by name.

"I'm a regular," he admitted on a shrug as they were led to their table. She didn't bother to protest even after catching a glimpse of the prices on the lunch menu, although she did mutter, "Nothing about you is regular, Max. Do you ever do anything halfway?"

"Why would I? Besides, only the best for you," he said lightly. "I'm trying to sweep you off your feet, remember? Only three months till your wedding. I don't have much time to make you change your mind."

"What would you do if I did?" Dayle couldn't believe she'd thought the question, much less asked it. Silently she blamed stress, nerves…her mother, and then laughed aloud, hoping to turn it into a joke. Max laughed, too. Interestingly, though, he didn't have a comeback handy.

After the waiter took their order, Dayle poured out her frustrations, ending with, "And I can't talk Ryan into eloping."

"That's because he's a smart man. He knows there will be no living with Lorna or his mother, for that matter, afterward."

Dayle cast her gaze skyward. "Will no one agree with me about anything today?"

"It's not that I'm disagreeing with you. I just understand Ryan's point. And Lorna's. And his mother's."

"Max—"

"I'm not finished. I have a suggestion. A compromise that might suit all parties involved."

She narrowed her eyes. "I wasn't aware you knew how to compromise when it came to personal relationships."

"I know how it's done. I simply prefer not to do it.

Besides, we're not talking about me. We're talking about you. Are you interested or not?"

"I'm listening," she said.

"Your mother wants to showcase her only daughter's big day. So, let her."

"That's your idea of a compromise?" she sputtered.

His sigh was exaggerated. "You really need to learn patience, Dayle. You're always rushing things, pressing ahead."

"That's only because you take so damned long."

Brows arching, he replied, "I've never had a woman complain about that."

Heat suffused her face. It curled elsewhere in her body when, for just one moment, she allowed herself to imagine Max taking his time. "Mmm."

He glanced at her in puzzlement. Had she made that sound aloud? Just in case, she said, "This soup is heaven in a bowl."

His frown intensified. "You haven't eaten any of it yet."

"Well, it smells like heaven." She picked up her spoon and motioned with it. "Can you get to the meat of your compromise at some point before the dinner crowd starts to arrive?"

"No patience," he said again with a shake of his head. But he went on. "As I was saying, let your mother showcase your day. Inform her that you've decided you want to hold your wedding someplace special, at some romantic, out-of-the-way destination that will give her supreme bragging rights, but be pricy enough to limit whom she can invite."

"Sneaky," Dayle murmured. "And to think my mother trusts you."

"She doesn't just trust me," Max corrected. "She adores me. If she were a few years younger she'd be all over me, giving you stiff competition for my affection."

"Please." Dayle pulled a face and waved a hand. "I'm trying to eat here." But then she asked seriously, "So you think I should take the show on the road, so to speak?"

"Only a fool would presume to tell you what to think. I'm merely suggesting that an out-of-town site, some-place exclusive, would encourage a small and select guest list."

"Small and select." She smiled. "I like those adjectives."

"I thought they might appeal to you." He grinned in return. "No matter where it's held, I'll be invited, right?"

"Of course." Dayle dabbed at her mouth with her napkin before setting it aside. She'd been waiting for the right time to ask him something. This appeared to be it. "Max, I need a favor."

"Name it." His grin was magnanimous.

"You and I go back a long way. Besides Beth, I consider you one of my best friends," she began.

"Same goes. Of course, you're also the only female friend I haven't slept with." His grin turned wicked and his voice dipped to a husky whisper. "We could remedy that, you know."

She shook her head. "I prefer my status as the one who got away."

He nodded. "Smart. Makes you irresistible."

"Right." Dayle pressed on. "As you know, my father is gone. Mom wants me to ask my uncle Lyle to stand in on my wedding day. Uncle Lyle is a nice man, but honestly, I haven't seen him in half a dozen years and we were never what I would call close. And so I was wondering—hoping, actually—that I could persuade you to walk me down the aisle."

She finished with a smile. Max, however, was frowning. At the outset of her request he'd appeared touched, humbled even. Now he just looked surprised and not in a good way. His face had turned decidedly ashen.

"You're asking me to give you away?"

"Yes."

His voice was hoarse, although this throaty whisper no longer appeared to be intended as sexy. "But what if I want to keep you?"

Dayle blinked. Sure she hadn't heard him right, she leaned closer. "Max?"

Max sucked in a breath. It took him a moment to regroup, especially with her watching him, her Elizabeth Taylor eyes filled with confusion and even a little concern. Finally he managed his signature smile. "Of course I'll do it. I'd love to. In fact, I'm honored to be asked."

Her expression brightened. "Terrific. Thank you."

"Don't mention it." He adjusted his French cuffs, needing something to occupy his hands. "Besides, it will give me an excuse to buy a new tuxedo while I'm in Italy. No one makes a penguin suit quite like Armani."

Dayle reached across the table and laid a hand on his arm. "It means a lot to me."

Max smiled in return, helpless to do anything but. Dayle looked so relieved, so pleased. She looked so damned grateful. He felt that familiar white-hot poker jab just below his breastbone. The pain seemed omnipresent these days. He really should go see a doctor. Maybe he had an ulcer. Maybe something was wrong with his heart.

The latter seemed more likely, since when he replied, "*You* mean a lot to me," the pain grew worse.

CHAPTER FOUR

"I'm coming with you," Dayle announced.

Max's brows shot up at that. It was late on a Friday afternoon and he was just pulling on his overcoat, preparing to leave the office for the weekend. On Monday morning he would depart for Italy. "Where? Home?" he asked. Then he smiled. "Interested in giving me a private send-off?"

Her breath hissed out on an impatient sigh. "I'm talking about Venice."

It was his breath that hissed out then. "Venice?"

He must have been staring blankly at her because Dayle snapped her fingers in front of his face and added in a dry tone, "Yes, Venice. The city in Italy with all those canals."

"And you want to go with me," he repeated in an effort to buy some time, because for just a moment his heart had bucked out a few extra beats, thudding with the kind of robust intensity it did after he'd finished a particularly punishing workout…or a bout of passionate sex.

"Yes. I do," Dayle said on a nod.

I do. They were two small words that reeled in his

libido, for soon enough they would make her another man's wife. As they stood in Globetrotter's tastefully decorated lobby, he jingled his keys and considered how best to handle this situation.

"But you never go on buying trips," he began.

She merely shrugged. "Never say never. Isn't that one of the mottos you live by?"

Dayle had him there. Sort of. His gaze lowered briefly to her mouth. Her lips were tinted their usual respectable shade of peach and curved in a smile. *Never* did apply in one instance. Or rather, *never again*.

"Besides," she was saying, "you told me I need to gain more experience in buying since I'll need to go on some trips for Globetrotter's West Coast office."

Yes, he had said that, but he hadn't intended for the comment to be construed as an invitation. In fact, he'd been looking forward to his trip to Italy precisely because it would put an entire ocean between him and Dayle.

The closer her wedding came, the closer her move to the West Coast marched, the more restless Max felt. Oh, he'd always been restless, unable to stay put in one place for long. He needed adventure, craved excitement. He was addicted to new sights, sounds, scents and tastes. He was like his old man in that regard, always eager to be off, to try something new. Always eager to spend time with new people…new women, though in his case one at a time and without breaking any sacred vows.

This restlessness, though, was different. Exactly how, he couldn't say. But it stemmed from his feelings for Dayle, of that much, he was certain. He liked her. No, he *adored* her, he admitted as he studied her lovely face. Admiration came into play, too. She was smart, determined. She'd picked herself up after the heartache and betrayal of her divorce, and had made a new and better life for herself.

"You're an amazing woman," he murmured.

She nodded impatiently, taking his heartfelt comment in stride. He supposed her reaction was to be expected since he was a serial flatterer as well as a shameless flirt. In this case, however, he was being utterly sincere.

It struck him then that in his own limited way, he loved Dayle. Well, as much as he was capable of truly loving any woman. Perhaps because of that, Max wanted the absolute best for her. And though he generally entertained an exceptionally high opinion of himself, he'd always known she deserved better than the likes of him. He couldn't give Dayle the one thing she required from a man: stability.

He would never be the nine-to-five sort, the kind of man who would punch a clock, carve out a life with a wife and two-point-four kids in suburbia, coach Little League, host neighborhood barbecues and, heaven forbid, wear synthetic fabrics purchased off the rack.

That was Ryan. Good old Ryan. The lucky bastard.

"I had an epiphany last night," Dayle was saying.

"Oh? Were you alone at the time?" He sent her a lecherous smile, feeling his footing return now that common sense had been resurrected. Love wasn't for him. Not the "till death do us part" kind anyway.

"Max," she warned.

"Sorry. Old habits."

Apparently mollified, she went on. "Remember how you suggested Ryan and I get married out of town? Someplace select to discourage the large guest list my mother has in mind?"

"I recall that," he said slowly as apprehension did a tap dance up his spine.

"Well, I was flipping through a bridal magazine while eating some takeout the other night, and it had this entire spread on destination weddings. It got me thinking. I've always loved Venice," she said.

"Understandable. It's a great city, but, Dayle—"

She cut him off. "Really, of all the places you've traveled for business, the only time I've ever felt the slightest bit of envy was when you've gone there. The canals, the palaces, St. Mark's Square…" She smiled dreamily.

Her soft expression tugged at him. How many times while he'd been in Venice—or other places, for that matter—had he wished she was with him, seeing the sights, savoring them alongside him? "With the right person it can be incredibly romantic," he admitted.

"No doubt you have plenty of firsthand knowledge of that."

"I'm too much of a gentleman to say." He busied himself with the buttons of his overcoat. But he couldn't help wondering, did he? Oh, he'd found romance in Venice and other places around the globe, for that matter. Romance in its most earthy form. The interludes all blended together now. Not a single one, not a single *woman*, stood out. Romance with the right person? Apparently not.

Frowning, he shoved his hands into his coat pockets. What was wrong with him? That was what he wanted. That was how he'd planned it. He didn't want permanence, memories, ties. None of those suited his personality, his lifestyle. Unlike his father, Max trod carefully when it came to others' feelings and so he never made promises he wasn't capable of keeping.

"Getting married in Venice would be ideal," Dayle said. "It would be small and intimate, for the sake of logistics alone. My mother couldn't invite second cousins and neighbors I haven't seen since puberty."

"I don't know," he hedged, still feeling uneasy.

"Come on, Max. Venice is romantic, stylish. You said I deserved that."

He smiled weakly. Nothing like having one's own words tossed back in the face. They hit a bull's-eye, making it all but impossible to object. Still, he gave it his best shot.

"I'll only be there a few days, and if you're serious about going on sales calls with me, business will keep us busy for a good portion of that. Surely you'll need more time to make the kind of plans you're talking about."

"You're absolutely right," she agreed. But, damn, she was smiling. "Which is why I took the liberty of booking us rooms for another week and a half."

"Us?" he asked.

"You'll stay on in Venice with me, won't you? Please, Max," she pleaded. "You know the city so well."

"Like the back of my hand," he murmured as his gaze flicked to her left one and the ring that encircled her third finger. The diamond caught the light, shooting sparks. One seemed to land on his chest. Damned heartburn. He reached into his pocket for the roll of antacids he'd begun to carry.

"I'm due a vacation," she said. "You're always after me to take off more time and go someplace exciting. Do you mean it or are you all talk?"

"I've never been accused of being all talk," he replied.

"Well?"

Neither had Max ever been one to back down from a challenge, but he chewed the chalky tablet and took his time answering, coming up with more questions instead. "What about Ryan? What does he say?"

"He's all for it." She laughed then. "He finally admitted to me that his mother is driving him to distraction, too."

"Will he be coming to Venice with us?"

"I wish," she said on a sigh. "Unfortunately he has a training seminar for his new position. But don't worry. He has complete faith in my judgment."

"Excellent."

"And he trusts you."

"He trusts me?" Max asked, unable to mask his surprise. Were the shoe on the other foot, Max knew trust wouldn't be forthcoming.

But Dayle was nodding. "He's well aware that you have impeccable taste."

Max worked up a smile. "Yes."

"And he knows that you know quality when you see it."

Max's gaze lowered to Dayle's lips again, lingering for a moment longer than he intended. "Quality," he murmured.

Beth sat cross-legged on Dayle's bed, drinking some foul-looking energy drink she'd picked up at a health-food store on her way to the apartment. She was half a head shorter than Dayle, with an athlete's lean body. She always seemed to be in training for some marathon or grueling fitness event. Not surprisingly, they'd met at the gym. Beth had been going through her own divorce at the time. As a person who had been there, done that, Dayle had held her hand through the painful ordeal.

Officially Beth was at Dayle's apartment to help her pack for Venice and go through the many files Dayle had downloaded from the Internet. Unofficially she was there to play devil's advocate. Beth had a law degree and worked in the district attorney's office. She also had a streak of romance as wide as the Atlantic. Put the two together and her imagination had been working overtime ever since Dayle told her she was jetting off to Venice. To meet Max.

"I still can't believe Ryan is letting you go." She slurped the last bit of unappetizing green goo through the straw and set the cup on the nightstand.

"I'm thirty-six, Beth. I stopped asking people for permission nearly two decades ago."

"You know what I mean."

"I haven't a clue," she said, opting to play dumb, even

though her friend had long maintained that Max secretly carried a torch for Dayle.

"Mark my words, he's going to try to talk you out of marrying Ryan," her friend insisted.

"Max?" Dayle shook her head and snorted. "Yeah, right. Like he's interested in me that way."

"I've seen the way he looks at you," Beth supplied. "He wants you."

Her friend's blunt assessment made Dayle's hands shake. Even so, she took her time carefully folding a cashmere sweater set and setting it in her suitcase. Eyes downcast, she said matter-of-factly, "He looks at every female between the ages of eighteen and eighty the exact same way. He's a flirt, Beth."

"Okay. I've seen the way you look at him."

When Dayle glanced over, Beth offered her most confident litigator's smile. Dayle returned to the closet and began riffling through hangers in an effort to compose herself. After a moment, she turned, holding out a dress in one hand and a pantsuit in the other.

"What do you think?"

"I think you're avoiding my question."

Dayle tossed the garments onto the bed and folded her arms. "Oh? Is this a cross-examination? I thought we were having a conversation."

"It's a little of both." Beth shrugged, not the least bit contrite or intimidated.

The women had been friends for nearly a decade, offering encouragement, giving one another advice, whether solicited or not. They didn't keep secrets from one another. Which made Dayle feel especially guilty for keeping this one. The truth was, as much as she loved Ryan, as much as she appreciated his steadfastness, she'd never felt with him the smallest flicker of sexual satisfaction. Heaven help her, but Max could look at Dayle across a stack of invoices, smile in that debonair, dangerous way of his and spark more heat than Ryan could manage in a marathon of inventive foreplay. It wasn't right. It wasn't fair. But it was a fact.

Still, she said dismissively, "Max is harmless."

"We were talking about you."

"What's to talk about? I'm going to Venice to plan my wedding. *To Ryan,*" she stressed. "If I were interested in Max in any way other than professionally, I certainly wouldn't have accepted Ryan's proposal of marriage."

That was sound logic. She'd used it to quiet her own conscience. So she smiled confidently.

"About that," Beth began. "We've been friends for a long time and I like Ryan. You know I do."

"Of course."

"I'm glad. So, please, don't take this the wrong way."

Nerves fluttered and Dayle had the insane urge to stick her fingers in her ears and start singing at the top of her lungs.

Instead she opted to act like a grown-up. "Take what the wrong way?"

"Honey, are you sure about this?"

"About Venice?" Dayle asked, hoping that that was the "this" to which her friend referred. Of course it wasn't.

"No. About marrying Ryan?" Beth asked softly.

Dayle pushed away the niggling doubts that usually only crowded in late at night when she was alone and feeling the most vulnerable. In a brisk tone she replied, "Beth, honestly, Ryan and I have been dating for four years."

Unperturbed, Beth replied, "That's one of the reasons I ask."

"I didn't want to rush into marriage. You of all people should understand that."

"I understand caution." Beth nodded. "But there's a great deal of difference between rushing and moving at a reasonable pace. Four years is…well, glacial, especially at this point in your life. It's not like you were waiting for him to finish college and for you to get your career established. You were both doing well professionally when you met. So, ask yourself, what's been the holdup?"

"There's no need to ask myself. I know. The timing wasn't right. And it is now," Dayle insisted.

But later that evening, after Beth had gone home and Dayle had finished packing, she wondered if the timing felt right or if she'd felt cornered. The proposal had come out of the blue, their longtime relationship notwithstanding. Ryan had told her he was taking the job in California after it was already a fact. Dayle knew not many couples could make a go of a long-distance romance. So she had felt pressured to accept his offer of marriage. After all, saying no essentially would have ended their relationship, and that wasn't what she wanted.

Was it?

CHAPTER FIVE

DAYLE arrived at Marco Polo International Airport early in the day, at least according to the clock. Her body was still operating on New York time, which meant she should be sleeping or at the very least just waking up. Oddly neither the long flight from JFK nor the three-hour layover in Amsterdam had drained her of energy. She'd been awake for both legs of the trip. Wide-awake and thinking. And she didn't care for the direction of her thoughts.

She blamed Beth. Her friend's well-meaning comments had Dayle second-guessing not only her engagement but her entire relationship with Ryan. Doubts were normal, she told herself as the Fasten Seat Belts sign blinked off. And these really weren't doubts so much as prewedding jitters. Every bride was entitled to those. Now that she was in Italy to plan her wedding without her mother's sniping or interference everything would be fine. So convinced, Dayle stood, retrieved her carry-on bag from the overhead compartment and took her place in the queue of deplaning passengers.

Inside the airport, she spotted Max easily enough amid the crowd of people eagerly awaiting loved ones.

A man that classically handsome, that sophisticated and self-possessed was impossible to miss. Her heart did a funny little somersault when he spied her and a welcoming smile creased his cheeks. The jitters she'd just managed to quell staged a second uprising. She blamed these on jet lag and pushed through the crowd toward him. Max met her halfway. Ever the gentleman, he was reaching for the thick strap of her bag to transfer it to his shoulder even before offering a greeting.

"Hello, Dayle. Welcome to Italy." Max smoothed the hair back from her face, tucking it behind her ears. Then he kissed both of her cheeks. "I trust your trip was uneventful."

"Pretty much." She wouldn't think of those doubts now.

"You look lovely, as always. An absolute vision."

Max's comment was over-the-top, and Dayle couldn't help chuckling. "I look travel-weary and wrinkled. *You* look lovely."

His brows rose at the compliment.

"New suit?" she inquired. She brushed the coat's lapels before giving in to the urge to rest her palms flush against his chest. It was solid, warm and oh so inviting. She pulled her hands away.

"I got it while I was in Rome," he confirmed on a nod. "The tailor worked overtime to ensure it was ready before I had to leave." He took a step back. "So, what do you think?"

"Hmm, nice." It was more than nice, especially on Max. The man had a body that was made for suits. The soft wool gabardine of this one hung elegantly on his lean frame. She meant it when she said, "It almost does you justice."

"Now there's a compliment. You must be exhausted to so willingly feed my ego."

She hadn't been tired a moment ago, but she was now. So much so that when he put his arm around her shoulders and said, "Let's get your luggage," she leaned against him rather than try to step away. At the baggage carousel, he asked, "How many suitcases do you have?"

"Just one in addition to my carry-on." That bit of news had him scowling until he saw it come around on the conveyor belt.

"It's a good thing I'm physically fit," he teased. "How on earth did you manage to get it to Kennedy airport?"

"It does have wheels," she replied pointedly. But then admitted, "I gave a very generous tip to both the cab-driver and the porter."

"Generous, hmm? I'll look forward to claiming mine later."

He offered a sinful smile that sent heat slithering down her spine before it coiled in her stomach, as dangerous as a snake preparing to strike. She sucked in a breath and relied on practicality to tame it.

"The suitcase is way over on the weight limit. I had to pay extra when I got to the airport, so be sure to lift with your knees. I wouldn't want your back to go out."

"That makes two of us." His smile remained wicked and he winked. Dayle felt snakebit.

They took a water taxi to their hotel, which was in a prime location on the Grand Canal. Despite the overcast sky, chilly April weather and her own growing fatigue, Dayle couldn't help but be enthralled as the boat chugged through the city that had defied the sea for centuries. She'd seen pictures of the place. Dazzling full-color photographs in travel brochures and on the Internet that paid homage to the ornate architecture and colorful façades. But nothing had prepared her for the reality that was Venice. The city exuded an intoxicating mix of charm, whimsy and decadence. Just like Max. And it was definitely romantic, sensual and seductive. Just like…

"Incredible, isn't it?" Max whispered the words in her ear. His breath tickled like a feather, which surely was the only reason she shivered.

She turned her head toward him. "Yes. I love it and I can see why you love it, too. The place suits you."

"Oh?" He arched an eyebrow at that.

Dayle chose not to enlighten him. Instead she changed the subject. "It's the perfect destination for my wedding. I can't wait to phone Ryan and tell him."

Frowning, Max glanced away. "So, I take it that Lorna is on board with the change in venue."

"More or less." She shrugged. No sense recounting the blistering, three-hour war of words that had followed Dayle's announcement that she and Ryan planned to exchange vows in Venice. Of course, with Max, there was no need.

"Sorry. I'll give her a call when we return to the States, see if I can't help smooth the waters."

And he could, too. Not a woman alive was immune to the man's charm. Well, except for Dayle.

"She wanted to come with me on this trip," she told him.

"How did you manage to talk her out of it?"

"Actually I didn't. Ryan came to my rescue. He told her that he needed someone to keep an eye on his apartment while he's out of town at his training seminar."

"The man's a saint," Max said dryly.

"He is," Dayle insisted. "Especially since my mother probably will have poked into every drawer and cubbyhole before he comes back. I'm sure she already has the contents of his medicine cabinet memorized."

"Remind me never to ask Lorna to house-sit for me."

"Afraid she'd discover something that might change her high opinion of you?"

"We all have our secrets," he replied lightly.

What, Dayle wondered, were his?

They reached their hotel a few minutes later. Max was on a first-name basis with the entire staff, not to mention several of the guests. They greeted him with an enthusiastic *buon giorno*. The smiles of the women were far more frank than those of the men. Dayle tried not to be annoyed, especially since thanks to Max's familiarity she was checked in and ensconced in her suite in short order.

Her rooms were located next to Max's on the hotel's third floor. Both of their suites offered lovely vistas of the canal, a perk that was reflected in the price. Well worth the splurge, Dayle decided, as she let the sheer draperies fall back into place. The hotel would definitely make the list of possible accommodations for wedding guests. Not only was the view stunning, the interior was lovely. All of the furnishings were top-of-the-line reproductions that did justice to the building's architecture and Venice's storied history. A soothing color palette of soft rose and gold added to the sumptuous ambience.

Dayle was just getting ready to kick off her shoes and lie down when a knock sounded at the door. Max was leaning against the frame when she opened it. He held a bottle of red wine in one hand and a foil-wrapped box of truffles in the other. His smile was as enticing as the chocolates. Dayle ignored it and the accompanying tug low in her belly. In a bored voice she informed him, "If you've come to seduce me, I'm too tired."

Having said so, she moved aside to let him enter. Not in the least put off by her tone, he fell in step beside her as she walked to the sitting room.

"You always seem to have sex on your mind, Dayle. I wonder why that is?" He didn't give her a chance to respond. He set the wine and truffles next to the flower arrangement on the entryway table. "Actually these are compliments of the hotel. I'm merely the messenger. I ran into one of the staff out in the hallway and told him I'd be happy to see that they got delivered."

"You're the soul of accommodation."

"What can I say? I aim to please."

She dropped down on the sitting-room sofa with a sigh. "I know it's not quite noon here, but I'm beat. And I can't wait to get out of these shoes and clothes."

"I'll be happy to help," he offered. On a wink he

added, "It so happens I'm exceptionally skilled when it comes to assisting women in such matters."

"Yes, I'm sure you are. All that practice."

Max merely shrugged. "Practice makes perfect." Then his eyes narrowed. "Jealous?"

Because she felt an odd little prickle of possessiveness at the thought of him undressing another woman, she snorted. "Please, I'm engaged."

Max shrugged. "My father was married. That didn't stop him from being tempted. And acting on it. Again and again."

He said it flippantly, but Dayle knew him well enough to detect an underlying note of pain. Max had once confided that while he was growing up his father had betrayed his mother repeatedly. Rosalind Kinnick had stuck with him for years, hoping the man she loved would make good on his vows to reform. Finally she'd had enough. Max had been thirteen when his parents divorced—old enough to understand why Rolland had moved out, old enough to know why he had a place to move to.

Dayle was no therapist, but she didn't figure it took a degree in psychology to draw a correlation between Max's parents' fractured relationship and his inability to make a lasting commitment. Of course, people in glass houses... Dayle had enough issues with trust thanks to her previous marriage that she generally kept such observations to herself.

"How about I start with your shoes," Max was saying. Before she could fathom what he meant to do he had scooped up her legs and settled onto the opposite end of the sofa with her feet in his lap. She was forced to turn sideways, which put the armrest and a decorative pillow under her shoulders. Her position was now one more of reclining than sitting. She was grateful to be wearing pants.

"Max," she began, struggling to sit up and take back possession of her feet. But he held them firmly.

"Relax, sweetheart. I promise to behave. Scout's honor."

"You were never a Boy Scout."

"Got me there," he agreed amiably. "Still, you can trust me."

Dayle was too tired to argue. Besides, he'd already divested her feet of their flats and had begun to rub her aching arches through the thin material of her socks. If she were a cat, she would have begun purring. As it was, she moaned softly. She chanced a glance at Max, wondering if he'd heard. His smile was smug and purely male. She had her answer.

Though she knew it wasn't wise, Dayle closed her eyes and gave in to the sensations. No doubt about it, Max was exceptionally skilled with his hands. He knew exactly which spots to knead, to stroke and caress to deliver the most pleasure.

Her mind had begun to stray into decidedly erotic territory when Max asked, "Are you sure you want me to behave, Dayle?"

She kept her eyes shut. God only knew what they might reveal were she to let the lids flick up. "The only thing I know for sure at the moment is that if our business ever folds you would have a promising career as a masseur. I'd pay big bucks for this, and I'm sure I'm not alone."

"Oh, I couldn't do this for money." He removed her stockings then. His hands were warm on her skin and their heat seemed to transfer to her flesh. "I prefer other, more basic forms of compensation."

At his huskily spoken words the warmth spread, spiraling upward, spiraling out of control as unpredictable and dangerous as a brush fire. For one brief moment, Dayle felt consumed and almost welcomed her own combustion. Then, thankfully, sanity returned. She abruptly pulled her feet away and stood.

"I—I really need some sleep." She kneaded her forehead and muttered, "I'm not feeling like myself at all."

Max eyed her curiously for a moment before rising to his feet as well. "Sleep isn't a good idea. Give in to jet lag now and you'll pay for it later. It's better to stay awake and reset your body's internal clock to local time."

She nodded, knowing what he said made sense. "All right. Just a long soak in the tub then," she replied. "I'll call you later. We can make plans for dinner."

But he was shaking his head. "We have a client to see before then."

"A client? Today? But I've only just arrived." She glanced at her watch. It was just after eleven Venice time.

"It's not for a few hours yet. That will give us plenty of time for lunch and a leisurely stroll along the canal."

She held out a hand in protest. "But, Max—"

He laid the stockings he'd removed over her wrist. "Go and freshen up. You have time for a shower." Cocking an eyebrow he asked, "Need help scrubbing your back?"

"I can manage on my own."

"Really?" One side of his mouth rose. "That must mean you're flexible. Flexibility is a vastly appealing trait in a woman."

On a strangled cry, Dayle wadded up her socks and tossed them in his direction. It was just her luck that even with one of them draped over his head he managed to look incredibly sexy.

"Leave me alone, Max."

He removed the sock, retrieved the other one from the floor and set both on the sofa. He sounded serious when he replied, "I'm trying."

Max wanted a drink. If it were later in the day, he would have been tempted to indulge in something far more potent than the sparkling water he'd swiped from the suite's minibar.

Sipping the water, he paced the sitting room. It was a twin to Dayle's, which was why he had a hard time even looking in the direction of the sofa. God help him, but when she'd moaned as he'd rubbed her instep he'd come close to forgetting she was his partner, his friend and the woman whose wedding he had agreed to help plan. He'd wanted to push her feet aside and find out what other spots on her body might be sensitive to his touch. Good thing Dayle had put an end to what had come awfully close to foreplay.

He finished off the water and began pacing again. Right. Good thing.

This was ridiculous. *He* was being ridiculous. But there was no denying he was feeling decidedly proprietary of the woman and as a result decidedly jealous that she was soon going to be another man's wife.

He wanted her to be his.

The unprecedented thought came out of nowhere, catching him off guard. The idea was crazy, not to mention appallingly selfish. Kinnick men weren't hard-wired for commitment.

An hour later, when Max tapped on Dayle's door, his resolve was firmly in place. During the next several days, when they weren't seeing clients, he would walk her into every church, palace and reception hall in Venice. He would take her to every florist, caterer and bakery. He would see to it that come June she had her fairy-tale wedding.

Dayle deserved one…even if fate had decreed that Max wasn't to be the groom.

CHAPTER SIX

DAYLE desperately needed something to occupy her mind after Max left her suite. It must be this place, she decided. Venice was so romantic, after all. Wasn't that one of the reasons she'd chosen it for her wedding?

She decided to unpack her suitcase, hoping the mundane chore would put an end to her wayward thoughts. She'd brought only a couple of dresses to wear for special dinners out. She hung those in the closet right away, as well as a few of the other garments that were prone to wrinkling. That left her with the rest of the big suitcase. Even as she lifted out the first neat stack of sweaters, fatigue had her yawning. She removed a few pairs of pants. They really should be put on hangers. And then she emptied the side pouches that contained her lingerie and other unmentionables. Much of it, she realized as she glanced down at the swatches of crimson, had come from Max.

Max.

She sank down on the free side of the bed and rubbed her eyes. She really should call Ryan and let him know she'd arrived safely. Ryan was such a good man. So kind. So steadfast. So…not Maxwell Kinnick.

She leaned back and brought the feet Max had massaged up onto the mattress. She just needed a moment. She just needed to stop thinking. About anyone. About anything. She rolled to her side, pulled the pillow from beneath the duvet and when exhaustion beckoned, she gratefully fell into its embrace.

She woke to a lingering kiss that promised far more.

"I was lonely," a husky male voice whispered against her lips. "I've been so lonely."

"Me, too." At the admission, Dayle's heart began hammering, tapping so loudly that she swore she could hear its beating.

It took off faster when he began to undress her. He removed her clothes with agonizing slowness, lips kissing, teeth nipping at the sensitive skin his skillful hands exposed.

She'd never been vocal during lovemaking, but she was moaning now, begging actually, until finally the last of her garments was removed.

Then it was time for her to return the favor. She was far less patient, showed far less restraint. She was so ready for him, so unbelievably eager. The small, slippery buttons of his shirt slowed her progress. She tugged at the fabric, nearly rent the broadcloth when she grew tired of fumbling with them. His rich laughter rumbled, only to stop abruptly when she reached for his belt and unbuckled it. Then his breath hissed out as she lowered the zipper on his trousers. It was her turn to be slow, to be thorough. It was his turn to moan, to writhe and to want.

Finally neither of them could stand any more. Their bodies met in the center of the bed. Heated flesh molded together, burning hotter and brighter than the sun that had pierced the clouds outside and now illuminated the distinctive domes of St. Mark's Basilica through the window. She felt him slide into her, filling her so snugly that she let out a long, low sigh of contentment. Soon enough, however, she became greedy for more. She arched her back against the mattress and lifted her hips to make more room for each deep thrust. His tempo had been slow, but now it began to quicken as his breath sawed out.

"So good." She panted the words into the curve of his neck, kissing the pulse that beat in time with their movements. "So good."

And it was. Better, in fact, than it had ever been. That alone made her want to weep, but she blinked away the gathering moisture. Now was not the time for tears even if they were the result of triumph rather than the product of sorrow.

Together they rolled on the mattress, their legs tangling in the satin sheets as they traded places. She was on top now and sat up, bringing her knees to either side of his torso and bracing her hands on the solid wall of his chest. She could feel his heart hammering beneath her palms. It rapped as loudly and as erratically as her own.

A little thrill sneaked through her. She had never tried this position in lovemaking. It let her set the pace, to determine the depth of penetration. She savored the control, but she wasn't selfish. She used it to both of their advantages, alternately rotating her hips slowly and then pumping them faster up and down…up and down…up and down.

Sensations built. Her breathing grew more labored. She heard him moan. Then the hands that had been cradling her hips moved to her breasts. He flicked his thumbs across her nipples, causing them to harden, causing other places in her body to tingle before contracting. Delicious heat curled, taking her closer to the flash point.

Her movements grew faster, more urgent and far less controlled. Primal instinct kicked in as need wound inside her like a spring. It coiled tighter and tighter until finally she could take no more. She leaned forward, rose up until their intimate connection was nearly lost and then drove down on him. He said her name, his voice hoarse and barely recognizable, as she supposed was her own when she cried out on a shattering climax. It was the first real orgasm she'd experienced in years, a fact that once again made her feel like weeping. She smiled instead as she lay draped across his chest, sated and happy, at long last complete.

"I love you," she murmured.

"I love you, too."

When she finally found the strength to move she levered herself up, pushed the hair back from her eyes and smiled down at her lover. It was not her fiancé she straddled.

It was Max.

Dayle woke with a start and scrambled off the bed as if it were covered in molten lava rather than a satin duvet. Her body was still throbbing from what had been a very real, very lovely orgasm. She glanced down, half expecting to find herself naked, but she was completely clothed, just as she was completely alone.

"A dream." She exhaled heavily. "It was only a dream."

It took her a moment to realize the tapping sound was real. It wasn't coming from her heart but from the suite's door, and it had turned to pounding by the time she went to answer it. Max was in the hall, looking irritated, looking good enough to eat. Heat crept into Dayle's face, making it hard to meet his gaze.

"Are you okay?"

"Fine," she managed, fiddling with the cuff of her blouse. The very blouse he had removed with such maddening slowness in her dream.

He touched her cheek. "Are you sure? You look a little flushed."

"I'm…fine," she repeated. She chanced another look at his face. He was studying her.

"I know what happened here," he said softly. "I can read you like a book."

Dayle moistened her lips and felt her face burn hotter. "You can?"

"Always."

Dear God.

"You fell asleep, even after I told you not to."

She nearly laughed in relief. "Yes. I did." She bobbed her head. "I fell asleep."

"You're going to regret it."

Actually she already did. Because she couldn't look at him now without a totally inappropriate question nagging: Was Max as good in real life as he'd been in her dream?

"Are you sure you don't want to sit down?" he asked. "You seem a little shaky."

"No. I'm fine. Just tired. I started to unpack and then decided to lie down for a minute. I was just planning to rest my eyes," Dayle said.

Max smiled. "Well, you rested them for nearly an hour."

"Sorry," she said again.

"You're only sorry I woke you." He stepped into the suite and nudged her in the direction of the bedroom. "Go take a shower. I'll finish your unpacking and pick out something sexy for you to wear."

"I can pick out my own outfit," she informed him.

Max was relieved to see some of Dayle's usual pluck return.

"That's fine," he replied on a shrug. Then he sent her a smoldering gaze. "I was referring to what you can wear beneath it anyway. That way I can imagine you taking it off tonight."

Where a moment ago her face had seemed flushed, now she looked positively pale.

"Hey, are you sure you're feeling okay?" he asked. "I can reschedule our meeting for another day."

"No. That's not necessary." She shuffled off in the direction of the bathroom.

Max frowned after her. She was acting odd, but then he wasn't feeling quite like himself, either, and hadn't been since she'd arrived in Venice.

He wandered to the large bed. Clothes covered half of it, neat stacks of sweaters, carefully folded shirts and pants. There was also a tantalizing assortment of lingerie, the majority of which was made of red silk. His doing. He grinned.

Max liked knowing that she wore the things he gave her. He liked knowing that he got the sizes of such intimate apparel right. And though he knew he was being sadistic, he picked up the lacy camisole he'd purchased the summer before in Paris and pictured Dayle wearing it. The mental image his fertile imagination produced had him groaning.

He dropped it back onto the pile and circled the bed. The opposite side was empty. Dayle hadn't turned down the covers to sleep, but she had pulled the pillow from beneath the spread. Max sat down on the edge of the mattress and placed his hand on the indentation her head had left. It was still warm. Because he heard the shower running, he gave in to temptation, leaned over and sniffed. He closed his eyes and sighed as her scent curled around him. The woman was going to be the death of him.

He stood and paced to the window. What was it about her that made him wish he could be a different kind of man? She was beautiful, smart, funny, interesting, but so were many of the women he'd dated, bedded. He'd never regretted it when their liaisons ended, but he still couldn't quite face the fact that he was losing Dayle, not just to another man, but to another city. He'd never really had her, of course. Maybe that was the issue here. The one who got away. Hadn't they once joked that that was what made her irresistible?

Max was still staring out at the canal traffic when he heard the shower switch off. A moment later Dayle stepped out of the bathroom wrapped in a fluffy white towel. Steam escaped along with her. His breath hissed out. She stopped when she spied him, her expression oddly vulnerable. More than anything he wanted to take her in his arms, hold her. Keep her.

Instead he crossed those arms over his chest. "You look good in terry cloth. Got anything on underneath it?" He bobbed his eyebrows and settled into the comfortable role of flirt.

"Wouldn't you like to know?" she retorted, her vulnerability vanishing along with the steam. "Wait out in the sitting room while I dress."

"And miss the show?"

"Exactly." When he stayed, she raised her voice. "Max."

He lifted both hands in defeat. "Going, going." But he stopped when she was within reach and wound one thick, wet curl tightly around his index finger, squeezing a little water from it. He wiped the droplet on her towel at the spot where one end was tucked between her breasts and took some satisfaction when she sucked in a breath and her eyes went wide.

He meant it when he said, "Ryan is one lucky man."

CHAPTER SEVEN

ENZA LEONI was a jewelry designer who counted European royalty and American celebrities among her clientele. Her one-of-a-kind pieces commanded outrageous sums, but more recently she'd started a signature line she wanted to sell through select stores in the United States. The line wouldn't be inexpensive, but it would be within splurging distance for the less affluent.

If everything worked out as planned, Globetrotter's would be the importer that handled Enza's entry into the trendy boutiques of Rodeo Drive and Fifth Avenue.

Her studio was in Venice's interior, well away from the city's main tourism arteries. It was tucked amid the slim alleyways and tiny canals that Venetians traversed in their daily lives and that lucky travelers merely stumbled across. Max seemed to know exactly where he was going. Dayle followed him, literally, since some of the alleys were so narrow that she and Max were required to walk single file.

After what seemed like an eternity, they entered a small *piazza*. The weather had cleared, much like it had in her dream. Dayle focused on the sunshine that danced on the water pooling in a fountain in the middle of the square. She wouldn't think of that dream. No. She would think of Ryan, of their wedding, of their life together. He was going to like Venice. In the summer, when she returned with her intended, flowers would be spilling from the city's many window boxes and planters. It would be warmer then, steamy or so she'd read. Ryan didn't like the heat. She frowned, as the dream and its too-real heat beckoned.

"Here we are," Max announced, stopping in front of an arched doorway at the far end of the square. "Enza's studio." He opened the door and ushered her inside.

He spoke too soon, as far as Dayle was concerned. They didn't officially arrive at the studio for three more flights of stone steps. Despite the low heels of her shoes, her feet were begging for relief by the time they finally reached their destination. Her mind reeled back to the foot rub Max had given her as she'd reclined on the sofa. Desire curled at the memory. She swallowed and sought to banish it, as well as that intimate dream. That was easily accomplished when they reached the studio and Enza came to greet them.

The woman wasn't as tall as Dayle, but she was poised and self-assured, with the most amazing green-brown eyes set in a face that would have stopped Manhattan traffic at rush hour. Dayle felt positively plain in comparison.

"Maxie, it's so good to see you again," Enza cooed in a lyrical voice.

She kissed him enthusiastically on both cheeks, resting her ample bosom against his chest during the time that it took. Then she turned her attention to Dayle. A pair of dark, finely arched brows tugged together and lush, full lips pursed. Dayle recognized that scrutinizing look. She'd been on the receiving end of it often enough from the women in Max's life. It said, "Back off. I've got dibs."

She'd never grown accustomed to it, but it particularly grated now.

"Enza, this is Dayle Alexander, my business partner," Max said by way of an introduction.

Since the woman wasn't quite done inspecting her, Dayle decided to go first. "It's nice to meet you, Enza." She held out a hand.

"*Sì*. Yes. It is nice to meet you, too." But Enza continued to frown. "Forgive me for my rudeness, it's just that when we had dinner together the other evening Maxie neglected to mention that his Dayle was a woman."

His Dayle. The words held an accusation. Max seemed to know that, too, for he cleared his throat.

"It must have slipped his mind," Dayle replied dryly.

To which it sounded like Max murmured, "Never."

Both women turned to study him. He fiddled with one of his gold cuff links. "Dayle can be a man's name. Perhaps that's where the confusion came in."

Enza's scrutinizing gaze cut to Dayle again. "Perhaps," she allowed after a moment, but her tone resonated skepticism.

Dayle opted to show her hand, literally. She let the diamond engagement ring flash. "I don't usually travel with Max, but I couldn't resist coming to Venice. My fiancé and I will be getting married in June and we want to have our wedding here. Max knows the city so well. He's agreed to help me find the perfect location."

Enza's smile bloomed. "You're engaged. Congratulations. Maxie didn't mention that, either." She sent him a pointed look. He shrugged by way of apology. "May I see your ring?"

Dayle held out her hand. The diamond was just over a carat and set in platinum. She'd picked it out herself after accepting Ryan's proposal. That had taken some of the romance out of the moment, as far as she was concerned. But then Ryan never seemed to get her preferences right. Whereas Max...

"A solitaire," Enza said. "A very traditional setting."

"Dayle is a very traditional woman," Max said knowingly.

Both women frowned at him. Enza was the first to speak. "The ring is beautiful, don't you agree, Maxie?"

"Stunning." But he didn't look at it, and it struck Dayle then that he'd never asked to see her ring, though he was a self-described connoisseur of beauty in all its many forms.

Dayle decided it was time to get down to business. "Max tells me your designs are unsurpassed, especially your hammered gold pieces. We believe Globetrotter's can ensure they receive the right positioning in the American market."

"So Maxie says."

The nickname was starting to grate. Dayle continued. "I've seen some examples of your work, but I'd love to see more."

"Certainly." Enza waved a bejeweled hand. "Right this way."

* * *

An hour later, to Dayle's relief, they were shuffling down the steps from Enza Leoni's studio.

"You might have mentioned that you're sleeping with our client, *Maxie*," she drawled.

She knew Max flirted outrageously with all women, even those who were Globetrotter's clientele, but she'd always assumed he knew where to draw the line. That was why his apparent intimacy with the very lovely Enza Leoni had her so incensed, she told herself.

"Actually I met Enza before she became a client. There's nothing going on," he said as he held the door that opened into the square.

"Now." She brushed past him. He didn't correct her and so Dayle figured she had her answer. Fury swept in from nowhere. "God! I should have known."

"Known what?"

"She's female," Dayle snapped. "So, of course you've slept with her."

"Are you saying I'm indiscriminate?" He had the nerve to sound puzzled and to look almost wounded. Dayle lowered her chin and sent him a pointed look.

"I'm not indiscriminate," he mumbled, reaching for her elbow.

But she pulled it away. "Oh, that's right. You'll flirt with anyone female, but in order for you to sleep with them they have to be stunning, sexy and have a flair for fashion."

"I appreciate a good sense of humor and some intelligence, too," he inserted with his trademark smile.

Dayle was beyond being charmed. God, what was

wrong with him? For that matter, what was wrong with *her*? Even as she silently asked the question, she was snapping irritably, "I don't find this situation amusing."

She lengthened her stride and stalked ahead of him.

"Whoa, whoa!" Max caught up to her and grabbed her wrist, forcing her to stop and face him. "What's gotten into you? Since when do you care who I spend my personal time with?"

"I don't care." She didn't. No, of course she didn't. If she cared that could be construed as jealousy, and a soon-to-be-married woman had no right—*absolutely* no right—to jealousy when it came to a man who was not her groom-to-be. It was that damned dream. That damned foot rub. It was Venice and jet lag, prewedding jitters and Beth's off-base musings. Dayle shook her head vehemently in a bid to clear her mind. Images she could have done without stayed, stubborn as burrs. Even so, she claimed, "I couldn't care less as a matter of fact."

"Uh-huh." Max ran his tongue over his teeth. She gritted hers. But at least he wasn't looking smug at the moment. She couldn't have tolerated that.

"I just don't think it's very professional of you to blur the boundaries between your bedroom and Globetrotter's bottom line." Yes, that was the issue. Professionalism was *exactly* the issue that had Dayle feeling so damned agitated.

Max gaped at her. "You're being a little melodramatic, don't you think? Enza and I had a brief..." He waved a hand, as if a suitable description of their coupling escaped him.

"Fling," Dayle supplied succinctly. "You and Enza had a fling."

He wrinkled his nose. "I prefer the term interlude."

Of course he did. Interlude made it sound gauzy and strewn with rose petals.

"You can use a prettier word, *Maxie*," she drawled. "But it doesn't change the facts."

He frowned. "Well, here are the facts for you. My relationship with Enza was one between two mutually consenting adults who were both well aware that it wasn't going to be anything more than what it was."

"And it was?"

"None of your damned business."

He was right, absolutely right, but that didn't make his words any easier for Dayle to hear. Even when Max added, "Besides, that relationship was over long before she contacted Globetrotter's about the possibility of becoming a client."

His explanation should have mollified her. It didn't. Quite the opposite.

"Relationship?" Dayle spat. "You don't have relationships, Max. You have flings." She shook her head. "Oh, sorry. That's right. *Interludes*. In the dozen years I've known you you've had too many *interludes* for me to count."

His eyes narrowed, making it clear she wasn't the

only one irritated now. "And that's suddenly an issue for you because?"

His words had her blinking. "I-it's not an issue for me."

"Okay, then what are we standing in the middle of this charming little square arguing about?"

More than irritated, now he looked confused. Dayle was confused, too. She had been since that dream, which perhaps explained why she said the first thing that sprang to mind.

"Sex."

Max's eyebrows notched up, taking one corner of his mouth with them.

"S-sex with a client," Dayle added, but she wasn't sure if the clarification was for his benefit or her own.

His expression sobered on a sigh, and he rubbed his forehead with the thumb and index finger of his right hand. "As I believe I've already made abundantly clear, Enza and I are not sleeping together."

"But you aren't sleeping alone. Or at least you won't be for long." Something inside of her twisted violently. Dayle decided it was because the bald statements crossed a line that she had drawn very carefully herself.

Max seemed to know it, for he stepped closer, metaphorically putting one designer loafer over that line as well. His voice was pitched low and held not a hint of its usual teasing when he asked, "Does it bother you to imagine other women in my bed?"

Dayle knew she should back away and reestablish the old boundaries. She needed to redraw the rigid line that had served her so well all these years. Or maybe it was time to erect a high, impenetrable wall in its place. But she stayed where she was, captured, captivated by his sensual and very serious expression.

"Yes, it bothers me," she admitted softly.

Their faces were mere inches apart now. Their breath mingled in the charged air of the square. Max ran his fingers down her arm. When he reached her hand, he clasped it within his. "Why? Why does it bother you?"

She answered with what she knew was only part of the truth, but the rest wasn't something she was ready to explore at the moment…if ever. "Because I want you to be happy, Max."

"Ah, Dayle. My sweet, sweet Dayle." He leaned in and his lips brushed hers for one brief, torturous moment. In the time it took him to back away, his mouth had already curved with a familiar, cocky grin. "There's no need for you to worry about me. Happiness is my middle name."

Dayle begged off on dinner that evening. She couldn't face Max again. She felt too exposed after their bizarrely intimate talk in the square. She wasn't sure what had gotten into her, saying the things that she had…and suddenly seeming to want the very things that she couldn't have and knew would ultimately bring her heartache. Whatever the reason behind these rioting emotions—Beth's probing questions, jet lag or Dayle's cheating subconscious—she was sure that some time away from Max would help her make sense of them.

So, she ordered room service, put on some comfortable clothes and curled up on the sofa with a bridal magazine. She had just flipped it open to an article on rehearsal-dinner etiquette when the telephone rang. Dayle eyed the phone a moment before answering it, worried it might be Max. But the voice on the other end belonged to Ryan. Oddly she felt disappointed.

"Missing me?" he asked.

"Of course." She ignored the guilt that nipped at her. "So, how's Venice?"

"It's lovely and absolutely perfect for our wedding. I wish you were here with me to see it." And she did. If he were in Venice, everything would be…normal. For hadn't she long known that Ryan was the perfect antidote to Max?

As if she'd spoken that thought aloud, Ryan said, "Is Kinnick behaving himself?"

She cleared her throat. "Oh, you know Max."

Ryan chuckled. "Yes, I do, which is why it's also a good thing that I know you."

This time guilt didn't merely nip. It snapped down hard and sank in its razor-sharp teeth. Coward that she was, Dayle opted to change the subject.

"So, how's your training going?"

Twenty minutes later, after ending their call, she was once again convinced that Ryan was the right man, the right choice. So what if she experienced no fireworks, felt no delicious urgency during their lovemaking. She could do without those things. He was a good life partner, a safe choice. Unlike her ex—and unlike Maxwell Kinnick—Ryan would never break her heart.

He can't break what he doesn't have.

CHAPTER EIGHT

FOR the next couple of days Max and Dayle had business appointments that took up many of their mornings. Max let her take the lead in wooing a couple of new clients, getting her feet wet for when her new duties kicked in on the West Coast. She was very persuasive at laying out the benefits of signing with Globetrotter's. He sat back and watched her, pleased and proud. Even though she'd always been content to stay in the shadows, he'd known Dayle would shine at whatever she tried.

Though neither of them mentioned it again, it was clear to Max that their argument—or whatever the hell it had been—in the square on her first day in Venice remained on their minds. For a moment, he'd almost sworn she was jealous of Enza, maybe even jealous of all the other women in his life, past and future. It had scared him to death, but at the same time it had stirred something he dare not think of as hope.

He wouldn't categorize their personal dealings since then as strained. He still flirted with her. She still put him in his place with a glib reply or a pointed look. That had always been the give-and-take of their dealings. He supposed one could call it their routine. Even so, something was different, something was…off. Dayle seemed on guard around him. He scrubbed a hand over his eyes and called himself a fool. Perhaps that was what his ego needed to believe. More likely, she was preoccupied. After all, she was in Venice to plan her wedding.

Before arriving, she'd researched possible sites for the ceremony on the Internet. In typical Dayle fashion she'd made a detailed list of those sites, what amenities they offered, how many guests they could accommodate and so forth. Max suggested a couple of other places that would match the mood and tone she was seeking. They would require him to cash in some favors since they were privately owned, but so be it. He'd promised her a romantic and stylish Venetian affair and he was determined to be a man of his word, no matter what it cost him personally.

The price was proving to be quite steep. He hadn't slept well since her arrival. How could he when his mind kept picturing her in that big bed in the adjacent suite clothed in silky bits of crimson he'd picked out himself? She was so close, yet further than ever beyond his reach. He comforted himself with the knowledge that soon enough their time together would be over, and he and Dayle would return to the normalcy of New York. That meant she would be in their Manhattan office and he would be jetting off again.

Max already had begun laying the groundwork for his next trip abroad. The Far East, he'd decided, for at least one week, maybe two, with stops in Hong Kong, Shanghai and Taipei. For the first time in his life, though, he wasn't looking forward to traveling. Perhaps it was because this time his plans seemed more about the need to run away than a remedy to restlessness.

Dayle met him in their hotel's restaurant at nine as he sipped espresso and glanced through an English-language newspaper. He'd been up since dawn after another fitful night's sleep. Two espressos later he'd still been dragging, until he caught sight of her. The woman sent the blood pumping through his veins at lightning speed. A man didn't need caffeine when she was around. The casual black pants she wore drew attention to the long line of her legs, especially since she'd apparently decided to ditch comfort for the day and had donned a pair of heels. He loved it when she wore them, the higher the better.

He folded the paper and set it aside. The tingle of attraction wasn't so easily dispatched. He opted to ignore it. "Good morning, beautiful. I trust you slept well."

"Fine, thanks." She signaled for the waiter to bring her an espresso and settled into the chair opposite his. "And you? How did you sleep?"

"Like hell. I tossed and turned. Visions of you wearing red kept me awake all night long."

It was the truth, but she rolled her eyes. "Right."

He shrugged. If she only knew. "So, what's on the agenda for today?"

They had wrapped up the last of their business

meetings the morning before, meaning her and Ryan's wedding plans would receive their undivided attention from here on out. Max's stomach burned at the thought.

Dayle pulled the small notebook from her handbag and flipped it open, consulting her lengthy to-do list.

"Let's see. We took care of flowers yesterday afternoon." She made a little check mark next to the entry.

"After what seemed like a lifetime of indecision," he remarked dryly.

"Don't start," she warned.

He held up his hands, palms facing out. "I'm just saying that someone who is as picky as you are has absolutely no right to label me high maintenance ever again."

Her utter fussiness still surprised him. It had almost seemed like foot-dragging. But what reason would Dayle have to drag her feet?

"I wanted white calla lilies."

"Yes and the blooms had to measure a certain number of inches in diameter and be uniform in all other aspects."

"I like uniformity." She shrugged.

"And the stems all must be wrapped in rose-colored ribbon. Not pink, not mauve. Rose." He mimicked her voice as he spoke.

"There's nothing wrong with knowing exactly what you want," she replied.

Max couldn't argue with that. Still, he felt compelled to point out, "But as the song says, you can't always get what you want."

And didn't he know it?

She glanced up from her notebook. Dark eyes studied

him a moment. Oddly Dayle sounded resigned when she said, "No. You can't always have what you want. That's why it's good to have a Plan B."

"So, you settle." When she frowned, he added, "That's what you're really saying, isn't it?"

They weren't talking about flowers or ribbon colors any longer. Max was sure of it when Dayle said quietly, "Sometimes the backup plan is the wiser choice." She moistened her lips before adding, "The safer choice."

Her words surprised him. "Safer?" he asked.

"Infinitely." She cleared her throat then and went back to her notebook. "I'd like to place the order for my cake today. I have a list of bakeries near St. Mark's Square that I'd like to visit, but I'm open to other suggestions if you have any."

Apparently she'd decided that the previous topic of conversation was now closed. Probably just as well, he decided.

Safer.

The word echoed in his head. Max ignored it and worked up his patented smile. "Cake it is."

"I'd also like to pick out some gifts for the wedding party. Perhaps we could get that out of the way first. I'm thinking jewelry, maybe something that can be engraved."

"You can't go wrong with jewelry," he said. "It's the perfect gift for any occasion."

"I thought that was red undergarments." She made a sound that was half laugh, half harrumph.

Max shook his head. "Oh, no. Those are only acceptable when you are particularly fond of the person."

"Then you must buy undergarments often—perhaps you even purchase them in bulk quantities." She smiled sweetly after issuing the dig.

"As it happens, I hand select each item and I only buy them for a certain someone when I've been away."

"I'm the only one?" Her expression was doubtful, although he noticed that she had edged forward in her seat, as if anxious to hear his response.

"The one and only," Max confirmed. But because the words left him feeling unmasked, he added a wink.

Dayle shook her head on a sigh and settled back in her chair. "So, can you recommend a place where I can find some quality pieces?"

"Of lingerie?" he asked, purposely misunderstanding her.

Her eyes narrowed. "Of jewelry."

"Well, as you know, Enza Leoni does exceptional work." It was petty of him, but Max took a perverse amount of pleasure from watching Dayle's upper lip curl at the mention of the other woman's name. "Her pieces are expensive but since she's a client she'll probably cut you a sweet deal."

"No, thanks. Her work may be exceptional, but it's a little too ostentatious for my taste."

Max sipped his espresso to hide his smile. Dayle might not be jealous, but she gave a good impression of it and his ego needed that at the moment.

With it sufficiently bolstered, he said, "It was just a thought. I know a few other places. Venice has no shortage of jewelry stores."

A couple of hours and several shops later, Dayle had purchased a lovely glass-bead necklace for Beth, whom she'd asked to be her maid of honor, and a watch for Ryan's best man. With a little prodding from Max she'd also picked out a strand of pearls for herself and a beaded handbag for Lorna as a make-peace gesture.

Finally, she had ordered favors for her guests. *Bombonieras* were an Italian tradition. Since the wedding was to be held in Venice, he'd suggested that hand-blown glass roses would make the perfect gift. After some dithering she'd agreed. Foot-dragging, he'd thought again, only to change his mind when they'd walked past another shop and she'd said, "I bet I can find something for Ryan in there."

Max shrugged and opted to wait for her outside with her bags full of the day's other purchases. The minute she ducked inside, he was digging into his pocket for the roll of antacids.

For small swatches of time as he showed her around Venice, it was easy to forget the true purpose of their visit. But it always came up, followed by heartburn. Max thumbed off a second tablet and popped it into his mouth, scowling as he chewed. He'd worked his way through half the roll by the time Dayle finally exited the shop.

"All set," she announced with an enigmatic smile.

When they reached the famed Rialto Bridge, he put his hand on her lower back, guiding her progress. The bridge was bustling with people, many of them tourists snapping pictures of the distinctive structure or the gondolas gliding on the canal beneath it. At the elevated center of the span, Dayle surprised him by taking his hand and drawing him to one side.

"Do you want to take a photograph?" he asked.

"No. I have something for you." She pulled a small, gift-wrapped box from her shopping bag. "I was going to wait to give it to you, but I can't. It's to thank you for all of your help."

"Oh, there's no need for that." Max meant it. Gratitude was a poor substitute for what he really wanted.

But Dayle shook her head. "I think there is. You've even agreed to stand in for my dad."

Max blanched at that. "Please, comparing me to your late father makes me feel perverse given the very vivid sexual fantasies I've entertained about you." He wasn't quite joking. They both managed tight laughter as people jostled past them chattering away in a variety of languages.

"How about this? You've agreed to give me away."

"Better," he murmured, though those words didn't sit right with him either.

"And you've been a huge help, showing me around Venice, helping me make decisions. Honestly, Max, I don't know what I'd do without you," she said.

"You'd be fine. You're a born survivor."

He, on the other hand, was becoming increasingly worried about how he was going to manage the day-to-day act of living after she married Ryan and moved away.

Dayle pressed the box into his hand. "Go on. Open it."

As he untied the ribbon and began peeling off the paper, an odd sense of anticipation built. She'd given him gifts before, jewelry even, which he figured this was. But the mood surrounding this gift was different. Or maybe *he* was different. Not a changed man, but a changing one, and the reason for his metamorphosis was standing opposite him, smiling.

The last of the paper was removed. He wadded it up and stuffed it into his jacket pocket, wanting to draw out the moment. Finally he lifted off the lid and looked inside the box. It held a gold chain and a medallion of some sort. He pulled them out, laying the medallion flat on his palm.

Dayle edged in closer. "I saw it and I thought of you. It's a St. Christopher's medal," she said.

"The patron saint of travelers." He stroked the face of the medal with his thumb.

"So you'll always return home safely."

Max attempted a laugh, but it caught in his throat. *Home.* He frowned. Where exactly was that for someone like him? First-class on an international flight? A suite in one of the world's choicest hotels? The Manhattan apartment that he kept but didn't quite live in?

Home is where the heart is.

The old saying plunked into his mind, sending out ripples like a pebble in a pond. He glanced over at Dayle. She was smiling, her expression open and inviting. Welcoming.

Home. Maybe Max did know where that was after all.

CHAPTER NINE

MAX was quiet during much of their lunch at a charming café in St. Mark's Square. He was wearing the St. Christopher medal she'd given him, and when he didn't think she was looking, she'd seen him finger it through the fabric of his shirt.

Dayle had stumbled across the medal as she'd scoured the shop for something for Ryan. She'd come up empty-handed for her fiancé, but not for Max. If Beth were there, Dayle knew what her friend would say about that, just as she would have something to say about Dayle's uncharacteristic indecisiveness over even the most basic of her wedding plans.

But Beth wasn't in Venice, leaving an ostrich to her sand.

Max was touched by the gift if his initial reaction was any indication. Indeed, Dayle wasn't sure she'd ever seen him look quite so moved, even when she'd given him pricier or more practical things. Since then he'd been lost in thought. He seemed to snap out of it when they started on their quest for the perfect wedding cake a little later.

She consulted her notebook as she waited for him to pay the bill. "I think Salvatore's is just on the other side of the square," she said when he joined her.

"I have another place in mind. It's not as well-known as some of the places here, but no one in Venice can outdo Franca Celli when it comes to dessert," he promised her.

They took a water taxi part of the way and then shuffled down a labyrinth of narrow passages. All the way, Dayle braced herself to be greeted by another curvaceous Mediterranean beauty, but when they reached the bakery that wasn't quite the case. Signora Franca Celli was a pleasantly plump widow who was pushing sixty. It was also clear from the way she patted Max's cheek and then came around the counter to wrap him in a robust hug that she adored him. What woman didn't? But at least Franca didn't call him Maxie. No, she called him by his full given name, with the fond lecturing quality of a parent. For this reason alone, Dayle liked her.

"Maxwell, you stay away too long," Franca accused.

"I know. My apologies. But I'm here now and I've missed you," he said with his usual charming smile.

Franca shook her head and laughed. "You cannot fool me, Maxwell. You miss my cannoli. You miss my tiramisu. You are not pining for an old woman."

"You're not old. You're experienced."

"Bah!" But she laughed. Then she turned to Dayle. "And who might this be?"

"This is Dayle Alexander, my business partner."

"*Bella,*" she murmured and sent a wink in Max's direction. While Dayle's grasp of Italian was sorely limited, she did understand that word. Beautiful. She felt her face heat when Max smiled and nodded in agreement.

"Buon giorno," Dayle said in greeting.

"Buon giorno," Franca replied. "It is nice to meet a friend of my Maxwell."

Where Enza's possessiveness had been annoying, Franca Celli's was endearing. Dayle smiled warmly in return.

"It's nice to meet you, too. Max tells me that this is the place to come for the best sweets in all of Italy."

"Ah, Maxwell." She patted his cheek again before asking Dayle, "What woman can resist such a charmer?"

"Actually *that* woman," Max murmured. "Which is why we're here."

"Scusi?"

A little louder he said, "Dayle would like your suggestions for her wedding cake."

"Wedding!" The woman's eyes widened first in surprise and then in excitement. She wrapped him in another bear hug. "Oh, Maxwell, so you are finally going to settle down."

"Oh, no. No, no." He sent an apologetic glance in Dayle's direction. "It's not what you're thinking, Franca. I'm not the groom. Come to that, I'm not even the best man."

Was that regret in his voice? She didn't have time to ponder it now. Franca ushered them to a table, calling over her shoulder for the young girl at the counter to bring them some espresso. For the next two hours she came out of the kitchen with one calorie-laden confection after another. All of the dishes were traditional to Italian weddings and vastly different from the icing-coated cakes that Dayle had been expecting. Not that she minded. These were feasts for the eyes and palate.

"First, you will try my *crostata di frutta*," Franca said, setting a slice of fruit-covered tart in front of them. A decadent vanilla cream voided out any of the fruit's nutritional qualities, but it was a worthwhile trade in Dayle's mind. If one was going to have dessert, why skimp?

Next Franca brought them a sponge cake filled with Bavarian cream, and then one topped with thick whipped cream and white chocolate shavings. All of the desserts were excellent, melting in her mouth. But Dayle knew she'd found the perfect one when she bit into a puff pastry filled with Chantilly cream.

"Oh my God, Max. You've got to try this one."

Max had relaxed enough to start enjoying himself, but then he heard Dayle moan. If that weren't bad enough, she'd held out her fork and offered him a bite off of it.

"It's heaven," he agreed, though the flavor didn't register. In fact, background noises and the bakery's scrumptious scents fell away. The only thing he was aware of at that moment was Dayle and how she looked smiling at him in expectation while sunshine streamed through the window behind her and teased highlights from her dark hair.

That stabbing pain lanced his chest again. God help him, but Max welcomed it. At least he knew he was alive.

"Are you sure you like it?" she asked. "You're frowning."

"Sorry." He worked up a convincing grin to go along with his lie. "Just thinking of how long I'll have to spend in the hotel's fitness center to work off all these calories. I'd hate to have to have my new tuxedo altered so soon."

After leaving the bakery, they took what Max intended to be a scenic detour back to their hotel. The weather was mild for April, nudging up near sixty degrees, and he thought Dayle might enjoy strolling amid the shops and boutiques. He knew he could use the air. But she walked at a New Yorker's pace, brisk and purposeful with her shoulders squared, her head up and her eyes focused forward.

He reached for her elbow. "You're going too fast. This is Italy. They believe in taking their time here."

She glanced sideways. "Sorry. Habit." And though she modified her pace and began to glance around some, she continued to walk as if she were late for something. Her feet had to be killing her in those heels. Maybe he'd offer to rub them later. He recalled the last foot rub he'd given her and the lingering effect it had had on him. Maybe not.

He was wrestling with his demons when she all but skidded to a halt on the uneven cobblestones.

"Ooh, look at that." She pointed to a mannequin in the shop's window. It was clothed in a pale blue silk dress accented with tiny darker blue beads around a low-plunging neckline.

"Do you want to go in?" he asked, somewhat amused by her uncharacteristic reaction. Unlike most of the women Max knew, Dayle wasn't the sort who enjoyed shopping. Yet despite laboring through a long day of it, she apparently was game for more.

"Do you mind?"

"Anything for you."

He followed her into the shop, hanging back a couple of steps in the hope of finding his footing. He needn't have bothered. The rug was pulled out from under him completely when he caught up with Dayle several minutes later. As he stood at the back of the boutique looking around for her, she stepped out of a fitting room clothed in the dress that had been on display in the window. It looked far better on her than it had on the mannequin. It flowed over her soft curves in a waterfall of blue silk. He balled his hands into his fists, which he stuffed into his trouser pockets.

"What do you think?" she asked.

Words he couldn't possibly give voice to piled up on his tongue. He swallowed every last one, grateful when he caught a glimpse of red peeking from her décolletage. The sexy distraction was just what he needed to regroup.

"I think you'll need different undergarments if you plan to wear that dress."

"Could you take your eyes off my chest for a moment and give me your honest opinion?" She tugged the neckline higher. Max sighed dramatically. Then he was left without pretense.

"It's lovely, Dayle. You're lovely."

"You think so?" He saw her swallow. Nerves?

"Stunning." The moment stretched. Finally he

cleared his throat. "So, are you thinking of wearing that to your rehearsal dinner?"

For a brief moment he swore the question had her puzzled. But then she nodded. "Yes. The rehearsal dinner." She fussed with the fabric that gathered at her waist. "Ryan says I look good in blue."

Max managed a smile even as his molars ground together. "Well, it's what Ryan thinks that matters."

Dayle stretched on the bed the following morning. She and Max had stayed out late. They'd dined. They'd danced. They'd drunk a toast to Italy, to life, even to love. She'd been a little tipsy after that, but as she recalled, Max had been a perfect gentleman. He'd issued no off-color comments. He'd made no inappropriate advances. He'd walked Dayle to her suite's door in the wee hours of the morning and, after unlocking it, he'd handed her the key. He hadn't asked to come inside. He hadn't even kissed her on the cheek. She should have been relieved. She'd felt disappointed. When she should have been sleeping, questions had bubbled like the champagne they'd drunk.

Just what was going on? Not only with Max, but with her? Ever since her divorce Dayle had been able to keep foolish needs and damning desires in a box. But the lid was off now and no matter how hard she tried, she didn't seem to be able to stuff them back inside.

CHAPTER TEN

MAX slapped at the alarm clock when it began to beep. Not that he needed the thing to rouse him. He'd been awake most of the night. Again. He'd pulled plenty of all-nighters thanks to a woman in the past, but those had left him satisfied afterward, relaxed. He was far from relaxed now. He was growing more frustrated, sexually and otherwise, by the hour.

And another day of helping Dayle plan her damned wedding loomed. On the bright side, the woman's lengthy to-do list was growing shorter, although she had yet to pin down the actual site for her nuptials. That was on the agenda for today. He rolled out of bed and stumbled in the direction of the bathroom. He'd take a shower, a nice long cold one. Then he'd wash down some breakfast with a carafe of espresso.

Who knew? Maybe the day wouldn't be as bad as he assumed.

By noon, he knew he'd been right. It was worse.

They'd only visited two sites from her list with three more scheduled before they called it a day. In both cases the people they met naturally assumed that Max was the groom-to-be. He and Dayle were quick to set them straight, tight smiles and forced laughter accompanying the explanations.

We're old friends.

We're business partners.

The benign descriptions of their relationship had really started to grate. Was that it? Was that all they were to one another after all these years? Maybe it was just as well that he wasn't feeling brave enough to discover the answers.

Max braced himself for more uncomfortable misunderstandings as they headed to the Palazzo Cavalli just before noon.

"It's a city-owned palace complete with eighteenth-century furnishings and it's considered a premiere venue for a civil ceremony," Dayle said, consulting her notebook.

"Lovely," he mumbled.

They were in a gondola, hips touching as they sat side by side. Their gondolier, a young man named Fabrizio, called out cheerful greetings to the other gondoliers they passed as he used a long pole to guide the vessel down the canal.

Buon giorno. Good day. What was so good about it? Max thought sourly. He reached up to loosen his necktie, only to discover he wasn't wearing one. Dayle glanced sideways at him in question. He abandoned the open collar of his shirt, folded his hands in his lap and ignored her.

When they reached the palace, though, he wasn't immune to her enthusiasm or to the building's impressive façade.

"Wow. It looks like something out of a fairy tale," Dayle mused.

She looked like something out of his fantasies with her hair floating loose around her shoulders and her cheeks turned rosy from the chilly air. Max stepped out onto the landing to help her from the gondola. He offered Dayle his hand, though a part of him wanted to offer much more.

"This would make pretty picture on your wedding day, no?" Fabrizio said in halting English. "You helping your lovely bride from my boat."

"She's not my bride," he replied.

"Just good friends," Dayle added.

Max was thankful that her grasp of the language was limited when Fabrizio continued in Italian. "What bad luck that you are in love with her, too."

Max opened his mouth to deny it, to explain that someone like him wasn't capable of the kind of love that marriage required. But his stock spiel about the wayward Kinnick genes never made it past his lips. He nodded instead.

"Very bad luck," he agreed in Italian.

"What did he say, Max?" she asked, smiling politely at the gondolier.

"He said…" Max glanced down. He was still holding her hand. What would she do if he told her the truth? He chose a safer version of it. "He said your fiancé is a fool to trust you alone with me."

"Max."

He offered a negligent shrug. "He also said you'll make a lovely bride."

"Oh." She smiled then, looking a little embarrassed. "Tell him thank you." She turned and added her own "*grazie mille*" before starting inside.

Max caught up with her and a guide as they climbed the palace's restored marble staircase to a large hall replete with frescoes and antique paintings. He usually appreciated fine art, but he barely spared these a glance. He needed a few minutes. While Dayle peppered the guide with questions, Max slipped out onto a balcony, sucking in air as he gazed sightlessly out over the Grand Canal. By the time Dayle joined him, the façade he'd worn as easily as a Venice carnival mask was once again firmly in place.

He nodded in the direction of the formal reception hall. "So, what do you think? Will this palace do for your 'I dos'?"

"It's lovely, but something's not right. I'll know it when I see it." She bobbed her head for emphasis. "I'm sure that I will. When it's right, it's right. You know?"

"Absolutely."

But Max felt certain of nothing as they made their way to the villa outside the city an hour later. The estate dated back several centuries and was located in an area where Venice's nobility had once passed their summers. The charm grabbed him instantly, despite the building's imposing façade. As had happened previously, the person showing them the villa's many amenities assumed Dayle and Max were the couple to be wed.

"You will find our honeymoon suite very luxurious and exceedingly private," the man told them with a smile.

"This is gorgeous." Dayle sighed and walked ahead of them.

"I'm sure the two of you will be most comfortable here," the manager said. If she heard him, she didn't let on. I should correct him, Max thought. But he didn't.

They went outside then, Max growing more uncomfortable with each sexy ooh and aah sound that Dayle issued. She found the site's storied history and its old-world charm appealing, but the possibility of a garden ceremony had her looking enraptured.

"The gardens are resplendent in June," their guide assured them as they walked the curving path between box row hedges to a vine-covered pergola in the center. "Many of our guests have had their ceremony performed here."

"I can see why." Dayle turned in a semicircle underneath it, taking in the expansive view. "This is it. This is the one." She turned to look at Max, her grin fading by degrees as she whispered, "It's…it's the right place."

It was. He felt that, too. He could see it, a little too clearly for comfort. In his mind, the current brown foliage greened and the small lawn area beyond the pergola filled with formally attired guests. The wedding march, a tune that he'd long likened to a death knell, played. It filled Max with anticipation rather than dread as he studied Dayle. She was a vision in pale ivory against a backdrop of wisteria and roses.

You may kiss the bride.

He obeyed the imagined command, leaning forward and kissing her not on the cheek as he'd been so careful to do all of these years, but on the mouth. When he heard her sexy sigh, he closed his eyes and surrendered what little remained of his sanity.

Dayle didn't pull away, at least not at first. She blamed her delayed reaction on shock. But need played a role, too. The desire she'd subjugated for so long staged an all-out insurrection when Max wrapped her in his arms. One of his hands was at the small of her back, pressing her body snuggly against his, though she needed no encouragement in that regard. His other hand was buried in the hair at her nape.

His body was solid, unyielding, and his mouth was proving to be every bit as erotically skilled as it had been in that dream.

"Dayle." He whispered her name against her lips. It sounded like a plea. When she opened her eyes, he was watching her. For the first time in all the years she'd known Max, he looked lost.

A discreet cough broke the spell. Belatedly she remembered they weren't alone. The villa's manager stood to the side, his smile indulgent and knowing, though he didn't have a clue about the true inappropriateness of what had just occurred.

"It is a romantic place, no?" he asked.

She wanted to believe the idyllic setting was the impetus behind that forbidden kiss, but she knew better. God help her. She knew. For when she had turned to Max to tell him that the site was exactly what she'd been looking for, a panicky inner voice had whispered that her groom-to-be was not.

"I will let you talk in private." The man gave a sly wink.

Dayle felt her face grow warm as he walked away, leaving her to face not only Max but her own worst fears. When she turned, however, Max had his back to her. His shoulders were held at a rigid angle and his hands were stuffed into his trouser pockets. She thought she heard the faint jingle of loose change. I should say something, she thought, but was at a loss as to what.

Max broke the silence. Without turning around, he said, "I'm sorry, Dayle. I had no right to do that."

His words were heartfelt, his tone sincere. She'd wanted him to treat the incident differently, she realized. She'd wanted him to joke about it, turn on the old Kinnick charm. This reaction was far too damning, especially given the insinuations her subconscious was making.

"Max—"

"I had no right," he said again, this time a little more emphatically, making her wonder which one of them he was trying to convince.

Fairness demanded that she point out her own culpability. "Neither did I. I'm hardly innocent in this matter."

He turned. "Nothing is your fault."

She'd never seen him like this, so open, so off his game. He was no longer a smooth player, his every word and move calculated in advance. He was unguarded, utterly exposed. If she'd thought the man dangerous before, he was deadly now. And that was before he admitted, "I wish I could say I was merely caught up in the moment, but the truth is I've wanted to do that for quite some time now."

Her heart tripped. Guilt? She twisted the engagement ring around her finger. *Please, please let that be guilt.*

"Well, Venice is a very romantic city," she began.

His gaze was direct, his voice husky. "I'm talking before Venice. *Long* before Venice."

She twisted the ring again before fisting her hand. The diamond solitaire bit into her palm. "But…but I'm engaged."

"I know." Max shoved a hand through his hair and swore ripely. "Believe me, Dayle, that fact has not escaped my notice." Half of his mouth rose in a smile that never reached his eyes. "You know, you're the only woman I've ever met who's made me wish I were a better man."

She frowned. "I…I don't know what you mean."

"I wish I could be good enough for you." He shook his head then. "Sorry." And before she could say anything in return, he was walking back up the cobblestone path.

Dayle's heart tripped again as she watched him go. She had a name for the emotion that was causing the sensation. It wasn't guilt. No. Not guilt.

The question was, what was she going to do about it?

Max called himself a coward and an unchivalrous one at that. He'd left Dayle at the villa with only a note of apology and money to make her way back to their hotel. He'd needed to get away before he said anything else. As it was, he'd revealed way too much.

The pain was back in his chest. He didn't bother with antacids or excuses. He knew its cause now.

He'd always been determined to steer clear of emotional entanglements with women, telling himself he was doing it for them, for their good. He was a confirmed bachelor and a Kinnick. He was like his father. Or was he?

He'd made it a hard and fast rule never to cheat on a woman. Each relationship was exclusive no matter how casual or short-lived. What if the heart he'd been so driven to protect from being broken all these years was his own? Well, if that were the case, the joke was on him. It was breaking right now.

When he arrived back at the hotel, Max called to see about getting a flight out of Marco Polo airport. The destination didn't matter. While he waited on hold, he started packing his bags. His hands stilled when he heard the knock at the door. Dayle. He knew it would be her, but he didn't answer it. A moment later, he spotted the slip of paper on the carpet just inside his room.

Max,
We need to talk. Please come by my suite when you get in. I'll be waiting.
Dayle

He crumpled the note in his hand, determined to ignore it. But an hour later, as he wheeled his bag past her door, he slowed. One last goodbye, he decided. She deserved that. When Dayle opened the door, she was wearing the blue dress. Max sucked in a steadying breath. He could do this without making a fool of himself.

"I got your note."

She glanced past him to the suitcase. "Going somewhere?"

He nodded, but didn't elaborate.

"So, you stopped to say goodbye," she guessed.

"Yes."

Her expression dimmed. "I was going to see if you wanted to go out for dinner to that fancy restaurant by the square, but…" She tilted her head to the side. "Got time for a drink?"

"Sure."

He parked the suitcase just inside the doorway and followed Dayle to the sitting room. A bottle of wine sat breathing on the low table in front of the sofa. She poured them each a glass.

"What shall we drink to?" When he said nothing, she said, "I know. How about happiness?"

"To happiness," he agreed somewhat warily.

"Yes." She smiled. "Your middle name."

He lifted his glass and clunked it against hers before taking a sip. The Chianti's mellow undertones soured. *Happiness.* It was all Max could do to swallow.

"Sorry about leaving you today. It wasn't a very gentlemanly thing to do."

"And you're always a gentleman," she said.

"I try." He set the wine aside and walked to the far side of the room. Outside, the sun was setting. Apropos since something inside of him seemed to be dimming, too. "I hope you didn't have any difficulty getting back to the hotel."

"None. I'm a big girl, Max."

"I know. But I am sorry."

Dayle sipped her wine and regarded him over the glass's rim. "Is that all you're sorry about?"

He kneaded the back of his neck. "I believe I already apologized for kissing you at the villa."

"Yes, you did. But that's not what I mean." She set her glass next to his and started toward him. The dress's skirt swayed along with her hips. She wore her hair up. Diamonds caught fire in the light and shimmered on her earlobes. Thanks to her heels, they were eye to eye when she stood in front of him. "Why are you leaving Venice, Max?"

He cleared his throat. "Business—"

"Is an excuse."

Yes, but excuses were all he had at the moment. So he offered another one. "Well, you know me, Dayle. I can't stay in one place for long. I thought I'd pop back to New York before heading out again."

"Running, Kinnick?" It was too close to the truth. Max said nothing. His silence didn't appear to bother her. She went on. "You're not who I thought you were, or rather who you've let me believe you are."

The words left him feeling vulnerable.

"Something occurred to me today when I was standing in the garden at the villa," she began. "I said I'd know it when I found the right place for my wedding."

"Yes, and the villa's garden was perfect," he said tightly.

"I'm not finished."

Max motioned a hand, urging her to go on. Wrap it up, already, he thought. He couldn't stand much more.

"Yes, the place was perfect, but something was off. Something was absolutely wrong. I'd known it for a while. I just had a hard time admitting it to myself. And then you kissed me." She brought her hands up to his face. "Like this."

Dayle placed her mouth over his, slid her tongue along the seam of his lips until he allowed it inside. But then he was pulling away. "Wait a minute. Hold on." He shoved a hand through his hair. "What are you saying? What *exactly* are you saying?"

He looked terrified, confused…hopeful. Dayle knew those feelings. She was experiencing the same ones at the moment.

"Do you really need to ask, Max?"

"I'm usually not slow, but—"

"Actually, slow is good for what I have in mind."

"But Ryan—"

"I called Ryan when I got back to the hotel. I told him I couldn't marry him. I'd been feeling that way for a while, but standing in the garden with you, I knew it for sure. I'm not in love with Ryan." She tipped her head sideways. "It turns out I've fallen for someone else."

"And that would be?" But he was smiling now.

She kissed him passionately for an answer and sighed afterward. "Sparks. I love sparks. I love you, Maxwell Kinnick."

His expression was as sincere as his words. "I love you, too."

"So, I take it this means you no longer need to catch the first flight home?"

"No," he said, walking her backward in the direction of the bedroom. "I'm already there."